PRAISE FOR CLARE NAYLOR

Dog Handling

Selected by *Cosmopolitan* as One of the Summer's Best Beach Reads

"[A] spunky heroine . . . Amid the comedy, the novel has a quietly confident, smart-girl sensibility. . . . Yip, yip, hooray!"

—*People*

"Comically wicked . . . Reminiscent of *Bridget Jones's Diary*."

—*Publishers Weekly*

"Highly creative and wildly entertaining."

—*Romantic Times*

Love: A User's Guide

"A perky tale of a glossy magazine fashion assistant's adventures in wonderland."

—*The Guardian*

"Tasty, rich . . . It's a read as luxurious as a pound of Belgian chocolates."

—*Open Book*

"A quirky look at twenty-something female angst with an uncommonly happy result—the hunk actually loves the heroine back. . . . A wry commentary on how a girl's wildest dreams can suddenly and unexpectedly come true."

—*Publishers News Daily*

"The rags-to-riches story of the year . . . [A] sparkling story of young love, fame, and fashion."

—*The Resident*

"A funny, sexy, bubbling bestselling debut."

—*World Books*

Also by Clare Naylor
Published by Ballantine Books

Love: A User's Guide
Dog Handling

CATCHING ALICE

CLARE NAYLOR

BALLANTINE BOOKS • NEW YORK

A Ballantine Book
Published by The Random House Ballantine Publishing Group

www.ballantinebooks.com

Library of Congress Catalog Card Number: 00-106434

ISBN 0-449-00557-7

Cover art by Anne Higgins

Manufactured in the United States of America

First Ballantine Books Edition: November 2000

10 9 8 7 6 5 4

CHAPTER 1

Food is the new shopping and shopping is the new sex. Alice wasn't really getting very much shopping or sex in her life right now, so she thought she might as well eat something. Yes, food. Not hard cornflakes that grazed her gums or char-grilled toast, but proper food that could feasibly, if she closed her eyes and let her imagination run riot, masquerade as sex.

She opened the fridge. Not a thing. And certainly not a host of sun-dried tomatoes or a bar of rich Belgian chocolate. She wanted something that would make up for all that she was lacking in her miserable life. She wanted something to make her forget the bitter aftertaste of her tyrannical, unfaithful ex-boyfriend, Jamie. She wanted something so sweet that her teeth would rot just thinking about it. A sponge. A light sponge smeared with seedy raspberry jam and double cream. She pulled the round cake tin from the drawer beneath the oven and set about weighing out her flour. But as she reached for the self-rising flour, her arm wobbled dangerously. She really should go on a diet. She opted for a carrot cake. Fewer calories, she reasoned. Except the fridge revealed only half a moldy carrot. Alice wiped a floury hand through her hair and set off for Chelsea Green.

The houses on her street were the color of sugared al-
monds and were dappled with sunlight this Monday morning. Bywater Street was the gypsy caravan of Chelsea.
Myriad baskets of flowers and rare lilies adorned the door-
ways. Her neighbors were, as far as she could make out,
Woodstock refugees and grandes dames, opera singers
and retired colonels, practicing their scales, getting to
grips with elementary taxidermy and feeding lobster ther-
midor to the roses in this first flush of May. Spring was
here, and if she concentrated, Alice was sure she could
hear birds above the traffic noises on the King's Road.
Wearing her holey leggings and a dyed-in-the-wash T-shirt,
hoping that her cousin Simon's Turnbull & Asser size-
eleven slippers could pass for the latest in Gucci footwear,
Alice attempted to mingle with the tawny-skinned women
and heroin-chic men hanging around outside cafés and
chewing the fat over their modeling portfolios. But catching sight of herself in the window of an exclusive lingerie
boutique, she realized that there wasn't a cat in hell's
chance of her flour streaks being mistaken for the labor
of love of a top Toni and Guy stylist. She ruffled her rebellious chestnut curls in a bid to liberate some of the baking ingredients and dashed around the corner to take
a shortcut away from the withering glares of the beau
monde.

Alice rounded the corner to Chelsea Green, a curious
place. Those who had never been to the city would recognize it instantly as London and break into a rendition of
"I've Got a Lovely Bunch of Coconuts" in a Dick Van Dyke
cor-blimey-me-old-treacle sort of way. Surrounding an
elegant patch of manicured grass, it boasts shopfronts
from a film set: a fishmonger's whose rainbow trout leaped
from stream to weighing scales with a casual flip of the

fins, a greengrocer's whose pears and potatoes nestled in a blissful time warp on a bed of AstroTurf and a newsagent who sold penny chews and sherbet fountains. Those who knew better regarded it suspiciously as London's answer to the *Stepford Wives*, lots of impossibly perfect women whose racehorse legs deemed it impossible for them to have given birth to a soufflé, let alone the pristine toddlers huddled in the back of the Mercedes. Alice, realizing that the only part of her anatomy that could be mistaken for that of a racehorse was her rump, stood behind one of these beings in the greengrocer's and tried to pull her T-shirt down to her knees. The woman was squeezing a peach so perfectly blushing it should have been made of marzipan. Alice helped herself to a more humble carrot, trying to imagine a life where the only grocery shopping you had to do was to buy soft fruits, where you kept your Egyptian bed linen in a trunk scented with patchouli and fretted only over the consistency of your polenta.

Alice wasn't cut out for a life of jobs and bill paying. She wanted to live in an Aga saga. She longed for a rectory with a crumbling wall and dogs. She couldn't quite picture the children just yet, but she thought she could manage responsibility of a dog kind. She accepted that she'd probably have to marry a vicar, though she wasn't quite sure where you found young vicars. They all seemed fifty if they were a day. Perhaps there was a seminary nearby.

The Jane Asher tea shop next door seemed as likely a place as any to find a member of the clergy, so Alice talked herself into a spot of tea and a cream cake. She sat alone, her spoon stirring up a diminutive whirlpool of Earl Grey in her cup, as she carefully surveyed the street outside for cassocks. Was that what they were called or was that something Russian? God, she couldn't really pull it off at the rectory garden party if she couldn't get a grip on her husband's clothing preferences.

"Absolutely, Lady B. I find that Ariel automatic does wonders for the marks on the reverend's dresses."

In the ideal vicarage life she wouldn't have to worry about washing, of course; in those Aga sagas there always seemed to be heaps of vicar groupies around to do all the unsavory jobs—arranging the flowers, pouring tea, wiping choirboys' noses. Yes, they'd have to be very choosy about which parish they plumped for, Alice and her vicar. The only other problem she could envision would be her looks—they weren't terribly chaste-vicar's-wife looks, they were the messy kind. Her hips were far from virginal—she'd look atrocious in a pleated skirt—her lips were plump enough to put the congregation off holy communion, and her curls would never in a month of Sunday sermons agree to anything as organized as a bun or a French pleat. Maybe it was a lost cause. Except, of course, that she'd make a fabulous Mary Magdalene in the Easter pageant.

As her carrots had sat in their brown paper bag on the table in the tea shop, they must have been mysteriously imbued with the spirit of Jane Asher, because Alice's cake rose magnificently and was much improved by the maverick touch of adding a few poppyseeds. "Inspired," declared Alice as she licked the mixture off the whisk and contemplated a future of cake baking for special occasions instead of typing. But right now she couldn't even afford a dozen eggs, so that put paid to that.

If you thought that Alice had come into this seemingly charmed life as some genetic freak with a trust fund and ever-so-*bijou* flat in a fashionable part of London, you'd be wrong. Alice is a girl like any other. Less fortunate than most, really, if you consider losing your job, flat, and boyfriend in the same fortnight a misfortune. One minute she had a somewhere career in PR, the next the company was merging with a corporate giant and Alice was surplus to requirements and thrust headlong into a life of daytime television. The adage, kick a dog when it's down, became grim reality when dastardly Jamie decided to dump her and move his new girlfriend into the conjugal bed of their shared flat just days later, leaving Alice nursing her pillow and her paltry redundancy check on the assorted sofabeds of various friends.

Thankfully for Alice, and for the friends whose Kleenex supplies were proving woefully inadequate for their guest's needs, she just happened to have a dashing cousin called Simon Benedictus. Simon had left London six months earlier for a stint in Brazil as a wildlife photographer. As far as Alice could make out, the only wildlife he'd encountered, or certainly photographed, was female and delectable, but who was she to judge? He'd generously loaned the desolate and destitute cousin from Clapham his house for a while. As well as leaving his house keys, he'd also left a legacy of heartbroken females who phoned day and night and occasionally called around in all their finery, leaving the engines of their convertibles purring in the street outside.

At first Alice had dealt badly with the Legacy. Wouldn't you? If a constant shimmy of satin dresses and honeyed flesh made its way to your door, leaving you to answer in fraying leggings circa 1987 crowned with unwashed hair? I thought so. And at first the Legacy was pretty peeved, too. Who, they wanted to know, was this alarming creature answering the delectable Simon's door so proprietorially? Had he secretly wed one morning after a particularly heavy night at the Ministry of Sound? Had the well-documented family history of insanity come back to haunt him?

So you can imagine how relieved they were when they found out a) that Alice was his cousin and consequently an unlikely choice of bride and b) that her limbs were far from honeyed. In fact, it was usually at this juncture that Alice stopped being a threat and became an ally. For who better than reliable cousin Alice to persuade Simon on his return of the wisdom of marrying Trinny/Sophie/Tamsin/whoever. And Alice was only too happy to oblige as they'd each insisted that she join them for some night-club opening or select soirée.

"So, darling, what do you want a horrible job for?" asked Trinny, one of the less alarming members of the Legacy, as she picked the seeds out of the cake and left the cake part in a heap on her plate. (Have you any *idea* how many calories per slice?) Alice had just plucked up the courage to tell Trinny that she wouldn't be able to make it to her girls' lunch party tomorrow because she planned to make herself available to the Office Trollope's temping agency. She'd been on their books for the last two weeks, but all they'd offered her was packing frozen yogurt into cartons and rearranging the Denby crockery in the Debenhams sale. However, an increase on her overdraft was nigh if she didn't make some money soon.

"Bills, Trin: food, clothing."

Trinny looked uncomprehendingly at Alice. She had nothing to add to this list of mundanity.

"I'm seeing Simon next week." She smiled, the cat who'd got the cream.

"Cousin Simon?" Alice swirled her finger around in the orange icing on her plate.

"Yes, Simon B." With just the merest alteration to his name, Trinny managed to turn the cousin Simon with bat-wing ears who had once peed in her terrapin's tank at a family barbecue into the indispensable social gadfly who loved and left women in mud huts and avocado plantations the length of the libidinous world. "He's invited me over. Well, I called him at some hill station and said I was doing a competition in Venezuela and wasn't that near him. Anyway, he said I should pop in and see him. So I shall."

Alice wasn't exactly *au fait* with the finer nuances of the map of South America but thought that Venezuela and Brazil were probably more than a cab ride apart. But she stuck the icing in her mouth and kept quiet. Trinny's life consisted of ceroc dancing and kite flying. Her days were a whirl of apple-green and Schiaparelli-pink creations that she flew high in exotic skies. The airfares it took to get there resembled phone numbers. Alice didn't really understand why the breeze above Clapham Common wasn't good enough for a spot of kite flying, but for Trinny it was an art form.

"So when you get this horrible job we won't be able to have lunch ever again, will we?" Trinny said sulkily.

"Well, I suppose that even people with jobs eat at some point, Trin."

"Don't you believe it. And your bottom will spread as well, you know." Trinny swept back a curtain of blond hair and shuddered at the thought. "Have *you* heard from Simon lately?"

Alice thought it better not to mention the phone call last night when Simon, drunk on some local spirit made from the saliva of a hallucinogenic Amazonian tree frog, said he'd fallen in love with a pygmy. "Oh, you know Simon," she muttered in an opaque way, and polished off another piece of cake.

·   ·   ·

"Last one to the top has to clear out the slops bucket," Simon yelled, and sprinted as fast as he could to the corrugated iron shack perched precariously on the sheer face of the mountain. Of course, he made it well ahead of the others, leaving his fellow travelers scrabbling on the rubble at the bottom of the path. He looked out over the peaks and pulled the icy air into his lungs, yanking his yak's-wool deerstalker farther down on his head. "Don't know what you're missing, guys," he muttered to himself as he took in the numinous South American landscape. Ahead of the pack and twice as laid-back: Simon's life had always been thus.

His mother, Alice's aunt Meg, had met Teddy, his father, in Nepal in the late sixties. They'd done what all good hippies did best and in the much-fêted summer of '69 Icarus Benedictus was born to the bobbing rhythms of a houseboat in Kashmir. There was a slight fracas early in '71 when Teddy, in a lucid hashish-free moment, had informed Meg that they really ought to take the boy child back to England for a proper christening. Meg thought a child born to Buddhist parents could probably do without that particular rite of passage and put it down to a bad acid trip on Teddy's part. Only when he started mumbling about *Debrett*'s needing to know about the birth of Lord Icarus of Kirkheaton did Meg pack her sari and a particularly lovely piece of amber in a suitcase and return to England to investigate. After tussles with the in-laws in their baronial castle she took the pragmatic approach and left Icarus (unforgivably christened Simon the second her back was turned) to attend Eton and Cambridge and only visit the ashram during the school holidays.

"I've just thought of a fantastic way to get us out of this mess," said Simon to Gibbo when his friend eventually made it to the top of the path. Open spaces and communing with nature always helped him with eureka moments. And this was one time in his life when he needed a bright idea more than ever before.

Alice poured the last four Cocoa Puffs into a bowl. She hoped that today would be the day that she'd be offered her old job back with bells on and an extra few luncheon vouchers. No such luck. She waited for the dreaded phone call from Office Trollopes. If they asked her to wash up in the Harvester on the M4, she'd have to say yes. She bit her nails and arranged the cake crumbs from the bottom of the tin into "HELP!"

Only when she'd eked a token breakfast out of Vegemite and some of Simon's raw Guaraná did the phone finally ring. It was Tamsin, one of the Legacy, asking Alice to lunch at a new café in Westbourne Grove.

Still quite peculiar on the Guaraná buzz, Alice laughed merrily. "You know, Tamsin, there's always some poor sod in life who has to sew the strings on tampons. Today that just might be me."

Tamsin hastily put the phone down and contemplated husband material other than Simon Benedictus. He may have lean blond-haired legs, but did she really want to marry into a family so patently barking?

Alice banged open the back door and, taking a quick look around to make sure the neighbors had all safely set off for the office, darted the entire six meters to the bottom of the garden. Well, it's London, she told herself, this postage stamp of a garden is practically a country estate and surrounding paddocks by London standards. Her nightie was so see-through, she was surprised that the Chelsea arm of Voyeurs Anonymous hadn't cottoned on to her daily forays to the greenhouse. In fact, she couldn't be sure that at this moment they weren't glaring at her from some Louis XIV chaise longue while sipping Earl Grey. At least there was probably a better class of Peeping Toms in Chelsea, she thought, as she bent over her twelve-day-old seedlings.

They looked up at her with their little green leafy faces, all adorable and optimistic. Alice breathed on them gently and poured water into every one of the thirty-two pots. She wasn't sure exactly where she'd put the sunflowers when they came of age (she liked to think of them as individuals with thoughts and feelings of their own), but she'd seen a photo of Provence or somewhere in a book and its fields of sunflowers looked just what Bywater Street needed. The other photo was of lavender, but when she'd explored that option at the garden center, the price was rather prohibitive. Either lavender or no food and electricity for a week. She'd pondered for a bit, where most sane people would balk instantly, but in the end she knew that shredded wheat and the dishwasher would win the day.

"And then there's this witch of a woman from the temping agency," she told her attentive offspring in hushed, oxygen-giving tones, "and every day she rings me and says in this whiny voice, 'I know it's not exactly what you're looking for, Alison, and it's only £3.57 an hour, but it is sort of creative, if you count doodling on the in-house notepaper while you're on the phone as creative. And you get to wear whatever denier tights you choose, which in today's job market is a bonus. Let me tell you. And the other girl only left after two hours because she was allergic to the boss's aftershave—not anything more sinister. Really.' So I had to lie to her and tell her I had a doctor's appointment. I know I shouldn't have, but . . ." Alice plucked a particularly lethal-looking weed of at least a millimeter from one of the pots and longed for the day that her flower children would reach maturity and this tiny part of London would become the South of France, with sunflowers and azure skies.

In fact, so lost was she in this fantasy that at first she thought the merry tinkle she could hear must be the cowbell on some Provençal cattle in the lane nearby, but then she realized that it was the phone. She ran inside, nearly shattering the greenhouse door, her nightie flying up and leaving nothing to the imagination and no doubt giving the V.A. next door the biggest thrill since Lady Caroline at number 17 got locked out in her Rigby and Peller corset. Alice hurled herself at the phone just as it stopped ringing. "Bugger." She dialed 1471 and discovered that it was Angela from the Office Trollopes temping agency. Did she or didn't she want to call back? She decided to have a cup of tea and think about it but on the way was accosted by the scarlet demand for loadsamoney from BT. Some usually absent vestige of common sense in Alice dragged her to the phone and made her return Angela's call.

"Well, Alison, you'd be doing me a huge favor if you could fill this job just for a few days, just while the company secretary's on maternity leave." Alice failed to register that this, if true, would be the shortest maternity leave in history. "I can't tell you how grateful I'd be, Alison. And it's £3.23 an hour."

How could Alice resist? Practically the crown jewels of £4.80 an hour. And she was a sucker for anyone who remembered her name, even if they didn't quite manage an accurate rendering of it. Of course she knew that that's what those women were taught in their sales and manipulation colleges: use the victim's name as often as possible. Play on their conscience. Make them feel as if they're your best friend. But Alice fell for it every time. She couldn't bear to think of the career of this poor woman being on the line just because she, Alice Lewis, thought she was worth more than £3.23 an hour.

"Okay. I'll be there at 8:30. And at least forty-denier tights then? Fine. No problem. Oh, really? Navy, above the knee. I don't think I have any, but I don't mind buying one. It's bound to come in useful. Bye."

What are you *like*, Alice Lewis? she asked herself as she pulled on her jogging pants in preparation for her shopping mission. She headed straight for M&S, bastion of all things navy. And there, sure enough, she encountered just what she was sure her job at Know Your Personal Computer required. Well, it was her own fault after all. Hadn't she told the woman at the agency that she wanted a change, that she wanted to get into journalism? Wasn't this the first step on the ladder?

Alice pulled the zip up and felt as though she'd regressed fifteen years. The gentle A-line of the skirt actually revealed her unshaven and pasty legs but could equally have been covering the over-the-knee socks and scuffed attempts at stilettos she'd sported throughout school. She could have been standing on the loo seat bitching about third years over the top of the cubicles and having a Silk Cut cigarette, she thought fondly. But no, life was harsh. She was going to work in this monstrosity tomorrow whether she wanted to or not. No skiving now, Alice.

CHAPTER 2

Alice woke to find her forty-denier navy tights on the pillow beside her. They had that school-dinner smell of the office. She shrugged them away and opened a bleary eye. She'd dreamed of Jamie again last night and now she was the waitress at his wedding to the Tart.

He'd taken a vol-au-vent from her tray and smiled his feudal smile. "I know you're only a serving wench, but I wouldn't half mind one anyway—what about on that table over there?"

Alice had obliged because he'd been dressed in black tie and she'd always fancied Jamie in black tie. But it was only a dream. When she woke up, she tried to turn herself against him by focusing on his supercilious smile, the only realistic part of the dream. She knew what a bastard he really was, but she kept coming back to the melting moment when he'd unbuttoned her waitress blouse. Stop it, Alice. Stop it.

She flung the tights across the room and noticed with horror her ink-stained fingernails. Three days at Know Your Personal Computer and her hands looked like a toddler's after a rainy afternoon of fingerpainting. She'd stood by the photocopier for so long yesterday that she'd been tempted to photocopy her face for the obituaries page. "Girl Dies of Frustration in Onetime Broom Cupboard."

How hard could it be, she'd thought as she'd smiled at her new boss and, taking a manuscript the size of a small toddler in her arms, trotted innocently off to the copy room. But what lay in wait was a fate worse than a phone bill. The machine spewed and spat and performed feats with paper that Houdini would have been proud of. How was it that page 3 was now where page 77 once was? And how did the article on Bill Gates's favorite holiday destination get onto the "Websites We Love" page? Alice banged the machine and tore at jammed paper with what was at first a cathartic passion because she imagined it to be the Tart's hair, but it soon became an exhausting round of kicks and tears. When her boss came to look for her two hours later, she was gnawing her own limbs in frustration.

"I can't go back on Monday. I can't go back," she chanted as she showered under the one-drop-every-three-seconds excuse for plumbing that Simon had installed himself. Her stomach roared its hunger over the trickle of water. What could she do today? What did working people do on weekends? She didn't have a house in the country. She didn't even have a boyfriend, for heaven's sake. Maybe she'd been on the wrong lines when she'd tried the carrot-cake thing, maybe she should have gone for more exotic food as her sex replacement. Maybe she should try something a bit more savory this time.

Alice stood chilled by the air from the fridge as she popped a herbes de Provence kalamata olive between her lips. She rolled it around her mouth, sucked the herbs off it, bit into the flesh, and opened her eyes to see the shop assistant looking crossly at her.

Eleven o'clock on a Saturday morning in Tom's Deli in Notting Hill Gate is neither the time nor the place to reenact your warped little fantasies, the girl's look told her. Alice hastily gulped down the perky little fruit and hurried over to the cheese counter. The boy with the blond bob wielding the knife looked like an altogether more open-minded type of person.

"No, no, no. That won't do at all. It tastes like a goat's backside," a large man in front of her tutted. Alice refrained from even contemplating how he came by this simile and elbowed her way between him and the wall.

"And for you?" The boy with the knife winked at her and it was all she could do to squeeze out, "I'll just have a bit of the Cathedral City cheddar, please." Bloody hell, Alice, is that the best you can do? Could she not have rolled her tongue seductively around "Some *chaumes*, please" or hinted at the more potent side of her nature by suggesting he help her to some vintage Stilton? It was the blond hair. Whenever she saw hair a shade lighter than mud, she thought of Jamie and her stomach gave birth to kittens, an unfortunate position to be in as it was turning summer and every Tom, Dick, and Harry in London was bound to be nurturing their highlights in this warm spell.

Alice accepted the cocktail stick sporting the very pe-destrian Cathedral City cheddar and was just wondering whether some sort of aversion therapy would do the trick, perhaps sticking red-hot pins under her nails whenever she thought of Jamie, when a French-manicured hand pulled the stick from her fingers.

"Oh no. That's dairy, you should know better."

Alice turned to confront the owner of the perfect digits. "How dare you—?" She was halted in her tracks by five foot ten inches of blond unfairness with an American lilt. Na-tasha Beauregard, Alice's best friend from school.

"Tash, my God . . . what?" At the sight of Natasha, Alice turned into a moron with the vocabulary of a budgie.

"I knew it was you, sweetie. You haven't changed one jot." Despite the newly glamorous veneer, this creature was definitely Tash. Tash who spoke like a Tennessee Williams heroine who's drunk too much champagne. Adorable Tash who had insisted Alice have nothing to do with "those frightful boys in the sixth form" and instead date the more cultivated specimens from the art college. Tash who Alice hadn't seen for "My God, it must be seven years," shrieked Alice as she skewered herself on the cocktail stick that Tash was still holding. "Ouch!"

"Hush, we're too old to be admitting our age in public anymore. Now are we going to loiter around this sheep's-ass smell all day or have a cappuccino upstairs?"

Alice grinned broadly as she trotted up the stairs behind Tash's floor-sweeping fur coat. She had certainly matured as well as any vintage cheddar. Tash's mother was a diplomat and her father an ahead-of-his-, and even our-, time, homemaker. They'd decided that flattest Norfolk was the perfect place to put some color in their rather pasty-faced only child's cheeks. Alice had often thought that the Florida sunshine or some Alpine meadow might have done the job equally well but never pointed this out in case her partner in all manner of boy-related crimes was whisked away from her. When Tash's father tired of the rather limited jam-making options available to him in Norfolk and decided to relocate to Boston, Alice and Tash were finally wrenched apart at Heathrow airport in a post–A level gloom. They swore to write nightly to each other. But the nightly turned into fortnightly and then only Christmas and birthdays as they both slipped seamlessly into university life and no longer had snogs and cider hangovers in common. Later, as a film-school graduate, Tash would occasionally call Alice from Heathrow, where she'd stopped

over on her way to work as a runner on some remote Scottish film set, and they'd swap essential details: No children,
thank God; Seeing this reformed glue-sniffer with a cute
bum; If you're ever in Los Angeles/Norfolk let me know.
Then they'd hang up, think fondly of each other, and carry
on where they'd left off before the phone rang. Such is life.
It didn't mean that Alice wasn't thrilled to tiny bits to see
Tash again after so long.

"So I left Martino to his goddamn Tuscan pile of bricks
and came over here. I was going to recuperate and regain
my self-esteem with a spot of retail therapy. I'm going back
to the States on Tuesday to start work on a new film. But
let's forget the shopping, we can play instead." Tash with the
rangy limbs and ink-blue eyes was now also Tash with a
chest men would pay to move in with. Alice had heard of
boob jobs and she'd seen *Baywatch*, but she'd never really
believed it could happen to real people. She tried to stop
addressing her potted history of the last seven years to
Tash's chest, but it was easier said than done. If she did
manage, it was only to marvel at the absence of roots on
the once-mousy-now-suicide-blond head. Alice wrestled
briefly again with the concept of blond hair without the ac-
companying Jamie image—this time Jamie sunburned in
Antigua last summer. Stop it.

"Darling." Alice had glazed over and Tash was now
looking at her intensely, waiting to hear all about Alice's
man. "I could just tell by the way you seduced that olive
that you're in love."

How could Alice tell her that it wasn't love, just wishful
thinking, that had led her to the olives? She couldn't face
going into The Carnage yet again. Besides, she was in public, she couldn't risk what had happened the last time when
she'd gotten so upset in a restaurant that the manager had

offered to call an ambulance. But Tash was looking so ex-
pectant, so enthralled, that Alice just couldn't bear it any
longer.

"There was someone, Jamie, but well, like Mick Jagger
said, it's all over now." Alice rushed through this sentence
at breakneck speed, leaving Tash confused. But only for a
second.

"But it's not that you used to love him, you still do. Don't
you?" she asked kindly.

Alice nodded.

"I'm so sorry. What happened?"

And she was sorry, Alice could tell by the way she furrowed her usually creamy-smooth brow. Not sorry in the
way Trinny was—only sorry so that now we've got that out
of the way, we can go down to the pub and talk about
something more interesting. Or sorry in the way that Alice's mother had been: "I always told you never to trust a
small man, dear. I knew it the moment I met him—he didn't
have a soul. I'm just sorry that he had to do the dirty on
you and you didn't get there first." That was the way Alice's
mother was sorry. But Tash was genuinely heart sorry in
the way that only best friends can be. They feel your pain
for you, they quiver in time to your misery. Oh God, there
was no stopping Alice now.

"And he told you this four minutes after you'd had sex?"
Tash shrieked, leaving the quiet Saturday-paper readers in
no doubt as to whether they'd prefer to find out what was
on telly tonight or eavesdrop on the loud American and
her unfortunate friend.

"Well, it could have been longer. Maybe six minutes,"
Alice conceded, suddenly aware that she was of more inter-
est than the exciting variety of lattes the café had to offer.
She buried her burning cheeks in her polo-neck sweater.

"Anyway, the thing is, Tash, he's living with her now, this lawyer tart, Helen, and I haven't a cat in hell's chance of getting him back, even if I wanted to."

"I take it that when you say getting him back, you mean punishment-wise, revenge-wise, CASTRATION-wise. And not love-wise?" The male observers crossed their legs.

"Of course I meant that." Alice back-pedaled rapidly. "Anyway, as I said, even if I had wanted to . . ."

"It's obvious I can't leave you alone for a second, Alice Lewis. Now let's pick up my stuff from the Lanesborough and I'll move in with you."

CHAPTER 3

"**C**up of tea?" Alice said as she wandered into a room strewn with designer clothes and clouds of perfume. On stepping foot through the front door Tash had instantly commandeered the master bedroom. She removed Simon's war books and *Penthouse*s from the bedside table and set about replacing them with her extensive array of miracle face savers. Seven different bottles for seven types of disrepair in the eye area. Fine lines, crow's-feet, too much booze, too little water, wrecked from the night before, etc. Alice imagined the last was probably the most in demand. Tash was a hardened partygoer and even as a seventeen-year-old Alice's vitality levels had struggled to keep up with Tash's. Now that Alice was an over-the-hill twenty-six she shuddered and ran for the nearest duvet at the mere mention of clubbing. Tash was sitting on the edge of the bed.

"Just as I suspected." Alice laughed as Tash zipped up a silver knee-high boot. She was already bedecked in a pair of silver angel's wings and her new Butler & Wilson tiara.

"So, are we going to answer the prayers of every man in London tonight, angel?" Tash winked and straightened out her fishnets.

"Oh, Tash, I'd love to. Really. It's just that . . ." Alice

struggled for an excuse. Ironing. Thank-you letters. Weeding. Feeble, feeble, feeble. She tried the honest approach. "I can't be dealing with going out, Tash." She plumped down on a chair in the corner of the room and felt a hundred years old.

"Hold your horses. This is about thingy, isn't it?"

"Jamie." Alice nodded. "Yes."

"Alice!" Tash yelled, and her wings reverberated with the force of the bellow. "He cheats, lies, and dumps you—and you feel guilty? I don't *think* so. I think you are coming out with me and we'll show him what he's missing." Their bodies may have soared into the wide blue yonder of the Grand Canyon but Alice was amused to see that the spirit of Thelma and Louise was alive and well and occupying her best friend's larynx.

"Tash." Alice looked down at herself. Her thighs spilled from one side of the wicker chair to the other, and her hair looked as though it hadn't seen shampoo since 1985.

Tash eyed her friend carefully. Even her Californian optimism was replaced with healthy pragmatism in the face of Alice's disastrous appearance. She could see this was going to take more than a little MAC lip liner.

"Okay, okay. How about we compromise? I'll run you an aromatherapy bath and prepare you a delicious salad and you'll stay away from those cakes while I'm out."

Alice could have hugged her had it not been for the forbiddingly angelic protrusions on her back. She nodded eagerly. Escaping from a night in deepest clubland right now was like being given a stay of execution from the gallows. She had never felt so warmly toward a *Casualty* repeat in her life.

"But I do need somebody to dance with," Tash demanded.

"My friend Trinny'll take you somewhere lively if you like," Alice volunteered as she examined one by one the bottles that held the secret of Tash's perfect complexion.

"Trinny. What kind of a name's that?" Tash trilled as she added a series of diamanté clips to her locks. "Sounds like budgie food."

"Stop pretending to be shocked by the British, Natasha Beauregard. You know they're all called Bunny and Pickles—you went to school with them."

"I'm just teasing. I'd love to go out with Trinny. What's his number?"

Alice waited for at least half an hour after the taxi's engine had burred away before she plucked up her courage and stole into the kitchen in her nightie only to be greeted by a brazen waft of Eau Hadrien. She knew Tash well enough to know that this guilt-inducing reminder of her friend was no accident. Tash had probably squirted her scent all over the kitchen so that when Alice approached the cake tin she'd be reminded of Tash's orders. Tash's brief stint at UCLA as a psychology major, before she decided that Fellini was cooler than Freud and switched to film, was far from wasted. She used it to lick friends, men, and colleagues into shape, playing mind games with them before they even realized she existed.

"Too smart for her own bloody good," muttered Alice as she prized the lid from a cake tin. Now she wouldn't be able to use a plate in case Tash noticed it in the dishwasher; she'd have to eat it with her fingers and feel all sly. "Bugger," she moaned as she carefully broke off a symmetrical-looking wedge and balanced it on her left hand, replacing the lid with the other. If it weren't for the bastardly Jamie, she wouldn't even want cake.

Since she'd split up with Jamie, Alice's evenings had stopped being the eternally merry round of Fridays in the Pitcher and Piano, Saturdays at one of Jamie's friends' girl-friend's dinner parties, and Sundays basting a chicken and waiting for him to come home from his game of golf. She should have listened to all those people who had told her never to trust a man who played golf. She couldn't remember on what grounds you weren't meant to trust them, but it had probably had something to do with the wearing of polo-necks and dubious footwear. How easy to be wise after the event. But now her Saturdays were devoid of clinking glasses of red wine and a luxuriant brunette hostess in Miu Miu mules apologizing, "It's just a little something I threw together from the *River Café Cookbook*, sorry, folks, hope that you don't mind *Patate al Forno con Aceto Balsamico e Timo* again," naturally delivered in flawless Italian accent on Jerry's Home Store's finest crockery. At this point in the evening Jamie would abandon talk of football for the only five minutes of the week and regale the hostess with tales of his year out in Florence, addressed softly and flirtatiously to her right earlobe or another such erogenous zone. Alice would be left listening to the auditing woes of the accountant from Balham. Well, things had certainly changed.

Now it was much more likely that Alice could be found in the very salubrious environs *à la* sofa on Saturday nights. In fact, she had spent so many evenings thus that she was sure the cushion fabric was thinning on her side. No matter whether she watched *Terminator II* or *Love Story*, she felt sick. Every actress seemed to have the nose or hair of the bitch Helen. Alice molded an effigy of Helen from the tin foil at the bottom of the empty cake tin. Ha. But there'd never be enough to make her bum. She chuckled bitterly and took the last swig of rosé from the bottle.

When she woke up, her sleeves were still damp from wiping her tears on them and there was a poltergeist-type wind whirling around the room. Stifling a scream, she listened as voices filled the hallway.

"I think that if Trinny had wanted to invite you back for sex she would have. Turning up here in your slinky black Porsche isn't going to make her desire you any more. Don't you realize that?" The words were enunciated terribly s-l-o-w-l-y, as though to a miscreant five-year-old. A male voice mumbled and a door slammed. Shit, thought Alice. I'm lying here in my wincyette nightie with cake crumbs in my hair and a man's coming into the house. The first man to have been in this house since Simon left for Brazil several months ago. In her bid to make a hasty exit and hide herself, she stood up and nearly crippled herself on the errant empty rosé bottle. She pushed it under the sofa just as Tash entered the room, closely followed by a desolate-looking Trinny.

"I don't know where these guys get off. You say you're going home now because you're tired and he thinks he can come along for a nightcap and sex. It's a little presumptuous, isn't it?" Tash was shocked to see Alice in all her gory glory frantically brushing crumbs from her hair and twisting the foil effigy nervously behind her back. "Alice, didn't the juniper work? You should have been asleep hours ago."

Alice ho-hummed and plumped up the sofa cushions.

"But we do that every Saturday! He stops for a bacon sandwich at Vingt-Quâtre, picks me up from wherever I am, and we go back to my place for a shag." Trinny was still reeling from the shock of missing out on her weekly oats. While she was heartbreakingly in love with Simon

Benedictus, so was every other girl in London. She had to get her kicks somewhere and she'd been sorted out, so to speak, on a weekly basis by Tim with the Porsche since New Year's Eve 1996. It was a mutually beneficial arrangement. At least until Simon finally realized he was madly in love with Trinny and abandoned his life of photography and women for Putney and a family.

But now this American had come along and tried to ruin a beautiful relationship because she thought that Tim was expecting too much. Trinny sulked. It might be five in the morning, but her lipstick was hanging in there and she was damned if she was going to waste her new satin dress. Tash was looking at her as though she'd just confessed to having an affair with John Major.

"I don't understand you English girls at all." She shook her head sadly. "Well, go and catch up with him then. I'm sure his engine's still purring away." Tash shooed an ecstatic and grateful Trinny from the room and then turned her attention to Alice, who was now turning all the blues of a Dulux color chart in the corner due to the arctic wind blustering around the room.

Why was it that Tash seemed to create a hum of fun and life around her? If Alice wielded just a thimbleful of that magnetism in the face of Jamie she'd probably still have a boyfriend. Or at least she'd have given him hell. As it was she hadn't even sent him off with a flea in his ear and guilt burning a hole in his conscience. Instead she'd told him that she still loved him and if he ever wanted her back he knew where she was. My God, it's a good job Tash didn't know the half of it.

Tash dispensed mango zinger tea and sound advice until Alice almost fell asleep at the kitchen table. The angel wings were now lying discarded in front of her and could happily have improvised as a pillow. Alice's eyes closed and her head nodded drowsily.

"Don't you agree?" Tash's voice hit her like a breeze-block from a fifth-story window.

Alice started, only to be greeted by the even more shocking sight of her friend looking like a supermodel at seven in the morning without a wink of sleep. Alice made a mental note to borrow some of the obviously voodoo potions by Tash's bed if Jamie ever called her up and asked her for a reconciliation supper.

"You see, you have to reclaim your life, darling," Tash was stating. "You can't just give it over to other people. If there are too many demands on you, you stop knowing what you want. Your boss. Your mother. Your boyfriend." Tash saw Alice flinch. "Even your ex-boyfriend can take up your time and energy if you let him."

How right she was. But right now Alice wished she had the courage to reclaim her life from the kitchen table and take it upstairs, where it could flop down on the duck-down duvet and carry on where her dream had left off this morning. With Jamie standing at the altar looking grave and saying, "I'm so sorry, Helen, but I've made a frightful mistake. It's all over between us. I never stopped loving Alice Lewis. I intend to marry her. So move over and let the woman of my dreams say 'I do' instead." Alice couldn't wait to live this moment again and again. No matter that she'd been cheated out of a romantic marriage proposal on some Balinese beach at dusk. She was marrying Jamie, that was enough for her.

"Well, I'm bushed," said Tash finally, not looking even shrubbed, let alone bushed. "See you at teatime." She dropped a kiss on Alice's furrowed forehead and sashayed upstairs.

But if Alice thought she could escape the wise utterances of Tash in sleep she was wrong. Tonight, or this morning to be precise, no Jamie appeared in rakish clothes and caddish behavior. Not a nuzzled neck to be had. Oh no. Alice got a kind of mutated Naomi Wolf diatribe from Jamie's admittedly-still-delectable lips. She woke up at midday feeling perplexed and cheated. How dare Tash walk into her life and disturb her perfectly happy misery? She stormed downstairs, expecting the kitchen to be alive with the sound of a step aerobics class and a carrot shake in the blender. But no, thank God, she found only her sun-dappled window box and the newspapers on the mat. She sat quietly at the kitchen table tucking into a bacon sandwich, the butter dribbling down her fingers, and read her horoscope. No sooner had she waded through the boring technical parts about retrograde Jupiter and ruling Mars, about to embark on the juicy advice about her love life, than the doorbell rang. Alice licked the butter from her fingers and made her way to the door.

"Only us." The visitor laughed merrily. Alice didn't know any "us." She made a strict point of steering clear of gruesome twosomes. An evening in the presence of a couple and she'd invariably wanted to go home and slit her wrists in a bathtub of Matey. She'd learned this in the week after her split with Jamie.

Taking the advice of a gay agony uncle in a magazine, she'd put on a brave face and confronted her demons. She'd accepted every social invitation within a fifteen-mile radius only to turn up to find the place awash with couples smoothing down each other's hair and munching convincingly on each other's tonsils. After fifteen minutes she'd turn into a snarling Beelzebub whenever love or romance was mentioned. "Hsst. Psst. Urgh," she'd burble, or "Ha. Love!" in a cynical manner, until nobody invited her anywhere anymore. At least not couples. So who, she wondered, was the "us" on the doorstep? She peered through the spyhole and saw the exceptionally large forehead and distorted grin of Trinny.

"Open the door, Alice, we're freezing." She did and it was easy to see why. In their eagerness to get to Alice's, Trinny and Tim had almost forgotten to dress. Trinny was wearing last night's satin dress with trainers and a cardigan and Tim was dressed only to put the milk bottles out.

"We want you to be the first to know . . ." Trinny held out a bubblegum ring and kissed Tim's cheek. "We're getting married."

Alice gulped back a million feelings and smiled bravely. "Come in. Congratulations!" She hugged them as they skipped past her into the kitchen.

A disheveled Bardot figure made her cautious way down the stairs and said huskily, "Hey, what's all the fuss about?" Tash gleamed even through the hangover from hell.

"Trinny and Tim got engaged," Alice related, still not able to take this kind of news on a Sunday morning and certainly not before she had read what the stars had in store for her own love life.

"They did what?" The last thing Tash had thought before she slipped off into a champagne slumber last night had been that she must take Trinny aside and explain that it was no good playing hard to get with men; honesty was a nobler, and frankly more successful, policy in the nineties. She hadn't even had time to remonstrate before Trinny was popping the cork on yet more bubbly and pouring out teacupsful.

"You see, we have you to thank, Tash. If you hadn't made Tim realize that I wasn't always going to be there for the taking, then heaven knows when we'd have tied the knot."

"Yeah, we'd still be settling for the weekly pash in five years time most probably." Tim hiccuped. They'd obviously been at this celebratory lark for a few hours now. Alice wondered if this was the first household they'd woken this morning.

"You know that I'm in love with Simon, but the thing is that Tim's here and Simon probably never will be. He'll always be photographing wildlife in Brazil and then it'll be too late to have babies. I have to be realistic. Anyway, Tim's great. And when he's sitting down he's really quite handsome. And I can always wear ballet pumps to make him look taller. They're really in this season, you know." Trinny had cornered Alice in the downstairs loo.

Alice dried her hands. "I'm really pleased for you both, Trinny. You're right, maybe we have to be realistic sometimes, and Simon's not exactly ready to settle for Putney and a Volvo just yet. Good for you." Alice kissed Trinny's cheek and made her way through the hallway back into the kitchen. Word had gotten out in London and the intimate lunch *à quatre* was rapidly turning into the feeding of the five thousand without the miracle of loaves and fishes.

As the revelers took over her kitchen, Alice felt terrible for not being able to muster up much enthusiasm for Trinny. She'd never imagined herself as one of those women who reached a certain age and panicked because there was no potential husband on the horizon, but she was afraid that she might be turning into one. She'd started to view her four years with Jamie as a wasted investment. Maybe Trinny was doing the right thing in settling for Mr. Right Timing rather than Mr. Right. God, Alice hoped she wasn't going to turn into one of those women who bought *The Rules* in a bid to turn themselves into "a creature unlike any other" who wouldn't accept a date for Saturday after Wednesday. It was too frightening to contemplate.

"I blame London," a tipsy spinster of thirty-four said as she plucked bits of cork out of her wine by the kitchen sink. "Everybody's had everyone already. There's nobody left that we don't know. Well, nobody worth marrying anyway."

"Maybe you're right," Alice mused, rescuing a smoldering garlic baguette from the microwave.

"It's like musical chairs. You dance around and stop for the odd relationship, then the music starts again and you get up, have a trot around, only to find that there are no chairs left anymore." The spinster had gotten her hand stuck in the wineglass and was now busy squirting washing-up liquid around the rim in a bid to help it slip off.

"That's really beautiful," Alice said drunkenly, then burst into tears.

At five o'clock, when the remains of the hastily prepared roast from Cullens had been cleared away and the ever-increasing influx of strangers were still topping up their red wine from Simon's cellar, Alice was just a peeved, cranky old cow. She emptied another ashtray and contemplated setting off the burglar alarm to clear the house.

"Darling, you're green. Are you ill?" Tash flounced in with a plateful of mutilated Sara Lee Pavlova.

"Oh, ignore me, Tash, I'm such an old crone. Why can't I be happy for Trin?" Alice warbled.

Tash's party persona vanished and her wise head appeared. "Remember what I said about reclaiming your life? Well, until you do you can't possibly be at one with others." She smiled sympathetically. "Remember that. Oh, and remind me why the Brits smoke so much? Is it to do with coal mines?"

Alice smiled at her friend and took herself off upstairs for a good cry. After all, she was only reclaiming her life.

CHAPTER 4

The sun bounced off the train windows as Alice hid behind her sunglasses. She'd had another bad night. She'd repeatedly played the footage of The Carnage in her head again from start to finish. From the moment when Jamie had tightened his arms around her that morning in bed and she'd been sure he was going to ask her to move in with him. She'd noticed for weeks that he had something to say. He'd often gaze at her for a long time; "Alice?" he'd say nervously.

She'd stop chopping lettuce for a moment and turn to look adoringly at him.

"Oh, not to worry." He'd smile timidly and carry on with the crossword. But that day. . . . That Sunday morning he'd blurted it out just as she'd relaxed into his shoulder in postcoital warmth. "I've been seeing Helen Caudwell for four months now."

A steel hawser tightened about her neck and her body went limp.

"Alice. Did you hear me? I'm sorry."

Even now, as she sat among a carriage full of commuters, she had to catch her breath. Stop it, Alice. Stop tormenting yourself. She punched hard at her arm and looked up to see the man opposite obviously assessing her symptoms as some only-seen-on-television-documentaries form of insanity. Like the people who wander around super-markets swearing loudly at packets of fish fingers. She picked up her bag and waited by the train doors for her stop.

The thought of another day at Know Your Personal Computer had been almost enough to finish her off. She thought of her friends who had proper jobs. They seemed happy enough. A stint in the gym before work, lunchtimes browsing in Jigsaw, and hair that just got better and better with each pay raise. How was it, she wondered, that more of her money went to NI contributions than Jigsaw garments and that she'd landed herself the only job in London that was in an office where the average age of the staff was about fifty-seven.

All her friends worked in trendy young places where to be over thirty was to be approaching the golden handshake. If Alice had to be a secretary, she wanted to be able to talk about sex with her workmates over the fax machine and have a crush on her sparkly-eyed, married boss. But this never happened to her. It had been just the same when she was fourteen and all her friends had gone on holiday and had a fling with the local Adonis while their parents turned a drunken eye and can-canned on the hotel bar. Alice's parents always went to resorts without a disco and where all her fellow holidaymakers only spoke German and had blue mohicans, not being aware that punk had been and gone for the rest of the world. That feeling of being on the wrong side of a happening existence was a pattern that seemed destined to repeat itself throughout Alice's life.

Her desk was in a dark corner buried under a jungle of spider plants that crept and sprouted creepily all over the place. The only sign that there had ever been any form of interesting life in the office was in the top drawer of her desk, where she had found several herbal teabags and a

Joseph Sale receipt. But that person had obviously deemed Know Your Person Computer an unfit place to cultivate a proper life and made for the hills, many moons ago judging by the sell-by date on the teabags. Alice was busy painting her fingernails with Wite-Out and drawing navy-blue hearts on them with a Biro when the sole male in the office to have been born after the blitz came and sat on the edge of her desk.

"All right?" he charmed.

Alice looked up. Nothing charming about him. He was in the PC-support section and spent all day on the phone coaching housewives how to turn on their modems. And the rest.

"Fine, thanks," said Alice curtly. The only good thing to have come out of Jamie's heinous betrayal was that as far as she was concerned all members of the species were tarred with the same brush and consequently she'd learned to be curt with men. This was no mean feat either. She was the archetypal girl who couldn't say no. She'd spent her life wriggling out of dates with men who'd followed her around Boots for fifteen minutes before accosting her in Prescriptions for her phone number. She'd always had to dance to "Careless Whisper" with the lecherous best man at the end of family weddings. Simply because she couldn't say no. Hail the New Alice, she thought as she coolly received this new admirer.

"How's your hard drive?" He leaned over her and circled the mouse suggestively.

Yuck, thought Alice.

"I beg your pardon?" she asked.

"You all in working order then?" He winked.

Oh God. She was going to be sick. The roast-beef-and-onion sandwich he'd had for lunch was obviously repeating on him and Alice was getting the full benefit. She gulped hard and Tash flashed before her eyes like an angel at the foot of her deathbed. "Reclaim your life, darling. It's the only way."

She took another look at his glistening, oily ponytail. "Absolutely, thank you. Now if you wouldn't mind getting off my desk, I have work to do." Alice scoured her desk furiously for something to do. She hadn't actually lifted a finger since the photocopying incident on Friday and wasn't even sure that she knew what she was meant to be doing. She picked up a folder lurking dustily in the corner and purposefully opened it.

"So you think you're too good for us, do you, you jumped-up cow?"

Alice glared at him. "Fuck off, you moron," she said, trying some of Tash's Stateside charm. She enjoyed it.

His face crumpled until his eyes were just two piggy slits amid his spots. He emptied the remains of his salt-and-vinegar crisps over her new navy-blue skirt and walked away.

At lunchtime Tash met Alice for an emergency summit in Prêt à Manger. At first Tash had walked past her as she sat in the corner with six mirror images of herself reminding her of her post-Jamie image—an ever-increasing number of chins and a stomach that before long would doubtless be reclaimed by the Vietnamese potbellied pig to whom it had originally belonged. Well, at least she was eating the low-fat vegetarian sandwich—it was all she could afford.

"I hardly recognized you. That navy's so school," Tash remarked, pointing to Alice's skirt. "You look seventeen. Actually, it's a good look. I may re-create it back in L.A. The guys there'll go to hell for it."

"Oh my God, you're leaving tomorrow?" Alice was suddenly mortified. She'd forgotten that today was Tash's last day. How could she have wished her on the Concorde heading for New York yesterday? Now she'd have given the world for this fount of wisdom in Lycra to stay a bit longer. She needed her.

"Tash, you can't go, it's great having you around."

"Have to, babe, I'm starting on a new film next week. The director has legendary sex appeal, wouldn't miss it for the world." Tash grinned. Alice imagined all that Tash would be going back to: Los Angeles. Hollywood. She probably had a mansion with a pool and Joan Collins around to lunch and Tom and Nicole for barbecues. And what did Alice have? Well, a very nice flat, but only until Simon came and reclaimed it; she also had very large thighs that could have been mistaken for the EC butter mountain were they painted yellow. Hell, she didn't even have a job anymore. "I've been sacked," she blurted out.

"Sacked?" Tash asked. It was obviously not a word in her vocabulary.

"Sacked, heave-ho, elbow. I suppose I'm getting used to it. If it's not Jamie, it's my boss." She pulled the slices of red pepper from the goat's cheese. "There are dumpers in life and there are dumpees."

"No, no, nooooo." Tash was adamant. About what, it wasn't clear, but her words stopped Alice from having a minor breakdown with a sandwich in her hand.

"What happened?" Tash asked. Alice was sure she was looking at her navy skirt in a disapproving way. Maybe Tash thought it served her right for wearing calico to the office.

"I tried to reclaim my life like you said. This disgusting lech in PC support asked me out and I said no." Tash smiled down on Alice, a teacher admiring an A-grade student. "Only it turns out he's the boss's son. I should have noticed the resemblance. Sweaty palms and dandruff. Anyway, I got the sack."

"Oh my God, I feel so responsible. Don't worry. We'll sort something out."

"What am I going to do, Tash? Nobody wants me!" Alice hiccuped the last part and burst into tears.

Tash wrested the goat's cheese mess from her hands and hugged her. "Trust me, darling. I have just the solution. And you just have to stop all this crying. It's hell on the crow's-feet."

CHAPTER 5

Alice plugged in her hair dryer and promptly blew every appliance in the house. "Bugger." She felt her way along the walls of the passageway toward the kitchen. Where had Simon said the fuse box was? He hadn't. That wouldn't be a very Simon observation to make. But Alice wasn't complaining. So she had no idea whether the hair dryer, or indeed the washing machine or the fridge, would ever work again. But she didn't actually care very much because tonight Alice Lewis was going out.

When she said out, she meant to-the-pub-out, not black-tie-champagne-swilling-starve-yourself-for-two-days-beforehand-out. But it was out. It was out of the house and down to the pub, which was farther than she'd been in quite a while if you didn't count the charity events that she was taken to by Trinny and the rest of the Legacy. Tonight was a legitimate Alice-goes-out-in-her-own-right evening, so there was almost a buzz of excitement in the house, if no electricity.

"Tash, do you know what a fuse box is meant to look like?" she yelled as she opened yet another cupboard door only to find even more LPs from the early eighties and another blow-up doll.

"Do I look like I do?" Tash appeared in the doorway looking more like Gina Lollobrigida with va-va-voom cleavage than Stanley the electrician with a navy boiler suit.

"Sorry I asked," Alice mumbled, noticing a few switches beside the boiler. Aha. "Don't worry, I've got it!" she yelled triumphantly to Tash, who wasn't in the least bit fretful. She began to click away blindly at the buttons. Room by room the house was illuminated and restored to full working order.

All except for the hair dryer. "Bugger." She ran to the bedroom window and heaved it open. She hung her head out and shook it backward and forward until the blood distorted her cheeks into a kind of boiled-piglet look. She opened her eyes only to see two accountant-style men cross over to the other side of the street, undoubtedly fearing some American-college-campus-type massacre in the heart of Chelsea. "Deranged woman leans from window and opens fire on innocent businessmen." She was half tempted to point her hair dryer at them and yell, "Stick 'em up," but she'd noticed that this sort of humor didn't go down as well in Chelsea as it had in Clapham. Come to think of it, she'd never tried it in Clapham either. Never even had cause to dry her hair out the window there.

The accountants trundled away with little more than a backward glance and Alice jumped up. After the inevitable bang on the head, which came from showing off to passersby, she put her mind to this evening. Her Last-Night-in-London Party. So what on earth was she going to wear? She knew that when she turned up at the bar at nine she'd be kissed and hugged by a bevy of girls who looked like they'd just walked out of a Helmet Newton shoot. Tight, shiny dresses and unfeasibly shiny hair. She looked down at her once-white-now-ish-colored robe. And her matted, damp hair. With Tash's expert hand they set about in a frenzy of transformation in ten minutes.

The girls wandered down to the pub arm in arm, partners in crime. They cut through the gardens of St. Luke's church and admired the municipal flowers in the park. It was so good to be with a friend. Trinny and the others were great, but they didn't really know Alice in the warts-and-all way that schoolfriends knew you. Knew your every snog from fourteen onward and your every bad haircut. And since Alice had come to London and started going out with Jamie, she'd all but lost touch with her friends from her native Norwich. Jamie had thought them too boring, or if they were a bit more exciting and happened not to have boyfriends, then they were confirmed dykes.

"Just wait and see, Alice. Louise is just dying to get you alone in the ladies," he'd mutter salaciously as they sat across some restaurant table from her schoolfriends on the rare occasion that Alice managed to persuade Jamie that her friends were actually worth giving up an evening for.

"I've known Louise since I was seven, Jamie," she'd chide him.

"Doesn't mean a bloody thing except she's never forgotten how exciting it was seeing you in your P.E. knickers." Nothing if not a dyed-in-the-wool male was our Jamie. Not that he didn't love the idea of getting a threesome going one night with Alice and one of her mates, though he'd most definitely have run a mile if put to the test. Alice had begun to blush recently when she remembered some of Jamie's remarks. If she didn't still love him so much she'd have thought he was just another predictable right-wing Sloane Ranger for whom wearing a tie with copulating frogs on it was being wacky. Just as well he wouldn't be meeting Tash, Alice thought as she hurried to keep up with Tash's strides, six inches longer than hers.

The Blenheim was heaving with smoke and a very particular assortment of London life. In one corner an alcoholic ex-footballer who was as much a regular as the dart board slugged back his last whiskey of the evening. His peroxide girlfriend had just walked in the door and was about to give him hell. He pegged it to the loo, knocking Alice's warm white wine as he went.

"Sorry, love," he chortled, giving her bum a swift pat for good measure. Alice had been coiffed into existence by Tash and her Velcro rollers and looked almost like her old self with the seven brands of eye cream all slathered under her bags and a smocky-type vertical-stripe ensemble concealing her forays into the cake tin.

"Alice, I can't believe you're leaving us. You will come back for the wedding, won't you?" Trinny took every opportunity to mention her impending nuptials, and Alice just smiled complicitly.

"It's only a three-month trip. Unless I get a job, I'll be back in September; you won't even have chosen the napkins by then."

Tash came over to the table with a pitcher of beer. She filled everyone's glass to spilling and then raised her own.

"Fresh starts," she prompted.

"Yeah. Fresh starts." The assortment of broad grins and chinking glasses along with a Pimms-too-many brought tears to Alice's eyes. Her last night in England.

"Westward ho!" Tim tipped his beer at her glass.

"What on earth are you going to do there?" asked Sophie, who was slightly bitter that she'd spent months nurturing a friendship with Simon Benedictus's cousin only to

have her zip off to Los Angeles at the first sniff of excitement. Oh well. Sophie looked down at the ring finger of
her left hand. At least Trinny was off the scene: for a while
the odds on her being the girl most likely to ensnare Simon
had been good. Now Sophie's position as an outside con-
tender was shifting. She was almost the favorite, if you
didn't count the minor European royals who were rapidly
entering the stakes as dark horses, even now busily buffing
up their tiaras for Simon's return.

"Who knows?" Alice laughed nervously. "Get a suntan.
Maybe even find a job and stay a bit longer. Oh, and get
away from the specter of Jamie." Everyone fell quiet as Alice mentioned his name. They knew that this usually pre-
ceded tears. But not tonight. Tash had counseled her well
and she was eyes front, looking to the future, not harking
on a past who'd run off with the female equivalent of
Rumpole of the Bailey in a pencil skirt.

"We'll miss you, darling," Trinny said, putting her hand
up to Alice's cheek. Alice, as predicted, shed a tear. But nobody seemed to notice. It was Trinny's beringed left hand
that oh-so-casually went up to Alice's cheek. All the girls'
eyes snapped to the replacement for the bubblegum ring. A
diamond the size of a gobstopper. Didn't she do well, their
eyes echoed.

Alice was secretly pleased to be leaving all this behind. The marriage market. Every night of the week. Seven
P.M. until midnight. Plenty of stalls still available but not
enough goods to go around anymore. Maybe in L.A. Alice
could forget about Jamie and not being married at the
grand old age of twenty-six and concentrate on herself and
her career for a change. God, had the suffragettes died under racehorses for nothing? Having Tash around was definitely a good thing for Alice's feminist spirit. The men, who

usually had quite a laugh at the marriage market, were oblivious to the mating overtures of the female marketeers this evening. They were too busy eyeing Tash's cleavage, which was having an outing all of its own. So Alice's tears went unnoticed. Or so she thought.

On a bench in the corner, waiting for his friends to arrive, sat Patrick Wilde. He ran his hand through his short black hair as he drained his pint of Guinness and fixed his eyes on Alice over the top of his glass. He'd noticed her as she walked over toward the bar, wearing the most terrible striped-tent creation he'd ever seen. Well, certainly in a London pub where even on a Wednesday night the female clientele were satin-shirted and boot-cut. But she didn't care; she stood at the bar, dropping first an ice cube into her glass and then one into her mouth. A couple of seconds later the cold would get the better of her and she'd take the ice cube out and put it into her drink.

Patrick was mesmerized. He'd never seen such unconscious behavior in a woman. Never seen anyone quite so real. Her messy dark curls and burning cheeks. He just couldn't stop staring. He prided himself on his highly developed taste in women, but this one was not up there. This one was a scruffy moorland pony among a stable of racehorses. So why was he even bothering to look? He waved to his friends, who'd just walked in through the door, grateful that he wouldn't have to stare at this girl with the terrible clothes and a weird way with ice cubes any longer.

CHAPTER 6

Alice hurled her suitcase into the back of the yellow cab at LAX airport and contemplated her blistered hands. She had no idea what traveling light was. Tash, surprisingly, seemed to be the only woman on the planet who had truly understood the essence of a capsule wardrobe and as a result her wealth of face creams, essential oils, Jimmy Choo mules, and Agent Provocateur undies all seemed to fit into a space the size of a pillbox. Alice, whose luggage always bred en route, marveled and decided that this trip would be a learning experience. Even if she didn't make it down to Mexico or learn to drive on the wrong side of the road, at least she'd figure out the secrets of economical packing. No small feat.

"Even the air smells different," said Alice as they drove down Pico toward Santa Monica. The evening was close and balmy and she'd already discarded the mountaineering socks she'd worn on the plane. "This is so beautiful." There were palm trees as tall as her house in London and the roads were wide enough to hold carnivals on. Lights flashed by and Alice wondered just how well she'd be getting to know this town.

"This is a really dangerous area. Never come here after nightfall," Tash warned.

"Oh well, I suppose I'll learn quickly." This area was

probably a bit like Notting Hill, thought Alice, the more bo-
hemian part of town; Tash probably lived in the equivalent
of Fulham, somewhere a bit safer. They passed a six-foot-
four transvestite and Alice could have sworn he was chatting to some bloke she'd seen on *Eastenders*. Oh well,
maybe it was more like North Notting Hill.

"This," Tash announced with a drumroll in her voice, "is
your bed." Tash set down Alice's battered suitcase by the
door and Alice flopped down on the magnificent creation.
She had never seen such a beautiful bed.

"Oh my God. This is absolutely amazing." Alice was
awestruck. It was a vast rosewood creation, and behind
the crisp white pillows, down a sheet of glass, trickled
rivulets of water lit up by cathedral candles that glinted
from behind. Alice swooned.

"Every man in Los Angeles wants to have sex in this
bed," Tash matter-of-factly informed Alice, who was now
bouncing on this nocturnal love temple.

"Is that a promise?" Alice laughed happily.

"No, it's a threat. You don't know what the men in L.A.
are like yet." Tash made her way through to the kitchen.

"Just so long as you don't introduce me to any English
lawyers called Jamie I'll be happy," Alice said as she followed Tash down the long hallway to the kitchen.

"Have fun in L.A., but it would be too horrible to fall in
love here. So don't," Tash warned.

Alice was now wandering around the plush living room.
"Are you sure this place didn't belong to some silent-movie
starlet?" she asked as she ran her fingers over scarlet velvet chaise longues and silver candlesticks.

"It was only built six years ago," Tash yelled above the
noise of ice cracking in a blender.

She walked through with two giant strawberry daiquiris. "Welcome to L.A." She handed Alice a glass.

As she sipped her way through it, all thoughts of Jamie drained from her mind. Up on the balcony, beyond the garden wall, she caught a glimpse of Venice Beach; the swaying groves of palm trees swept away all her yearning thoughts of him and she was grateful for once that she wasn't Helen Caudwell sitting in her dusty lawyer's office in Temple with her stuffy career and perfect bob. No, this was the life: sunshine, open-top cars, and cocktails. Who needed Jamie and his dirty blond locks?

"Wake up." Tash swept open the curtains of Alice's room with a flourish. "Just time for breakfast before your interview."

Alice's head nearly rolled off her shoulders. Interview? Breakfast? Oh God, this was getting worse.

"Buddamjetlagged." She groaned, shoving her head into the sanctity of the duvet.

"Wheatgrass. I knew it. It's just what you need."

Alice had known that Tash was harboring some potion that had turned her from an averagely clever, averagely pretty schoolgirl with braces into the Amazonian goddess who could talk about Jungian symbols and Fellini's cinematography standing on her head. So this was it. This was the secret that Tash had until now cunningly concealed. She'd known when she'd seen her radioactive healthy glow that it hadn't come from a merely balanced diet in which all the food groups were represented. Oh no, it had to be something far more sinister. At first Alice had suspected drugs. But then she'd noticed that Tash's superhuman energy levels came without the incumbent red eyes, nostrils, and bank balance of a drug addict.

Wheatgrass. She'd read about it in the *Daily Mail*. She'd seen it in the window of Planet Organic in Westbourne Grove, growing as innocently as you like, masquerading as AstroTurf. You could even grow your own if you wanted. Alice had resolved at the time to stick with her sunflowers and wilting kitchen-windowsill basil. When the *Mail* health editor had said it wasn't terribly palatable, Alice had suspected journalistic license. No such luck, she would soon discover.

Tash led Alice down Fourth Street and out onto Main— a wide, Roman-straight street fringed with shops selling everything from hot-pink beach-babe bikinis to every strain of blue-green algae mineral supplement and authentic Woodstock caftan. This was quintessential California. Outside the surf shops sat middle-aged men whose sun-baked bellies spilled over their damp denim shorts, humming to the strains of Tom Petty from the transistor in the fly-carcassed shop window; a whole block was dedicated to the windows of Gold's Gym, which flaunted taut bodies on going-nowhere exercise bikes and grimacing bodybuilders glaring into mirrors. Only on closer peering did Alice notice the less lean hamburger-casualties tucked away from the public gaze on the rowing machines on the far side of the room. Main Street was indeed a mecca for the West Coast lifestyle.

Café upon café catered to every need, from alfalfa to triple-choc muffin to frozen yogurt, and enlightened souls from every corner of the chilled-out world had abandoned the lay lines of Druid Dorset and youth hostels of Byron Bay to Rollerblade and meditate in Santa Monica. And it was so consumer friendly, too—should Alice ever find herself not able to live for another second without a six-foot natural sponge or a personal trainer for her pooch, then this would be her destination.

In fact, she'd almost walked off her hangover by the time they made it to Herbal Heaven. Drinking in the intoxicating atmosphere of her new surroundings had made her feel as close to bouyant as she'd felt for months. That was until she watched the razor-sharp blades of grass vanish through the blender and emerge as a gloppy species of pond slime. Alice imagined suddenly that she'd forgotten to pack her stomach. It certainly wasn't residing in its usual place tucked neatly beneath her rib cage. She wanted to dash for the loo, but Tash's evangelical grin weighed down upon her conscience like the face of the goldfish she'd forgotten to feed at age seven that had died an emaciated death.

"It's a total cure-all. Here." Tash proudly handed Alice the bilious-looking liquid. "Cincin."

If only she hadn't had that final round of daiquiris, she'd be able to stomach this cud juice. The thought of mashing cow's mouths and biology lessons learning about their double stomachs made Alice feel worse. Rheumy something. What was it now? If she focused on scientific facts, she might get through it. The periodic table. Sodium—Na. Potassium—K. That should do the trick, thought Alice, relocating her stomach at last.

"Let's eat alfresco." Tash joyfully led the way into a verdant glade at the back of the organic café.

"This place is nice." Alice smiled fakely, playing for time.

"Oh, it's totally full of major granolas, but I like it." Tash nibbled on a fat-free tofu cake.

"What's a granola?" Alice asked, relishing the opportunity to converse rather than do a down-in-one.

"Granola is like a breakfast cereal. Like muesli?" Tash said. Alice nodded, yup, she knew muesli. "Well, people

who are, like, herbal, organic, y'know, we call them granolas. They wear Birkenstocks and stuff. Kind of crunchy
people."

"Oh, okay." Alice nodded, pleased to have been enlightened on that point and even more pleased to have postponed the inevitable for thirty seconds. But there was a
menacing-looking empty table lurking in the far corner of
the café. Tash determinedly made her way over, plonked
down, and knocked back a mouthful of bilge as though it
were the ambrosia of the gods.

Why the hell did this bloody garden have to be so bloody
green, thought Alice, wincing, green, green, green. She
slipped her sunglasses onto her nose so that at least if
her eyes smarted Tash wouldn't be able to tell. But Alice
and wheatgrass just weren't meant to be. " 'Scuse me."
Alice hurtled for the nearest potted plant and promptly
deposited her mouthful of neat chlorophyll and a good
deal of last night's nachos and daiquiris onto the roots of
an organic lemon tree. Organic no longer.

As she came to with her head propped against a cool ter-
racotta pot, Alice suddenly remembered the latter part
of Tash's threat. Intersomething. Not inter-railing surely.
Interfering. Well, that was par for the course with Tash,
that was why Alice loved her so much. No, something else.
Tash was now crouching down next to her and the deluge
of Eau Hadrien acted like smelling salts on a Jane Austen
heroine. She opened her eyes to catch the tail end of
Tash's rallying cry. ". . . or you'll miss your interview."

Tash's cream-colored Armani trouser suit was a sooth-
ing oasis amid all the green. Alice reared her head groggily
as the words sunk in. That was it—inter-view.

"Interview? Where?" She ignored the unamused glances of her fellow wheatgrass imbibers and concentrated hard on Tash's lips.

"It's okay, they're friends of mine, they'll love you."

"But . . . I don't have my CV," Alice improvised hastily.

"They don't need a résumé, darling, I've already told them how sweet and talented you are. Don't worry, you'll be fine. See, once you get this job you'll get a green card and then you can stay longer than three months. Great, huh?"

Dusting a mangy lemon leaf from her hair, Alice contemplated her talents. Now let's think, she always hated those parts of the interview when they asked her what her strengths were. Better to be prepared. She racked her brain. She was loyal, oh yes, she'd stuck with Jamie long after his sell-by date; and she had initiative—had she not had the inspiration to sprinkle her last batch of carrot-cake mixture with some rather delicious and nutritious poppyseeds? And she could hold a ruby in her now rather obscured-by-all-the-aforementioned-cakes-she'd-eaten belly button she was certain, not that she'd ever quite had the opportunity, but once she'd gotten drunk and practiced with a fruit pastille. A ruby couldn't be much different. Hmmm. She was, after all, a particularly talented individual, and if Tash was convinced that she really was sweet, so hot on the heels of the vomit-in-the-potted-plant scenario, then it must be so. Sweet, talented Alice. Wheatgrass aside, this American positive-thinking thing was suiting her rather well.

"So what experience do you have that actually qualifies you for this position, Ms. Lewis?" asked the woman who'd shaken Alice's hand so fracturingly firmly and looked her square in the pupils as she'd walked into the room.

"Erm. Well, you see, when you say experience . . ." Alice trailed off. She glanced around the boardroom: the ludicrously expensive butter-soft leather sofas; the multimedia equipment so superslick that it would have made her coworkers at Know Your Personal Computer think they'd gone to heaven and were having sex with Scully from the *X-Files*; and the stunning rooftop view of the convertibles in a traffic jam along Wilshire Boulevard. Never in her career had she even taken minutes at such a high-powered meeting, let alone been the object of such mind-bendingly important people's attention. Why on earth were they bothering with Alice, thirty-two words a minute on a good day and capable of making a pig's ear of even the simplest envelope-stuffing task? She suspected that they were beginning to wonder the same. The other four members of the interview panel were looking penetratingly at her from behind their individual desks and limited-edition Armani spectacles. Why did she get the feeling that any second now they'd hold up placards declaring United Kingdom zero points? The green card vanished over the horizon of Alice's imaginary new life.

"What can you offer our company?" Even the man with the aging rocker's ponytail on the end whom Alice had thought would be a pushover—just mention REM and offer him a spliff—had gone all terse on her. And these were Tash's *friends*. What would an interview with proper interviewers be like? Alice saw creeping up on her from behind at best an illegal career stacking the fridges at Blockbuster video with Häagen-Dazs and at saddest a lonely plane ride back to Heathrow.

"You see, the thing is . . ." For all their cool professionalism they couldn't conceal their contempt any longer. The panel's eyes rolled en masse, making them look like one of those strange Magic Eye pictures of dolphins beneath the sea. Perhaps if she squinted hard enough . . .

"Ms. Lewis?" Oh dear, she was in trouble now. Could she be deported for cocking up her interview so monumentally?

"I haven't a clue what the job is. If you wouldn't mind telling me, then I'm sure I can come up with the pertinent experience." She smiled benignly. Was *pertinent* the right word?

The representatives from every Ivy League college you could name, and some you couldn't, breathed in sharply. She'd soon find out.

Alice had eaten three onion bagels and some things she'd found at the back of the fridge called ranch-flavored chips. She wasn't altogether sure what a ranch was supposed to taste like—but for some reason sprawling plains and log cabins and Kevin Costner sprung to mind—but squashed into the cream cheese they could have passed for Walkers salt-and-vinegar chips. She heard Tash hang up the phone in the kitchen and kicked the ranch chips under the sofa. What was the point of having Alice join the most elite gym in Santa Monica if she was going to just munch junk food all day, she could hear Tash say. What point, indeed, other than that Alice was convinced she would not be joining this elite haven of Southern California's finest torsos.

She'd eaten herself into a trough of depression since her interview two days ago. No job. No green card. No life here, basically. She'd be on the next plane back to London, where all the men reminded her of Jamie every time they opened their mouths to utter "See the game on Saturday?" and where the only romantic opportunity available to her was to go out with Nick from PC support and be promoted to head photocopier once she'd married into the family firm. She scoffed up the last bagel before Tash could confiscate it.

"So you got the job." Tash strolled into the room with her cell phone tucked under her arm. "But I'm just gonna call them about a pay raise. I can't have you working for less than forty grand. It's an insult."

So insult me, abuse me, tell me I'm crap. Alice didn't care. FORTY THOUSAND DOLLARS. She poured the remaining ranch chips down her throat in shock. Wow. Grown-up salary. Did they have Jigsaw over here? She was longing to call Lloyds Bank in Norwich and tell them where to stick their interest rates and say, "No I won't be needing a seven-thousand-pound overdraft limit anymore, Ms. Turnbull. Yes, I'm quite sure, thank you."

But Tash was still far from happy.

"What, no clothing allowance?" yelled Tash as she resumed her negotiations with the head of human resources. "And how is a member of your staff expected to perform the tasks demanded of her in clothes from Banana Republic?"

"Don't push it, Tash," Alice muttered nervously. God, she could buy out Donna Karan for forty grand a year, what was Tash getting her knickers in a twist about?

"Good. Now let's talk expense account," Tash negotiated. Alice buried her face in the sofa and waited for the phone to slam at the other end with a resounding "Don't call us, we'll call you."

Instead Tash's smile broadened into "Thanks, Melissa, I'll have her there first thing on Monday. Ciao."

Alice unplugged her ears and looked in anticipation at Tash. "Well, don't keep me in suspense."

"You start at ten on Monday. Which only gives us two

days to make you look the part of publicist to the stars. Come on." Tash was already swinging her handbag over her shoulder and setting the burglar alarm as Alice took in the news. So that's what the job was. At the interview she had been so busy trying not to regurgitate the rest of the green slime all over the shagpile that she'd been completely deaf to her job description. Publicist to the stars. She didn't know whether she should laugh or cry at this juncture so instead she licked a blob of cream cheese from her fingers and ran out of the door after Tash.

CHAPTER 7

"**Y**ou see this absolutely has to go, Alice." Tash was tugging at Alice's bobbly black cardigan. The thing Alice loved most in the world—now that *he'd* gone, she added as a caveat. It had been squashed on the back of her chair when she grappled with the Franco-Prussian war in sixth form; it had dangled over her shoulders like a talisman on her first date with Jamie and kept her warm on summer evenings in pub beer gardens. Tash's drawing attention to its sartorial shortcomings made her sad—it was like suddenly realizing that her mother had wrinkles and was no longer the bell-bottomed young woman who graced the dusty photo albums. She pulled it closer over her fraying T-shirt.

"Do what you will with me, Tash, but the cardigan stays, you know that."

Tash laughed and tossed her hair back as they sped along the freeway to Beverly Hills in the silver convertible.

"And those shoes. Urgh!" Alice hid her feet under the seat and had to admit to herself that her old Pumas were less than fragrant and had a considerable amount of London Transport debris stuck between the grips on the bottom. She wasn't going to complain if Tash persuaded her into a pair of café-au-lait suede loafers, that was for sure.

They pulled up in the shady carpark of the Beverly Center only to be set upon by a man in black tie.

"Argghhh!" Alice screamed as he opened the driver's door. "Help!" Certain death flashed before her eyes. Her mother and father, grief-stricken on the sofa, oblivious to the whistling of the kettle in the kitchen; her fifth-form school photograph emblazoned across the front of the *Daily Mail*; a BBC2 debate on the increasing hazards facing tourists abroad.

"Alice honey, he's the valet. Get real," Tash said, handing over her keys and throwing her handbag over her shoulder.

Alice got out of the car with still-quaking knees.

"Alice, this thing with Jamie hit you really hard, didn't it? Now I know perhaps you don't want to tell me this, but I'll ask anyway. Was Jamie ever violent toward you? Did he ever hit you?" Tash was looking hard at Alice, looking for further signs of mental scarring.

"Ha, ha, ha! Noooo," Alice belted out in her relief at being spared her life and at the random ridiculousness of the question. "Unless of course you count the time he walloped my face because he said there was a mosquito on it. And personally I never really believed that. I swear to this day it was because I jumped up and down on his golf clubs."

Tash backed off, obviously startled by this revelation. "Wooh, that's way too messy for me to go into. I think we should look at getting you some professional help." And with that she led Alice by the arm toward the elevator.

Rodeo Drive was blisteringly hot. All Alice could see was rising waves of heat and fragmented groups of Japanese tourists laden down with slick shopping bags. Her jeans were beginning to stick to her hot legs and she couldn't help feeling like Nick Nolte's female counterpart in the film *Down and Out in Beverly Hills*—a complete tramp. When the stares from women dripping with gilt and poodles became too much, she just pretended to herself that she was a method actor deep in character. It didn't stop the stares, but it gave her a kind of superiority that convinced the onlookers that to be so scruffy and confident, she had to be a grunge actress or a member of the English aristocracy.

"I've made an appointment with Randi, who'll do your hair. You'll then have a mani and pedi with Andi. I'll meet you in three hours in the coffee shop across the street." Alice had been so engrossed in her Stanislavsky method acting that she hadn't realized they'd come to a halt beside a building that had obviously been uprooted from Athens sometime before Plato died. Magnificent columns and pruned bay trees adorned the entrance. Blimey.

"So where do I go for my trim?" Alice blinked, wishing she'd remembered her sunglasses. She wondered if Tash had a squinting-too-long-at-the-sun eye cream.

"Here." Tash pushed open the front doors of the Athenaeum to let Alice through and then hared off around the bend.

"Oh, and none of this 'trim' crap. I've told Randi what to do, it'll be no use arguing," she yelled behind her as she made for Melrose Avenue.

Alice contemplated her options. Run, cab back to Santa Monica, pick up my suitcases . . . No, that plan fell short on the second leg. She couldn't even afford a cab back to Versace at the end of the street. Besides, there was a tall Rudolph Valentino look-alike loitering in the doorway trying to grab her cardigan from her. What did these bloody Americans have against her cardigan? She resolved that it was a shampoo and set or nothing at all. It was her hair, she was damned well going to decide what happened to it. Reclaim your hair, Alice, she thought crossly.

Alice sat with a head heavy with foil. She could see Randi only through the gaps in her metal helmet, but she could hear her.

"So would you say porous, dry, or oily on occasion?" Randi twirled her suicide-blond locks around her four-inch-long pierced fingernails and drawled her way through the twentieth question.

"Not applicable," mumbled Alice. She was becoming woozy from the smell of bleach. She'd once seen this woman on *Watchdog* who'd been left bald after routine highlights. She looked nervously around her at the other clients to assess the risk, but they all had enough foil on their heads for a month of Sunday lunches.

". . . never, sometimes, or mostly?" Randi continued, squinting intently at the customer care questionnaire and filling in the boxes with the precision of one much prac-ticed in the "How Deep Is Your Love?" and "Will He Leave His Wife for You?" questionnaires in women's weeklies.

"Mostly," Alice said with conviction. This was beginning to be like the test at the optician's, where they ask you which circles are brighter, the green or the red. After a while you get bored and lie. Then you spend the next two years worrying that maybe you've got the wrong prescrip-tion spectacles. Shit. I'd better pay attention.

"I'm sorry, Randi, you'll have to repeat that last one. I think someone's got a hair dryer on." A remarkable obser-vation, Alice. Try a hundred and fifty hair dryers. This was no ordinary hair salon. No siree. This was an emporium of vanity. Four floors of pristine Hollywood female. Hair sculpted and set and an eyebrow wax on the way out. It was like *Charlie and the Chocolate Factory* without the joy of chocolate. Only oompa lumpas and staircases leading to strange instruments of torture—one of which was wielded before Alice two hours later in the manicure chamber.

"It's only a cuticle clipper, dear. Don't look so anxious." Andi was looking at her curiously now. Oh my god, it's my hair, isn't it? Alice wanted to scream. It's falling out. She looked for telltale clumps in the foot spa. She'd tried to catch a glimpse of herself and see the results of Randi's handiwork, but she'd been whisked between the tinting chair and the wash basin with such vigor that she'd only seen a blur with big hair as she passed the mirror. But why on earth was Andi still staring at her?

"You know you have beautiful eyes?" He cupped her chin between his hands in the way that only a gay man can without a slap in the face. She smiled. She liked this warm, honest approach Americans seemed to have. "Now if you'd just let me tweeze that brow we'd have you looking like a doll in no time."

Alice was cross again now. "If I wanted to look like some ditzy bloody Hollywood airhead, then I'd bloody ask for it, wouldn't I? And haven't you ever heard of Brooke Shields?"

She regretted her loss of temper instantly, but Andi remained unperturbed. "Brooke? Of course, I trimmed her corns only yesterday actually." Alice burst out laughing. Were these people for real? Still, living in the artifice capital of the world was going to have its compensations, she thought as Andi dealt with her hangnails. At least with all this peroxide going on I'm not likely to encounter anyone with muddy blond hair.

When they met in the coffee shop, Tash made a big deal of pretending not to recognize the new, improved Alice and Alice pretended not to look at her reflection in the pictures on the wall next to them.

"My God, but, Ms. Lewis, you're beautiful!" Tash kept saying between sips of her latte.

Alice could see her new self reflected in the lines of a Mondrian print—her hair was the size of a small European country, her eyebrows reduced from cabbage-fattened caterpillars to anorexic tapeworms. Did that constitute an improvement? And she couldn't really be sure about the color of her hair, as it varied depending on which Mondrian square it was revealed in, but the curl that she could see out of the corner of her left eye looked to be a pleasing Cadbury's milk-chocolate sort of color.

"Now we just have to get you into some halfway decent clothes and you'll be able to pull significantly more than the PC support manager on Monday."

Alice looked at her warningly.

"Okay, I know you're not ready for another relationship, sweetie, but the best thing to do is get back in the saddle. Truly." Tash crossed her heart with her newly lime-greened nails and winked at Alice.

"One step at a time, Professor Higgins," said Alice, rather enjoying the attention for once and longing to hit Bloomingdale's or wherever it was she was going to go to buy clothes.

"The Gap?" she whined like a teenager being taken to Clarks for her shoes.

"For someone who doesn't give a shit what she looks like, you're making an awful fuss."

"Who said I don't give a shit?" said Alice, now almost

scraping her feet along the floor as she walked among the chinos.

Tash looked pointedly at her current attire.

"I happen to have spent my first month's salary on turning my hair the shade it would be after a week in the sun if I'd waited. I'm not about to scrimp on clothing." Alice was not unaware of how brattish this sounded. An hour in the 90210 zip code district had obviously been an hour too long. She buried her head in her chest and flicked through a rack of sundresses, but Tash's accusing gaze was too penetrating.

"Well, maybe you have the makings of a Valley girl in you after all." Tash grinned. "Come on, let's do some proper shopping, I was just testing to see how much room for improvement there was beneath that frumpy exterior." Alice flicked her cardigan at Tash, who ducked behind a rail of black turtlenecks. "Besides, I have a reputation to uphold. It's bad enough that you're English; they've become a totally humdrum accessory in this town since *Four Weddings*. For a while everyone wanted one, but now they're passé. You're just gonna have to make up the brownie points on novelty value: being a well-dressed Brit."

They strolled out of the Gap and along the street to Ralph Lauren. Alice bought a belt that was so blissfully lovely, she knew that it would transform her life, in the same way that every purchase always promises elevation from oneself into a glistening new person. She couldn't wait to take her holidays back in London and parade her hair and nails up and down Blackfriars Road and accidentally bump into Jamie and the Tart.

When they arrived home laden with Barneys bags, most of which admittedly belonged to Tash, the girls collapsed on the sofa. Alice pulled out her new garments one by one.

"I'm still not sure about the beige," she said as she fingered some silk trousers and matching cashmere sweater.

Tash winced. "Blond, sweetie, not beige."

"Same thing. You sure I don't look too much like porridge?" she queried as she pulled the sweater over her head.

"Which reminds me. Gym tomorrow."

Alice wondered what had prompted that stream-of-consciousness remark from Tash and decided it must have been her thighs. Oh yes, nothing like Alice's lumpen thighs to remind people of all manner of breakfast fodder. Jamie had once likened them to his favorite Cumberland sausages.

CHAPTER 8

Patrick sweated anxiously aboard the Boeing to L.A. Next time he'd remember to go economy. The first-class seats were beige leatherette affairs with sheepskin trims that reminded him of the time he was seduced at age twelve by his best friend's mother on some late-seventies rug in front of a glowing log-effect fire. He squirmed at the thought. Since then he'd gotten used to it—being seduced, not sheepskin. It happened with predictable frequency; not that he was an Adonis or anything, he just had this look about him. Women wanted to take care of him with his urchin crop and magnetic green eyes. And his Irish lilt certainly added to his appeal.

Being imbued with this sense of the possible as far as romance was concerned from such an early age had left Patrick with none of the vanity but all of the optimism of a Casanova. He fell in love on an almost daily basis and had he ever been asked by *Who's Who* for his favorite pastimes, he would undoubtedly have said kissing, women, etc. His career in the theater heightened his sense of the romantic: as one of the youngest and most talented directors in London, he was forever coaxing Heros and Leanders and Anthonys and Cleopatras into passionate clinches.

"Can we not have a bit more frisson there, you two?"

he'd wail from the darkened shadows of the pit as the actors worried what their other halves sitting in the front row on opening night would say when they got home.

And it wasn't as though he was traveling all the way to L.A. just to see her, was it? He'd been meaning to come for ages. Not that he'd ever worried before about crossing the world for a woman. That was part of the joy of romance. It's just that Alice hadn't really been his type, but as he'd been thinking about her almost every waking, and some sleeping, moments since he'd first seen her in the pub, then he might as well try to kill two birds with one stone while he was out there. Anyway, she wasn't his type at all, he usually went for blondes—granted, there had been one or two redheads, but they'd all played irresistible parts like the tragically noble Duchess of Malfi or Bernard Shaw's Saint Joan. In the case of the redheads, it had been their lines he'd fallen for, if he was being honest. And it wasn't as though he'd deliberately tried to find out about her, was it? He'd finished his Guinness and bumped into one of her friends at the bar, quite a beautiful friend, too.

"Someone's birthday?" he'd asked Sophie as she waited for her Tanqueray and lime.

"Engagement party," Sophie said, bestowing her brightest smile on him. Could this be a man worth having who she didn't know about? She made a mental note to look him up in her *Tatler's* Most Eligible Bachelors when she got home.

"You're not from London, are you?" Sophie asked, taking a sip of her just-so Tanqueray.

"Dublin," said Paddy, looking over her shoulder at Alice. "Is that the bride-to-be?"

"Alice? God, no. She's leaving. Trinny's getting married.

Great ring from Theo Fennell." Patrick gave Sophie the once-over—very long legs, mermaid-green eyes, very nice. So that was her name—Alice. It suited her.

"And where is she going, our Alice?" he asked. Maybe he'd take Sophie home.

"Oh, America. L.A., I think. I hear Dublin's beautiful; do you actually live there?" She circled her finger around the rim of her glass and took in the full effect of this man. Beautiful. Just tall enough, slightly on the skinny side, but nothing a few long dinners at the Bluebird café wouldn't remedy, and his hair was a bit shabby, but she knew this great guy in Notting Hill who did wonders with men's hair. Yes, she could picture them now, ring shopping hand in hand at Bulgari—Theo Fennell was all very charming, but would it stand the test of time? Bulgari and then on to Catherine Walker for the dress. It would probably be a simple city wedding, maybe at St. Luke's. Oh, but maybe he would have other ideas. "Does your family live in Dublin?" she'd asked, just to ascertain any impediments to her plan.

"Some of the time," he'd replied vacantly, staring over her shoulder again. God, they lacked concentration, these Irish.

She'd been pretty irritated, he recalled, when he turned up at her soiree straight from the RSC rehearsal studio in Clapham with his only-fit-to-paint-the-spare-room jeans and shirt on. But she'd unconsciously gotten her own back by excusing him to all her friends as "rather an arty type" and then giggling uncontrollably. Somehow the conversation turned to Alice, he presumed that that was because she was all they had in common really. Eventually Sophie told him that it was okay if he wanted to pursue Alice because she was still in love with Simon B. and anyway her mother would kill her if she married a socialist. He had no idea what she meant about pursuing Alice, Sophie was much more his type. They'd even shared a few glasses of flat champagne when her guests had left.

When Paddy got home that night, he called Jack, his closest friend in L.A. "Jacko, you don't still have that spare room, do you?"

"Aha, has Patrick Wilde decided to sell his soul to Hollywood?" Jack had asked between the mouthfuls of smoked salmon and scrambled egg he enjoyed daily on his balcony overlooking Manhattan Beach.

"Nah, I've got this meeting with this producer who wants to finance a film of *The Seagull*."

"So you have sold your soul. I thought you didn't want to make films."

"Ah, and there's the beauty—he'll just film my play with a few great props. Anyway, there's this girl . . ." The champagne was making him say things that he didn't even mean.

"What a surprise. Let me guess. Five-ten. Peroxide. Ex-RSC, now starring in a daytime soap?" Jack knew the scenario. The second one of Paddy's productions ended he followed the nearest dearest thing into the sunset.

"Wrong. Wrong. Wrong. Actually I probably won't see her at all because she's living in Santa Monica and you're in Manhattan, right? But I've got a few weeks before I'm due back here, so how about we paint the town a lurid shade of scarlet?"

"Aren't you getting a bit old to be doing this, Pat?" Jack asked affectionately. "I mean after *The Playboy of the Western World* you were off chasing some woman to Sydney, last summer it was that gym instructor in New York. They obviously pay you too much money for being this wunderkind. Don't you get bored?"

"You're kidding. It's fabulous. You just don't appreciate women, Jacko, there's infinite variety, each one has something amazing about her—the way she strokes the hair at the back of your neck, the way she rubs her leg up and down yours during the night—idiosyncracies, that's the joy. But this one's not the same. I absolutely don't fancy her. And even if I do come over I probably won't even see her."

"Sure. I'll make up the bed." Jack had known Patrick Wilde since he'd been directed by him as Ariel in drag in some grotty theater in Camden. The production had been a disaster, but they'd remained firm friends. Paddy sometimes put Jack up in his surprisingly lavish flat in Soho when he had an audition in London. Jack took a bite of toast and wondered what on earth was going on. Paddy was never shy about his women. He'd tell you straight up which ones he wanted and then he'd get them. As he'd never really suffered rejection, caution was not part of his repertoire. All very simple really. And then they'd have sex ad infinitum until the next woman came along.

Paddy stretched his legs out into the aisle. Of course he wasn't getting too old to do this. He worked hard and played hard. He and Jack could have a fantastic time in L.A. He opened his peanuts and calculated that if everything went according to plan he might even be able to squeeze in an affair with some babe and be back for casting of *A Chaste Maid in Cheapside* in just under a month. The whole love thing, start to finish, never usually lasted that long anyway—the flowers, the seemingly innocuous lunch at an airy restaurant followed by the steamy siesta followed by approximately two weeks of wanton passion— no more than a month. And Patrick was nothing if not realistic. He closed his eyes and tried to get some sleep. If only he could get Alice out of his head.

CHAPTER 9

"**E**ven God rested on Sunday," Alice complained as she pulled the duvet over her head.

"God obviously didn't have unfortunate flabby thighs. Forty minutes a day on the StairMaster and you'll be a new woman," yelled Tash between toothpaste spits from the bathroom. "I'll take you to the omelette parlor afterward."

"And how many free periods are there between then and lunch, miss?"

"I'll pretend I didn't hear that," said Tash, turning off the bathroom light and putting her head around Alice's door. "It's for your own good."

"I know, I'm an ungrateful cow, but you've gone from being this sweet teenager with bad taste in leggings to this organized, disciplinarian goddess. I can't cope."

Tash patted the lump beneath the duvet that was Alice and grinned cheekily. "We'll soon have you reclining in the dewy glades of Mount Olympus, don't fret. Good night."

I've done my reclining, thought Alice as she recalled the month after she and Jamie parted when she'd refused to get up. Her space had become a large ashtray littered with full-fat-yogurt pots and cream-egg wrappers. The curtains hadn't been opened since the morning they broke up. If it hadn't been for Simon's offer of the Bywater Street house and an irritating number of messages from her bank

manager demanding money, she'd probably still be sobbing under the blankets in the same jogging pants. And
she was pleased the reclining was over as she twiddled her
new, split-endless hair around her finger, but she wasn't
quite ready to be a goddess yet. Not that there was much
chance of that even if she moved into the gym on a sub-
letting basis and kept Andi and Randi in attendance twenty-
four hours a day. Still, she thought, as she flipped the switch
to turn on the waterfall behind her, perhaps just for one
night, just to see if this bed's all it's cracked up to be. And if
it hadn't been for the strange muddy yellow light of the
candles reminding her of what she didn't want to be reminded of, namely Jamie's hair, she might have fallen
asleep without crying for once.

It's a total myth that if you go to the gym in your holiest
black leggings and your Joshua Tree Tour T-shirt that you
won in the college raffle, nobody will look twice at you. Instead they look four times at you, as Alice was discovering.
She'd just fallen off the StairMaster again and an *über* babe
behind her was tutting noisily because she couldn't see
herself in the mirror for Alice's bum.

"Ritual humiliation," she groaned as she stalked off to
burn up some calories on the treadmill. At least she couldn't
go far wrong with walking. She climbed aboard and applied her elementary knowledge of computers to program
the thing. Where was the PC-support lech when you needed
him? The supermarket conveyer belt began to shift beneath
her feet. Yup. Still standing, she thought proudly. The machine bleeped and demanded to know her heart rate.

"How the bloody hell do I know?" she told it.

"Just hold the sensors, dear, and it'll tell you." A

desiccated-looking old bird on the next-door treadmill yelled over the din of Bryan Adams. Alice was staring so hard at the woman's creepy arms she nearly fell off.

"Here." She patted two silver handles and flashed a smile with the most perfect teeth Alice had ever seen outside a Pearl Drops advert. Spooky. Alice wondered if perhaps they were filming her for a special edition of the *X-Files*.

"Thanks." She clutched the bars and watched as the machine failed to register the fact that she even had a heart. Well, I could have told it that anyway, she snarled, thanks to *him*.

"Ready for the weights?" Tash bounded up behind Alice with the energy of a labrador in heat. She had chosen to reveal a lot of thigh and even more stomach. Plus that chest again. But she was far from alone in the not-quite-as-nature-intended stakes. Everywhere Alice looked a crop top was spilling the spoils of Hollywood's finest plastic surgeons. Jamie would have a field day, she thought, noticing miserably that her T-shirt was virtually concave by comparison.

Alice held on to the handrail for dear life as she teetered down the stairs from the gym. Her legs trembled. She'd known that two minutes on the inner thigh press had been two minutes too long, but would Saffron listen? Saffron was now her personal trainer, the young Australian who'd shared the glorious news that she'd probably burned about fourteen calories in what had felt like a month on the treadmill. Alice had bitten her lip and resisted the urge to push Saffron's bendy little body headlong into a steroid-crazed weightlifter.

"Ah, don't worry about those," the delightful Aussie had

twittered as she prodded the lumps visible through the holes in Alice's leggings. "Drink plenty of water and you won't see yer cellulite for dust."

I won't see my cellulite for the view of the bathroom door from the loo, you mean, thought Alice, contemplating the inordinate amount of water it would take to shift her surface-of-the-moon-through-a-telescope thighs.

"You're a pom, aren't you?" Saffron smiled warmly as she readjusted her perfect ponytail.

Alice nodded.

"My mother's from Wales." Saffron was chuffed to bits to impart this news and Alice smiled with genuine warmth this time. At least this girl wasn't trying to wrest her cardigan from her and make her assert her female rights. As fellow members of the Commonwealth, she thought they should stick together. Saffron obviously thought the same.

"Haven't got a boyfriend, have you?" Saffron was very certain of this point.

"Erm, not at the moment, no," Alice replied defensively. "Just . . . taking a breather."

Saffron obviously didn't believe her, and there was fat chance that Alice would find a boyfriend in this town if all the women looked like bloody Saffron. She thrust her card into Alice's hand. "Listen, anytime you need to tighten up those inner thighs, just give me a bell." And with that she darted off like the India rubber man to her next aerobics class, leaving Alice unsure as to whether she'd just been insulted or picked up by a woman.

"All I'm asking you to do is to sew it to the inside of yer boxers and take it through customs."

At the time he'd thought that the perfect solution to getting rid of the South American gangsters who'd been pursuing his best friend, Gibbo, would be to just comply with their wishes. Do as they said. Donatello and his men were small and swarthy but tough as Brazil nuts—all the boys had to do was smuggle a few bits and pieces across into Mexico and they'd be off their backs. But now it wasn't looking so appealing.

"If you're implying I stick it up my bum . . ." Simon Benedictus clenched his buttocks, perished at the very thought.

"Of course I'm not, look at you, you're a pom, you're practically royalty. They'll never stop you in a million years. I only have to say g'day and they arrest me for heroin smuggling." Gibbo pushed his blond dreadlocks back from his smooth bronzed forehead and looked imploringly at Simon. "If we don't get it through to Mexico they'll kill me, man."

"And if we do then that'll be it. Finito. Are you sure, Gibbo?" Simon turned over on his hammock and drew circles with a stick in the sand. " 'Cause I'd hate to go to all this trouble just to be chased by the evil bastards through Mexico."

"No. We take it to Mexico, give it to Donatello, and I'm on the next flight out of there back to Melbourne. Sod this traveling bollocks, me old man needs a partner for his accountancy firm, reckon I'm just the ticket." Gibbo stood up and paced around, the crisscross lines of the hammock emblazoned across his broad surfer's shoulders.

"I'll only do this if you swear they're going to kill you. If all they said in the note was that they'd torture you, then you can take it like a man." Simon squinted at the stunning horizon and wished that he hadn't offered his Nikon to Donatello as security against Gibbo. But then again maybe he didn't really want to take too many more photos. The last decent roll of film he'd shot had been at a strip club in Rio. *The Sunday Times* magazine would probably lap it up, but he was bored with South America. Maybe he should move on to Asia after this. The locals were less intimidating.

"My Spanish is good enough to know the difference between pull yer fingernails out and murder you in cold blood, okay?" Gibbo was clearly terrified.

Simon took a thoughtful swig of his beer. "All right. I'll do it. But if anyone touches my bum you're dead anyway."

CHAPTER 10

"So what happened to this guy in Italy?" Alice dug her spoon deep into the melon and eyed the double pancakes and bacon on the next table covetously.

"Oh, actors schmactors. He was the lead in the film I was working on in Milan. We decided maybe we should have children, so went back to his family place in Tuscany. After a few weeks playing the wife and sun-drying tomatoes from the vine, I got bored and we started throwing unglazed Umbrian pottery at each other, so I left."

"Do you miss him?" asked Alice, who at this moment was missing Jamie more than she'd ever admit. It was something about Sunday mornings. Lazing in bed till noon, a few Bloody Marys at the pub, and a roast. Couldn't beat it.

"Miss him? Not at all. I'm thinking of having an affair with the DP on the film I'm working on here."

"DP?" Alice queried.

"Director of photography. They're much more creative than actors and there's something about the way they hitch the camera up on their shoulder . . ." Tash paused and licked the cappuccino froth from her spoon thoughtfully. "Makes you wish it was you . . ." She was lost now, obviously being hauled over some brawny creative shoulder in her mind's eye.

Alice drifted back to Sunday morning on Fulham Road,

realizing it was probably quite a poor domestic daydream in comparison to Tash's full-blooded fantasy.

"Did you ever want Jamie's children?" Tash interrupted her steaming up of the camera lens and popped a raspberry in her mouth.

"Well, not exactly, we weren't really ready for children." Why did it sound so ghastly and weak? She felt like one of those women who allow fifteen minutes twice a week for lovemaking—no passion, no *joie de vivre*. She'd wash Jamie's rugby kit and he'd fluff up her hair on his way to the pub. "See you later, alligator. Oh, my pink shirt, would you mind just running the iron over it, it's just that I'm seeing a client tomorrow."

And the tragically pathetic thing was that Alligator didn't mind at all. She'd lapped it up. Even rubbing Vanish into his shirt collars to get out those nasty raspberry coulis stains (did she ever believe that? she wondered incredulously) out.

"I wanted to have a brood. Still do, but I'm looking for the right gene pool. It's one thing ending up with a dysfunctional husband because you can divorce him and keep the Bel-Air home, but if you have a kid by him, then you're stuck with a dysfunctional child. You have to be really careful."

Alice wondered what Jamie's child would look like. Probably have a power bob and a penchant for miniskirts, seeing how the person most likely to be giving birth to Jamie's child certainly wasn't her.

Tash read her thoughts. "You're moving onwards and upwards, Ali-Baba. We'll have you fixed up with your dream man in no time."

Alice gulped. She thought of reminding Tash that no one in her right mind would sleep with a guy from L.A. but realized it might seem ungrateful. "I really think that a man is the last thing I need right now. Why is everyone so obsessed with my love life?" She was peeved. "Does having a man make you a better person?" she asked chippily.

"Absolutely not. Of course not. Only . . ." Tash paused and bit into a slice of papaya. "I'm sure if you were having good sex then you wouldn't cry so much."

"Did I keep you awake again last night?" asked Alice, instantly feeling guilty.

"Just for two hours, then I took a handful of melatonin and dropped off like a baby."

"I'm sorry, Tash, I'll try to keep it to myself."

"Even better, let it all out. There's a tantric sex course starting in a week or so out at Manhattan Beach. If we haven't sorted out the problem by then, we'll enroll you. That'll kick-start your hormones again."

"And what makes you think I need to learn about sex?" demanded Alice incredulously.

"Well, babe, if you were doing it right in the first place you wouldn't be able to get enough. Don't worry, you're English. Nobody expects it to be any other way, but what a pleasant surprise when a man takes you to bed and expects to find the usual frosty knickers and strikes gold." Tash smiled patronizingly.

Bloody, bloody Americans, Alice thought. Rude, crude, crass. Think the world revolves around the genitals. Too many of those smutty movies. "And I'll have you know that the English are not priggish in the slightest. We happen to be renowned for our sexual perversions. Haven't you heard of the Tory party?" Alice spluttered. A man at the next table winked at her and licked his lips. Yuck. She shot him a disdainful look and shuddered.

"That's great, Alice, speak your mind, don't repress it anymore. Anything goes in California."

"I just want to go on record as saying that I am not averse to sexual activity. But only if the man is handsome . . ."

"Oh God, you're not going to tell me you have to be in love with him?" Tash threw her head back and laughed, revealing two rows of perfectly capped teeth.

"No. In fact, I'm open to offers. Yes, I am. If I find a man who fits the bill, then I'll happily abandon myself to the throes of grand passion. And that's a promise," said Alice resolutely, not meaning it for a minute but considering it her own personal National Service. A duty to the nation. Can't let the reputation of her fellow countrymen down. Cry God for Harry England and Saint George!

Laying her new clothes out on the chair in the corner of her room for her first day at work, Alice felt as though she were going back to school after the summer holidays. All she needed was a new pencil tin and some unscuffed shoes with stiff buckles for the picture to be complete. Never mind that within two days she would have chewed her way through her new Biros and scribbled pop stars' names all over her homework journal, it was the thought that counted. The sparkling-clean slate. She'd make a go of this job, she thought with a surge of enthusiasm, make her life work for once. She'd show Jamie and Helen that they may have been sleeping together under her duvet in Clapham, but they hadn't won yet.

CHAPTER 11

Paddy sat outside a bar on the beachfront in Santa Monica sipping a *caffé latte* and wondering when he should arrange the meeting for. He wasn't even sure if the guy was in town. So what else could he do? What about that girl? He conned himself beautifully. He knew at the moment that Alice would be staying with Tash, who was working as the first assistant on a film called *Whiplash*.

Paddy had made some inquiries among his friends in the film industry, of which there were numerous owing to the fact that they were always phoning him asking him to direct the next Stallone film: "Hey, Patrick, it's practically Tolstoy, it's called *Vengeance Is Mine and I Will Repay*. We'll throw a car into the deal. And a cut of merchandising, Fisher Price has these great samples of the Sly Vengeance doll with detachable grenades—you'd love 'em." Invariably he declined. Cameras just weren't his thing, he didn't understand them. They paid him enough in London; he couldn't imagine what he'd spend silly money on.

Anyway, they pointed him in the direction of where *Whiplash* was shooting and now all he had to do was turn up at the studio tomorrow, follow Tash home, and he'd be led like Hansel and Gretel through the forest to Alice. Even though he didn't fancy her, she looked like the type who

might be quite a laugh if he just asked her out for a drink—
as a friend. And now that he knew where she was he
might as well. He had nothing better to do. In fact, Col-
umbo couldn't have pulled it off better. Paddy was good at
tracking women down and wooing them. Not in a preda-
tory way—he liked to think of himself as some medieval
knight who, finding a delicate lace glove, simply has to
have the woman to whom it belongs. His ancient quest, his
holy grail.

The sun sank low over the pier and, lighting a cigarette,
he noticed a pretty girl at the next table. Santa Monica was
full to brimming with neo-hippies, but some of them were
lovely, the original flower children's children. And Woodstock was nothing if not good for ensuring a certain liber-
ality of body and spirit, he thought as he winked lazily at
the girl whose denim shorts barely concealed her perfect
California-peach behind.

Tash dropped Alice off in the carpark and waved her
good-bye as Alice walked stomach in mouth to the reception desk of Star PR. The lobby was a vast open space
where every move one made was replicated twenty-four
times on the television monitors on the wall. Alice looked
like a walking bowl of custard in her new cashmere outfit.
There was nowhere to run and nowhere to hide. The other
walls were hidden by a veritable planetarium of celebrity
photographs; never had the vase of stargazer lilies standing anemically on the reception desk been so aptly named.
But despite the fact that you would notice an ant if it were
to sashay through the swing doors and make its way
across the open-plan marble floor, Alice was having some
trouble making the receptionist notice her. She waited for

a good fifteen minutes for the inevitable blonde to finish telling some random caller about her audition as an extra on *Beverly Hills 90210.*

"Bodies like you've never seen," she grumbled as she checked her ice-blue nails at arm's length. "Can I help you?" she asked at last. Her cheery voice was betrayed by a look as cool as her nail polish.

"Hi." Better start on the right foot. "My name's Alice Lewis, I'm starting work here today." The receptionist looked blank.

"Uh. I don't think so." Her collagen lips came to an abrupt purse.

"Oh really?" Alice wondered if maybe she'd been mistaken after all.

"See. If you were starting work here, I'd know." She was now obviously auditioning for the part of Queen of Sheba.

"It's in the publicity department, I think," Alice ventured.

"The business of this entire company is publicity. I really don't know what you mean." With that she began to massage her temples and ignored Alice altogether.

Fortunately at that moment Alice recognized one of her panel of interviewers coming through the doors. "Erm. Excuse me. I'm Alice Lewis. We met at the interview. Only I'm here to start work but don't know where I'm supposed to be."

The woman smiled her professional smile and whipped her immaculate head to face the now miraculously capable-looking receptionist, not a head massage or nail-polished finger in sight. "Kelly?" she quizzed her.

"Oh, I was just checking the various departmental memoranda to ascertain whether Ms. Lewis here was expected." She smiled crisply at Alice, defying her to say anything to the contrary. Ms. Beachbunny had turned into Miss Money-penny. Alice suspected it would only be a matter of time before Kelly put in an Oscar-winning performance in a proper motion picture.

"Good. I'll leave you in Kelly's hands, Ms. Lewis." The woman sped off in the direction of the lifts, propelled by an expensive Italian leather briefcase, as Kelly clattered into action on her switchboard.

Three seconds later: "Take the elevator to the seventh floor and you'll be met by Lysette." Alice noted the gauntlet of contempt that had already been cast down by Kelly. Great, Alice, fall out with the receptionist on the first day, that way she can sabotage every personal phone call you get for the rest of your working life. Alice optimistically envisaged Kelly deliberately confusing Simons with Kevins and asking Nathan if he'd enjoyed his date at the opera with Alice when she knew she'd been Rollerblading with Paul instead. Hmm. In my wildest dreams perhaps. Alice dismissed the notion as the doors sprang open onto the seventh floor.

"Lysette Jackson. You must be Alice?" A sleek brunette with a Louise Brooks bob held out her hand as Alice stepped out of the lift into an open-plan office space with a spectacular view of the Hollywood sign.

"You're sitting at the desk right beside me. Follow me." She smiled warmly and led Alice past groups of people sitting around workstations, hermetically sealed to their phones. The walls were a collage of glossy photographs of clients, some of which Alice recognized from her nights in the King's Road cinema, others she had to trawl her memory to recall. Big-name starlets next to early-eighties cop-show heroes now playing only on cable. Alice instantly knew which category of celebrity she'd be asked to promote.

"Here." Lysette plumped down on a desk and gestured for Alice to sit on the ergonomically sound swivel chair. "You'll be sitting here, I'm there. I'll just call Jennifer and she'll come down to explain your duties to you. If you want French fries and chicken wings for lunch, I'm going to Koo-Koo-Roo. You're welcome to join me."

Alice couldn't have been happier if she'd been invited to lounge by a pool with Tommy Kelly, the pinup of the moment whose picture steamed down on her from the wall nearest her new filing cabinet. Did that mean that he was a client of Star PR? Would Alice get to meet him? She smoothed her skirt down at the thought. Tommy Kelly, the Hollywood wild man every woman wanted to reform. What would Jamie say to that?

"Love to, thanks." Alice beamed and swiveled in her chair, overcome with the excitement of owning her own bookshelves and stapler. She felt a fully fledged professional woman beginning to stir beneath her beige cashmere sweater. Yes, she was going to enjoy this career-woman lark, even though she still hadn't quite grasped what it was that a publicist to the stars was actually meant to do.

"And Jennifer is a total *man*." Lysette licked her fingers clean of Koo-Koo-Roo mayonnaise and slurped the bottom of her Coke. Alice looked up in surprise from her Cajun fried chicken. She'd been relieved that her officemates hadn't whisked her off for a whole-wheat bean feast for lunch. Tash was trying to starve her and she had to get her calories somehow.

"In what way?" she asked, not sure that she wanted to be enlightened.

"Well, not in a bad way, she's just not really one of the girls." Then, leaning in closer as if about to divulge classified information straight from the Pentagon, she said, "In three years nobody's seen her legs." Lysette on the other hand did have legs. Long crossed ones that waiters kept tripping over. And she had a Southern drawl that would charm a snake from a basket.

"The receptionist wasn't very friendly." Alice ventured her most gossipworthy observation for Lysette's dissection.

Lysette nodded sagely and leaned over the red Formica tabletop. "Oh, well, that's because she's screwing Huey in accounts and he's in love with Tommy Kelly."

"Really?" Alice felt herself metamorphose into the role of garden-fence gossip. It'd been so long since she had a life worth gossiping about, it was as delicious as the French fries dolloped in ketchup. "Well, I never."

"And how long have you worked there?" Alice asked Lysette.

"Oh, ages. I'm waiting for the London branch of Star PR to open, then I can go over there and find my husband."

"You're married?" Alice asked, not sure how anyone could manage to lose a husband. She lost things all the time, lip liners, umbrellas, even her mind occasionally, but to lose a husband . . .

"No. But my husband's in London. I went to see this fortune teller in Venice Beach. She didn't tell just an ordinary fortune blah blah handsome stranger . . . she was, like, 'Oh yeah, your cake crumbs tell me real clearly that—' "

"Cake crumbs?" Alice was puzzled.

"Yeah, you, like, eat this cake. Mine was lemon sponge, but I guess you could use chocolate or something instead. Anyway, she was, like, 'Your crumbs tell me that your twin soul is waiting for you in Engerland.' Can you believe it?" Lysette was radiant at the prospect. "So I'm just waiting till next year. Then I'll go over. I've always known that I should be in a castle. And I've always wanted a man to open doors for me. So it kind of figures that my twin soul should be in England. Doesn't it?" She looked at Alice as though she were the oracle at Delphi munching laurel leaves, about to give out some invaluable advice.

"Oh yes." Alice didn't want to disappoint on her first day. She bit her tongue and refrained from mentioning the number of times she'd been battered out of the way by door-slamming males trying to jump before her in the petrol-station queue.

"So I've started to buy sweaters in the winter sales and I've been watching *My Fair Lady*, just so I can understand the language and all." Lysette sat back in her orange plastic seat and imagined her husband's family's heraldic crest, something noble. And his family portraits that would grace the walls of their castle, all those men with huge noses— God, she couldn't wait—the huger the noses, the better.

Alice spent the afternoon being awestruck by her Rolodex. She had the home phone numbers of every name in Hollywood. Every film she'd ever seen, every pop star she'd ever fancied, and every washed-up alcoholic this side of Vegas. They were all there in the loopy turquoise handwriting of her predecessor. She acquainted herself with her computer whose screensaver rather disconcertingly announced "What do me and Burt Reynolds have in common? We're both fucking awful actors."

Lysette leaned over and drawled, "She was sleeping with Tommy."

My God, Tommy Kelly obviously was a client. Alice wondered if she'd get to bring tea into a meeting with him. She remembered one day at her old job when Richard Madely had come into the office and Alice had asked him if he wanted one or two sugars, she hadn't been able to type a

word for the rest of the morning. But Tommy Kelly. He
really must be something, Alice thought. She'd seen every
one of his films since he was the leader of the brat pack
when she was about fourteen and he'd played a motor-
stealing hoodlum in some Francis Ford Coppola film. For
the next two years his name on the front of a *Just Seventeen*
cover had been Alice's cue to buy every single copy that
she could carry out of the newsagent.

But there was no way that she'd be working with
Tommy Kelly. She knew from life experience that she was
the girl in the photocopying cupboard, not the one at lunch
with the superstars. Never mind, just to touch the hem of
his garment would be enough for her, she thought as she
tried to change the screensaver to some witty Oscar Wilde
quote like "I can resist everything but temptation," but
there had to be a silk stocking clogging up the hard drive,
so she couldn't.

Alice arrived home spent with the exhaustion of looking
the part of a businesswoman all day. Of trying not to
squeal when an extra from *Knots Landing* entered the office and of trying not to gaze too moonily out of the window with a vacant expression while she dreamt of lunch.
She'd kept her eyes on her computer screen all day and
even managed to keep her shoes on under her desk. Yes,
she was evolving into quite the professional. She opened
the fridge and found nothing but a moldering bit of root
ginger and an off pint of milk. Perfect. Just to be expected
from a woman too busy with life to do grocery shopping,
she thought with satisfaction as she rooted through the
telephone book for a takeaway pizza number. Tash wasn't
there, so longing to tell someone about her first day at
work, she called Trinny, the only person she knew who
wouldn't mind having her sleep interrupted for a gossip.

"Tommy Kelly. Oh, hang on a minute, is he the bloke on *Pets Win Prizes*?"

"Trin, how can you say that? He's the most talented, handsome, sexy thing since chocolate, but never mind. I suppose you've got other things to think about. How are the plans going?" Alice doodled 'Tommy Kelly 4 Me' on the phone book.

"Hell on toast. Peter Jones or Conran Shop. What do you think?"

"You've lost me," said Alice,

"Wedding list, darling. Peter Jones for practicality, *naturellement*. But there's this umbrella stand in Conran that I think I'll die if I don't have."

"Well, why don't you buy the umbrella stand at the Conran Shop yourself, then have your wedding list at Peter Jones. If you need a break from all this prenuptial stress you can always come here," Alice volunteered.

"Maybe we'll come for our honeymoon. Tim's got a cousin in Santa Barbara and Antigua's so passé. You have to break new ground with these things, otherwise there's nothing exciting for Dempster to write about."

"That'd be great. Anyway, I'd better go; this is probably costing me a fortune. I'll call you soon and you can fill me in on the guest list. Give my love to Tim."

"Will do. And if you speak to Simon B., will you break the news to him gently? He left a message on my answerphone the other night asking if I was still sleeping with that hot-shit lawyer 'cause he might be needing him. I think he must have been in the sun too long. Anyway, send him my love. Oh, and one last thing—gold or silver leaf on the invitations? Is gold just too crass?"

Alice poured every one of Tash's fifteen essential oils into her bath and began to feel very strange indeed. The

schizophrenic blends of everything from arnica to rose-
mary and ylang-ylang promised to evoke all manner of
feelings from passion to relaxation, as well as stimulating
memory loss and aiding sore throats. Hmm. Maybe she'd
overdone it. She escaped the vapors as soon as possible.
She watched a video and ate the middle of the pizza, leaving the crust, a gorgeous sin that Jamie would never have
permitted. Alice hoped that he was urging the same re-
straint on the Tart. But of course there was a time difference, they'd probably be sleeping like spoons in his bed
right now. She wished that Tash would hurry up home
from work, but she, too, was probably having her inner
thighs toned in a far more interesting fashion than those
birthing-type machines down at the gym. Oh well, some
of the greatest people of our time are celibate, Alice reassured herself, like, well, like Kennell Williams and . . .
Mother Teresa.

By midnight Alice had given up on Tash. She skulked off
to her bed, leaving a note to wake her early tomorrow, she
wanted to go to the gym before work. An hour into sleep
she heard a curious noise from the kitchen. At first she
thought it was a neighbor's cat stuck on a barbecue but
then realized it was probably Tash's strangulated giggle on
reading that Alice, sloth Alice, wanted to be woken at six
to go to the gym. How the worm had turned.

CHAPTER 12

On Wednesday the girls overslept monumentally. Tash hammered crossly on Alice's bedroom door at ten to seven. "Too late for the gym. I'm leaving in ten minutes. Do you want oatmeal?" Tash yelled from the kitchen, where she was managing to digest *Variety* and a bowl of porridge at the same time. Alice clambered from beneath her sheets and into yesterday's clothes. So much for good intentions. She picked up her bowl of oatmeal and followed Tash, who was crossly kicking some rubbish lying on the doormat.

"This fucking junk mail. I've told them not to send it." She shoved it to one side with her stiletto and stormed into the car. Alice forced down two more spoonfuls of lumpen porridge and decided that she'd buy some Lucky Charms on her way home from work, at least they'd cheer her up and kick-start her day. Alice was about to close the door behind her when she remembered the company charter she'd brought home to study but naturally hadn't so much as glanced at. She ran back to her room and picked it up.

"Hurry up, Alice, or we'll be late," Tash shrilled as she revved the engine like a racing car driver. It was obvious she'd had a pig of a day on the set yesterday and was sulking because the cameraman or whatever he was hadn't asked her out to dinner yet.

"Coming!" Alice hopped all the way to the door trying to put one of her new shoes on, but her foot had grown two sizes overnight. "Ouch!" She slammed her hand in the door behind her and kicked the same pile of rubbish in the porchway. Bending down to prize her blistered foot into her shoe, she noticed that it wasn't in fact rubbish but some flowers tied about with a piece of string.

"Alice, ten more seconds and I'm leaving." Tash had begun to reverse out of the drive now.

"Hang on. I'm there." Alice picked up the flower rubbish and hobbled into the car.

"What are you bringing trash into the car for?" Tash skidded down the street.

Alice examined the bunch closer. They were deep purple violets with pinhead yellow faces and hooked under the string was a tiny piece of card. She plucked it out and gasped.

"What?" Tash narrowly missed killing a Rollerblader; she wound down the window. "You moron. Go play on Venice Beach!" Alice had fallen silent.

"Tash, they're for me."

"What?" Tash turned briefly and screwed up her eyes to see them. "What are they?"

"Flowers."

"Yuck." Tash clearly wasn't impressed. "Who sent them?"

"Doesn't say. Just says 'For Alice with love.'" Alice's cheeks had turned pink. She thought for a moment they might be from her mum. Had she sounded so homesick the last time she spoke to her on the phone? Then she realized that there was no way her mother would send her twelve violets. They'd be gladioli and crysanths, or not at all.

"I'd toss them away, you might catch something from

them." Tash had obviously left her heart in the shower this morning. Alice wrapped them in a tissue and bundled them in her handbag.

"So sweet. Where d'ya get them?" Lysette stared over the partition between her and Alice's desks and examined the mystery gift.

"Well, it's weird, because I don't know a soul here. And nobody knows me." Alice was puzzled but flattered. She couldn't remember when the last romantic mystery in her life had been. Probably Killian Madden sending her a Valentine's card in fifth form. And even then he'd signed it. The only mystery had been why, as he patently wanted to snog Sharon Dickinson that night at the Valentine's Disco.

"Beats me." Alice placed them carefully into a plastic cup of water. "But I quite like them."

"Well, I'll tell you one thing for sure. They're not from any guy in this town."

Alice looked at Lysette, whose infuriatingly elegant appearance gave no hints of her penchant for Koo-Koo-Roo's wares. "Why?"

"Because the closest the guys in L.A. get to flowers as pretty as those is to stand on them. If they send anything, their secretaries order them and charge it to their Amex platinum cards. I'd say your admirer is either broke or romantic. And there aren't too many men in either of those categories around here." Lysette ducked back behind her wall as Jennifer made her way across the office.

"Alice, I'd like you to come and meet one of our most important clients." She bent down and fingered the posy on Alice's desk. "Better get those chemically treated or we'll have all kinds of bugs making this place home." It was meant kindly, but Alice suddenly felt like the office freak. "Tommy's in my office. Go and introduce yourself and I'll be through in a minute."

Tommy Kelly. She said it slowly and with as much composure as she could muster, but it came out as Tommy-Kelly-wildly-famous-dated-models-front-of-*Vanity-Fair*-I-can't-go-through-with-it. Alice flung a backward glance at Lysette, who gave her a good-luck thumbs-up. Oh my God, she suddenly noticed a dollop of Saturday night's Thai green curry that had attached itself to the sleeve of her cashmere cardigan. If Tash hadn't been in such a bloody rotten mood she could have borrowed some little Ferragamo number from her. Bloody cameraman's fault, wasn't it? She pushed Jennifer's door open slowly. Too slowly. She'd been so quiet in her entrance that he hadn't noticed she was there. Now what was she supposed to do? Clear her throat? Go out and come back in more noisily? She was loitering in the doorway like a spooky fan.

But it was too late, he looked up. He wasn't going to say a word, so, "Hi, I'm Alice Lewis, Jennifer suggested we meet." God, it sounded like a blind date. She squirmed. But obviously he wouldn't contemplate her as a potential date under any circumstances.

"Hmm." He looked at her and then buried his head back in the script he was reading.

Alice was about to dart out through the door in shame but heard Jennifer's purposeful strides behind her.

"Alice, I thought I told you to introduce yourself to Tommy," she said, closing the office door behind her. Alice was trapped.

"I already did." Alice looked feebly at Tommy to vindicate her but to no avail. He just stared blankly at the green Thai curry. Fucked-up two-timing junkie. She thought back to the last article she'd read about him in the newspapers before she'd left London. And anyway he's really short.

"Alice, I thought you could sit in on this meeting and discuss with us the best way to repackage Tommy in Europe. It would seem to me that his profile there has suffered as a result of recent events and we have to put that right before his new film comes out next month."

Alice could barely find her way back to her desk after lunch. If it hadn't been for the beaconlike poster of Tommy announcing her partition, she might have spent the rest of the day in the ladies' loo. She clutched at the arms of her chair and begged it not to swivel. Stay still, she pleaded. But the chair was very firmly in situ. What was spinning was her head. Or her thoughts, to be more precise. The meeting had gone so well that Jennifer felt they should continue over lunch. As they drove to the restaurant Alice had scratched at the remains of last night's dinner and wished she'd washed her hair after the gym the other morning. Her scalp was beginning to itch and her hair had hardened into a style that sat at a 180-degree angle. They'd been ushered into such a trendy sushi bar that Alice felt like she had stumbled into the presentation of the Academy Awards, so star-studded was the clientele. She'd been given sake to drink from a box. A messy enough business at the best of times, but when your hand's shaking because your foot keeps brushing against the hottest actor in town's shoe then it's well nigh impossible.

Alice had been petrified. Tommy had been silent. It was only after several boxes of sake that her tongue began to loosen and she persuaded herself to imagine that Tommy Kelly was the greengrocer from Chelsea Green that she managed to utter a few words. In fact, once she'd polished off her fourth box there was no shutting her up. She enlightened them on the finer workings of the British tabloid press, of which she actually knew nothing but for which they seemed grateful. And by the time the sashimi had arrived she had also enlightened them on a good deal more, including her unceremonious dumping by Jamie. In fact, she was pretty sure that she'd done a good job of lunch. She'd gone down as well as Pamela Anderson on a stag night and felt rather self-congratulatory. She managed to remain professional and informative despite being disgracefully drunk. It was only when they were leaving the restaurant and someone asked Tommy for his autograph that she forgot he wasn't the greengrocer from Chelsea Green and jumped six feet in the air when he kissed her good-bye.

Now, sobering up in the arctic air-conditioning and attempting to pick up her e-mail messages from her computer, she was beginning to cringe with embarrassment. Tomorrow morning's regretful shame wasn't even worth contemplating, she thought as her mouse seemed to take on a life of its own beneath her shaking hand. Had she really told Jennifer that she'd worked with celebrities all the time in her last job? And Tommy. He'd been much nicer than she'd expected—so kind and deferential to her throughout lunch.

Then she remembered why—she'd told him that he was too old to be behaving like a teenager at a rave and despite what he might think there was no glamour in ending up a fat old drunk with a heart problem, he should pull himself together and be grateful for what he'd got. It was obviously the schoolteacher in Alice's genes that had said it—her mother was a gym mistress and her father a music teacher and every so often, in vino veritas, she became a bossy person with a whistle doling out detentions. Fortunately, it had struck a chord with the impressionable Tommy, who, instead of spitting in her eye and telling her to fuck off, had poured himself a glass of mineral water and decided that she would be his new mentor. Still, her headache was horrendous and she'd sworn off sake forever.

The last thing she was ready for when she got home was to be wrenched from the sofa and its host of attendant chat shows and made to behave like a civilized human being. But Tash phoned with wrenching firmly in mind.

"Honey, I feel so guilty about being so cranky this morning. I'm gonna take you to a dirty big dinner to apologize."

Alice wanted to say that a dirty big dinner just might clash with the dirty big lunch and positively filthy amount of sake she'd had, but the line went dead. Eurgh. She curled up on the sofa and waited for the whirl that was Tash to arrive home.

"You know what you said about having good sex and all that?" Tash opened the conversation as they whizzed down La Cienega toward Drai's.

"Vaguely. I think I was just being patriotic though," Alice managed through her sybaritic saked state.

"Too late. I've invited this guy Charlie to dinner. He's an absolute dream. Looks like Brad Pitt on a windy day."

"And so what makes you think he'd want to go out with me?" Alice asked suspiciously.

"Well, he's good-looking and stuff and he's got a great job, but he just can't seem to find a girlfriend. Insane, isn't it?" Tash threw her hair back in the wind and laughed.

"Not really. You see, men who can't find girlfriends usually have some kind of innate character flaw. Especially if they're rich and handsome."

"Now you're being unfair, Alice. Some men just find it a little difficult."

"In *this* town?" Alice choked on all the fresh air she was inhaling. "Can't you put the top up a bit?"

"No. I like to feel the wind through my hair. Anyway, what do you mean in *this* town?" Tash seemed mildly offended.

"Well, you can't leave a handsome, rich man unattended in a supermarket for five seconds without all the local females sniffing around in his shopping basket to make sure he isn't buying athlete's foot medication, and if he isn't, he's in their beds before you can say Jack Nicholson."

"Just because women here are more forward . . . It's not a crime, you know, Alice, we can't all be shrinking-violet English roses." Tash squealed to a halt outside the restaurant and let the valet take the strain.

"I know. I'm just saying that this Charlie character can't be all *that*, otherwise he'd have been snapped up by now. But . . ." Alice was fully aware that Tash was providing her with a lift home. "I'm prepared to keep an open mind. Is that all right?" She finished as they stepped through the doors of the restaurant into the air-conditioned bliss of Drai's.

"That's absolutely fucking fantastic." Tash kissed her on the cheek and, taking her hand, led her to the table.

"Just don't embarrass me, Tash." Alice remembered many a teenage nightclub encounter when Tash had bribed the object of Alice's affections to dance with her friend. She could be horribly unsubtle. But it was too late.

"This is Alice. She's my single friend from London. Alice, this is Charlie." Oh God. Alice smiled tightly and avoided his gaze. Trying not to take in the fact that actually he did look remarkably like Brad Pitt, only kind of more rugged. Quite handsome actually, thought Alice as she mentally prepared a list of all the things that could possibly be wrong with him given the lack of girlfriend situation. Nostril hair? No, didn't seem to be a problem there. An olfactory problem perhaps? Rank-smelling feet? Nope, his shoe leather showed no signs of wilting. It didn't appear to be a physical problem anyway. At least not one that could be discerned with his clothes on. Alice put the naked Charlie to one side to contemplate later and concentrated on trying to remember everybody else's name at the table.

Unfortunately, her suss-out-Charlie mission had to be postponed as she was seated at the far end of the table next to a record producer, none of whose bands, Alice discovered to her embarrassment, she had ever heard of.

"Ulcer? Morphine?" he tried.

Alice shook her head yet again. It was in danger of becoming unscrewed if she rotated it one more time. "Sorry, but it's just that I never really listen to pop music. Just Radio Four really." Alice tried to pacify him. He was frowning with incomprehension. "Well, that was when I was in England. Honestly. I've practically never even heard of the Beatles." Alice laughed.

He didn't. "The greatest band in the world ever and you've never heard of them?" he asked solemnly.

"Well, when I say I've practically never heard of them, of course I've heard of them, otherwise, well, otherwise I wouldn't have mentioned them, would I? It's just that, well, that was a way of demonstrating how little I actually know about music." Alice was exhausted. Was this what they meant when they said that Americans had trouble with irony? She hoped that conversing with Charlie wasn't going to prove so laborious.

"So you were lying then?" The record producer battled away and Alice took to the bottle.

She floated through the rest of dinner on a tide of

Chardonnay and about two and a half strands of tagliatelle. Unfortunately for them an assortment of Tash's friends had turned up to welcome Alice to L.A. Unfortunate because she was there in all but mind.

Such perplexing questions and comments as:

"So you live in London? Do you know my friend Elizabeth?"

and:

"Sure, I've been to England, but I really can't understand why the queen built Windsor Castle so near to Heathrow airport."

volleyed around all night.

The girls were mostly beautiful and fake-breasted and the men were mostly turning in the other direction having given Alice up for dead. She tried to check out Charlie, but her focus wasn't so great anymore. He was looking less and less like Brad Pitt and more like Brian Blessed after a particularly grueling stab at Everest. Alice thought he was probably beautiful, too, but couldn't be sure if that was a result of her inebriation.

"If you cast *her* in your next movie, I swear I'll cut your balls off." A Latina lovely and her beau were obviously having a domestic.

"Just because she has a reputation for going down on anyone with a dick doesn't mean she's not a damned fine actress, Marcie."

But Marcie was far from convinced. She spluttered incredulously, "Oh, well, excuse me. I thought that fine actresses took their talent to Julliard or at least some bumblefuck acting class at UCLA. She was only discovered when she lap-danced on the head of the studio."

"You're just jealous, honey. Settle down, I wouldn't sleep with her if she paid me." He put a placatory hand on Mar-

cie's cheek and she bit it. A domestic, eh? God, even the do-
mestics in this town sounded fabulously glamorous. Alice
imagined a comparable ruck in the Slug and Lettuce on Fulham Broadway.

"You been at it with that Lorraine in accounts again?"

"What Lorraine in accounts?"

"The one who wore the Wonderbra to the Christmas
party. Don't give me that."

"Oh, that Lorraine."

"Yeeesss. That Lorraine."

"Nah. Anyway, 'er old man's a black belt in judo." So
that put paid to that. Once more unto the shandy and a bit
of banter about last night's episode of *Harry Enfield*.

Alice certainly felt she was broadening her horizons.
Even if nobody was bothering to converse with her anymore. She settled back in her chair and the next thing she
knew Tash was lifting her face from the uneaten tagliatelle.

"It's just jet lag. I'm so sorry," she said to her departing
friends. "Alice, are you okay? You look kinda ill. Let's get
you home."

The last thing Alice could remember was being told that
her skin would suffer if she didn't remove her makeup and
not to forget the gym tomorrow.

CHAPTER 13

"**C**an we get the first assistant here right away? Hello? Natasha, we don't have all day." The camp director, who looked like a refugee from *Apocalypse Now*, with his khaki fatigues and omnipresent mangy dog, was standing with his hands on his hips waiting for Tash to take charge and do what he was paying her to do instead of trying to sneak off for personal phone calls and make eyes at his DP all day. "Honey, now. Puhleeasse."

"Yup. It's done. Baz, can you make sure that you're watching the monitor? And where's the goddamn runner?" Having delegated her duties for the next five minutes, Tash wandered behind the bit of the set that was about to get blown up in the next scene and tapped Alice's work number into her cell phone.

"So Charlie called me this morning. I think he really likes you," she said gleefully.

Alice was nodding wisely and pretending to be booking a car for some decrepit rock star. "Yes. Absolutely. Thank you." Why was it that some people had the art of pretending to be on a business call when their boss was nearby down to an artform and others, namely Alice, managed to make even their calls to the tax office sound as though they were talking to their best friend about a hot date last night. Whatever the reason, Alice thought it unfortunate and wondered if there was a course you could take that was designed to convince your employer otherwise. Especially as Jennifer was now glaring at her, ready to pounce with some sound advice on the profligate nature of personal phone calls during the working day.

"Charlie was the waiter, right?" Alice asked in hushed tones.

"No. Charlie was the talent agent. Don't pretend you've forgotten, Alice." Tash had to dive down as a piece of exploding backdrop nearly decapitated her.

"I haven't forgotten, but I wasn't exactly on mastermind form last night. He was Rob Lowe, right?" Alice asked, then added, "If you'll just let me have the invoice for that I'd be most grateful," as Jennifer popped up by the fax machine.

"No. He was Brad Pitt. Remember? Anyway, I was thinking that I might just give him your phone number. Whaddayathink?"

"What like . . . hi Charlie . . . yeah, great food . . . 310-555-7298 . . . and what was going on between Marcie and Rob? Why don't you just wait until he asks for my phone number? Look, I have to go, Tash. I'll call you later." Alice hung up.

Last night she wouldn't have been averse to a spot of digit swapping with Charlie, but right now her mind was elsewhere. This morning when she'd arrived at her desk, somewhat the worse for wear, there'd been a little pale blue box sitting on top of her in-tray. She'd opened it cautiously, not being sure how powerful a letter bomb of six centimeters square could prove. But inside, scattered with magnolia petals, was a crumbling piece of paper. She'd lifted out the paper and smoothed it flat on her desk.

Your riot of angelic beauty brought me here,
Love and a thousand flowers could bloom,
Alice, we'll meet soon.

Trembling, either from her one-too-many the night before or more likely from what she'd just read, Alice hugged her coffee in her hands and racked her brain. Who could it be? She tried to work it out. Beauty, flowers, meeting soon. It was all quite standard stuff. If it wasn't for the fact that this person seemed to know her name, she'd have presumed it was maybe somebody who'd just seen her in the street. At lunchtime she and Lysette worked through it.

"Yeah, but even if he'd just seen you in the street he could have heard someone call your name, you know."

"That's true." Alice pondered, fingering the already slightly crumpled piece of paper. "But then I haven't really been anywhere. It's not likely to be somebody from the health juice bar. I threw up in a potted plant."

"Hmm. Have we decided that it's the same guy as the violets?" Lysette asked.

"Well, as I've never had a single secret admirer in my life, the idea of two appearing at once is highly implausible. You see, I haven't ruled out foul play."

"Like what?" Lysette crammed in a mouthful of chickenburger.

"Well, Tash wants me to feel good about myself right now. This is just her kind of tactic." Alice didn't really believe this theory. If it was Tash, she'd be phoning Alice every five minutes to ask whether Alice had received any "erm . . . interesting packages" recently. She hadn't an ounce of secrecy in her glorious body.

"I'll ask Tash tonight and update you tomorrow," Alice finally promised Lysette, who had been totally wooed by

the romance of these gestures and was already planning what she'd wear to the wedding. "We have to get
back. Jennifer wants to see me in her office at two sharp. I
think she'll probably fire me after my disgraceful behavior
yesterday."

"No way. I think Tommy's really warmed to you. I
haven't seen him smile so much since he was sleeping
with Julia Roberts."

Out of the thick darkness the waves came up high on the
beach. Despite the outdoor bonfire heating the terrace of
the restaurant, it was still chilly. Alice pulled her jumper
down over her head. Much as she wanted to tell Tash
about the letter, it was all she could do to squeeze in her
food order between Tash's, "I could just tell by the way he
looked at you" and her, "He never calls me usually." And
before the main course had arrived she'd broken the news
to Alice that she'd arranged for Charlie to take her out on
Saturday night. Alone. Alice choked back her swordfish
and tried to enjoy the view of Malibu beach.

"But I don't want to go on a date just yet, Tash."

"Getting back in the saddle, that's what it's all about, my
dear." Tash laughed, obviously not for a second imagining
that Alice wasn't just playing the coy English rose.

But Alice could genuinely think of at least seven thousand things she'd prefer to do on Saturday night. Christ,
she couldn't even remember what he looked like. There
were the Brad Pitt vagaries, but in the cold light of day she
thought that that was probably just a red herring. She tried
to come up with hair and eyes, but the sake had put paid to
that. Shit. And what kind of weirdo would fancy a girl who
spent most of the evening with her head in her dinner?
This was the most disturbing aspect of all.

"Well, why don't you come along, too, Tash. Bring your cameraman," Alice ventured.

"He's a director of photography, not a cameraman. Anyway, Charlie would very much like to take you out alone. Don't worry, he knows you're a bit out of practice and doesn't mind one bit." Tash waved her forkful of king prawn in a blasé way.

Alice pushed her swordfish to one side and spluttered helplessly. "He doesn't mind. What about me? Don't I get a say? I mean it's not as though I'm some kind of charity case."

But Tash wasn't paying any attention. She was picking the batter from the other prawns and doing a bit of mental arithmetic as to how many minutes on the treadmill she'd need to do tomorrow now that she'd ordered chocolate cake for dessert. "So whaddaya think of Malibu?" she finally asked.

It wasn't until the last crumb of chocolate cake had been guiltily polished off that Alice tentatively removed exhibits A and B from her handbag. The violets now resembled an amateur attempt at perfume making, all mangled leaves and browning petals, and the box came attached to a handful of hair from her brush.

"You know these flowers I got the other day?" Alice put forward exhibit A. Tash furrowed her brow trying to decipher the mess before her. "Well, I think that the same person may also have sent me a poem." There. She'd said it.

Tash was still looking perplexed and, for the first time Alice could remember, was rendered speechless. Alice waited, lightly fingering the little box.

Finally Tash spoke. "These are flowers?" she asked dubiously.

Alice nodded. "They're a bit crumpled now, obviously,

but they really were quite sweet when they first arrived, apart from your footprint on the stems, that is. That's probably why they didn't survive. Didn't stand a chance really with damaged stems. That's how they get nutrients and water, you see . . ." Why was she so nervous? It was only a couple of adolescent love tokens, not like she'd nicked the crown jewels and was now laying them among the prawn husks and cake crumbs for the world to see.

"Okay." Tash had now taken in the horror of the flowers. "And what's in that"—she hesitated to call it a box, but generally that was what one called square things—"box?" She finished quickly, as though speaking the word would somehow contaminate her.

"Well, that's the poem." Alice barely noted Tash's distaste. She was thinking what a lovely, unassuming box it was. She opened it and took out the letter, unfolding the now familiar words. "Here." She pushed it gently toward Tash, who stared at it for a moment but couldn't make out the words for the creases across the paper. So she picked it up carefully with just the tips of her fingers.

"It's okay, Tash, it's not really as fragile as it looks," Alice encouraged.

"Oh, but you never know where it's been, really, do you?" Tash said as she peered at it. " 'Your riot of angelic beauty brought me here, Love and a thousand flowers could bloom, Alice, we'll meet soon.' Ohhh." Tash said this as though somebody had just told her that she'd inadvertently consumed five hundred calories. "That's really freaky. Are you okay?"

Alice nodded. "Fine. Why?" she asked, hoping that Tash could help her work out who the sender could be.

"Well, this is really spooky, Alice. Why didn't you tell me earlier?"

Spooky? Alice hadn't thought it at all spooky. "Why spooky?" she asked.

"Well, this guy is obviously a weirdo."

Alice laughed out loud at this. "What, because he fancies me? Oh, thanks a lot, Tash."

"No, just because normal guys don't do this kind of thing. They may ask you out or call you up, but to send these . . . dead . . . flowers and that crazy letter, that's odd even by your standards, Alice."

"But, Tash, the flowers weren't dead when he sent them, you know. They were pretty."

"But why not just use Interflora like everybody else, huh?"

"Maybe because it's a little more romantic to pick your own, show you've put some thought into it." Alice wasn't going to concede defeat on this one.

"Oh sure, just like it's romantic not to have a clue who this guy is. Don't you think that if he was remotely attractive or socially acceptable, he'd have the balls to meet you face-to-face?"

"There's a long and rather wonderful tradition of secret admirers, Tash. Haven't you ever heard of Cyrano de Bergerac?"

"Sure, and look at the size of the guy's nose."

Alice realized there was nothing she could say to persuade Tash otherwise right now. But she'd be sorry. Riot of angelic beauty. That wasn't the product of a warped mind or even an ugly guy. Alice could just tell.

CHAPTER 14

"**J**acko, do you mind if I borrow your car tonight, only I've said I'll have dinner with this girl I met in a café?" Paddy ran into the house sweating. It was a sizzling Saturday afternoon and the cabdriver had refused to go any deeper into Manhattan Beach because of its minuscule streets and death-defying hills, so he'd had to run the last two miles.

"No, I'm taking the masseuse out tonight—I need it." Jack was sitting by his Caribbean-tiled pool flipping through *FHM* magazine's One Hundred Sexiest Women to get him in the mood. Poolside was his favorite place since he'd arrived in L.A. He'd had one part in *Days of Our Lives*, where he had to be a perverted dentist, but he seemed to enjoy being a lounge lizard more than the rigors of auditioning; besides, he had a sizable trust fund and was starting to think that maybe he was more of a producer than an actor anyway. "I'll drop you off."

Paddy pulled off his shirt and sunk onto the grass. "Christ, but I'm unfit. How did you get that six-pack, Jacko?"

"By expending in the gym all the energy I don't use up having sex. It's kind of a native thing."

"But you'll get it with the masseuse to be sure?" Paddy coughed and took a crumpled cigarette pack out of his back pocket.

"Not if I don't have a bloody car, I won't." Jack decided that the masseuse looked a bit like Kate Moss, who was number 37—not bad going at all. Maybe with such a hot date he could afford to be generous. "Tell you what, you can drop us off at the restaurant and pick us up at eleven thirty and bring us back here. I can tell her you're my chauffeur."

"Done deal." Paddy shook Jack's hand, not really taking in the fact that he'd therefore have to abandon his own date before midnight.

"So does this date mean you've finally scored with what's-ername?" Jack asked, wondering if maybe the masseuse actually, apart from the hair, looked a bit more like the hippie from *Friends*, who was a disappointing number 78.

"Alice? Nah, I told you, Jacko, I'm not interested in her like that," said Paddy, wishing that Jack wouldn't make such a big deal of it.

"So you sent her some handpicked flowers because you're not interested in her?" Jack threw down the magazine. Maybe he should meet this Alice chick and try to work out what was going on.

"Well, she wasn't in when I called round her house, so I thought I might as well leave her a note. And I think that if I just turn up unannounced she might just freak out a bit. I reckon she's kinda shy." Paddy stroked the back of his neck slowly.

"So are you trying to get her into the sack or what?" Jack was confused, but then so was Paddy.

"I really don't know. The thing is that I think I must like her or I wouldn't be here. She's so different from all the others though, Jacko. You wouldn't look twice at her. 'Cept of course I did. And now I can't stop thinking about her. It's a bloody pain in the arse, actually."

"Sounds like the real thing to me." Jack threw *FHM* at Paddy, who just tugged at his hair.

Surely not? "Ah, get outa here. She's all right. That's all." He sighed. "I called by her house again today, but there was nobody there."

"Again? Do you mean you've been there before and still not managed to pull her?" Jack laughed and bummed a cigarette off Paddy, who trailed his hand in the cool water of the swimming pool, his eyes half closed with expectation, his hair damp from his recent exertions. "Well, I reckon your days as Wilde man are numbered. Who's tonight?" Jack asked.

"Isabelle. She looks like the girl from Ipanema . . . tall and tanned and young and lovely." Paddy smiled. He ran his wet hand through his hair and sat up. Where the hell was she anyway, this Alice? Didn't she go to the bars on Main Street like normal people? Jesus, but she was elusive.

Tash added the final diamanté clip to Alice's hair.

"There, you look stunning. He's gonna love you." She stood back and admired her handiwork. Alice was wearing a turquoise Versace catsuit with ladybirds crawling all over it, a pair of ballet pumps, and hair that had lost a fight with a Force 9 gale.

"I look like Marie Antoinette on acid. Can we just dampen it down a little bit?" Alice pleaded. Wearing jeans and manky Pumas would have been overdressing as far as she was concerned. If Charlie saw her like this, he'd think she was gagging for it. And she wasn't, certainly not with some totally forgettable-except-for-his-windy-hair-and-suntan type of man. Suntans went out with the ark surely? She thought of the accouterments of suntans—white sports socks, open-topped cars, playing tennis before breakfast, always carrying an egg timer so you knew when you'd got toasty brown enough on your back. All these things were repellent to Alice. All of them made her want to flee, screaming, back to the safety of Chelsea and men who didn't wash very often. At least they were real men, she thought, not shop-dummy replicas.

"Tash, this has been great fun, but I've got stacks of work to do on this campaign for Tommy Kelly. I should really stay in." She practiced it to the mirror while Tash ran into the kitchen to get an ice cube to rub on a spot that had appeared on her neck. But she knew there was little point in protesting. Charlie had called that morning to check whether she had any food allergies he should tell the restaurant about. It was too late to stem the tide.

"Here. Just hold this to your neck until he arrives and the redness will go down." Au contraire. By the time the doorbell rang, the ice cube had melted and formed a small river that ran from Alice's neck to her cleavage, thence leaving a damp trail to her belly button. And an attack of frostbite had broken out where the spot had been. Oh, well, perhaps if I tell him I'm contagious, he won't kiss me at the end of the evening. Alice tripped to the door in her gold mules.

"Hi, Charlie, good to see you again." Tash had beaten her to it and was air-kissing him.

Alice stood in the background feeling like a fourteen-year-old in some American sitcom waiting for her date for the prom.

Not that her dating life had ever been thus. For Alice it had been more like, "Oy, my mate fancies you," followed by a fumble in the cloakrooms at the disco, perhaps outside if you were keen and then embarrassment at school on Monday when the male in question pretended never to have laid eyes, let alone sweaty palms, on you. So here was her attempt to have a chocolate-box date.

"Alice, good to see you again." Charlie emerged from the air-kiss and shook her hand. Oh God, he was going to be formal. She didn't think she could bear it. As Tash played sitcom mother and asked where they'd be going and the like, Alice gave him the once-over. Height: 5'11" (passable, not ideal, but it would suffice); Hair: brown and perhaps in danger of having been doused in some sort of setting solution or mousse (dubious); Eyes: yes; Teeth: lots of (from her limited experience Alice had found kissing men with lots of teeth conjured unsettling images of Ken dolls); Dress: chinos, probably Armani, nondescript shirt and loafers (probably the less said the better). So she was going to be dating Ken. Perhaps Barbie was having a wanton affair with Action Man and he was trying to get back at her.

"Have fun, guys!" Tash waved from the doorway and had she been wearing an apron and carrying a handkerchief in her hand Alice could have sworn she'd stumbled on to the set of *Happy Days* by mistake.

And it goes without saying that the car was open-top. Alice forfeited a considerable number of diamanté clips to the winds as they zipped along the freeway toward Beverly Hills. She wished that Charlie would forfeit some of his perfunctoriness, too, but to no avail.

"So, this job must be quite stimulating?" He indicated even though there were no cars for several miles. Something tells me here's a man who plays by the rules, thought Alice as she salvaged her diamanté earrings from her hairdo. At least the wind had dried up her damp patch.

"Well, I suppose so. It has its interesting moments.

Actually I trained as a milliner." Alice hadn't a clue why she was lying, but it was the first thing that came into her head and she had to liven this date up somehow.

"Right. So that's like what? The architecture of mills or something?" Charlie looked puzzled as he negotiated the road ahead at sixty miles per hour. If he had been able to converse on the subject of pillbox versus boater, then she'd definitely have given him a second chance. But it seemed that Charlie had just burned his boaters.

"And you're a talent agent, Charlie. That must be quite stimulating." She supposed she should at least make some conversation. After all he'd probably be paying for dinner. At least she hoped so since Tash had warned her that it was the most expensive and exclusive restaurant in town. Charlie reeled off a list of celebrities she'd never heard of and regaled her with tales of budgets and the complexities of casting. She smiled politely and checked out his profile through the corner of her eye. Fabulous nose actually. And really nice lips. Firm and quite generous. But not icky slobbery generous. Nice. And clean ears? She craned her neck to have a quick peep. Yup. Spanking clean. So why not, Alice? Why not? Just too bloody handsome really. And too bloody boring actually. Not to mention too clean. Charlie was Mr. Safe.

Alice, dressed as she was for virtually anything, was in the mood for a spot of debauchery. She'd been locked up in her office all week and was having one of those hormone fests that crop up in your life with random inconvenience and make you fancy everyone from the cable TV man to chat-show hosts. Everyone, that is, except the man sitting next to you in the car.

Charlie led her down many a back alley to what she had to admit was a really beautiful restaurant. Nothing as trite as a ceiling: this was open-top dining with just the stars for lighting and a beautiful fountain in the middle of the courtyard. The clientele was decidedly hip and although Alice hadn't actually got a clue what this place was, he proudly informed her that the waiting list for a table was six months.

"My, my, you must have been to that fortune teller on Venice Beach." She giggled.

"What?" Charlie's beautiful eyes clouded over with vacancy.

"Well, imagine knowing six months ago that you'd want to take me out to dinner tonight," she explained lightheartedly.

"Oh, but you see I didn't. I just booked the table and then found a date," Charlie told her earnestly.

"That's so romantic, Charlie. Thanks." She laughed, hoping to see the corners of his mouth move in a northerly direction. But to no avail. The waiter came over to them with a bottle of champagne that had no doubt been on ice for the last six months, too. Never mind the company, Alice thought philosophically, they were dining in a beautiful alfresco restaurant beneath the stars, sipping expensive champagne; she was buggered if she wasn't going to enjoy it. She'd just have to drink him sexy, she thought as she downed her first champagne cocktail. They then progressed to neat champagne.

If Alice hadn't known Charlie to be possibly the most boring and upstanding member of the Hollywood community, she'd have suspected him of trying to get her plastered. But chance would be a very fine thing. Thus far he'd opened the car door for her, asked her if she had a preference as to which table they sat at, and told her about his mother's sciatica. Had fluffy kittens with balls of wool suddenly

appeared, the scene couldn't have been more unthreaten-
ing. Needless to say, by the time Alice sat down to her
starter of white mussel soup, she couldn't quite see straight.

Dinner was merely a succession of courses punctuated
by much champagne, a to-be-expected-but-definitely-not-
cherished experience. They had just about successfully
kept alive the corpse of conversation from the car with
more of the same agent-movie-budget-hats banter. Alice
would occasionally throw in a comment or joke that would
sail unobserved over Charlie's head at a height of 30,000
feet and she'd conceal her private mirth in yet another
glass of whatever was handy. By the time they eventually
left Alice had to be bodily carried to the waiting car. Perhaps a slight exaggeration, but she was leaning heavily on
Charlie's shirt, leaving her new indelible blusher all over
his sleeve. Charlie then got it into his head that he was
sober enough to drive home. Alice wasn't sober enough to
decide whether he was or wasn't and she was definitely
too drunk to protest coherently. Besides, it looked like being the only remotely dangerous thing that Charlie would
do all night, so as there were no cars on the roads and
even fewer pedestrians around, she conceded.

"Ohh, Charlie, this isn't where I live," Alice said as they
pulled up into the driveway of what must surely be Aaron
Spelling's house. The gate swung open automatically and
Charlie positively glided up the gravel. Perhaps he hadn't
had too much to drink after all, thought Alice, then re-
tracted nervously. Nooo, the prospect of her having consumed all three bottles of champagne unaided was too
alarming to contemplate. The car pulled to a halt.

"I thought you might like to take a swim." Charlie turned
to her and raised an eyebrow.

Wow, coming from any other man right now Alice

would have been knickers off and skinny-dipping at the merest suggestion, but Charlie was just so smooth. No thanks. "I might drown," she explained helpfully.

"I have a rubber ring," he said without a hint of humor.

"Well, maybe I'll just have a look, then you can take me home, all right?" she suggested. It was obvious to Alice that the only thing she would be checking out the size of tonight was Charlie's swimming pool. Was she a trifle disappointed? No, of course not, she thought, but then maybe his eyes *were* nice. And this place, she could quite handle a day spent poolside in a turban with a glass of iced tea and an impromptu lunch party.

"Absolutely fine." He closed the car door and walked ahead of her to the house. So he wasn't interested then. Why not? Did she look hippy in this Versace thing? She'd told Tash that she should tie a cardigan around her waist to hide her bulges, but had she listened?

"This is quite a place, Charlie." Alice skipped to catch up with him.

"Glad you like it. Can I get you a coffee?" he asked as he opened the front door. Ah, now was that coffee coffee or coffee *coffee* with an infinitesimal rising at the left-hand corner of the mouth, with the gentle arcing of a carefully trained eyebrow? Alice couldn't tell because Charlie was now marching seven paces in front of her. He obviously just wanted to get to the front door before her and lock her out, leaving her to wander the grounds all night until his security people could be woken at seven and made to escort her from the premises. Maybe she should have listened more carefully to his mother's ailments. Maybe he was just convinced that she was selfish and uninteresting. It probably wouldn't be the first time that she'd been mistaken for somebody with those characteristics.

"And your mother, Charlie, is she a lot better now?" Alice asked, desperate that if she wasn't going to fancy Charlie herself he'd at least be left with a vaguely rose-hued impression of her.

"My mother's dead." He put his keys in the door and walked into the cool oak-lined hallway. Alice stood outside, mortified in his wake, waiting for him to ask her to leave. Then whose sciatica had they been discussing?

"Are you going to come in, Alice?" he asked, his eyes . . . sparkling. How had Charlie gone from being the romantic equivalent of an egg sandwich to a crusty brie and tomato baguette?

"I'm coming in," she said, losing another diamanté clip as she tripped up his front step and flew headfirst into the house.

"It's just that I have a couple of phone calls to make, do you mind?" he asked, showing his perfectly white, perfectly perfect teeth. He was handsome. In fact, he was now positively a sun-dried olive foccacia and parma ham sandwich. Bloody hell, maybe she had drunk him sexy after all. His ruffled hair was certainly starting to nudge Jamie's blond mop off the top of the charts. And his forearms were almost ravishing, with their light tan and dusting of fair hair.

"Absolutely fine by me, Charlie, I'll just sit down and make myself comfortable . . . somewhere." She gestured with a flick of her wrist and smacked it bang into a . . . a Picasso? Surely not. Surely yes. Blimey.

"Go through to the den, I won't be long." He opened the door to a room that would probably have answered just as eagerly to being called the lair. Deep burgundy velvet sofas, rugs that once graced Moorish harems, deep, luxuriant shagged-pile carpets. Alice flopped back gratefully but not gracefully onto an emerald-green slipper chair. She leaned her head back and opened her eyes.

"Arrgghh!" She sobered up for a second. There, staring down at her through suspicious eyes, was herself. Then she burst into nervous laughter. A mirrored ceiling. In fact, a silver-leaf ceiling reflecting back on her, but Alice didn't know that such extravagances existed. Charlie came back into the room, only he seemed to have gone terribly Noel Coward. He was wearing a silk dressing gown.

"Charlie!" Alice tried to sit bolt upright in the chair, but it was designed only for reclining and something else that she absolutely wasn't in the mood to do now. A swift kiss before bedtime out in the cool breeze by the swimming pool was one thing. Being pawed and goodness knows what else in this—Alice looked around her, noting with terror some very unerotic erotica involving a donkey staring down at her from the wall—brothel was quite another. Charlie was gaining on her. She pulled her knees tightly into her chest, then, realizing that this wasn't very likely to make a blind bit of difference to the outcome of the situation, quickly sprung up and made for a piece of art.

"It's great. Is it Henry Moore?" she asked of a twisted piece of metal in semihuman form.

"Early Beth Derbyshire." He nodded grimly and draped his silk-clad . . . His silk-clad what? Hell's bells, she didn't even want to think about what was underneath the dressing gown, although now that her mind had alighted on the subject, as it were, she couldn't seem to shift it. "Go away," she instructed her head. "Stop it." But still Charlie and the donkey and the silk and the slipper chair designed for *that* were all mixed up in her head. She hurled herself onto the most Draconian piece of furniture in the room. A little

wooden stool. Safe as houses. Could have been sitting in
an RE class in the Convent of the Sacred Heart. She wiped
the perspiration surreptitiously away from her upper lip
and breathed again. Charlie was on his sofa at least three
meters away and all was well with the world.

"Do you like it?" Charlie asked, gesturing to her resting
place.

"It's great. Very sturdy," replied Alice, rocking slightly on
it as if to demonstrate the sturdiness but not rocking too
much lest she should be propelled headlong into Charlie's
silk lap.

"It's a Puritan birthing stool." Charlie smiled, but this
was New Charlie. New Charlie with a leer, all mention of
kittens and sciatica had vanished into the ether. "It's not
only sturdy but surprisingly versatile," he leched.

Alice nearly screamed for the LAPD there and then but
decided that her first move had to be to remove herself
from the chair of sin. Just as she was filling up her lungs
with air, he deflated her.

"I invited some friends over. I hope you don't mind?" he
said, leaning forward and scrutinizing her hipbone. So it *was*
her hips that had put him off. But to be honest she didn't
care. She was a free woman. All she had to do was prance
around the room a bit until his friends arrived and then
when they'd chuckled over their fiftieth baseball joke and
stubbed out their third cigar she'd just get up, casual as
you like, and call for a taxi home. Perfect. Hell, they might
all even go for a late-night dip. It was menacingly hot and
now that sex in the swimming pool was off the agenda she
might quite enjoy a spot of breaststroke.

"That one's an old girlfriend . . ." Charlie was filling Alice
in on the art adorning the room. She'd asked at least seven

questions about every piece on every wall and this was the last one. After this she'd have absolutely nothing to say. But old girlfriend. This was great. This was a topic she could sink her teeth into while simultaneously proving that she regarded herself as totally out of the picture as far as current girlfriends were concerned. She could establish herself as a friend. Not a lover.

"She's very pretty," said Alice, though she wasn't quite sure which part was the girl's face or even which was round or . . .

"She *took* the picture. It's actually *of* me." Charlie came over and stood too close to Alice. He took her finger and traced it over what had previously looked like a nose and mouth in shadow but was now quite patently not. "But I'm glad you think it's pretty." He smiled.

She pulled her finger away as though to touch the photo was somehow tantamount to touching the real thing, which she had absolutely no intention of doing. *Briiinngg.* Saved by the bell. Charlie vanished into the hallway and Alice darted back to the birthing stool and waited for the room to fill with beer-can-wielding, baseball-cap-toting males.

"This is . . . I'm sorry, I've forgotten your name." Charlie gestured to a dark-haired beauty on his left.

"Chakira and this is Courtney." She spoke with a cigarette smoker's rasp and took her equally pretty blond friend's hand. They walked over to the sofa and sat down, legs crossed to reveal just a glimmer of suspender belts.

"Drinks, girls?" Charlie wandered happily over to pour a couple of brandies. "Oh, on second thought let's have champagne. It's Saturday, after all." He grinned, pulling a dewy bottle and four chilled glasses out of the fridge. Alice watched the women for signs of glee at the appearance of vintage champers, but they merely took their glasses dutifully without so much as a thank-you. Californian women, honestly, so spoiled. Alice made a huge, teach-them-by-example point of displaying her gratitude.

"Thanks so much, Charlie, wow, and icy glasses, too. Lovely," she rambled histrionically.

The girls looked at her as though she were a few bubbles short of a bottle of the stuff. For friends of Charlie's there didn't seem to be much merry banter being exchanged. Not much jolly or frothy conversation. In fact, it was all rather gloomy.

"Chakira and Courtney, what pretty names." Alice leaned forward on her stool and looked intently at the girls. She was darned if she was going to stoop to low standards of personal politeness just because they were. She rounded all her Lucie Clayton charm up and sallied forth. "So what do you both do?"

"Is she for real?" the Courtney one turned to Charlie and asked.

He looked panicked for a second and then smiled broadly. "Girls, why don't you just go and have a stroll around the garden. Alice and I are just going to have a quick chat. I'll call you in a moment." He took their glasses and they obediently but rather sulkily stood up and walked toward the door, where he whispered something to them, handed back their drinks, and closed the door behind them.

"What odd girls," Alice commented as Charlie turned back and began to walk toward her. "Have you known them long?"

"Oh, not that long really. I think they're probably quite sweet," Charlie said, smiling. Quite a winning smile actually. In spite of his silly dressing gown he looked quite fanciable again.

Alice wondered if she were in the early stages of schizophrenia and watched him closely. He was physically perfect. Very lean, muscular in just the right places. And if that photo on the wall was anything to go by . . .

"Why don't you sit somewhere more comfortable," said Charlie in a languid drawl. If she closed her eyes it was almost sexy. She moved over to the slipper chair so that she could observe him from a safe distance. Watching Charlie was like looking at one of those Athena posters of hunks you had on your bedroom wall. Easy on the eye but not a great deal to say for itself.

"Those ladybirds on your suit." Charlie moved over to Alice's chair and looked closely at her right thigh. "Do they mean something?" he asked earnestly.

"I don't think so."

"Well, they're pretty. I thought maybe they were a fertility symbol or something. Ladybirds are notoriously . . . randy." Charlie's perfect lips were very close to Alice now.

"Ladybirds are randy? Well, fancy that!" Alice laughed so loudly that he was forced to move backward a bit. Her leg had gone a bit quivery.

"Very," he breathed.

She closed her eyes. That goddamn drawl again. It got her every time. This time she kept her eyes closed. In fact, she almost fell asleep. She could feel Charlie take her hand in his and stroke it gently. She felt a soft warmth around her wrist. Then he took her other hand. The same sensation. Mmmm. She was almost nodding off now. Charlie's aftershave was warm and leathery.

"You can open your eyes now," Charlie breathed softly

into her ear. She didn't want to open her eyes; it was very pleasant just lying there dozing off. "Alice," he said. Oh God, he would go on. She opened her eyes.

"Yes?" she said, not focusing properly.

"I'll be back in a moment." He stood up and left the room. And that was it. She'd gone to all the effort of opening her eyes for that? She closed them again and went to rub her eyes, God, she was more tired than she'd realized. But her hands were so heavy, they wouldn't budge. She put a bit more effort into it, but still her hands remained glued to the arms of the chair. She opened her eyes and looked at her right hand.

"Arrrgghhh!" she squealed to herself. She looked at her left hand. "Arrggghhh!" again. Both of her hands were not glued but handcuffed to the arms of the chair. "Aaarrgghhh!" She tried to swivel her head and see where Charlie had gone, but the slipper chair made it impossible for her to see anything other than what was in front of her, namely Charlie's framed poster-sized genitalia. "Arrrgghhh."

Panic gripped her head and the handcuffs gripped her arms. She looked closely at them and examined them for signs of toyishness; maybe they were a joke pair that came apart at the hinges or something. Maybe the key was in the lock. But no. No easy escape route here. But she did notice rather reassuringly that they were designed for comfort. Oh yes, beautiful fur lining, mink if she wasn't mistaken. In fact, Alice felt as though she had been mistaken for a mink, put in a trap, and was about to be turned into an object of desire for a very rich person. Shit. What on earth was she going to do?

"Ahhh, Alice. There you are." Charlie grinned broadly as he stepped back into the room, followed by the still surly Courtney and Chakira.

"Of course here I bloody well am. Where the bloody well else would I be?" she spluttered. Maybe if she smiled warmly at one of the girls they'd help her out. She needed all the allies she could get right now. She tried a wide smile at Chakira, who frankly looked slightly more friendly than Courtney, though still only marginally more approachable than a rottweiler. But as she smiled at Chakira, Charlie turned around and winked at her. Chakira rolled her eyes in a bored fashion and went over to where Alice was sitting. She knelt by her feet and took her left foot in her hand; she pulled off the admittedly killingly painful stiletto and put Alice's big toe in her mouth.

"What the bloody hell . . . ?" Alice yanked her foot away, mainly with the fear that after a good eight hours in a too-small shoe it would whiff to high heaven but also because she wasn't really sure what was going on here. It would have been more apt if Kim Basinger was sitting in her place and Mickey Rourke was perving from Charlie's vantage point. This was not Alice's life: this was a harmless perv when it's on the video but another thing entirely when it's your own bloody toe that's being turned into a Walls ice lolly.

"Excuse me, but I really wouldn't do that if I were you, it's just that . . ." Alice came over all English and was just about to apologize for her none-too-fragrant feet when suddenly Chakira's hands were fumbling with the shoulder straps of her catsuit.

"Oy!" yelled Alice, only to find that Courtney was standing behind her kissing her neck. Bloody hell.

"Charlie, can you just take these things off my hands, please, and take me home? Tash'll be waiting up and I'm sure she'll be worried," Alice lied, knowing full well that the longer Charlie kept her out, the happier Tash would be.

Charlie probably realized the truth, too, because he was sitting on the sofa opposite gazing avidly at the spectacle before him, his eyes narrowed with pleasure.

"Excuse me, Charlie! Tell them to get off!" Alice shouted, and kicked Chakira in the stomach. Chakira merely took Alice's foot in her hand and sat on it. Courtney meanwhile was doing a very deft job of removing Alice's underwear from beneath her catsuit. Charlie suddenly snapped his fingers.

"Okay, girls, let's give Alice a bit of a break. Let's see what you can do without her." At which the two Cs began to remove each other's clothes and wrestle on the rug.

Alice closed her eyes firmly and tried to remember the periodic table again. "Copper—K. No, not K, that was potassium. Shit, what was copper? Iron—was that In?" She screwed up her face and hummed in her head to blot out all the groaning that was emanating from the vicinity of the rug, and occasionally and rather unsavorily, she realized, from the sofa. "Magnesium—Mg. Nice and easy, that one."

Finally the moaning stopped and Alice drifted off to sleep through sheer exhaustion. She wasn't sure which happened first, she was aware only of waking up and seeing the washed, shaved, Ralph Lauren–ed Charlie standing in front of her drinking a cup of Earl Grey. She seemed to have the use of her hands back and apart from the fact that her bra strap was rather irritatingly undone and halfway around her waist, she appeared to be unscathed. Had last night really existed? She shook her head and tried to remember what would have happened if she hadn't fought off two hookers from the confines of her fur-lined handcuffs. She really had to give up drinking, it did her no good at all. Then she looked up and saw a framed picture of a pretty girl's smiling face gone all hazy . . . oh no . . . wait a minute . . . not a smiling face at all . . . oh no!

"Morning. Can I get you anything?" Charlie smiled. Alice jumped ten feet in the air.

"A lawyer," Alice was tempted to say but didn't. But he was so clean-cut. Maybe it had just been a particularly torrid dream induced by the erotic art. Rather imaginative, given her usual pedestrian shagging-of-her-ex-boyfriend-on-their-honeymoon ones.

"I'm really sorry about last night, Alice," he said as if apologizing for a simple faux pas, serving white wine with red meat or something. "I usually pride myself on knowing which women will get turned on by that sort of stuff. I guess I misjudged."

"I guess you probably did," Alice said, grinning anxiously. What on earth had given him the impression that she was that sort of girl, she wondered, deciding that she just didn't have the bottle to carry off Versace.

"It won't happen again, I promise." He put his hand on his heart with "I vow to thee my country" sincerity and Alice relaxed back into her chair. He couldn't really be all that dangerous, Tash had known him for years. Maybe that was normal in L.A., maybe it was Alice who was the weirdo.

"Can I get you anything?" he asked with a reassuring absence of lechery.

"No, erm . . . I'm fine, thanks, but maybe you could give me a lift home. I've got tons of ironing to do before tomorrow."

Patrick woke up alone, tangled in Izzy's white satin sheets overlooking the ocean. He lifted his heavy head and looked around, no sign. He pulled on his boxer shorts and decided that today he might just go for a dip in the sea—he had to get over his morbid fear that every stretch of water would be as cold as the lead-gray sea of the coast of Cork, where he'd swum as a child.

"Izzy," he called out down the hallway but got no reply. He presumed she was welded into the lotus position somewhere. She'd spent most of yesterday evening telling him how fantastic her kundalini yoga teacher was and that they should go have lunch with him tomorrow. Patrick thought he'd rather not. Besides, he had to face Jack's wrath. He'd been so entranced by Izzy's talk of the nude gymnastics class she went to that he'd completely forgotton his role of chauffeur.

He tiptoed past the bathroom only to see out of the corner of his eye Izzy standing stark, staring naked plucking her eyebrows. Last night's athletic marathon should have told him to keep on walking or he'd be in danger of not being able to move a muscle for a week, but instead he turned and smiled.

"Morning." Wow, if that was what kundalini yoga did for these girls.

"Hi." Her grin was broader than her hips. "Have you seen the shower?" Patrick was hauled excitedly into the bathroom. The shower curtain was made of live bamboo and the window overlooked the ocean.

"It's an exhibitionist's fantasy," Izzy drawled, her zaftig body making his eyes water. "Do you wanna try?" Did he have a choice? Paddy's shirt had already left his back and his belt was being expertly undone by pistachio-green fingernails.

Two exhausted hours later he put on his sunglasses and drove as fast as Jack's clapped-out Volvo would take him toward Santa Monica with the radio on. The Beach Boys,

Bon Jovi. God, Jack's taste in music had obviously taken a serious nosedive since he arrived in L.A. Paddy stopped at a phone box in some very dusty and dodgy part of town and called Jack, but he wasn't home. Either that or he wasn't speaking to Paddy.

"Jack, it's me. Listen, I am so, so sorry. I completely forgot about you last night. I'll pay for the cab. I'm just going to call by and see if Alice is up, 'cause I'm kind of in the area, but I'll be home soon. I owe you a large beer." Paddy raced back to the Volvo before it got its hubcaps stolen and raced off toward Santa Monica. Driving past Noah's bagels and getting a waft of the irresistible baking smell, he pulled over and ran in for some much-needed sustenance—ran was perhaps too agile an adjective, he limped at a muscle-achingly slow pace into the shop and opted for a toasted poppyseed with marmalade. He munched it down in his car and drove along Main Street to Tash's house. No sign of life came from the house and the cat sat patiently at the front door. He rightly assumed the inhabitants were recovering from a heavy night all around and was so tired himself that he wished he was curled up behind the shutters, too, maybe with the soporific Alice.

He knew exactly what he'd do the second he saw her: open the car door and follow her down the street for a few minutes before calling out, "You know, I don't usually stop strangers in the street, but it strikes me that you're not only beautiful but you're also English. Am I not right?" Well, that was what he'd usually do, but maybe it wasn't the right approach to take with Alice. Christ, he wished he didn't have so much time to think about it. It was doing his head in. It wasn't as though he'd even recognize her when he saw her, unless she was wearing that terrible striped thing again. He could still smell Izzy's patchouli on his jacket.

Izzy, now there was a woman who knew how to dress, and undress, well. He rummaged on the backseat for a spare shirt or sweater. Just crisp packets and unraveling cassettes. And that thing with the ice cubes. What was that all about?

God, this was boring. Ordinarily, if he'd been waiting for a woman outside a theater or in a restaurant, he'd have kept himself amused by imagining the nuances that made her so perfect, the little twitches of her face, her cascading locks and things, but with Alice he kept coming back to the way she'd smiled absentmindedly at him when she'd caught him staring at her later on that night in the pub. She'd obviously presumed that he was just staring blankly into space. Most girls he knew would have presumed, quite rightly, that it was because he fancied them. Alice would never have dreamed of presuming. I mean, wasn't it dangerous for such a naive woman to be out alone in the world, she obviously needed someone to look after her.

He was just contemplating scribbling another poem onto the back of a cigarette pack when he saw the door open and the cat vanish inside. Aha. Someone was up. But then nothing for another half hour. If he stayed out much longer in Jack's car, he would be in danger of being evicted from the spare room. Sod this for a game of cards, he thought, stuffing the keys in his pocket and hopping over the garden wall to see if Alice was ever likely to make an appearance. But just as he nipped behind an oak tree he saw the shutter being thrown back and a bedraggled Tash with a full complement of rollers and face cream staring out. She screamed and, gouging his leg on the wall on the way, he ran headlong back to the car. Shit. He didn't imagine he looked such a pretty sight either, but Tash in her rollers with a scream that would curdle milk was a bit much for a Sunday morning.

He put his keys in the ignition and was about to start the engine when a convertible BMW drew up in front of the house and out rocked Alice. But this wasn't the Alice he remembered, this one looked like she'd fallen off the catwalk in Milan and walked the rest of the way home, stopping for a game of pool and a whiskey along the way. My God. What a woman. Where had the girl in the pub gone? But he didn't have time to ponder the conundrum. No sooner had she stepped out of the car, followed swiftly by a man from the driver's seat, than Tash came hurtling down the garden path pointing maniacally in his direction. She was screaming at him.

"I've called the police. I know just what you're like! Oh yeah, flee when there's danger, you pervert . . ." Paddy didn't stay to hear the end of the tirade. He put his foot down and sped along the street, leaving only dust. These American women were certainly forthright, he thought, as his pulse returned to normal.

"What's going on?" Alice asked as the streak of Volvo disappeared around the corner.

"It's your stalker! I caught him about to steal your underwear from the washing line."

Alice stifled a snigger. She was still quite drunk from last night's preprandial bubbly and the idea of a stalker driving a symbol of middle-class predictability made her laugh. She caught sight of Tash's and Charlie's faces. Stone-cold sobriety. Whoops. She feigned nervous hysteria at the prospect of a maniacal nutcase livening up her day-to-day existence and they led her gently inside.

"I think you should enroll in some self-defense classes." Charlie was all grave concern. My God, he'd only gone on a date, albeit an idiosyncratic one, with her, not given birth to her. What right had he to worry? And excuse me but weren't sado-masochists just the sort of people her mother had warned her about when she'd told her not to take sweets from strangers? Well, not that her mother would have known S&M from M&S, but she certainly would have forewarned her only child had her roots and life experience stretched just a bit further than Norwich. Bloody hell, rich or what? Alice thought. Imagine, Pervy Charlie suggesting I need self-defense. She kept her mouth shut and wondered who the mystery man was and then felt guilty for wondering.

"Absolutely. And from now on you should only go out when you're with somebody. Either myself or Charlie," said Tash. Alice wanted to argue, but her head was beginning to throb and she longed for her bed.

"Look, I'm feeling a bit fragile, I'm going to bed." She stood up and her head spun.

"Of course, let me help you." Charlie walked her to her bedroom door and followed her into the room.

"This is it then?" He stood serenely and contemplated the bed. "It's wonderful." He turned to Alice and gave her a lecherous look. "Come here, baby." He lay back on the bed and held open his arms. Alice backed toward the wardrobe. If at least seventeen units of alcohol the night before weren't enough to make her feel hungover, then Charlie calling her baby definitely did the trick.

"I think I need a shower," she said in the vain hope that the idea of whiffy armpits might put him off grappling with her unwashed body.

"That can be arranged, sugar." The endearments were pouring forth with alacrity. "Want me to soap you up?" The very idea.

Alice blanched and backed toward the door. "Another time maybe, Charlie," she said boldly, and held the door open for him. "I've got a headache."

This was obviously music to Charlie's ears. There was nothing he liked more than being turned down. It made the cherry seem so much sweeter. "Until next time, honey." He took her hand and licked her palm in a manner obviously intended to leave her gagging for it. When he turned his snake hips toward the door, Alice stuck her tongue out in horror and shuddered at the narrow escape.

"Jacko, where are you hiding?" Paddy walked through the house and out to the pool. Still no sound. He pushed open the bathroom door—no one. But a razor, a pastel pink one, was hanging out next to the coal-tar soap. Aha. Paddy went to Jacko's room with a grin and hammered on the door; it was about time Jack saw some action.

"Anyone home?" he called. No reply. "Come on, Jacko. I know you're here."

"Excusing me. Jacques is not 'ome. 'E is at ze droggerie— drugstore. We 'ave used all condoms in 'ouse and 'e 'as gone for *d'en plus*." A petite woman stood in Paddy's dressing gown in the doorway of his bedroom. Had he missed something?

"I am Beatrice." She held a tiny hand and brushed her long dark hair over one shoulder.

"Patrick. Good to meet you." Paddy hoped that she might just make her way back to Jack's bedroom or something or maybe lock herself in the bathroom and shampoo her admittedly very-clean-already hair, but she didn't. Instead she stood in the doorway of Paddy's bedroom smiling at him like a very beautiful character in a fairy tale.

"You're French, aren't you?" Paddy asked when the hypnotic staring became a bit disconcerting for him.

"*Oui,* from Lyon. But now I live 'ere." She smiled brightly.

"L.A., yeah, it's a great place to be, sure." Paddy tried to maneuver his way to his much-needed bed but, short of rugby-tackling her, didn't stand a chance.

"Ah, you've met." Jack walked in through the door in his pajama top and jeans, clutching an industrial-size pack of condoms. The beguiling Beatrice finally skipped away from the doorway and to Jack's side, where they slurped happily over the industrial-size promise of lots more sex and slurping. Paddy took advantage of the lull in conversation to dash into his room.

"Oh yes. Just what I've been waiting for," he murmured, utterly exhausted after his all-nighter and disastrous Alice-chasing session, "a wee nap." He tugged his T-shirt over his head, but just as he was about to hurl himself headlong into his duvet, he noticed that it had become a rather Draconian-looking massage couch. Steel legs. White plastic. And his duvet was folded up neatly in a corner next to a crate of cellulite oil.

"Oh yeah, sorry about that, mate," Jack yelled between slurps, "Beatrice is moving in, those are just a few of her things. You don't mind the sofa, do you?"

Alice slept like a baby, except for the dream about being tarred and feathered by Pervy Charlie, and woke at four that afternoon to find Tash sitting looking concerned at the end of the bed with a cup of chamomile tea in her hand.

"Alice, if you're feeling up to it there's a policeman in there who'd like a word."

A policeman. What had she done? She racked her brains. A video she hadn't returned to Blockbuster? Not tipping a cabdriver enough? What could it be? She took a sip of the chamomile tea and calmed down a bit. Of course, it had to be something to do with Pervy Charlie, she just knew it. What else could it be? Tash took Alice's hand in the way a nurse soothes a geriatric. "It's about the stalker."

CHAPTER 15

Alice walked through the door to find Tash sitting on the sofa watching the end of some staggeringly boring-looking road movie. "I've got muscles—look." Alice pulled up the sleeve of her T-shirt and flexed her arm. "My kickboxing instructor says I have naturally dynamic posture. It won't be long till I have shoulders like Elle Macpherson." Alice practiced a few left hooks and kicks in the direction of the television.

"Hey, move out of the way, that's DP's genius you're threatening," Tash said, wafting a hand in Alice's direction.

"Really?" Alice sat down on the arm of the sofa and watched. "So have you guys got it together yet?" she asked, hoping that they had because at least then Tash would have more important things to worry about than Alice's security twenty-four hours a day. She didn't mind the kickboxing or even the fact that she had to watch *Psychological Ways to Intimidate the Enemy* videos instead of *Melrose Place* every evening, but she hated not being able to go anywhere alone anymore. She had to have lifts to and from her kickboxing classes with a high-security taxi firm and felt as though she couldn't even pop out for a blueberry muffin from around the corner without an armed escort.

"I figure that if I delve into the genius of his creativity, then it won't be long before I can tap into his sexuality," Tash said, pausing the video on a frame of bleak desert road.

"God, how amazing to meet such a brilliant man and have a meeting of the minds," Alice said, slightly enviously, trying to find the symbolism in the lone boulder on the desert road.

"Well, yeah, but I think I caught him looking at my tits today, which is a huge breakthrough." Tash laughed and turned off the television. "We have to be out of here in twenty minutes. Are you sure that Lysette doesn't mind me coming along? It's not as though you need a minder while you're there, I can always just drop you off and pick you up later."

"Don't be ridiculous. Anyway, she wants to meet you, she's heard so much about you."

Despite her pretensions to be Lady Blah or Duchess Something-or-other, Lysette was also the consummate publicist and her dinner parties were like a torn-out page from the *National Enquirer*. She gathered dysfunctional actresses, eligible men, and gossip columnists together in the same room and she never adhered to her guest's yeast-free, no-alcohol, low-sodium dietary requirements. As a result everyone went home high as kites and twice as happy and the party was talked about for weeks to come. Tonight was no exception. There'd been enough additives and preservatives in the scattered bowls of Kettle chips to spell Engelbert Humperdinck.

Alice and Lysette squeezed into the cramped kitchen, adding liberal sloshes of red wine to the pasta sauce and dairyloads of butter to almost everything else within reach.

"I tried really hard to get some dripping, but they don't do it here. Apparently there's some amazing deli in New

York that sells it, and stuff like mushy peas and marmite,"
said Lysette.

"What on earth do you want dripping and mushy peas
for?" Alice asked, grimacing at the very thought.

"Traditional English fare. If I'm going to live there I have
to know how to cook the basics." Lysette tossed her California green salad with orange dressing and took a sip of
her wine. "I make a great steak and kidney pie, with those
little pastry leaves on, y'know?"

Alice smiled at her—standing there in a cool lilac sun-
dress in front of her shelf of commemorative royal china:
Elizabeth II Silver Jubilee plate, HRH the Prince of Wales
and Lady Diana Spencer mug with a telling chip—it was
hard to imagine her in tweeds with only her Labrador for
company while her husband dined at his club yet again.
There was no way that Lysette's dream earl could live up
to expectations. Alice shuddered at her friend's potential
fate. There was no doubt about it, if Lysette ever made it to
London and into the company of the landed gentry, she'd
be snapped up like a fox by hounds, which wouldn't do at
all. No, what she needed was someone less traditional, a
more cosmopolitan member of the aristocracy. . . .

"Lysette, this Englishman—does it have to be a castle or
would any ancestral pile do?" Alice asked, suddenly struck
with inspiration.

"Oh, you know, castle schmastle, I guess as long as it
has a coat of arms and this twin soul guy of mine owns it
I'm not gonna be too choosy. Why?"

"Oh, just a thought. Now what am I going to do about
my mystery admirer?"

"The poor guy. I can't believe Tash called the police." Lysette ladled iced watercress soup into eight bowls. "I
thought he sounded sweet. Here, can you take these out

for me?" She handed Alice some spoons and led the way into the dining room.

"So. Natasha tells me you have some weirdo tailing you?" said the girl who was sitting next to Alice, a beautiful actress who was allegedly dating a film star.

"I think that's a bit harsh. He probably got the wrong person or something."

Yes, he probably did, Izzy thought, looking Alice up and down from her flip-flops to her mousy hair. Izzy had tried so hard to get a stalker. She'd even hung around Internet cafés in the hope that some nutter would follow her home, but as yet she'd been unsuccessful. What did this girl have that she didn't, apart from terrible dress sense?

Izzy smoothed down her chiffon dress and took another sip of her wine. Her nutritionist would kill her, she could feel the yeast-bloat creeping up on her already, but who cared, she was feeling reckless, she'd had fun the other night with that Irish boy. She'd fantasized that he was JFK's forgotten son and that if she married him and then the Kennedys discovered his true identity, then she'd be clasped to the bosom of the family, taken to Martha's Vineyard, and become a sought-after actress. Hmm. She definitely felt better now. Maybe she should take to the bottle more often.

"Lysette tells me you're an actress. I don't think I've ever met a working actress before," said Alice, swirling cream into Izzy's soup. "Most of the actors I knew just did panto once a year and went on the dole. Do you do any television work?"

The table fell silent. Who was this girl? Didn't she know the cardinal rule of L.A. etiquette? Nobody works in television. Nobody will admit to it anyway. It may pay the kid's college fees and you may appear on a daytime soap seven days a week, but you certainly never acknowledge it to anyone other than your agent. Alice wondered why everyone seemed to be playing musical statues with their spoons glued to their lips. Then she realized.

"Oh, it's fine. The soup's meant to be cold." Then added generously, "But if it's not to your taste then I'm sure Lysette will heat it up in the microwave." But no. The spoons remained. Until Tash took charge as usual.

"Alice has only been in Los Angeles a short while." Then, icing on the cake, "She's from London." Ah. The bubbles of conversation whizzed to the brim again. A murmur spread and everyone relaxed back into party mode. Except for Izzy, who was glaring threateningly in Alice's direction.

Lysette pulled Alice into the kitchen.

"I know I made some kind of faux pas in there, Lysette, but what?"

Lysette was shaking a balsamic dressing for dear life. "Just don't mention television in this town. It's a kind of snob thing."

Alice was none the wiser but tried to commit the tip to memory. "How do you know Izzy?"

"She lives with my sister up in Malibu. Actress. Does daytime soaps when she's lucky. She's a bit wild but quite fun."

By the time the *tarte Tatin* was sitting on the table, Izzy seemed to be veering around a hairpin bend at speed, probably due to the inordinate amount of additives she'd consumed. She was telling the gossip columnist from the *L.A. Times* that she was dating a member of the Kennedy family, but don't tell anyone, promise. At this she'd slip her hand between his thighs and bare her teeth in a wildcat sort of way. Probably something she learned at drama school, thought Alice, little knowing that this particular pose was aired seventy times a day on national television in Izzy's latest acting role, that of a satisfied kitty in a cat-food commercial.

On Alice's other side was an empty place. The napkin still lay unopened and the wineglass unfilled, but nobody seemed to have missed the absent guest. Alice leaned over to Lysette, who was busy pouring oil on the troubled waters between Tash and a girl who claimed to want to marry a millionaire and have his tea waiting on the table every day when he got home.

"What, and let him keep you?" Tash wailed over and over again before adopting a hybrid Australian accent for her Germaine Greer speech on the rights of women.

"Well, I don't actually see what's wrong with that," mumbled the girl into her soup.

"What's wrong with it is that it's essentially demeaning and retrograde!" Tash brayed.

"Who's supposed to be sitting here?" Alice asked Lysette, not wanting her to see that she was desperate for somebody to talk to now that Izzy had taken an instant loathing to her and was studiously avoiding her.

"He'll be here soon." More and more mysterious. Alice fiddled with her cutlery and tried to add her middle-of-the-road views on feminism to the Tash vs. Sugardaddy debate without much success. Then into the room through the French windows strolled Tommy Kelly. Lysette jumped up to greet him.

"Tommy, you made it!" she said and was about to give him a run-down of the assembled company when Izzy stood up.

"Tommy, it's been ages. Remember me? Uma Thurman's housewarming party. Why don't you sit here next to me."

With which she glared at Alice, who was supposed to move her far-too-fat-for-this-town bottom to another seat. Tommy smiled blankly at her, pretty much in the way he'd done to Alice the day they'd first met. Alice kept her head down. Despite having a merry lunch with Tommy and helping to solve his image problem on the other side of the pond, she wasn't risking humiliation. Tommy followed Lysette into the kitchen, leaving the others aghast. It wasn't often that one of the real stars came down from their homes in the Hollywood Hills to sup with mere mortals. The struggle that ensued in the room to have Tommy park his leather-clad bottom on the seat nearest their own was epic. Even the would-be cookie-cooking housewife became embroiled on the premise that the way to a man's heart was through his stomach and offered to do macrobiotic for him one day.

Alice slipped away and sat on the sofa to escape the fray. She fell back onto the "Englishman's Home Is his Castle" hand-embroidered cushion and flopped. Alice never felt lonely when she was alone, but now, sitting alone in a room full of strangers with so much to say and laugh about that didn't involve her and that she didn't want to be involved in, she thought of Jamie. She'd packed up her room in London and left behind all the reminders: his rugby shirt that smelled of Eau Sauvage, the shells they'd collected on holiday in Greece, and the wrapper of the first condom they ever used. But still, devoid of all these mementoes of love, she found herself thinking of him. And thinking how even before the pervy incident she hadn't really been able to make herself fancy Charlie. God, maybe she'd never meet anyone she could fancy again. Maybe Jamie had been her twin soul. But then she remembered the letter and the flowers. Just who was her mystery admirer? The last thought made her smile and pull the threads on the cushion until the moat of the castle had almost completely disappeared. She quickly stuffed them down the side of the sofa and hugged the cushion.

"Penny for them?" It was Tommy. His hair was dyed blue-black and his skin was almost translucent. Alice remembered his *Just Seventeen* likeness being wrapped around her fifth-form chemistry book, but strangely she didn't feel any excitement. After her lunch with Tommy and Jennifer she'd realized that Tommy was a universal male and would happily sleep with anyone without a skirt. He certainly wasn't her type, though Alice liked him and could envisage hanging out with him and having a laugh, but he certainly wasn't Bunsen-burner material.

"Oh, you know," she said, moving the cushion behind her head. "The usual."

"And what is the usual for you, Alice Lewis?" He'd remembered.

She smiled. There you go, sweet. No famous actor was obliged to remember the name of his new publicist. Especially when the glorious likes of Izzy, Tash, and Lysette were present.

"Shells and condoms," she replied honestly.

"Ha, my analyst would have a field day," he replied. He then proceeded to tell her about his problems with drink and drugs and how as a teenager he'd hear his parents arguing and just sit in his room and play his guitar. Alice had been tempted to add that if those were the grounds for needing an analyst they'd have to have a séance with Freud himself in her case. She'd thought that all parents hurled chairs through kitchen windows and lobbed rolling pins at each other. It was certainly part of the domestic landscape in deepest Norfolk.

"Why's your dad got a broken foot, Lucy?"

"Oh, Mum ran him over 'cause he was in the pub all night." What was unusual about that?

Alice still nodded sympathetically though. "Maybe it'd help if you took up a hobby, kung fu or something. Better than going to a shrink. And cheaper. I go to a great kick-boxing class." She laughed and Tommy looked at her with overawed respect.

"You're amazing. Do you know that, Alice?" At which point the entire room had somehow fallen silent and noted that the man they were fighting over was no longer in their midst. He was sitting on the sofa gazing at the girl from London as if she were going to vanish in a puff of smoke if he took his eyes off her.

"Totally lost the plot on drugs. It's so sad," Izzy mumbled to her gossip columnist, "You have to promise me that you won't mention the fact that Tommy and I are seeing each other, will you? It'd be so bad for my career to be romanti-cally linked to such a fucked-up loser."

The gossip columnist laughed. "You and Tommy?"

"Sure, me and Tommy." Izzy wouldn't take her eyes off him now.

"So what about you and Kennedy's son?"

"Oh, that's precisely why you have to keep quiet about Tommy." She was obviously completely gaga, but he was used to these wanna-bes. Couldn't move for them in this town. What he was much more interested in was what exactly was going on between the scruffy chick on the sofa and Tommy Kelly, local Lothario. Izzy saw the keen interest on his face and vowed to sort that pathetic English girl out once and for all. Jesus, hadn't she even heard of Callanetics?

CHAPTER 16

The Fourth of July. The sun was veiled by a milky mist this Saturday morning and the tops of the palm trees along Venice Beach were swathed in fog. It could have been a winter morning. The air seemed to be filled not only with flags flapping against masts but with portents of a wonderful day ahead. Market traders from Manhattan Beach to Santa Monica ordered in extra ice cream and Cokes. Animals seemed to know what lay ahead: dogs strained more vigorously on their leashes and cats sought out shaded places to retire to later on. The Rollerbladers were doing up their laces early, their denim shorts and midriffs already seeking out the weak rays of sun.

The only people who didn't seem to have a sense of glorious anticipation of the day ahead were Paddy and Alice. Not being native they didn't have that headstart. Weren't accustomed to the promise in the air. But if they had known, what difference would it have made? Maybe they'd have hopped out of bed a little more eagerly, maybe Alice would have slicked on a little lipgloss. But nothing earth-shattering, nothing that could alter the course of their destinies at this late stage.

Alice showered in some chocolate-scented shower gel she'd bought in Melrose yesterday and pulled on a pair of white lace Victorian bloomers with a T-shirt and a thinning lavender cardigan. It was the weekend, she felt she deserved a few home comforts; the strange dress sense and a body smelling like a bar of Galaxy were today's chosen luxuries. Tash had gone away to Big Sur with a bunch of people from the set and would probably right now be fluttering her brainwaves in DP's direction. So Alice could go out; she was free. She had promised Tash that she would make Lysette or Tommy or someone accompany her if she left the house, but what harm could she come to? She could even skive her kickboxing class and go to the flower markets instead. She noted happily that her legs no longer wobbled dangerously around inside the bloomers; instead they tended to go in the same general direction she was traveling in. To have your legs and bottom lead and not follow you was a great joy in life.

Paddy was only just getting used to his new bed. He'd decided to give Jack some privacy to be massaged by Beatrice whenever the fancy took him. After trawling the *L.A. Times* for property to let, he finally came across a slightly pricey but very simple place that he could spend the next couple of weeks in. Most of the others he'd seen had dangerously lurid floor coverings and live-in maids, which he was quite happy to do without. Besides, he liked to have a bit of space to himself. Lately he'd developed a sort of homing instinct. No matter where he was or how well the evening was going, he wanted to wake up in his own apartment, with its view of the Love drugstore up in the Hollywood Hills.

The block was one of the oldest in town and all the apartments overlooked a cool shady courtyard, which the landlord had liberally scattered with all manner of *feng shui*–inducing objects. There were Japanese fish in a small pond, a trickle of water, and so many windchimes that the fish must imagine themselves in a perpetual tidal wave. Paddy's place consisted of a large workbench and a mattress in a white room. It had belonged to an architect who obviously charged a fortune to impose his own brand of garage minimalism upon the unsuspecting rich of California, but it suited Paddy.

The curtainless window revealed that it would probably be a cloudy day. The Hollywood sign was barely visible and Paddy longed for some greenery. A lawn, a field, a forest. He missed home on days like this. He pulled on a navy jumper and some shorts and decided to eat breakfast out. He wasn't in the mood for the kind of spiritual breakfast his kitchen warranted. He'd prefer some sausages and eggs—bacon, he'd sadly discovered, was a no-go zone throughout America, stringy bits of pink the width of your little finger were the best one could muster. He decided to drive down to Santa Monica and leave his car somewhere along Main Street, then he could walk up to Alice's and see if she'd put in an appearance today. Though he was beginning to think that unlikely. He had to do something about her today.

Part of the reason why he'd stopped seeing Izzy and the rather sporadic series of other dates he'd picked up in various cafés and bars was that he was becoming bored. The fleeting glimpses he'd caught of Alice since he arrived had left so many contrary, jarring yet enticing images in his mind. The wanton party girl with the curious catsuit and dagger heels, the red-faced, glistening athlete in her workout clothes at the gym, kickboxing her way to emancipation,

the dowdy child-woman in her wincyette nightdress collecting the post from the doorstep. It really was so frustrat-
ing. He wanted to know what she was all about, then he
could get her out of his system. And much as Jacko teased
him and said that he was in love, Paddy knew better. He
knew what love was: it was the incredible happiness he
felt when he was around the woman. But this was nausea.
Fear. In short, it was horrible.

Alice strolled down toward Main Street with her espa-
drilles flapping loudly on her heels. She had a straw
basket bigger than a Provençal housewife carries to market by her side. In fact, there was still a moldy potato
lurking in the bottom. She stopped at Noah's bagels on
the way.
    "No, no, no. You must order properly, if not I ban you,"
the owner was yelling for the umpteenth time today to
some poor woman who had just driven down from San
Francisco to celebrate the Fourth of July with a famous
Noah bagel. San Francisco, where anything goes and life is
carefree. The woman didn't know what had hit her, so in
her pacifist way she ordered a plain with cream cheese,
untoasted thank you. The owner, known locally as the
bagel Nazi, calmed down. How many people forfeited their
toasted onion bagel with taramasalata and capers through
fear, Alice wondered, thinking that today she'd take the
plunge and go for toasted sesame cream cheese. You can't
expect to go native all in one day.
    "Get out, get out!" Noah was now screaming at a red-
faced man. "You were banned for a year. It's only been
four months. Come back in eight months and I serve you."
The red-faced man snarled under his breath and sloped off
to the inferior Jack's Deli down the street.

Alice sat looking out of the window of Noah's onto Main Street. Today was the only blissful day of the week when it was impossible to tell who was film industry and who wasn't, for the trades weren't published on Sunday. The trades consisted mainly of *Variety*, which anyone who was everyone would tut over and scour for mentions of their latest projects.

"Ha, whaddathey wanna give Demi Moore that part for?" they'd snarl when it was evident that they themselves hadn't earned a mention. No, today they all stopped being generic industry types and differentiated themselves by their reading matter. From *Forbes* to *Vogue*, it was evident whether they were in the business for power, money, or just plain old-fashioned sex. Alice pulled out her battered Jane Austen and marveled at how a bit of toasting and a few seeds had transformed her breakfast.

If she'd looked up then, she'd have noticed the ill-fitting figure of Paddy Wilde wandering past the window. Having waited for half an hour and seen no sign of Alice at her house, he decided to take a breakfast break. He eschewed the orange juices and smoothies in Noah's fridge for a Coke from the liquor store next door. As he delved into the deep freeze to try to weed out the only full-fat, heavily caffeinated can in the whole state from the bottom among long-forgotten ginger ale, Alice walked past the fly net of the liquor store and out toward Venice Beach.

The day was warming up considerably. Alice had already taken off her woolen jumper and put it in her basket. As she passed the regulation-Lycra crowds heading for the beach, she felt slightly self-conscious of her pallid limbs and baggy bloomers. Maybe she should have left her bolder personality statements to the days when she was accompanied by Tash, who would have happily performed a citizen's arrest on anyone who dared poke fun at Alice's antiquated clothing. Never mind. She hitched up the waist of her bloomers so that they could be mistaken for mutated Bermuda shorts and carried on walking. Walking down Venice Beach, past the bodybuilders and rap artists, and weaving her way through the cyclists and Rollerbladers, she felt an amazing sense of liberation. For the first time since she'd arrived a month ago she was experiencing all this for herself. Not with Tash or Lysette as well-intentioned tour guide, or with a detailed map of how to get herself from the taxi to the front door. If she got lost it didn't really matter. She looked up at the palm-fringed apartments overlooking the beach and promised herself she'd spend her first million on one. Or maybe she should go up the coast to Malibu?

Paddy sipped his Coke and was just about to set off to continue his vigil of Alice's house when he saw Izzy coming in the opposite direction. She was immaculately made-up and heading for a spinning class at the Main Street Gym. He ducked behind a limo carrying an eminent politician to a rendezvous with an actress downtown and watched her cross the street as she spotted a pooch-wielding girlfriend. Looking at Izzy, he felt an absolute hollow. Not a pang for any of the nights he'd spent with her, not even a stirring of the flesh. He took a large swig of Coke and, throwing the can away, headed toward the organic fruit market until he could be sure that Izzy had her feet firmly on the pedals of her exercise bike.

The sun was now arcing its way up beyond the palm trees and even Paddy, with his poor Irish circulation, found it warm enough to slough off his navy sweater. He tied it around his waist and loitered beside some dismal-looking organic carrots being sold by a woman with an organic smell all her own. He moved away toward Orange County pineapples, and as he did so he saw the most extraordinary sight. A girl coming toward him who looked like a cross between a rag doll and a supermodel. She was wearing a tattered Liberty bodice and bloomers and her face was hidden beneath a straw hat the size of a wagon wheel. Her shoulder was red-raw from carrying a basket bigger than her, but still she looked beautiful. Still he knew it was Alice.

Alice decided that the only way to fill this godforsaken basket she'd been lugging about town was to buy the largest, heaviest fruit the state had to offer. She also wanted to buy some sunflowers; it was about the only thing she missed about London and she often wondered at the fate of her sunflower children. Had they had much rainfall in England? Would they have grown into towering beauties? She kept her eyes peeled for surrogate sunflowers, but the flower stalls seemed to be all on the other side of the market, so instead she went straight and poetically, in Patrick's mind, for the watermelons.

As she ran her diminutive hands over the gargantuan fruit, Patrick chewed his lip. It was a bit like being given Christmas in July. You wanted to dive in and tear off the wrapping, but you also knew that once it had been, you'd lost that moment forever. And to tell the truth he was nervous. He tried to recollect how much alcohol he'd downed last night to make him feel this queasy. None. He almost took off at that thought. The moment when a confirmed Lothario's life of seduction reaches its natural end is like the moment you tie the breezeblocks to your legs and haul yourself over Putney Bridge. It's not pleasant.

Patrick was suddenly the sheep in wolf's clothing. He

milled over to the next stall and bought two blood oranges
as a means of getting closer to this extraordinary vision in
car-boot clothing.

"These, please." He couldn't take his eyes off Alice, who
was now loading two vast watermelons into her basket.
Any second now they'd fall right through its rotten bottom
and roll down the street like a scene from a nursery rhyme,
scattering people and animals in their wake.

"Seventy-three cents, please."

Paddy fumbled in his pockets for change. Credit card.
Phone card. Not a bloody dime.

"I'm really sorry, I don't think I have enough change. I
think I'll just put them back. . . ." But he carried on rum-
maging, not knowing where to put his oranges and not
wanting to let Alice out of his sight. Then she turned
around. She looked at him and tipped the brim of her hat
up out of her eyes. He looked incredibly familiar.

"I've got three cents if you need it," she offered. She'd
heard his voice and warmed instantly to it. If there was
one accent destined to get Alice where it wanted her, it
was Irish. Actually there were two—Scottish ranked a
close second. But this, this was the vocal sublime. And
when she had pushed her hat up ever so slightly, he had
dropped his oranges, sending them crashing among the
pears. She smiled. How nice to have such an effect. But
still he hadn't answered. She began to wonder if he'd
heard her or if he was just too startled by her frighteningly
freckly face. She pulled three cents out of her purse and
handed them to him. "Here, for your oranges."

A fraction of a second longer and his hand would have
begun to shake and then she'd have thought he was a
wino like the rest of his countrymen and been off. But in-

stead there was long enough just for that necessary frisson, for that locking of eyes. For the thunderbolt of cliché
to crash.

"Thanks." He took the three cents and handed it to the
woman, who'd had enough of this moron and his weirdo
girlfriend. She wrote off the remaining seventy cents as
a bad debt and turned to serve a young woman with a
child.

"That was really kind of you," said Patrick, taking both
oranges in one hand and putting his hand out to shake
Alice's with the other. He was beginning to regain some of
his composure. "Patrick Wilde." He smiled and delved his
hand deep into his pocket to find his Marlboro Lights. This
was very definitely not an abstemious moment.

"Alice. Alice Lewis. I thought that probably you might be
new in town. I know what it's like when you don't understand the currency." Even in the face of this beautiful new
man Alice couldn't resist the urge to imagine that she'd
been in L.A. longer than somebody—anybody. She was fed
up with being new. She wanted to seem cosmopolitan and
well traveled. Then she noticed his sweater tied around his
waist and the way he was struggling to light his cigarette
in the breeze and it didn't seem to matter whether she was
new or not. He wasn't really the sort of person to be impressed by this.

"Want one?" He held out his pack to her and sucked
hard on the cigarette in his mouth, holding his whole hand
over it, dragging for dear life.

"No thanks." Alice was faintly amused by his nerves.
How nice to make a man tremble. Thank God she was
feeling positive today or she'd never have even dared to tip
her hat to him, let alone offer him money. She smiled. But

then she realized with a pang of regret that it was probably the psychopathic bag-lady attire that was causing him panic.

"So you're new in town?" He smiled from behind a veil of smoke. Alice didn't take up the smile gauntlet. Snide bastard. All good-looking men were the same, intent on demeaning you at every turn.

"No. Actually, I live here." Alice thought that strident-but-vague was the best stance to take against such attacks; at least with vague she was covered in case he gave her the third degree about which zip code of L.A. she considered the hippest.

"Sure," he drawled, taken aback by her tone but not wanting her to slip out of his reach at this stage. "How about you show me a good place to have brunch?" he suggested.

Alice lit up and racked her brains. The only places she knew were Noah's and the Omelette Parlor. Unless you counted the home of the wheatgrass fiasco. "The Omelette Parlor it is then." She grinned, leading him proudly onto Main Street, her melons straining at her basket and one shoulder sloping pavementward in a dangerous and Hunchback-of-Notre-Dame manner.

"I've never quite understood why Americans cram all three meals of the day and several betweentimes snacks into one breakfast," said Paddy as he dipped some hash browns into the clotted cream he'd mistaken for mayonnaise. He couldn't believe he was coming out with such idiotic ramblings. Jesus, he'd lost his vocabulary, mind, and heart in one fell swoop.

"Looks like you've made it to high tea already. That's clotted cream," Alice answered as she spotted his mistake. She'd made it herself last Sunday. "So what are you doing over here?" she asked him, taking in the fact that now that he wasn't hiding his mouth behind a hand and a cigarette, he had the most remarkably curved lips, all undulating bow and curling smile.

"I'm a theater director." She wasn't sure what the smile denoted, but it could have been a ruse to show off the curling mouth again.

"So what do you direct?"

"You know, stuff."

She didn't know; she raised her eyebrows in inquiry.

"Well, mostly tragedy. Jacobean usually. Lots of lascivious bishops and incest." Those lips. Wicked this time.

Alice nearly dropped her forkful of overeasy eggs. If she wasn't careful she'd be overeasy herself in a minute. It was the way he snaked around his words, sooo sexy. But for some reason she didn't believe him. "So you're putting on a play in L.A.?" she asked, trying to elicit further information. She had an instinct about men like Paddy Wilde. Words came easy to them and there wasn't a woman in the Western World who wouldn't fall for them. If she'd had to bet what Paddy's preferred activity of a Sunday morning was, she certainly wouldn't have opted for sharing ham and eggs with a rather witless English girl in Santa Monica. It would probably have involved bronzed bodies and at a pinch maple syrup, but certainly not on his pancakes.

"No, actually."

Ha. Suspicions confirmed.

"I'm sort of over here for a meeting." Meeting of minds. Bodies. Souls. How could he lie to her? Maybe he should just come clean? No. That was too terrifying. "I was staying with a friend, but he's just moved in his girlfriend, so I thought I'd get out of their way. I'm renting a house up in the Hills." Paddy felt it necessary to get that in as soon as

possible. Ordinarily he'd leave the gender of his host am-
biguous until the last moment under the play-hard-to-get
clause, but this was a bit different. Alice was too soft
around the edges to take the jealousy card. But firm elsewhere, he noted. Yes, he knew that she'd run at the first
sign of competition. He wasn't sure why, she seemed
clever. And beautiful. God, actually, she was all right. She
had this really straight nose with about seven freckles on
the bridge. One day he'd count them. One day he'd brush
her hair from her face and count them.

"And you?" he asked, laying his knife and fork aside in
favor of coffee. "You've lived here for years, have you?"

Alice was suitably flattered. Ha-ha, no. "No, I'm staying
with a very bossy friend who's enrolled me in everything
from aerobics to kinky sex with the locals." Alice wished
she hadn't said that last bit. She always spilled just one
bean too many. Anyway, what was she doing here telling
some random stranger, granted he was a random sexy
stranger, her life history? Well, Alice, it's because he's sexy,
really, isn't it? You're not likely to tell him you'd rather be
at home making coleslaw, are you?

Paddy's green eyes were staring at her in anticipation.
This was just the kind of detail he loved. "Really, and does
one have to be a local to volunteer?" he asked, not being
able to resist the incorrigible habit of a lifetime.

Alice pretended not to understand, although she turned
as pink as watermelon flesh. "I work for a PR agency. Pro-
moting actors mostly." She tried to sound blasé about her
job, which was hard when you still couldn't remember
your way to the fax machine.

"Exciting?"

Why did he have to stare so hard? And how could anyone be as incisive in just three syllables? He could probably be incisive with no syllables at all. She blushed even harder.

"You know. Actors." She swept her hand in a nonchalant Gallic way and managed to dust a waffle off her plate and onto the next table, where a famous boxer was brunching with his mistress.

Paddy rapidly plucked the waffle off the boxer's table and swept Alice out of the door with practically a single flourish. "You'll get us beaten to a pulp, darling," he told her laughingly in the street.

She wanted to go home and start all over again. The awkward boy with the jumper around his shoulders and not enough change had turned into a devastating charmer with better things to do than hang around with Alice Lewis. Maybe if she came back in the beige cashmere she'd feel happier, more valid. What on earth had possessed her to wear these terrible bloomers in the first place? And just where had her vocabulary gone? How dare it desert her when she needed it most? There was nothing for it; she had to escape.

"I'm so sorry, but I've just remembered that I have to be at a friend's lunch party in ten minutes. It's been very nice to meet you." She bit her cheeks. "Nice." Hardly Pulitzer Prize–winning dialogue. Paddy looked rather nonchalant, slightly hurt, but not, she conceded, surprised. He probably has an actress waiting on the beach for him to rub Hawaiian Tropic into her protruding shoulderblades, she thought bitterly.

"It's been delightful, Alice. Thanks." He kissed her on the cheek and watched her as she walked away.

Alice felt like she was on a piece of bungee elastic.

She no more wanted to walk away from him than to eat
her own limbs, but that most tedious of the seven dead-
lies, pride, was preventing her from springing back, from
turning around and asking him if he'd like to come back
for a slice of melon, as it were. And it had all been going
so well.

CHAPTER 17

"**W**hat in hell's name did you want to go and do that for, Alice?" Lysette grilled her on Monday morning. "An Irishman! That's almost English." She melted into her computer keyboard with a sigh.

Alice was suitably shamefaced and still hadn't fully recovered from the fact that she'd walked away from possibly the most romantic moment of her life simply because she was wearing the wrong trousers.

"But he'd have given me his phone number, wouldn't he, if he'd wanted to? Or at least asked me for mine?" Alice knew her argument by heart. She'd pondered it all night long after all.

Lysette fell deeper into her home keys. "Are all English people so hard to woo? I mean, the guy takes you for breakfast and you run away. Yet you expect him to beg you for your phone number. Am I missing something here?"

But Alice knew that he didn't want to call her again any more than she wanted to go out with Charlie again. My God, Paddy was gorgeous, he wouldn't want to be with her. Taking her to breakfast had just been his well-mannered way of repaying the three cents.

She suddenly felt sick to her stomach but couldn't work out why. It wasn't Paddy. That was churning and nerveshredding but not sickening. What was it? Then she remembered: Oh God, Charlie. He was still hanging around like a bad smell and she was meant to go out with him to L'Orangerie a week from Wednesday. He'd waited two weeks for the reservation and she knew that this was the night she'd have to give him the heave-ho. "What am I going to say to Charlie, he's calling tonight to check if I can make it?" she asked mournfully.

"I've told you, until Charlie grows up and realizes that not all women like being tied to pieces of furniture he doesn't deserve an explanation," Lysette stated crossly. That kind of thing happened so often in this town that it bored her. Why Alice was wasting her time when she could be pursuing a European was beyond her.

"But I can't just say thanks but no thanks. He's taking me to L'Orangerie."

"Oh, so put out the flags. It's only a fucking restaurant." Lysette knew better but couldn't bear to think of Alice sleeping with Charlie out of a sense of gratitude. If she told Alice just what a big deal dinner at L'Orangerie was, she'd be sure to give way. "Listen, just say yes, you'll go with him. I've got a plan."

Paddy had watched Alice disappear down the road yesterday with a heaving disappointment. He was surprised that she'd just vanished to some lunch but being of a disorganized disposition himself had fully understood how that kind of thing could happen.

It wasn't until Jack had pointed out the big flaw in his plan that he realized just how disorganized he'd been.

"It's not like you not to think ahead, mate." Jack laughed as Paddy chain-smoked and paced up and down the side of the pool. "You can't phone her now 'cause you haven't got her number."

"Of course I've got her number. I got it from operator services." Paddy was too all over the place to be thinking straight.

"But you can't phone her, can you?" Jack spelled it out as if to a child. "Because you *don't* have her number, do you?" More emphatically now.

"Fuck." The penny dropped. "I'm not supposed to know where she lives, am I? I can't even wait outside her bloody house because her flatmate'll see me and screw it all up." Paddy felt his usual control of a chase slipping away. He couldn't just follow her to work and watch from afar; he had to get in there before she realized he'd been the one sending her the flowers and stuff. He reached into his pocket. He'd smoked more cigarettes in the past few days than he did throughout the entire rehearsal period of a Jacobean tragedy. "So what am I going to do?" he asked Jack, genuinely baffled for once.

Jack just shrugged. He was enjoying watching Paddy squirm. He'd never seen it before and it was like watching an insect in a petri dish, it made you realize how surprising life could be sometimes. Paddy Wilde in love. A first.

"Patreek honey, you look stressed, I can almost see de knots in your shoulders, you want massage?" Beatrice appeared in her bikini and sat on Jack's lap.

"No thanks, Bee. But have you got any of those Gauloise-Blondes? These things aren't strong enough for me."

The scorching Venezuelan sun was already well into its ascent when Gibbo hammered on Simon's corrugated-iron door, a beer in one hand, some rare post in the other. "Mate, there's a postie here for you. Another of your chicks?" Gibbo Frisbeed the postcard over Simon's head. "Want some brekkie?" He made a beeline for Simon's

Calor gas stove and a dubious-looking couple of sausages that were only just discernible beneath their blanket of flies. Simon pulled the pillow over his face as the mid-morning glare invaded his dark room.

"Yeah, gotta keep my strength up in case we get stuck in the desert in Mexico with nothing but cacti for company," said Simon, picking up the postcard from the spider-infested corner by his bed.

"I've been thinking. We're gonna need to leave Mexico City pretty bloody sharpish after we've handed over the stuff, right?"

"Right." Simon nodded.

"Well, I reckon that Beirut might be an option, don't you?"

"Beirut? Why in hell's name do we want to go there?" Simon was sitting up in bed, squinting at the front of the postcard, wondering who would send him such a bad-taste picture of palm trees.

" 'Cause it's the last place anyone would think of looking for us. Not that there's gonna be much trouble or anything. Just that we should maybe lie low for a bit. Make sure we got these sick-puppy guys like Donatello out of our hair before we can go home."

"You're really gonna go back to Melbourne and work for your old man?" Simon asked, blagging a sip of Gibbo's beer. "Er, this is flat."

"Last night's." Gibbo turned the sausages. "Yeah I don't see why not. Being an accountant should be right up my alley. Don't you ever wanna just go home and have an easy life?"

"Nah, even the prospect of being chased around the world by underworld morons has its thrills. Guess it's in the blood."

"Well, then, you should love Beirut. I had a mate who worked in a merchant bank there, reckoned the chicks were real tigers in the sack."

"Sorry to disappoint you, Gibbo, but it looks like we're not going to Beirut at all." Simon waved the postcard above his head. "My cousin Alice, she's living in L.A. How's that for the lap of the gods?"

Gibbo bit into his too-hot sausage. "L.A.? Yeah, maybe that's just what the doctor ordered."

CHAPTER 18

Alice cut the cheese-and-pickle sandwiches into tiny triangles and wrapped them in something called Glad wrap, an altogether more cheerful prospect for sandwiches than being squashed in Clingfilm. She poured milky instant coffee into the thermos flask and wrested a couple of packets of Ranch Munch'ems from the back of the cupboard. They slightly defied the spirit of the car-journey packed lunch—a family bag of Walkers cheese and onion would have been better—but ninety-eight-percent fat free was all America had on offer, so Munch'ems it was.

"You're sure you can't be tempted?" Alice called to Tash, who had just emerged from purdah in the bathroom. She'd been there for over an hour and Alice took the opportunity to whip in and brush her teeth.

"Totally positive. Besides, I can just hang out, y'know."

Alice bumped into Tash who had emerged from the luxuriant steam of the bathroom wearing a very floaty Yardley-fragrance sort of dress.

"You're going to hang out . . . in that dress?" Alice looked on in awe.

"Actually, DP's coming around."

"When?" Alice squealed. She'd been longing to meet DP. Dying to know who this cerebral hunk was who could do marvelous things with his lens. "Has anything happened?"

"No. But we had martinis last night at Chateau Marmont and he promised to come around today and teach me about filter techniques. But he's absolutely not interested in a relationship; he says it's nothing personal but he feels married to his art."

Alice slumped against the wall and sighed. "God, how amazing. Just the fact that he's interested enough in you to want to teach you about filters is great, isn't it? I mean, if he really isn't interested in relationships but wants to hang out with you. Doesn't that make you feel really special?"

"Totally." Tash was orbiting Earth, she was so happy. "His arms, Alice, you should see them. When he rolls up his sleeves, you can see them, really hairy arms. God, I think I could love him." Tash moved over and stood in the window, looking out onto the garden.

Alice suddenly realized just how floaty the dress was. "Tash, if you want to borrow some knickers . . ." Alice wasn't too sure of the wisdom of such diaphanous garments in the California sunshine. Certainly if anyone wanted to examine Tash's plastic surgery scars they could do so without difficulty. But Tash laughed at Alice as if she were a small child.

"Darling, that's the whole point."

"Okay, if you're sure. Good luck." Alice kissed Tash on the cheek as she heard a car pull up outside. Lysette honked her horn in the street and Alice ran to the window to wave that she'd be out in a second. When Alice wasn't being tailed and escorted outside the house, she was pretty well safely locked in.

"Tash, can you help me with the alarm? I can't turn it off," Alice called out. The trouble was that she could never remember her security code; she wasn't sure if it was her birthday or the day that Jamie had dumped her.

Tash came over and expertly tapped in the magic numbers. "I was thinking of planting some rosebushes in the garden. Don't you think it'll add a touch of romance?" Tash asked Alice as she ran back into the kitchen for her forgotton packed lunch. "He was going to take me out onto the beach to shoot some film, but I figure once he sees this dress he won't be able to take me anywhere for fear of arrest. Or, at a hopeful pinch, cardiac arrest. Then he'll have to stay indoors and ravish me, won't he?"

Lysette was now causing the neighbors to pour from their houses with her incessant horn tooting. "Great idea, and can we have red roses?" Alice had to tap in her own personal two-digit security code while Tash turned her back; thankfully, it was her age, so she was just able to remember it. "I've no idea why you always lock this door. It's not as though we've heard any more from our resident pervert since last week, is it?" She tapped in twenty-six rather sadly. In the absence of more romantic missives she'd even begun to see her possible date with Charlie as something that may not have to be avoided at any cost, and that was pretty much the definition of desperate. Still, her weekend in Coronado with Lysette was intended to cast all thoughts of men from her mind and reestablish harmony in her life.

" 'Bye and have a great time," Tash said. She hadn't looked as pleased to be getting rid of Alice since the night she'd set her up with Charlie.

"Hope this weekend of passion means that you'll get off my case for a while." Alice laughed.

"Not a hope in hell, sugar. Your safety is my mission in life." Tash laughed, almost pushing Alice out the door.

"See you tomorrow night," Alice called back down the drive. She longed to make Lysette wait around outside until DP arrived and she could catch a glimpse of him.

"I'd love to, honey, but even more than I want to be a voyeur, I want to be in San Diego before teatime. So we'd better zip.

"You can be DJ," Lysette told Alice. "The tapes are under the seat." Alice rattled through a handful and settled for *Ella Sings Gershwin*. They sang along at the top of their voices and headed down the coast road. This was the life. Alice stretched her feet up on the dashboard and looked out through the sunroof. And she resolved to stop this living-in-fear-of-the-stalker business from taking over her life. If she wanted to go out and fetch the papers on Sunday mornings, she wasn't going to be stopped. She was free. She put her hand out of the roof and felt the air rush past.

Lysette smiled as she smoochily hummed "My Baby Just Cares for Me." The landscape whizzed by and turned from the wide roads of Los Angeles into a meandering coastal drive. They drove in almost total, relaxed silence apart from the odd burst of singing.

"So where are we going?" Alice asked.

"This great hotel. We can pretend we don't have a care in the world and lie in the sun and get massages by the pool. Just what we need after a hefty week under the beady eye of La Jennifer. You'll see."

"Fantastico." Alice lay back and dozed off to sleep in the warmth of the late afternoon.

It took an exhaustive amount of persuasion for Alice to make Lysette stop in a layby so that they could eat their sandwiches and crisps. "Can't we just eat them as we go? We'll get carjacked if we stop," Lysette reasoned.

"They don't count if we eat them as we go," Alice said, then decided to try some tactical persuasion. "It's a great English tradition. You have warm sandwiches with ever so slightly curled-up corners and stuff the crisps—we've got Munch'ems instead—into the sandwich. Then you sip the coffee. The driver usually gets the little white thermos cup with the handle and the passenger has the one without."

"Alice, these sandwiches are disgusting," said Lysette.

"Good," Alice said proudly as the margarine dripped onto her fingers and the car vibrated in the slipstream of passing traffic. Lysette only just managed to persevere with her curly white bread triangle by convincing herself that this was training for when she and her husband would take their children to visit Hampton Court for the day.

The sun dipped behind the mainland as they drove across the bridge to Coronado. From above the sea they looked down and saw the yachts moored in the harbor for the evening, the sunbathers rolling up their towels and leaving the beach. Through the streets of Coronado Alice noticed the beautiful sunburned marzipan color of the houses, the lush green. The feel of Mexico seemed to seep over the border and the night seemed more vibrant and alive. A little Latino magic was definitely in order, decided Alice. Eventually they pulled up in front of the most startlingly grand hotel Alice had ever seen.

"It's the one where they filmed *Some Like It Hot*. Can you believe that Marilyn Monroe stayed here? How old must it *be*?" Lysette was gazing up in admiration at the turreted, old stone building. Cars larger than Alice's bedroom slowly prowled the car park. The girls parked their banger in a space reserved for the Aga Khan and went indoors.

"Our cheapest room?" The receptionist looked down her surgically chiseled nose at the pair whose faces were by now shiny and pink from four hours in the car. "Well, our least expensive is the Lagoon Suite. It's haunted, though."

Say no more. The girls slapped their credit cards down
with plastic-bending ferocity. A ghost. Brilliant.

They took their shabby bags and wound their way up to
their turret. The room was dark with mahogany and their
bed was a huge four-poster. They bounced up and down
on the end and pulled out their weekend wear. Alice had a
two-dollar black petticoat she'd bought at a car-boot sale
and Lysette put on its more expensive Dolce & Gabbana
cousin. They showered in Chanel No. 5 as homage to Marilyn and adorned their slips with all manner of feathers and
false lashes. By the time they sashayed down the winding
staircase into the hotel foyer, they could have been ninety-
year-olds tiddly on port and lemon with their slightly
askew lipstick and feather boas. The middle-aged tour parties gathered on the sofas in the darkly lavish reception
area adjusted their bifocals and worried for a moment that
they'd had one too many sherries.

"Surely, Hank, that's not Jack Lemmon and Tony Curtis
comin' down them there stairs?"

It seemed a shame to waste such haute glamour
on bum-bag-carrying, sunhat-wearing polo-shirted tourists, but what the heck. The girls headed for the bar and
ordered double vodka martinis through lips gooey with
cherry-colored gloss and perched on barstools like birds of
paradise.

Alice felt truly happy and truly gorgeous. She was away
from L.A. and all her cares and she could have kissed Lysette for bringing her here. She looked around the bar. The
clientele could have passed for the residents of a retire-
ment home, but she didn't care.

"Do you think that all the men we know when we're
eighty will look like this lot?" Alice asked Lysette.

"Most definitely. Except mine will be more distinguished; he'll have that kind of curly white hair that old guys in England have," Lysette said dreamily.

Alice racked her brains. "Like what?"

"Like that curly stuff." Lysette took a pencil from behind the bar and drew a passable diagram.

"Oh, like a judge." Alice laughed. "You don't want to marry one of them."

"I thought all *lords* were like that." Lysette was bewildered.

"Nah. Lords are different. You have to marry my cousin Simon. There's no chance of him becoming a judge because of all the parking offenses and possession charges against him, but he'll be a cool lord."

"Well, just point him in my direction, I keep telling you."

"Actually, I've invited him to L.A. Not that he'll even get the postcard for another six months at least, which is a relief, I suppose."

"Why?" Lysette asked, stuffing down a handful of Japanese rice crackers in her excitement.

"Well, because he'd have to stay with me and Tash and they don't actually get on all that well," Alice said, not really wanting to go into detail.

"They know each other?" Lysette asked, suddenly slightly anxious.

"Simon took her to the Fourth of June when she was fourteen and he was at Eton. Anyway, she caught him kissing this guy on the cricket team behind the boat shed. She was a bit pissed off 'cause she'd spent her whole Easter holidays making a Madonna miniskirt for it."

"I'd be pretty pissed, too, I guess," said Lysette sympathetically. "Did he get over the kissing-boys thing?"

"I imagine so. There were more copies of *Penthouse* by

his bed than *Vulcan* anyway," Alice reassured her. "I can't wait for you to meet him. You'll love him."

Lysette was preening at the thought of the engagement announcement in *The Times* when the smile on Alice's face came to an abrupt halt. "Oh my God!" It was all she could manage.

"What?" Lysette asked, turning around to see what had caused this rigor mortis to set in.

"It's him," Alice said very quietly.

"Who, your cousin Simon?" Lysette scanned the room. It had to be him. He was sitting in a corner with a very average-looking woman. Lysette tried to check out his face. He turned around. Quite disappointing actually, she thought. She'd expected him to be a bit more like Alice, softly beautiful with curly blond hair. But no, he was obviously from the in-bred side of the family; he was quite short and unremarkable. Oh well, maybe he was wildly intellectual and witty.

"He's coming over," Lysette said, but Alice was just staring at the girl he was with who had stayed in the corner and was absolutely glaring in their direction.

"I really can't believe it . . . of all the bloody places . . ." Alice had gone white.

"Are you okay? Don't you like his girlfriend or something?" Lysette was growing concerned.

"He's coming over. Can you believe it?" Alice was speaking as though she were under water, the words bubbling to the surface from the depths of her memory.

"Well, he *is* your cousin."

"He's not my cousin. It's Jamie. Lysette, it's Jamie." Somehow Alice managed to stay welded to her seat as Jamie strolled over to where the girls were sitting.

"Alice, thought it was you. How are you, old thing?"

Jamie was smaller than she'd remembered, his voice quite thin and reedy. And was his hair receding? At twenty-eight?

"Very well, thanks." Alice kept her voice stone cold. He didn't appear to notice.

"Hezza and me are holidaying here for a week. What happened, d'you win a trip on a cornflakes packet or something?" He chuckled. Oh my God, he meant it. He actually thought that the only way she could have gotten over here was by a stroke of divine good fortune. Smug bastard.

"No, actually. I work in L.A. I'm just here for the night." Ha. That showed him. That'd teach him to dump her moments after sex and run off with Helen with the fake Gucci loafers.

"Blimey. Not bad going, Ally-bongo. Got a floor we could stay on for a bit? We're doing L.A. next week." He waved to Hezza, who was irritatedly twirling her watch around on her wrist. Alice played her moment of power for all it was worth. She tossed back her hair and pouted.

"I'd love to let you have the floor, Jamie, but my boyfriend would hate it. He doesn't trust members of the public. They usually sell their story or something vulgar. Not, of course, that you're vulgar. Just not terribly trustworthy, are you?" Alice smiled sweetly and pulled her skirt up a bit for the benefit of Hezza, who, she noticed gleefully, had ankles like milk bottles. This was fun.

"Oh, well, no, but that was kind of a bit of a cock-up, I admit, old girl, but . . ."

Alice rubbed her hand up and down her thigh and sent him into a bit of a sweat.

"So this boyfriend bloke. What does he do then that

means the public's after him?" Jamie was floundering. Any minute now he'd sink without a trace.

"He's a movie star," Alice said matter-of-factly. She didn't really want to lie, but the bull-in-a-china-shop approach was the only one that would sink in with Jamie. "I'd tell you his name, but you'd sell the story to the press. Once bitten, eh, Jamie?" Alice grinned and sipped her martini. Ah, yes, there was dumpy Hezza plowing her way through the tables like a farmer's wife feeding the chickens. Why, oh, why is it that we always see the light only after the suffering? If Alice had known months ago that Helen Caudwell had dodgy ankles and bad taste in clothes, would she have felt better? No, it would probably have added insult to injury. And as for Jamie . . . What a tosser. Had she really loved this inane ignoramus who was obviously going out with his mother? Why hadn't Alice noticed that before either? Is love not only blind but deaf, dumb, and downright brain-dead, too?

"Anyway, Jamie, it's been a revelation. I'm glad we ran into one another. Now if you'll excuse us we have more interesting fish to fry. Ciao." And with that Alice kissed him on the lips, left Hezza gasping for air like a garden-pond goldfish on a patio, and walked off with a little swing of her bottom.

The girls marched, giggling, out of the hotel and decided to walk into town for supper.

"If we hang around in there, we'll be put off our food by Jezza and Hezza. I swear, Lysette, she's the spit of his mother. Down to the ever-so-tasteful pearl earrings," Alice said, still reeling from the shock. Her hands were trembling.

"So he just has to murder his father and he'll be the perfect Oedipal case study. I have to say you had a major slipup on the taste front there, darling. God, he makes Pervy Charlie seem like heaven on a stick." Lysette took Alice's arm and they walked through the streets of Coronado to a little restaurant they'd spotted earlier. "Granolas galore in there, but I hear they make their own ice cream. Wanna give it a try?"

"Yeah, why not. Do you really think he's hideous?" Alice asked, not really wanting to know the answer.

"An absolute fucking werewolf if you ask me." Lysette wasn't one to beat about the bush.

"God, I wish I'd known you two years ago; you'd have told me that in a heartbeat, wouldn't you?"

"Oh yes. Most definitely. Did you really iron his shirts?" Lysette wondered, as if asking if the story of Little Red Riding Hood was actually true. Surely not!

"Yes." Alice wasn't really embarrassed. The person who sweated and burned her fingers putting creases in Jamie's Turnbull & Asser collars was absolutely not the same person who was walking with a swing in her step through the wide palm-fringed streets of Coronado. "I guess it's a bit like pain—you forget what it's like. If you remembered, you'd never do anything again, never run around without your shoes in case you stubbed your toes, never take a job that was too difficult for you. And most definitely never fall in love again. But I can put my hand on my heart now and say that I'm completely over Jamie and his floppy muddy-blond hair. And do you know what's even better?" she said as they slowed down outside the window of a shop selling beautiful Mexican ponchos and rugs.

"No, what's even better?" Lysette smiled, watching Alice lit up and happy under the streetlight.

"That I think I might be ready to fall in love again. Oh,

not with Charlie or anyone I know, and not yet necessarily. But just that I could do, if I had to."

"That's cool. It really is. Now shall we eat?" Lysette pulled Alice away from the window and along to Wild Oats restaurant.

Over *moules marinière* Alice tried to elicit from Lysette what a charming southern belle was doing in L.A.

"Same as yourself, I suppose." Lysette prized open a shell and scooped the creamy juice into her mouth. "I wanted to get as far away as possible from a particular man and if Hollywood wasn't exactly the ends of the earth, it was certainly a long way metaphorically from West Virginia. And I guess I must like it a bit, in spite of all my complaining."

"But doesn't it get you down, all the relentless glamour and vain men?" Alice asked.

"Hell, no. The men are great 'cause they're always so awful you don't need an excuse to dump them. Use them and abuse them."

"And when you meet your Englishman, will you just marry him? Crash, bang, and leave L.A.?"

"God, yes. I've met Englishmen in Hollywood, so I'm kind of getting practice, but they're actors over here because they have Californian values. I want the ones who prefer hunting to sunbathing and woo a woman with verse. A bit like your ardent admirer. I keep telling you he can't be from around here, but you won't believe me."

Alice was contemplative for a moment. "Do you really think that he's anything other than just a weirdo, my mystery man?" she asked cautiously.

"God, yes. I think he's fabulous. Trust me on that. I bet he turns out to be the man of your dreams."

"Aha, but so was Jamie, and look at the monumental

cock-up there," said Alice, brushing the subject to one side but more intrigued than ever as to who the man was who thought she was worth writing to and winning over.

"Do you play the piano?" Lysette leaned over and whispered to Alice. They were back in the hotel bar, nightcapping. Helen and Jamie were smooching in the corner, much to the dismay of the ninety-year-olds but most definitely not to Alice.

"Only 'God Save the Queen' and 'Frère Jacques,' " Alice said regretfully. Lysette was silent for a second, then called over a waiter, whispering in his ear. Before Alice had a second to wonder what was going on, she was being dragged wrist-first toward a baby grand in the corner, where the waiter was cracking his knuckles in a *Godfather* fashion.

"You can sing with me instead," Lysette said benevolently. Years of torment in the choir welded Alice to the spot. Her body wasn't taking her a step closer to humiliation, her mind was making sure of that. Miss Bull tapping her head as the perfect demonstration of tone deafness was a memory that would never leave her. Even if by some supernatural accident she was imbued with the spirit of Kiri te Kanawa, she wasn't going to reveal her larynx to strangers, and most definitely not to Jamie, who'd had more access to her tonsils than he'd ever deserved.

But Lysette tugged harder and before Alice could make a dash for the loo, the piano was belting out, "For you and I have a guardian angel . . ." It was a song that Alice vaguely remembered from *High Society*, but she'd been so preoccupied with poor Grace Kelly enduring Bing Crosby's legendary bad breath that she certainly hadn't taken in the

lyrics. And now she was expected to harmonize. She tried
to do it quietly at first, but Lysette, who was now sitting
atop the piano, kept kicking her.

"On high with noooothhing to ddooooo, and I giiivee to
yoooo . . ." God, Alice sounded like a caterwauling tomcat.
She surreptitiously shut up just as Lysette had come to the
conclusion that Alice's profession to be tone deaf was not
mere modesty. Lysette let her be and Alice sat back and
watched as her friend's wonderful voice enthralled the assembled oldies and her sex appeal distracted Jamie from
matters at hand. Alice longed for a talent. A gift. Though
she baked good cakes, she supposed. The smell of Chanel
No. 5 began to make her woozy and she suddenly realized
just how tired she was. She slipped out to a side corridor to
the main staircase and left Lysette to woo them all with se-
lected highlights of Edith Piaf.

The next morning Alice woke feeling slightly disappointed at not having heard a peep out of the ghost. She
rolled over, expecting to find Lysette sprawled out on the
bed next to her, but she obviously hadn't been back. Alice's feather boas had left a trail across the floor and she
sneezed as she extricated one from her nose. Oh well,
she'd be bound to turn up sooner or later, thought Alice as
she purged herself of Chanel No. 5 and tried not to think of
the ghost. She had left the shower curtain open for fear of
what might lurk beyond it and kept the bathroom door
open so that she'd have a head start on all spirits and gob-
lins that might be contemplating trifling with her. Suddenly
the bedroom door opened and Alice got a full view of the
bathroom, bedroom, and corridor beyond. And Lysette and
last night's waiter got a full frontal view of Alice.

When Alice had succeeded in swathing her modesty in a

bathmat and put green powder on her face to conceal the creeping blush that had filled her from the toes up like a glass of Ribena, she sat on the bed to find out where Lysette had been all night. Lysette had told the waiter to run along down to the bar and wait for her, and looked like a vaudeville music hall singer who'd been exhumed. Her lipstick, originally misplaced, was now positively AWOL, and her fishnets looked as though they'd narrowly survived a few skirmishes with Spanish fishermen protesting against EC regulations. But still, with her rich, shiny helmet of hair firmly in situ, she remained divine.

"I spent the night with the waiter on the beach. Men who play the piano, darling, there's nothing they can't accomplish with those fingers. God, I'm so into pianists." She smiled in recollection.

"You were great last night—the singing," Alice said as she pulled on an old pair of jeans.

"Too many hours watching musicals. But I hear that showbiz in your country is considered quite common. I wouldn't want to jeopardize my chances with the aristocracy," Lysette confided.

"That was years ago. Princes marry showgirls all the time now," Alice reassured her.

"Sure, I was forgetting about Diana," said Lysette. Then suddenly, "Look you don't mind if I push off with the waiter until lunchtime, do you? Only it'd be a crying shame to waste such musical talent."

Of course Alice didn't mind, even though she suddenly realized that she was possibly the only person she knew with the exception of Jennifer, her boss, who didn't have even a token male in her life. There was Lysette, out until breakfast making love on the beach with a man with wonderful fingers. Tash was seducing her DP person in her new rose garden and beginning a new and exciting affair. Even back in London she imagined that Trinny would be planning how best to squish her five hundred closest friends, mostly models exceeding five feet ten inches, into a Norman village church designed for the local congregation of twenty very short people.

Alice pulled on her smelly Pumas and made her way to the beach. But just as she was about to take her shoes off and stroll in solitary contemplation along the seafront, she saw Lysette and the waiter making the most of a small boat tied up on the sand. She hastily performed an about-turn and was about to head off into town when she saw Lysette's car sitting in the baking sun in the Aga Khan's space. She hadn't driven since Christmas in the Norfolk snow and she'd not touched a steering wheel in L.A. for fear of mortality, her own and that of innocent pedestrians. But how the hell could she be expected to take control of her own life if she couldn't even drive? The metaphor towered over her like a bad line of poetry or a Hunter S. Thompson novel. Learning to Drive in L.A. She ran at double speed up the stairs to their room, where she swiped her sunglasses and Lysette's car keys, and hared back down before this trite symbol of her own destiny deserted her.

As she opened the car door, Alice was accosted by the smell of warm plastic seats scalded by the midday sun. She laid her cardigan on the driver's seat and eased herself into position, blowing air onto the baking steering wheel. She put the key into the ignition and the seat belt dinged into position, in the way that American seat belts did, as if you didn't want to remember that you might be looking mortality in the eye when you drove. Alice certainly was. She grappled with the global logic that had insisted that nations who spoke the same language and watched the same television programs drove on entirely different sides of the road. But this was the practicality, she thought as she crawled out of the Aga Khan's space and into the car park at large. Her heart thudded and her hands began to slip with sweat on the wheel as she advanced on the real roads. What on earth was she doing this for?

Within half an hour Alice had narrowly missed killing the entire local pet population and several of the town's war veterans. Or at least she presumed that was what they were from the feisty way their desiccated bodies responded to their near-death experiences.

"You fuckin' crazy person," they roared from wrinkly gullets. "Get off the road!"

But she sailed on happily. She seemed to be getting the hang of the junctions when somebody chucked in a roundabout, rare in America but obviously put there by the gods to exasperate and maybe even finish her off. Holy shit. She started to go the right way, the way that the law of the land dictated, but all those years of leftness had left their mark. She couldn't; it was against nature. Like telephoning a man before he called you. She knew it was an accepted pattern of behavior, but she just couldn't bring herself to turn the wheel in the other direction. Until she saw a policeman. She then veered dramatically to the right and nearly polished off a motorbike and sidecar. The blue lights went on. Alice fluffed the policeman a whoops-I'm-a-woman smile, and remarkably it worked. He looked at her sternly from above his handlebar mustache, but he let her off. She put her foot down, proceeded in the wrong direction, and felt immensely happy.

CHAPTER 19

After two hours in the hot sun waiting for Alice to emerge from her house, Patrick gave up and met up with Jack in a smoothie bar on Santa Monica Boulevard.

"I just can't believe it. I mean, I send her flowers and stuff and no response. She's never home. If you had an admirer, wouldn't you hang your head out the window occasionally just to see who he was?" Paddy whined into his banana smoothie. "She's just gone and buggered off for the weekend."

Jack laughed. He enjoyed seeing Paddy thwarted in matters of the heart; it was a rare treat and would soon be remedied, he was sure. "Sounds like maybe she's not interested." He wound him up. "You say you saw her with some bloke with a flash car?"

Paddy nodded miserably. "But honestly, she's not that type of girl. Not a flash-cars-and-yachts type." Paddy's voice had the tone of a little boy who can't understand why he can't have all the sweets in the shop. He ran his hand through his thick black hair.

That's why all the bloody women fall for him, realized Jack, who'd spent years trying to work out why this scruffy Irish bloke was always knee-deep in salacious offers by the end of an evening. Little boy lost.

Then Paddy saw Izzy heading in their direction. Three

nights with her had been quite enough. Besides, he'd already overstayed his predicted week in L.A. and was no closer to success. He'd got the cast list for *A Chaste Maid in Cheapside* in the post this morning and was beginning to realize how close he was to having to go back. And how far he was from his L.A. raison d'être. He hadn't the time to waste on anyone else. He wanted Alice.

"Darling, hi." Izzy sidled over and put her skimmed-milk smoothie on his table, pulling up a nearby chair. "If anyone asks you, by the way, about your relationship with me, would you mind telling them it's purely platonic?" She rubbed his knee imploringly.

Jack was silent. He'd been here for a year and still hadn't overcome his fear of these creatures with their psychobabble—he called it shrink-wrapped confidence—and their unreal bodies. Neither though had they shown much interest in him. But the second he hooked up with Paddy life turned into a Beach Boys song. He looked at his watch—only two hours and he'd be lying on Beatrice's couch having his reflexology.

"Well, I tell you what. Why don't we keep it just that? That way you don't have to disappoint this young man and I don't have to lie," Paddy reasoned smoothly, happy to find a way out. But not so fast. Didn't he realize that hell hath no fury like an actress's ego?

"It's not a person. It's the press. I'm kind of seeing somebody else. A famous actor. If he finds out, he's likely to go ballistic. But you and I can still see each other." She was totally deluded, the poor love. But Paddy wasn't to know this. And her legs, they stretched from here to Malibu. Oh, what the hell, a night with Izzy was cold comfort, but it was better than staying at home and watching

Terms of Endearment on cable and wishing he was with Alice.

Alice arrived home at midnight to find Tash and DP lying on the sofa watching *Last Tango in Paris*. She tried to dart unseen into her bedroom, but Tash emerged from a smoochy fumble to see her handbag disappear around the door frame.

"Alice, you're home. Come and meet Alan."

Alan? Who was Alan? Alice rewound in slow motion as Tash uncurled herself from the hairy limbs sprawled across the sofa.

"Good weekend?" Tash asked, clearly dying to show off her new beau to somebody.

"Yeah, lovely." Alice was sure that this Alan guy probably wanted to kill her for interrupting his session with Tash. She smiled sweetly at them both. "You know it's been lovely to meet you. I'm really, really tired, so I guess I'll just skip off to bed . . ." Alice slunk backward toward her bedroom.

"We shot some great film, come and have a look." Tash switched on a lamp and the man on the sofa was suddenly visible. They shot some film. Ah, Alan must be DP, not quite as glamorous as DP—Alan. Alice tried to get a good look, which was difficult as he was obviously not the gregarious type; he just played with his fingernails while Tash rewound their weekend masterpiece.

"Look at this fabulous shot of me. Look at the angle."

It looked more like soft porn than film practice, thought Alice, who was simultaneously trying to check out DP. He was devastatingly handsome—and deeply married. Alice flinched slightly. That's how it is with married men, there's just this look. She wondered if this fit in with Tash's scheme of sisterhood and female allegiances and all that. She'd thought that now probably wasn't the best time to ask her. Best save those questions for tomorrow.

Alice had bitten her pencil down to a stump, leaving only flecks of yellow paint around her mouth and bits of wood between her teeth. When she looked up, Tommy was still staring at her. At first she'd thought she must be imagining it and that he was just still high from whatever party he'd been to last night, but then he winked. A great dirty wink. She looked down quickly, but not before she'd caught Jennifer's cross look. The board of directors was meeting to discuss how best to package the talents in their stable and the directors had some huge mystery project in mind, so they had invited Tommy and his agent along, as well as the hottest producer and director in the stratosphere, to listen to their plan. Alice was, naturally, taking minutes.

"This is so goddamn huge that I get goose bumps just to even think about it." The director with the ponytail who had interviewed Alice for her job, and who seemed to have completely forgotten who she was, rubbed his hand up and down his arm as if to illustrate his goose-bump point.

"My client is very pleased to have been asked, but I think we have to think about doubling the sum," said Tommy's agent, who had long ago accepted Tommy's mute disposition at all meetings.

"Alice, are you getting all this down?" Jennifer turned to Alice, who had now embarked on chewing her hangnails in the absence of a pencil. Alice nodded and scribbled with her stump, wondering how it was possible that someone of Tash's wonderful intellect and intuition hadn't noticed that the man she was sleeping with probably had the white mark where his wedding ring usually was suntanned into his finger.

"I think we can talk figures later. What I want to know at this stage is that we're all on board in spirit and that all associated parties will lie low for the duration of negotiations in order not to attract media attention to this highly sensitive project."

Alice had lost the ponytailed man on "talk figures" and was trying to make up what he might have said. Thankfully this came under any other business, so Alice knew that her secretarial perdition was nearly over.

As they filed out of the room, Alice shuffled behind, brushing the paint flakes from her skirt, wondering if Jennifer would notice if the minutes somehow never materialized.

"Alice, c'm here." Tommy was suddenly tugging on her elbow, pulling her back into the boardroom. "You got a minute?"

"I've, erm . . . got to type up the minutes . . ." She was slightly nervous about the way he'd been staring at her and was keen that Jennifer didn't think she was fraternizing with clients.

"It won't take a minute. Please, Alice, I really want your help." Tommy was looking even more like a member of the Addams family than ever before, his ludicrously expensive shirt was hanging off him; it'd probably been days since he'd had a decent meal. She softened. "Hold on a minute, I'll be back." She raced to her desk, dumped her notes, and pulled out a Tupperware box from her bag.

"Here. Now what was it?" Alice and Tommy sat at the boardroom table and Tommy fiddled with his huge watch as Alice laid two slices of homemade ginger cake out on the lid of her box. She hardly ever had cake these days and now that Jamie was officially exorcised she might never bake another one again.

"Well, the thing is I've been thinking a lot about stuff recently." Alice broke off the edge of her cake slice and stuffed it into her mouth; it was going to be a long session. She nodded. "And the thing is that you've kind of become my mentor, what you said about taking up a hobby and stuff . . . It was great, man." Tommy was looking suspiciously at the cake.

"Have some." Alice nodded.

He picked up a piece and toyed with it. "Anyway, I think that you were right. And I've cut out the spirits and haven't touched a narcotic for"—he looked at his watch and grinned proudly—"it's gotta be thirty-six hours."

"That's great, Tommy. Really great." Alice swallowed a mouthful of crumbs and patted his arm. "And have you found a hobby yet?"

"Well, kinda, but you might think that it's a real loser thing to do."

"God, I'm sure I won't. I used to collect stamps. How's that for a real loser thing to do?" Alice laughed encouragingly as he began to pull the hairs out of his head. "Ohh, Tommy, don't do that, it looks really painful." She took his hand and held on to it.

"I've started to go to church." Tommy turned to her with such a light in his eye, so expectantly that she knew better than to ask if he was serious. Hell's bells, he was. Alice, who until now had rather been relishing her rare role of bestower of wisdom, suddenly saw her job, salary, the car she was planning to buy, and the roof over her head flash before her eyes. If it ever got out that she'd encouraged

Tommy to find God, she'd be absolutely buggered. And these evangelists couldn't keep their mouths shut. She could just imagine it: "The day the light came into my life: we talk exclusively to former actor Tommy Kelly about his appointment as bishop of Beverly Hills."

Alice shuddered and patted Tommy's hand. "That's wonderful, Tommy, and I'm thrilled for you. I really am. But can I just offer you one word of advice?" Tommy nodded ecstatically. "Let's keep this our secret for now. Because it's between you and God, after all, and until you get to know Him a bit better, maybe it's best just to keep it hush-hush." Alice hoped that God would forgive her for robbing Him of a very high-profile convert.

"Like when I went out with Sandra Bullock?" Tommy asked.

"Exactly." Alice smiled her best mentor smile and breathed a sigh of relief, only noticing as she picked up her Tupperware box to go that Jennifer was standing on the far side of the office watching her very closely, indeed.

Izzy pulled on her boxing gloves and began to punch the bag hard. "One, two, hook, jab." She breathed hard, bouncing on her feet.

Paddy sat on a nearby bench and watched as the long muscle in her thigh flexed and tightened. She really did have superb limbs, but he was starting to view them more in the way he imagined a gay photographer viewed the body of a supermodel: a thing of beauty, but not for him. For him there was only one definitive woman in the world right now.

Izzy bent over and picked up a skipping rope. "You know, you still haven't told me where exactly your parents are from." Izzy wound the rope around her hands and looked at Paddy, who'd only agreed to accompany her to boxercise at the Main Street Gym so that he could keep an eye peeled for Alice—well, that and Izzy's thighs.

"Ah, y'know, all over the place. Mum and Dad live in Dublin, but they've got a place down in Cork."

"And do you look like your dad?" Izzy asked, displaying a rare interest in something other than Paddy's body.

"I don't really know, I suppose I'm more like Ma. Dad's got red hair. So have my sisters." Paddy picked up a boxing glove and picked at the fraying red leather. No sign of Alice, and he didn't even have a view of Main Street from here. "Are you nearly done here?" he asked.

"Sure. I just gotta shower. So it's kinda likely that your father could be somebody else, isn't it? Your mother's beautiful, isn't she?" Izzy was looking very closely at Patrick now, tilting her head to one side, observing if he had those famously sloping eyelids.

"To be sure she looks a bit rough around the edges now. But she was a bit of a looker in her day, so she was." Paddy couldn't quite work out what on earth Izzy was on about but thought the sooner he escaped the better. Surely her brain cells hadn't been bashed about enough in one boxercise class to result in any lasting damage. "Anyway, why don't you have your shower, I'll meet you outside in ten minutes or so." Paddy practically shoved Izzy into the shower, but she didn't care. Now that she was almost positive who his real father was, he could shove her about as much as he liked. And that explained why he liked her so much, hadn't his real father had a thing for blond actresses, too? There was no escaping genetics. She showered happily, practicing her pelvic floor exercises and vowing to be extraspecial in bed tonight.

Paddy meanwhile was standing at the reception desk

of the gym, trying to find a Biro that worked. Finally he begged one from the Pilates instructor who'd been demonstrating the sad state of his clients' torsos by making them hold pens under their bosoms. Paddy tore off half an aerobics class schedule and penned his note. Then, returning the pen to the southerly migrating bosoms, he tore up the street toward Alice's house. It was the middle of the day and he imagined that both girls would be firmly behind their desks/cameras. He checked to see that the car wasn't there and hopped over the wall again. This time he squeezed through the very narrow passage leading to the back garden, scratching his elbow on the brick as he did so. "Jesus, Mother, and Joseph," he muttered as he almost got stuck when he came to a drainpipe. "The things I do."

Then he remembered Alice's freckles, the way she'd laughed at his jokes. He breathed in and headed for Tash's new rose garden, spiking the note onto one of the thorns, kissing it for luck, and then he legged it all the way back to Izzy, who was checking her roots in her rearview mirror as she waited for him.

Tash came home from work and slung her bag onto the sofa. "Ugh, I can barely walk. DP is such a great love." She collapsed in the armchair and grinned in that early love way.

"He's very handsome," Alice said, wondering how she could broach the married-man conversation.

Tash was surprised at how calm Alice was being about her date at L'Orangerie. The first time Tash had been there had been on a blind date with an entertainment lawyer, and she'd waxed, wrapped, and exfoliated every part of her body into nonexistence. Alice was just languishing with an ice cream in front of Oprah Winfrey. "Sweetie, I hate to nag, but shouldn't you be getting ready?" she asked, feeling slightly guilty for neglecting Alice in favor of DP lately.

"I'll have a shower in a bit," said Alice, munching the cone. "He's not coming until eight."

"I'm glad you feel relaxed enough with Charlie now, anyway. Did you know that Mel Gibson's his new client? We'll have to have him around to dinner."

Alice didn't know this at all. It had probably been revealed at a point when she'd been drifting off thinking about one of the other problem men in her life: Jamie, Tommy, her mystery admirer. Now she could add Paddy to the list. But she'd put that off until she'd sorted the Charlie thing out, although she had been keeping one eye exceptionally peeled every time she wandered down onto Main Street, and she had been wandering down to Main Street with increasing frequency. Tash had only to sneeze and Alice was gone on the pretext of stocking up on tissues and lozenges for ticklish coughs. When she was there, she'd saunter past the Omelette Parlor and glance in the window, look at the table they'd sat at, and conjure up the ghosts of Alice and Paddy past. Not that there were any present or future ghosts, unfortunately. How on earth was she ever going to see him again? When she thought of the way she'd just run off, without so much as a backward glance, and when she dwelt on what could have been, she was consumed with regret and had to sing loudly to forget about it.

Tash had wandered into the bathroom and would commandeer it for the next hour as she prepared for DP to come around. Maybe Alice would have to save the inevitable tête-á-tête about his marital status until tomorrow when she could combine the blow and also tell her that she'd dumped Charlie.

"Oh, by the way, Izzy's invited us over to dinner tomorrow. Will you be around?"

"Sure. Are you positive I'm invited?" Alice couldn't imagine for a second why the terrifying Izzy had invited Alice. Perhaps it was just for sport. Bait the English girl. It was plain that Izzy loathed Alice. She thought she was a sad English prig who couldn't stop a man in a passage. Maybe she was right.

Charlie arrived bang on eight o'clock. Were all sadomaochists so precise? Alice supposed they'd have to be, really, one slip in those situations and you or your object of desire's a goner. Shame, really; she would have liked another few minutes to practice her facial contortions again.

"Are we ready?" Charlie's teeth asked.

"You bet we are," said Alice as she picked up her bag and tried to shrug his hand from her bottom. Oh God, already.

"Charlie, there's something I've been wanting to ask you." She gave a saccharine smile that she really didn't have the lipstick for. He didn't seem to notice; he was too busy smoothing his eyebrows down in the rearview mirror. Alice suspected he'd Vaselined them, but it could have been just the oil slick of his personality oozing through again.

"Fire away," he said, not taking his eyes off himself.

She couldn't resist: she stuck her tongue out at him and pulled V-signs for all she was worth. The man in the Ferrari next to her nearly dropped his cell phone in surprise, but Charlie didn't notice a thing. It probably happened to him all the time.

"Well," that syrupy loveliness again, "I've never been to the Havana Club, and I hear it's just great for a preprandial puff." Lots of seductive alliterations, that'll get him.

But it didn't, it just baffled him. "Pre what?"

Oh God, she should have known better than to try to impress him with vocabulary. "Prandial—it's like a meal thing. Preprandial. Before dinner." But he wasn't listening. She took the more direct approach. "Take me to the Havana Club, Charlie."

There. Message received. He turned to look at her.

"Sure, baby. If you wanted a quick suck on something phallic, you should have let me know earlier."

She contemplated pulling tongues again, but he was staring straight at her. And he'd begun to spin the wheel in the opposite direction, so she presumed they were heading for the Havana Club and part one of the plan.

The valet hopped into the car and once again Alice forgot to get out. She turned and smiled at the valet, who was looking at her as if she were a plate of chopped liver.

"Hi," she said with a smile.

More chopped liver. He didn't smile back. Then Charlie wrenched open the passenger door and she realized that she should have vacated.

"Ooops." She giggled at the unamused and contemptuous valet. "Forgot about that bit." She hopped out onto the sidewalk and was led like a dog show prizewinner into the Havana Club. Alice looked around and admired the bar; there's nothing more flattering to a man than having his club or his penis appreciated, Trinny had once told her that when they'd gone on a bender to try to find Mr. Ideally Rich.

"This. Is. Just. Lovely," Alice enunciated carefully, in case Charlie mistook the meaning of one of the words. She spun around in admiration, taking in the glittering ceiling and shimmering clientele.

"This isn't it," he said, with startling alacrity for one so slow, as he led her by the elbow into the lift. The elevator attendant shook hands with Charlie and another man who'd just walked in with his wife. But not with Alice and the wife. He didn't even look the women in the eye. As the lift pinged to a halt, Alice wanted to give him a swift ping to his ankle but was ushered out by Charlie before she could weigh up the consequences.

The room before her was awash with faces. And not a single woman. The man and woman in the lift had obviously progressed to higher and better things. The room was thick with cigar smoke and there was a sort of mini-Sainsburys in the corner displaying all manner of puffable wares. Oh God, she'd stumbled into some coterie of misogynists who made up for their sexual inadequacies with large cigars. In the corner she spotted Arnold Schwarzenegger with a large stogie. Well, if this place didn't make her hate Charlie enough to go through with the plan, then nothing would. Charlie led her to a low sofa in the corner already occupied by a group of generic cigar smokers, dull suits, mustaches, and a look of bored indifference on their faces as they appraised Alice's breasts.

"Can I get you a drink?" Suddenly another female appeared but naturally in a servile role. Jamie would probably love it here, Alice realized, finally finding the most appropriate burial ground for the ghost of the most outrageous misogynist she'd ever slept with. Well, thought Alice, taking in a deep breath and picturing Charlie's fur-trimmed metalware, if a job's worth doing, it's worth doing well. All she really needed to execute the plan was a great green glass of wheatgrass, but she was sure as eggs that a whiskey would do the trick equally well.

"A Jack Daniel's, please." She smiled wickedly. "Neat."
The men looked at her for a fraction of a second with what
in human beings could have passed for surprise but in an-
droids wasn't so easy to discern.

"And, darling"—she smirked, quite enjoying this now—
"you couldn't possibly get me a huge fat stogie, could you,
just to keep me going until later?" She undid a button on
her top and winked at Charlie. The men puffed on their cigars like Thomas the Tank Engine. God, she'd missed her
vocation. Alice merrily crossed her legs à la Sharon Stone,
revealing, if not what they'd have liked to have seen, at
least some passably lacy black knickers. If she'd been a
bored housewife in Clacton-upon-Sea she couldn't have
relished her foray into amateur dramatics more vigorously.
She'd have run off with the organist before you could say
Mikado.

Charlie meanwhile had fled for the hills. Or at least for
the cigar minimart at the far side of the room. Oh, so much
fun, thought Alice, whipping her legs together and standing. Let's see what goes on over there. So she shimmied
past Arnold and into the cigar store, where she dug a false
fingernail into Charlie's bottom. He jumped a foot and
nearly broke a Montecristo that the man next to him was
sniffing gratuitously.

"Careful, darling." She smiled, sidling up to him. "Now
show me what there is."

Charlie, who thought somebody had swapped Julie Andrews for Linda Lovelace during the night, began to stutter
his analysis of the cigars on display. Alice opened one
drawer after another and sniffily dismissed all the smokes
offered to her.

"I want the richest, juiciest one you've got." She turned

to the man who was selling these precious leaves and smiled. He pulled out a cigar the size of a Mars bar and handed it, not to Alice, but to Charlie.

"Sir, I hope this will be to Madam's satisfaction." She was about to click her heels in a girly strop when she noticed the three-figure sum indicated on the till. Fucking hell. For a bit of sunburned vegetation. Best keep quiet, she said to herself and pretended not to have noticed the dirty green cash being handed over by Charlie. I'm an expensive date, she thought happily. About time, too, I've spent a lifetime ordering the cheapest pizzas on the menu. From now on I'm going to be a four-cheeses-and-anchovies kind of girl. I'm going to enjoy this.

Back on her sofa, it took all the men at the table to light Alice's cigar. They'd now warmed up to room temperature as they realized that she was the kind of woman they could understand. Not a living, breathing, thinking one, but a caricature out of the movies they made. In fact, she wouldn't be at all surprised if some cigar-wielding demons weren't the next box-office attraction. How gullible can you get? she wondered as she slipped her hand between Charlie's thighs and watched them all shift uncomfortably in their chairs. The plan was simple, but she'd better get a move on, she thought, and stop having fun or she'd have to live up to all this phallus-charming behavior later in Charlie's bed. Think fur-trimmed, Alice, she thought as she downed another Jack Daniel's and nearly burst a lung with the effort of inhaling.

"It's not a joint, baby, you don't inhale." One of the tailor's dummies was leaning over and smirking as though he'd just been reincarnated with the wit of Oscar Wilde. Alice blew a mouthful of swirling blue smoke in his face. He sat back in surprise and coughed. She could see their cheeks puffing out in admiration. Who was this classy ball-breaking broad? they wondered.

Thankfully it wasn't long before Alice's stomach was hastening to its intended end. The cigar smoke and whiskey were lurching around like a bad crossing on a channel ferry. But she had to hurry, Charlie was looking at his watch and they'd be leaving for dinner at any moment. She knew that once she reached L'Orangerie, she'd be scuppered. Lysette's words rang in her ears. It had to be the Havana Club, no two ways about it. She spied the menu sitting in splendid isolation on the table in front of her and reached over for it. "Chocolate Ecstasy, please," she said in her best gangster's moll drawl. There was something about cigars that sent her haring around the bend of her imagination into some Prohibition bar of trilbies and Al Capone. And then to Charlie's rather peeved expression: "I just got to have one, honey."

The assembled workshop of dummies were on the verge of offering her a part in their next movie when the chocolate began to work its magic. The huge dessert had dissolved before their eyes into the mouth of this extraordinary woman. Not only did she smoke and drink like a sailor, she ate. Not something the women they knew did a lot of. And then she was sick. Spectacularly. The whiskey, the dark chocolate sponge, and a liberal splatter of neat Jack Daniel's. Straight onto Charlie's Armani suit. Alice almost gave the game away by laughing. The whiskey had swilled away any vestige of self-consciousness and all had gone according to plan. *Arrivederci*, L'Orangerie. *Au revoir,* Charles.

She'd expected a furious Charlie to thrust her into a cab bound for Santa Monica and wash his hands and Armani suit of her. But, like the best-laid plans of mice and women, he didn't. He steeled himself against the accusatory stares of the waitress and the elevator man and, doing his best with his suit and a damp napkin, scooped up Alice and deposited her safely back at Fourth Street with Tash. Granted, he hadn't offered to mop her feverish brow until the early hours, but he'd done the gentlemanly thing. Much to Alice's shame and dismay. She'd thought she'd be rid of Charlie and a few pounds in weight by Wednesday morning. No such luck.

To make matters worse, Tash was red-eyed and wrapped up in a comfortable toweling robe on the sofa. She'd put on a brave face for Charlie, but as soon as his car had pulled away she'd started sobbing afresh.

"The most awful thing's happened, Alice," she cried into a pile of crumpled tissues that were all too familiar to Alice. "He's married."

Alice waited for the rest of the awful thing to be revealed. But it wasn't. Oh my God, Tash really hadn't known. Alice was stone-cold sober thanks to her drive from the Havana Club with Charlie's roof down. She plucked a fresh tissue from the box and replaced it for the one in Tash's hand.

"You don't mean to tell me you didn't know?" she asked faintly.

More sobs and a vague head-shaking motion.

"And he told you tonight?" She wiped away Tash's tears, suddenly feeling about a hundred years old. How had she suddenly gone from being everyone's problem to listening to and solving all their problems?

"His wife came to pick him up from the set." Then a great heaving choke: "With his children!" Tash was racked with sobs now, her shoulders rocking.

"Oh, darling, I'm so sorry." Alice and Tash sat hugging each other until Tash's arms went numb and she had to sit up.

"And that bloody pervert's been hanging around again. Trampling over my roses. Have you noticed any of your lingerie missing?"

CHAPTER 20

Tash had cried off from Izzy's dinner party and declared a day of personal mourning. She'd left for the set that morning blue with fury and wearing her most slutty Agent Provocateur undies. Alice knew it wouldn't be long before DP regretted the error of his married ways. As Tash walked out the door—obviously having liberally applied an apt unction to her undereye area, for there wasn't a trace of froggy redness that Alice usually suffered from—she'd yelled, "Take somebody in my place tonight. Oh, and there's another note from your grubby stalker in the trash can."

For some unknown reason, possibly the absence of a real boyfriend in her life, Alice's stomach leaped at this news. She bent down and scratched among the cotton balls and crumpled tissues. Unfortunately, it was remarkably well disguised as a crumpled tissue itself, but she pinched it out with her fingertips and laid it on the kitchen worktop.

> *Alice! a childish story take,*
> *And with a gentle hand*
> *Lay it where Childhood's dreams are twined*
> *In Memory's mystic band*
> *Like pilgrim's wither'd wreath of flowers*
> *Pluck'd in a far-off land.*

Alice's brow knotted. She recognized the verse from her childhood. *Alice's Adventures in Wonderland.* Of course she knew it. Everyone from grandparents to baby-sitters had read it to her. It went with the territory. But why this? She read it again. She thought it was quite a sad bit to choose for somebody who was supposed to be trying to woo her. Maybe it meant she was to forget all this had ever happened. Lay it to rest. Typical, she thought miserably. The one ardent and secret admirer I'm ever likely to have has just thrown in the towel and resigned. Little did she know that, though he'd put on a production of *Alice in Wonderland* at the Barbican a few seasons ago this was the only line he could remember in the fifteen seconds he had to write the epistle while holding the still warm Biro in the gym. Alice ran to the front window in the hope of catching some mysterious stranger lurking around the oak tree as Tash had. How come Tash had all the bloody luck? He was Alice's stalker and she hadn't even set eyes on him. Shit, she was late for work. She grabbed her bag and pelted toward the door.

But Alice didn't have time to waste mulling over the injustices of her romantic life. She had two projects to complete before lunch and a meeting with Jennifer and Tommy that afternoon. She ran about the office with flaying arms making harassed noises; she didn't even have time to report back to Lysette about the progress of the evening. God, it was as if Charlie had never happened. She did manage a few thumbs-up, though, from her vantage point of the color photocopier when Lysette had made inquiring puking motions. Yup, all had gone perfectly to plan. Lysette smiled and carried on with her doodling.

"So we're agreed. We're almost there in terms of Tommy's off-screen image now thanks to Alice." Jennifer looked meaningfully at Alice, who pretended not to notice. "And we just have to work at making the next few movie choices intelligently, repackaging him for the European market. Of course, all these plans are dependent on our ability to keep Tommy away not only from interviewers but also the press in general; overexposure at this stage would kill our plans for the other project, the greatest move of Tommy's career."

Alice sighed audibly. Keeping Tommy quiet was the best idea Jennifer had come out with all morning. Until Alice had a chance to talk to him about the appeal of atheism, silence would be best for everyone. The team of top executives nodded their agreement to Jennifer's plan and jotted for all they were worth. Tommy Kelly was the jewel in their crown.

"Alice, we had no idea you'd been so influential in these plans; as you seem to have a pretty good insight into this area, I'd be really interested to know what you think," one asked, pencil at the ready to quote her. Alice looked around her in panic; she didn't actually think very much. Her stomach was growling like a caged animal and she was almost beginning to regret not having gone to L'Orangerie after all. She heard that they did the most delicious foie gras. She tapped her pencil on the table in a bid to hide the grumble emanating from her jumper. Quick, sharp Alice.

"Well, I think a nice costume drama wouldn't go amiss." She said this and instantly regretted it. The only role for Tommy in a costume drama would be as some gruesome phantasm in *Confessions of an English Opium Eater*. If you held him up to the light today, the sun would shine through him like plastic wrap. He bore no resemblance to the sultry but undeniably glossy young man on the front of his press package. But it was too late to renege on the idea of hoisting this wastrel into velvet breeches.

"My God, what a genius idea," the senior vice president gushed. Other voices rose in unison. Great. Fantastic. Jennifer managed a grudging smile. Until Alice had come along, Jennifer had been Tommy's publicist par excellence; she'd never really intended this English girl to have a thought in her head, and now she was practically stealing, not to mention sleeping with, her best client from under her nose. Alice blushed into her coffee. Only one voice was absent and they all turned to him to see what he thought. A thumping fist on the desk could indicate a hasty exit from the golden-girl seat for Alice.

"Yeah, I think I could definitely handle that." He was already pressing himself against heaving bosoms in his mind's eye, and he did a quick mental survey of the Best of British Breasts, picking his leading lady from the lineup. Alice read his mind—or rather his trousers.

"And you never know, it could be just the opportunity we're looking for to find that perfect romantic match for Tommy. A girlfriend and a career as a romantic lead in one fell swoop."

My God, where had they found this girl? Couldn't somebody give her a pay raise? Well, no, actually, talk was cheaper than salary bonuses, but it was the thought that counted. In the fracas of discussion about just whom Tommy should play, the desultory cad or the swoonsome horseman, Alice suddenly remembered that she didn't have a dinner date to take Tash's place. She'd rather cut off her head than go alone to Izzy's house. Shit. Then, in an unprecedented move, she asked a film star if he'd like to be her date for dinner that night. Even more unprecedented, if that's technically possible, he said yes.

Tommy was grateful for the invite, in fact. He'd spent the last two days trying to reconcile what he'd read about celibacy in *Christianity Today* with what went on inside his boxer shorts every time he thought about a woman. "Alice, I'd really like it if we could talk through this tonight," he said. "Yeah, course we can. I'll meet you by the cinema in Santa Monica at seven?" Alice darted back to her desk, anxious not to give Jennifer anything else to glare about.

As Alice showered in vanilla this time—nothing disconcerted people more than a person who smelled of food— she was quite pleased that she had the social cachet of Tommy on her arm to help her along tonight. That would teach Izzy to underestimate the Brits. Alice knew that she and Tommy were about as likely to get it together as Elton John and Margaret Thatcher, but Izzy didn't. Maybe Alice could enjoy this evening after all. She made up her face. An alabaster complexion and ludicrously red lips. Her lashes were dark and sweeping, and she piled her hair up and let some tendrils fall, like a wanton Pre-Raphaelite. She scattered fake flowers all through her hair and opted for the nightie again. This time she teamed it with a pair of monstrous cork-heel wedges.

Ha. Put that in your pipe and smoke it, Izzy, she thought. After years of playing the well-behaved girlfriend to Jamie's jolly-japes rugger-bugger, she'd finally found her rebellious streak lurking at the bottom of a dressing-up box. Maybe she did have a theatrical nature after all.

Tommy had agreed to drive tonight, swearing that he was on cranberry juice for sure. When Alice arrived at the bar, he was surrounded by girls who showed no signs of leaving when she sat down next to him and he asked her what she was drinking. Eventually he performed some magic shooing motion and they scattered to the four corners of the bar.

"That was an awesome idea you came up with today. Do you think maybe that chick from *Pride and Prejudice* would be up for it?"

Alice shrugged who knows—there was no accounting for taste.

"Of course, I'm supposed to have sworn off women, but I can just look, can't I?" Tommy asked, proudly taking a swig of his mineral water.

"Look, Tommy, I've been meaning to talk to you about this. You know that there's nothing wrong with enjoying female company and having fun. You should just try to concentrate on the basics like loving your neighbors and doing unto others as they do unto you to begin with," Alice said.

"Oh sure, you're absolutely right, Alice, but self-discipline is the key, and if I can stay away from the evils of the flesh then I'm on the right path. I've also been thinking about what you were saying about keeping quiet, and I think maybe it would be better if I told the world, spread the word and all." Tommy had a slightly manic look in his eye and Alice realized that he was obviously just an addictive personality. Take away his narcotics and some other substance would take their place. Much as she hated herself for it, when Tommy went to the loo, she got the barman to put a dash of vodka in his mineral water, reasoning that it was better the devil you knew than the Christian you didn't.

By the time they headed up to Izzy's, Alice had successfully administered two vodka shots to Tommy and was beginning to feel a bit more relaxed about the whole thing. He'd be back to normal in no time, she hoped. In fact, she was so relaxed that she toyed with telling Tommy about the letter she'd gotten yesterday—maybe he could shed some male light on the subject—but he'd driven so fast that they'd already skidded up the drive and practically landed in Izzy's swimming pool.

Alice had been slightly nervous about presenting herself *chez* Izzy without Tash, but she needn't have been. Izzy hadn't a clue who she was. Probably thought that she was Tommy's deranged transvestite bodyguard or something.

"Tommy, darling." She coiled her newly baby-oiled body around him and lured him into her lair, almost closing the door on Alice in the process. Izzy, it had to be said, looked devastating. She was wearing palazzo pants and a vest top; her arms were as long and rangy as Alice's were round and wobbly. She had the sort of horseback-riding-on-the-beach tan, all health and vigor, and her hair, still damp from the shower, flowed down her back. Alice felt like Little Red Riding Hood's grandmother in her ridiculous makeup and nightdress. Oh well, at least I wasn't hoping to meet the man of my dreams tonight, she thought.

Alice prized open the front door and went in. There were voices in the kitchen, but not having been formally asked in by Izzy, she thought better than to go in and introduce herself. Tommy was virtually underneath Izzy on the sofa, her rangy arms ranged all over him and her lips were skimming perilously close to his. All this was naturally designed to make the world, or at least their fellow dinner guests, thence the world, think they were lovers. The house was stunning, big and bright and airy with vast canvases of undoubtedly bank-breaking works of art on the walls.

Alice wandered out into the garden. It was high on a hill and looked out over the sea. The view was breathtaking with giant cacti and aloe vera plants scattered along the sandy cliffs. She lay in a hammock strung between two palm trees and took in the last of the evening sun. Just as she was nodding off to the distant lull of the waves, she heard somebody walk up the path toward the hammock. Fake sleep, Alice, and they'll mistake you for a sloth, she thought, hoping that sloths were from America and not Australia. But no such luck; she could never even imagine that she wouldn't be spotted with that lipstick on—in fact, it was probably the coast guard from Malibu beach mistaking her for a distress flare.

"Alice, we wondered where you'd gone. Come and have a drink, Izzy's made this mad punch." Tommy stood in the way of the dying rays of sun and took her hand as she made an ungainly exit from the hammock. "You have to meet Lysette's sister, Fifi; she's a complete babe."

Alice walked into the kitchen behind Tommy. If it hadn't been for his presence, she knew she'd have been mistaken for the cheeseplant in the corner and not spoken to all night, but as it was, a certain acceptable-by-association status had been prescribed to her due to the Tommy factor. Was that really his girlfriend? Was she his adopted and mentally subnormal sister that they'd read about in the *National Enquirer*? She could hear the cogs whirring. And her worst nightmare. A kitchen full of actresses, the witches of Eastwick, a blonde, a brunette, and a redhead. In L.A. the term *actress* was synonymous with glamour and was usually writ large, as if on a warning sign in red paint: No Mortals Beyond This Point.

Alice had learned this lesson when she'd contemplated joining the Main Street Gym. "Oh, actresses go there." But had she taken heed? She'd sauntered along to an Alexander technique class (she'd been trying to grow two inches at the time) in her black leggings with a hole in the bum and school plimsolls, thinking she was the last word in chic, like Audrey Hepburn in the film *Funny Face. Mais non, chérie.* The place was like a bloody *Baywatch* audition. She'd scarpered and contemplated asking the London Dungeon if she could borrow their rack next time she was over there for the desired height increase. A kitchen full of actresses. What a nightmare.

They stood around swirling the ice in their glasses and gazing at Tommy's crotch. Alice was wondering which one was Lysette's sister when a girl looking like Uma Thurman in *Pulp Fiction* walked in, barefoot and six foot, slick hair and milky skin. Look no further. She smiled warmly. Ah, outbreaks of sunshine in Antarctica, what a relief.

"Alice." She held out her hand and looked quizzically but not unkindly at Alice's ensemble. "Lysette thinks you're the best thing since the Queen Mother. It's great to meet you at last, *and* you brought Tommy."

She kissed Tommy on both cheeks and the icicles in the kitchen just glared.

"Now I want to hear all about this fabulous campaign you guys are planning, or is it top secret?"

The icicles' eyes had narrowed into extinction. My God, Alice thought, I hope they've invited some more men or Tommy may not make it through the evening, he's only slight, the poor love. Tommy's birdlike rib cage looked ever frailer with all the eyes boring into it, but he looked relieved to be chatting to Lysette's sister. What was her name again? Alice wondered as she was roped into dicing an avocado by the redhead.

"Do it real tiny, that way the calories work off quicker,"

she instructed, and carried on swirling her ice with her straw and ogling Tommy's nonexistent bottom. Alice felt quite like the maiden aunt. Honestly, you'd think they'd never seen a man before. But just then it was Alice's turn to look as though she'd never seen a man before. Into the room, his brown chest and legs gloriously exposed and wrapped in just a hand towel, walked Patrick. Alice diced her finger into small bits along with the avocado. What on earth was he doing here? His hair, too, was wet from the shower and tiny droplets of water covered his chest. He was holding his head back and laughing. Alice peered discreetly from behind the model's slick red chignon. Would he recognize her?

"Patrick, darling, you've left the top off my shampoo again." Izzy came up behind him and was about to walk past when she noticed the look of pale shock that had crossed Alice's face. So she put her hands on his waist from behind and sunk her teeth gently into his freckled shoulder, not taking her eyes off Alice. "Next time, darling, there'll be trouble." She moved her hand overtly around and slid it up the front of Paddy's towel.

Paddy flinched slightly. "Hey," he said warningly, "I don't want these poor girls here to be having me arrested, do I?" He laughed good-naturedly and gently moved Izzy's hand away. And as he did so he turned and saw Alice.

Alice, with gluppy-green avocado fingers. Alice, who was barely recognizable beneath her geisha-girl foundation and who was unable to take her eyes off him. She'd have sworn he blushed at that moment but then realized that it was probably only her own flushed cheeks casting a rosy glow around the kitchen. Izzy removed her other hand from his waist in a strop. That weirdo had had three seconds too much attention from Patrick for her liking. She spun Paddy around on his heels and dragged him back to the bedroom with much cavewoman ferocity.

"Let me show you something before the guests arrive." She led him away by the hand into her boudoir. Right then Paddy was too shocked at seeing Alice to protest . . .

And what was Alice if not a guest? That chopped-liver feeling washed over her again. She tried to resume her vegetable dissection but found that she'd squeezed one whole half of an avocado to guacamole in her bare hands. No wonder Izzy had looked at her as though she were insane.

Alice stayed in the kitchen with the vegetables until there was nothing left to chop. She was crunching her ice between her teeth and feeling very much as though she'd been bashed on the back of the head with a frozen lump of haddock. Everything she'd suspected had been true. When Paddy'd taken her to breakfast it had just been a philanthropic gesture, he'd listened to her nattering on about England and how she wanted an organic vegetable garden in Sussex out of politeness. She felt so embarrassed she could die. And now he was in the bedroom with the West Coast's answer to Aphrodite. Alice washed her hands and looked out on the ocean. She couldn't compete even if she tried. Great legs, great house, great view. Izzy had certainly pulled the long straw on life. Alice slid, unnoticed, onto the sofa beside Tommy, who was sitting with a full complement of disciples at his feet.

"Tommy, you were so wonderful in *The Elephant Man*. How any man can play that role with such . . ." The cleavage heaved and the redhead took a deep breath ". . . sexuality. Is beyond me." The blonde and the brunette froze again and Tommy just smiled, used to the attention but thankfully not in the least bit won over. "It's kinda fun playing those outsider kind of characters."

"Oh, tell me about it." This was the blonde's opportunity to shine. "I played a Russian agent's mistress in a Bond film. So fulfilling."

Alice turned to Lysette's sister. "You know, I don't think I even know your name, I'm so sorry," Alice said as the weird sisters continued their hubble-bubble in the background.

"Fifi. So has my sister enlisted your help in marrying royalty?"

"Oh yes, in fact, I've written to my cousin Simon in Brazil casually inviting him here, but I may not hear from him, he's a bit unpredictable, a bit of a law unto himself. In fact, that's the problem really, he'll never settle down and be a real lord-of-the-manor type, there's too many hallucinogenics in his genes. He'll never settle down and Lysette'll never get her Emma Bridgewater teapot." Mr. and Mrs. Simon Benedictus. Lord and Lady Kirkheaton. It sounded great, but in reality it'd never work. Alice tried to remember if she knew any other aristocrats.

A respectable thirty minutes after Izzy and Paddy had sequestered themselves in the bedroom, they returned, markedly more ruffled. Paddy was awkward, the fact that he'd just spent his time in the bedroom trying to persuade Izzy that he had no intention of selling the secret of his paternity to *People* magazine didn't seem to alter the general impression that he'd just enjoyed body-bending sex with Izzy for the last thirty minutes.

Alice looked away rather than catch his eye. There was always that horrible point beyond which if you hadn't acknowledged somebody already, you had to spend the rest of the evening either ignoring each other or falling foul to some elaborate charade in which you pretended that you'd never set eyes on him or her before. This point came and went. The only indication that these two knew each other was the fact that Alice was clutching a whiskey like a life raft and Paddy was chain-smoking. They both spoke too quietly and laughed too loudly at unfunny jokes and trembled in unison.

Always slightly off cue, Fifi took this opportunity to introduce Tommy and Alice to the assembled company.

"Guys, this is Alice and Tommy"—she turned to the outsiders—"Jenny, Rachel, Scarlet, Izzy you obviously know already, and this is Peter, a friend of Izzy's."

"I think we already figured that bit out," said a smirking Rachel.

Izzy smiled, always happy to be reminded of her ability to bed down any man at any given moment. In fact, she was also glad to stir imaginings of her rampant nymphomania in Tommy's mind—she could tell that he was coming around to her. She hitched her skirt up a little more.

"Actually it's Patrick," Paddy corrected nervously, but nobody but Alice heard him. They'd all moved on to weightier topics.

"Well, you know that Alice here has her very own stalker, don't you?" Izzy was grinning snidely. Everyone turned and looked at Alice as though she were something unpleasant they'd just stepped in with bare feet. "Yeah, tell us all about it, Alice," said Izzy, dying to find a hole in Alice's story. Surely if Izzy herself couldn't succeed in that department, Alice hadn't a hope in hell.

Alice shuffled uncomfortably in her seat. She couldn't begin to explain to them that there was a fundamental difference between a stalker and a secret admirer. Unconsciously she plucked a piece of ice out of her drink with her fingers and began to crunch on it.

"Well, he just sends notes and stuff." Okay, Alice, most people could dine out on this story for a month, you've made it sound as exciting as a repeat episode of *Crossroads*. "And Tash saw him hanging around the garden one day, but by the time she'd put her makeup on and gone out to have a look he'd vanished." Alice's little humorous aside fell flat. They all just looked at her with this look. This girl had a stalker? With a body like that? They were incredulous.

Only Paddy, sitting quietly in the corner and not taking his eyes off Alice and her wondrous ice trick, had smiled at the notion of how L.A. it was to put on full makeup to chase a pervert. He'd also been listening intently to every word. But Alice hadn't noticed that. Or at least she'd noticed but thought that she was only imagining that she'd noticed. After they'd all exhausted themselves with the amusing notion that Alice had a stalker and were talking among themselves, Izzy turned to Alice and, just loud enough for Tommy to hear, with the bitchiest of all smiles, said, "Oh, and the ice-cube thing?" presumably pertaining to Alice's nervous crunching. "You suck it like a dick or it just has the opposite effect, complete turnoff. Of course it helps if you have the lips." Alice curled her toes in anger. Who did the silly cow think she was? But by the time Alice had dreamed up some clever rejoinder about collagen, Izzy had fled to the kitchen to bring out the food.

In fact, the food consisted largely of Alice's avocado mash and a few rice cakes. Alice remembered when all the girls at school had gone through their longing-to-be-anorexic stage and they'd munched rice cakes until the common-room floor had been awash with bits of white sugar-puff things. She helped herself to a plate of avocado glup and matchstick carrots. The others dined heartily on rice cakes. The guys just drowned their hunger with more beer. The conversation revolved mostly around the usual who's fucking who and involved only the women.

Paddy was frantically trying to ascertain whether Alice was sleeping with Tommy—in a roundabout way, of course. "So, Tommy, you're a local, are you a great Frank Lloyd Wright fan?" he asked.

"Was he the bassist with the Grateful Dead?" Tommy pulled hairs from the back of his hand in concentration.

"The architect. I thought all film stars lived in his houses." Paddy smiled, slightly relieved. He thought that maybe Alice wasn't sleeping with Tommy after all.

"Architect, huh?" Tommy asked. "Well I kinda have this thing about church architecture, like they're this amazing symbol for the human soul, right?"

"I suppose you're right. I'd never thought of it like that. Though I'm not really up on churches, I'm afraid," said Paddy.

"Sure. But you see I am. You should try it sometime, it's cool." Nope. Alice was definitely not sleeping with Tommy.

Alice overheard Tommy veering toward God and quickly ran to the kitchen to top up his cranberry juice with vodka.

"Here, Tommy." She handed him the drink and he smiled fondly. The affection was not wasted on Izzy, who though she had never really known or shown this emotion recognized it from watching *Melrose Place*.

"So, enough already. We don't wanna hear about buildings. That's so eighties. Tommy, do you think that Generation X has been replaced by New Puritanism?" Izzy asked, but Tommy had just downed his vodka-cranberry in one gulp and was much keener on her freestyle libido than her *New Yorker* conversation. So as Tommy's and Izzy's hormones became entangled, Alice and Paddy continued their intricate ignoring game. Alice tried not to look at him at all and every time she did sneak a peep he caught her. She surreptitiously sought out the piece of watercress that her front teeth must be doing their best to harbor, or else why wouldn't he be looking at Izzy's legs, or chest, or neck, or some other erogenous zone he was planning to home in on later, if Tommy didn't get there first? She felt sick but compelled by the thought of Paddy in bed with Izzy. Two of the world's loveliest locked in passion. He wouldn't even have to touch me, she thought, just to hear his voice close to my ear would be quite enough.

Alice had vanished to the loo to clean her teeth, a sure-fire way of making sure you didn't indulge in dessert, and Tommy took the opportunity to hedge his bets of a bed for the evening. "But it's true, I have slept with every actress under contract to Paramount—and Disney, if you're not counting Minnie Mouse." He grinned wickedly. The actresses tittered like birds on a wire and hoped they'd join the salubrious ranks later.

Alice spooned the bio yogurt into individual bowls and Izzy diced mango into minuscule chunks. She'd made a big play of having Alice help her with dessert, if that was what you called it, and now that they were in the kitchen she hadn't said a word to her. Just watched her very closely when she thought Alice wasn't looking and dropped helpful hints like: "You should really ask your pedicurist to clip those corns. They may go down well in Britain, but over here we're quite particular about our foot hygiene."

Alice had a searing vision of Paddy sucking like a baby on Izzy's immaculate big toe. She smiled and turned mute. There was no reply bitchy enough to compete, and anything witty enough would have been misunderstood. But then, like the head of John the Baptist on a plate, Alice got what she wanted, the opportunity to piss Izzy off into next week.

"So are you fucking Tommy?" Izzy asked, scouring Alice's upper lip for facial hair.

So charmingly subtle, thought Alice, her superior English rose bursting into flower after a spell in the shade. "Well, that would be telling, wouldn't it?" she said, then gave her final flourish, a waft of her eyelid and a wink. Ha, bitch. Take that.

Izzy's tone changed. She'd left the bitchy remarks under the table along with the feet and made herself more sickly sweet than three sherbet dips in a row. "Oh, I bet he's just wonderful. So expert. Isn't he?" Izzy simpered.

Alice flexed her newfound superiority, like a fledgling muscle. "Well, let's just say I don't have any complaints." Well, of course she didn't, but if she had climbed into bed with Tommy she'd be sure that a scrawny chest and a lack of attention to the rigors of underwear changing might have numbered two of her complaints. But as she hadn't she didn't. It wasn't exactly a lie.

But Izzy flew into a rage. It was more than she could bear that this . . . English girl in drag had gotten herself a stalker, but another thing entirely that she should succeed where Izzy herself had failed so many times, in getting Tommy Kelly into bed. She was livid and would have picked up a jar of beetroot and tipped it onto Alice's head had a cunning plan not stolen into her mind. She tried Alice for size.

"Have you spoken to Patrick yet? You two must be practically related, England's such a small place." Her eyes bore into Alice's, waiting for the telltale flicker.

"Oh, he's from Ireland though. It's not the same at all," Alice replied, blundering under Izzy's scrutiny.

Yes, Izzy had her. She'd known they'd met before. "How do you know that?" she asked, quick as a flash.

Alice floundered, laughing. "Oh it's the accent, dead giveaway."

"Patrick hasn't said a word all evening."

Fuck. Alice held her breath. Then she remembered, of course he'd said a word, he and Tommy had been chatting away like old pals. It was too late. Izzy was looking at her like the cat that got the cream and still sported the feathers from the canary she'd had earlier.

"Patrick's the best lover I've ever had," she said, licking mango juice off the tip of her finger and looking Alice straight in the eye.

Alice felt that old wheatgrass-juice sensation again and nearly ran to the bathroom. Instead she looked down at her feet. Well, what did the bitch want her to say?" "I'm so pleased?" "Can I borrow him sometime?" For God's sake. Instead Alice just hmmphed into her shoes. A kind of non-committal grunt.

"Just in case you thought I might be putting him up for general release. Nobody, but nobody, is getting their hands on him."

Oh boy, and didn't Alice suddenly realize what side her bread was buttered on? She wanted to squelch a halved avocado onto Izzy's nose and twist it around, but part of her knew that she was absolutely right. And let's face it, when Patrick could have his hands on Izzy, why would he want to put them anywhere else? Instead of arguing, Alice just did what she did best. She picked up the plates, walked into the other room, and said, "Pud's up."

Because if we're honest, there are women who are made to be dessert, with skin as white as meringue and nipples as sweet as raspberries, and there are those, un-fairly or no, who are made to serve it. Apron and nonslip shoes. Natural-born dinner ladies. Alice felt she fell Hush Puppies first into the latter category.

Back in the dining room Izzy went straight for Paddy's lap and spent the next three-quarters of an hour trying to feed him mango slices. Paddy, though, seemed more concerned with closely reading the assembled coffee-table books, though Alice would never had had him down as a *Hairstyles of the Rich and Famous*–type man. Tommy at least seemed to have abandoned religion in favor of playing strip poker with the witches and Alice should have been grateful for small mercies.

But she was on the periphery. In fact, she wondered if this was really a dinner party at all. Maybe it had just been an event designed to humiliate Alice as much as possible. If only Tash were here or at least some other nonactresses. God, she felt as though she'd taken the wrong turn at Pacific Palisades and ended up in a Bedouin harem. She picked up her drink and wandered out through the French windows into the garden. The hammock was now swaying gently in the evening breeze and she could smell the wild jasmine that clambered up the cliff wall.

The whole man thing was just no good at all, she decided. She'd used Charlie to get over Jamie and then Paddy had prompted her to dump Charlie and now Paddy was hook, line, and sinker involved with one of the most desirable women this side of Manhattan Beach. Never mind La La land, she felt remarkably similar to poor Alice down the hole in Wonderland, with all the bloody wretched white rabbits and Cheshire cats. And Izzy was most definitely cast as the Queen of Hearts yelling, "Off with her head." Her stalker person had certainly known what he was on about when he likened her to her Victorian namesake. She just wished she knew who he was. But maybe that was best left a mystery; maybe Tash was right and he had a nose like Cyrano de Bergerac's. Right now she didn't think she'd mind, at least it'd be somebody to talk to.

"Hello there." Alice didn't turn around. She just swung in her hammock, presuming that it was Tommy.

"Hi," she mumbled, staring out at the sea.

"Don't know why I didn't say something back there, guess I just thought it couldn't really be you. And then it was. And it was too late." Alice started. Oh my God, it wasn't Tommy at all. The hammock tipped her almost headfirst onto the lawn. She clutched at the strings for dear life and regained her balance.

"Don't worry." She was curt. Bloody Izzy had probably sent him out here to get her to say something she regretted and then would turn on the floodlights and, ha ha, roll up for the freak show, ladies and gentlemen.

"I kind of hoped that I'd see you again." Oh yeah, pull the other one, you deceitful sod. "I really had fun on the Fourth of July," he said.

Alice sat back in her hammock and looked as relaxed as possible given that her stomach was doing arabesques. He crouched down beside the hammock. Alice turned to find him inches from her face. Shit. She pulled back and tried not to topple over again. She clamped one inelegant foot onto the ground and pulled herself back to horizontal.

"Won't Izzy be missing you?" she said to warn him from coming closer. Not that he could be much closer. He didn't reply. He just watched her as she swung back and forth trying to pretend that the air wasn't heavy with fragrance and that the sound of the waves wasn't lapping her body into a pit of excitement.

"Would you mind if I kissed you?"

Stop. Rewind. How on earth did I get here? thought Alice
in a fit of panic. She carried on staring up at the palm tree
overhead, its trunk narrowing into leaves. She felt giddy.
He put his hand on her bare arm. How easy to say yes.

"Only I have this theory . . ."

He leaned over . . .

Hang on a minute . . . theory? Alice balked, then Izzy's
voice carried in a shrill catcall from the house.

"Do you do everything she tells you?" said Alice crossly,
untangling one of the roses from her hair that had attached itself onto the hammock. Paddy stood up, shocked
but smiling.

Alice stormed past him back in through the French windows. "Tommy, I don't feel well, can we go home?" Tommy
was sitting on the sofa posing for a photograph, wearing
just his gray socks and Rolex.

CHAPTER 21

Alice arrived at the office the morning after the dinner party with that sinking feeling in her stomach. She was trying to work out what she was going to do about Tommy, but all she could see was Paddy's face. Focus, Alice. Tommy Tommy Tommy. God, the boy was incorrigible. Sitting there, buck naked except for his devilish grin. And she was supposed to be turning him into the Julie Andrews of the silver screen, preferably without the stain of religion. What hope had she now? If she'd felt brave she might have phoned Izzy to ask her for the redhead's phone number and tried to get the film back, but then there it was again. Paddy. He might still be there and he might just answer the phone. She wouldn't be able to bear it. Had he really asked her to kiss him? Oh, go back, go back, she told the niggle and tried to focus on the nude-photo story waiting to happen.

The next few days were such a whirlwind that Alice barely sat down. She would crawl out of bed feeling worse than if she'd drunk four bottles of red wine the night before. Water, water. She went to the tap and poured herself a tall glass of water and began to glug. This morning Tash seemed to have performed a Marie Celeste; her boiled egg was half eaten and one shoe remained on the floor, but she was nowhere to be seen. Alice went to the window to see if her car was still there. It wasn't. Oh well, the filming of the movie Tash was working on was over and they were pretty much in the editing room day and night; at least she'd soon be rid of Mr. Married DP when he whisked his children off to Maine for the summer to assuage his guilt. Which he inevitably would do. Alice had seen enough TV dramas about married men who had affairs to know the pattern. She couldn't begin to understand how worldly-wise Tash hadn't seen through him. Maybe she didn't watch enough TV.

Alice was about to go and damp down her Pre-Raphaelites-on-acid hairdo when she saw a figure dart from behind the dustbin and out into the street. But it was so quick that she barely even knew if she'd really seen it or if it had been the shadow of a tree. She looked closer, but there was definitely nobody there anymore. She wasn't sure whether she should be afraid. Whoever it was had gone now anyway. She toyed with the idea of calling Tash, but she'd just be told, "Call the police," and then not be let out for the next month. She was relishing her freedom too much for that.

Instead she picked up the spike-heeled mule lying beneath the table and pulled her T-shirt down over her bottom—she didn't want to give the neighbors a fright. Santa Monica was notoriously liberal, but she didn't think even Hugh Hefner would have been grateful for a flash of her bottom at this ungodly hour. She opened the door and, stiletto poised, sallied forth onto the porch. A cat moved behind the mailbox and she almost abandoned her mission to rid the neighborhood of demon dustbin lurkers. She took another bare step out onto the cold-morning red bricks and jumped back in fright. She'd trodden on a box of chocolates. Bugger. She pulled up her left foot slowly and with it several cherry delights and some rum supremes. The bottom of her foot was caked in broken chocolate and, welded to the chocolate with creme de menthe, was a piece of paper. Alice thudded down on the bricks and tried to extricate the note, but her bottom nearly dropped off with the cold. She stood up again and, hopping about, pulled off the paper, which was just a mass of soft centers.

Dearest Alice,
You probably need some nourishment—just save the caramels for me. It's about time we made this official. Meet me tonight at six by the fountain in the Rose Garden. I'll know it's you.
Me xx

Alice's mind sped faster than the Concorde. First she thought, Mexx, oh God, I can't meet somebody called Mexx, he probably wears a Stetson and rides a horse. Or maybe he's an oil baron from Dallas. Rich but not terribly romantic. Then she realized that "Mexx" was actually "Me" and two kisses. . . . Hmmm, very familiar. But "Meet me . . . in the Rose Garden . . ." If she wasn't mistaken, the Rose Garden was a slightly hovelly place down on Venice Beach, Formica tables and those ancient ketchup bottles made in Taiwan. But then it did sound like some Queen of the May romantic tryst out of Chaucer. Then she registered. Tonight. Six. My God, even if she didn't go, which she probably wouldn't, because, after all, he was just some perv with a big nose according to everyone she'd asked, she should still have legs like silk and smooth hair. Or was it the other way around?

She hopped to the shower and quickly tissued off the chocolate gunk that had become encrusted on her foot like some ancient caveman's shoe. Then she showered, none of your fruits of the forest fragrance today, oh no, today I'm doing sseexxxyy. She reached for Tash's Eau Hadrien and then thought better of it, too grapefruity; Annick Goutal's Passion was just jumping up and down on the shelf begging to be used. So Passion it was. She trickled it sensually everywhere from the crown of her head to between her breasts. She even used it less poetically to shave her legs with.

But hang on, talking of poetry. Shouldn't she feel quite cheated? This was an altogether more prosaic letter, no flourishes or flowers (unless you counted the Rose Garden bit) and no sweet Alice in La La land references. In fact, he'd even referred to something as mundane as hunger—surely the only hunger that should have been mentioned was hunger for each other, desire? Talk about short-changed. If she'd been contemplating turning up to meet this man, then his mean spirit had certainly put paid to that. There was no way that she was meeting him now, she thought, rubbing Passion body lotion into her left buttock.

Alice finally left the house an hour late. She'd spent a sizable chunk of that time deliberating whether she should borrow something of Tash's and then telling herself that she was too huge to get into it, then noticing that her own clothes seemed rather too roomy to wear on a date. Eventually she ventured into Tash's walk-in closet. Talk about the *Chronicles of Narnia*. She mistook a fluffy ostrich feather jacket for the snow queen and herself in the mirror for a hideous troll before finding the perfect garments.

She carefully slipped an ankle into the trousers—so far so good. Then pulled—yup, still a safe amount of slack around the calf. And crikey, they actually managed to stretch all the way around her bottom. In fact, it wasn't until she fastened the button with resounding ease that she realized she was now the same size as Tash. She contemplated sipping some Diet Coke out of one of Tash's gorgeous slippers in celebration. Wow. All those kickboxing classes were obviously warding off more than her stalker. Namely the pounds and inches.

Finally she pulled on the matching white jacket and pegged it out of the house to the waiting taxi. She glanced hopefully at her reflection in the car window. She'd wanted to achieve that Bianca-Jagger-on-her-wedding-day look but it was more of a wilting-lily thing. Never mind, she'd scrubbed the remnants of chocolate from the note with her toothbrush and now folded it carefully into her pocket. And how did he know that she'd need to be fed? Alice would have to have a thorough going-over of the nuances and implications of the note at lunch with Lysette. Oh God, the taxi driver was going the wrong way up La Brea, she'd be even later now.

An hour and twenty minutes late for work wasn't at all bad considering the adversity she'd encountered en route. Kelly the Cow flashed her a smug look that told Alice that her knickers were showing through her trousers. Bugger, she'd either have to tie her jacket around her waist tonight or buy a G-string at lunchtime. Not that she'd turn up anyway, she thought, remembering the fatty smell that always wafted out of the vents when she walked past the Rose Garden. A rose by any other name, and in this case a sausage. She took off her jacket in the lift to make it look as though she'd been there for hours, only to find a note on her desk summoning her to Jennifer's office.

Lysette raised quizzical eyebrows at her. "How was the date with Tommy?"

"You really don't want to know." Alice shoved her bag under her desk and looked more closely at the note. It had been written at 8:13—unlucky for some, it was now 10:23.

"I can't wait." Lysette chuckled as Alice ran full-speed to Jennifer's office.

"Come in," Jennifer said, her impeccable self-control in place. Sitting opposite her, looking as though butter wouldn't melt in his mouth, was Tommy. God, Jennifer did look cool, not at all ruffled and cross, maybe she had no idea what had happened last night. Now all Alice had to do was get Lysette to phone the redhead and all would be well with the world, apart from the obvious Paddy issue.

"And how do we think we're going to explain this little peccadillo?" Jennifer snapped, catapulting Alice headlong out of her reverie.

"My pecker isn't little," whined Tommy. Jennifer shot him a dark look. On the table in front of them she banged down the *L.A. Times*. Front page: Tommy *au naturel*. Except, of course, for the all-American Ralph Lauren socks and glittering Rolex. Alice winced. Tommy had on his wax-dummy expression. Help me out here, Tommy, she wanted to yell like some baseball coach. But she couldn't, Jennifer was staring at her. Alice picked the paper up with shaking hands. Forget a female boss being a positive role model, Jennifer was the last person on earth you wanted to become. Nine out of ten employees would rather wake up to find themselves in the ring with Mike Tyson than taking a meeting with Jennifer.

Alice pretended to read but she already knew the story. The still of Tommy sitting there beside Izzy, who Alice noted with envy was also stark-staring naked and right now probably turning down offers to appear in *Penthouse* on the strength of it, took her back to last night. Seconds before that picture had been taken she'd had Paddy breathing hotly onto her shoulder, his hand resting on her arm. She went weak at the thought. Now, seconds later, she also went weak at the sight of her own name in print. "Accompanied by his press officer, Brit Alex Lewis." Well, it was as good as her name. She looked up at Jennifer and wished longingly that she was in a bathtub of piranhas instead.

"If Tommy hadn't pleaded your case you'd be out of a job, young lady." Oh God, it was school all over again. Alice smiled weakly at Tommy. "But you do realize that you've set our campaign back at least a month. We're going to have to embark on a major damage-limitation initiative and you'll be the one burning the midnight oil."

Alice relaxed back into her seat. Phew, she still had a job. She thought about buying Tommy a beer later to thank him for standing up for her, then she remembered just who it was who'd removed his clothes last night. Not her. She decided to draw a mustache and spots on his poster.

"So as of now we're in phase one. Press releases. That should take you at least all day and all night. Then we'll see how you feel about letting Tommy behave like that again in public." Jennifer tapped her pencil firmly on her desk to indicate that Alice was now to leave and make haste with her penance.

But Alice didn't move. Tonight. Burning the midnight oil. "What about the Rose Garden?" she wanted to wail. But she knew it was no good. At six o'clock this evening she'd be cutting and pasting press releases until her head ached and he, perhaps the man of her dreams, would be waiting to declare his love for her in the Rose Garden. She could have joyfully garroted Tommy for his exhibitionist antics.

As Alice downed her thirteenth coffee of the morning she wondered if she could possibly enlist somebody else to turn up at the Rose Garden and pass on a note to her mystery admirer. Then she realized they wouldn't know who he was. Oh God, he was going to sit there, wasn't he, and wait until midnight watching the door and every time it opened he'd look up and long to see her face. Except he wouldn't.

"I could die of misery!" she wailed into the ink cartridge.

"It's only a machine, darling." Lysette was standing behind her. She'd been in a meeting all morning and Alice could have hugged her to little bits. Now she could talk about the whole thing to somebody.

"Lysette, I need a favor." She was crouching on the floor picking up stray pieces of paper.

"I'm not putting my hand in there." Lysette was about to stroll back to her desk.

"Lysette. Please. It's the secret admirer." Alice knew that this would make her spin on her heels and deposit her pile of papers on top of the photocopier as she listened.

"So, if you just turn up with a novel and watch all the men who come in, it'd be fantastic. At least then we could compile a sort of profile of possibilities." Alice tried to look busy as Jennifer strolled past.

"Hold it right there, Alice, I'd love to. But I can't." Alice's face fell a hundred miles. "I'm going out with this guy whose mother lives in Wales."

"What's his mother in Wales got to do with the price of fish?" Alice asked, feeling wretched.

"Wales, well, that's right next to England, right?" Alice nodded. "Well, ordinarily I'd agree to take my date to the Rose Garden and kill two birds with one stone, but this is different. This one is potential husband material. Wales and all." Lysette was obviously so excited by the prospect of a mother-in-law from Colwyn Bay that Alice would have felt mean had she exerted any more pressure but tried one final carrot.

"But I've told Simon to come out here. He's related to the Plantagenets," Alice said, feeling guilty because she was convinced that Simon was definitely a case of barking up the wrong tree.

"Well, darling, your cousin Simon sounds divine, but I'm just not sure that he'll want me, whereas Gareth definitely does," Lysette said in her kind but firm PR voice. It was obviously no good taking this further.

"I know, I'm sorry. And I don't mean to get your hopes up about Simon. The truth is, I don't think he'd ever really want to live in his castle," Alice said.

"Don't worry, honey, I figured that. Anyway, Gareth's great. He's gonna teach me how to make something called Scouse." Lysette smiled dreamily and wandered back to her desk.

What was Alice going to do now? She couldn't ask Tash, could she? Tash would just get the police to cordon off the area and have a stakeout. Bugger. There was nothing for it but to try to finish the press releases by six o'clock.

Paddy looked at his watch: 7:30. He stubbed out another cigarette in the Cinzano ashtray. She wasn't going to come. Maybe he'd been too hasty in sending the chocolates only hours after their encounter last night, but he just had to see her again. He hadn't even been able to muster up any of the poetry this morning; no lines he could come up with felt sincere enough. It was all a bit too glib. He wondered if he'd made it clear enough that it was him who'd sent the chocolates. He tried to drop as many clues as possible, like the fact that she must be hungry because Izzy had fed her nothing but rice cakes. The sooner all this was out in the open, the better. He'd never thought of any of his actions as sinister in the slightest until last night when they'd mentioned her stalker. Jesus, if that was where old-fashioned wooing got you, he'd almost rather be celibate. But then he remembered Alice.

He'd been trying for days now to figure out just what it was that made him feel like this about her. Surely it wasn't just the fact that he couldn't have her, as Jack had suggested? No, he'd had women play all those hard-to-get games before and it had always bored him. Unlike most men, he was usually much more thrilled by the actual getting than the chasing. All that anticipation was just wasting valuable time as far as he was concerned. He'd much rather be nestling in the bend of a woman's elbow than be wondering what it would be like. But this was different. He could remember every detail of Alice: her pale skin with cheeks that flushed pink whenever he spoke to her; the way she would push just the one escaping curl back from her eyes; the crease above her upper lip when she smiled. And when she talked, the lulling nursery-rhyme quality of her voice: he'd listened for hours last night and when she'd left the room it was as though everything had fallen silent, even though the others were squealing and cackling like a Borgia dinner party. And he just couldn't bear to think about her body, her soft marble-white curves that fell away and filled out. That seemed to defy any amount of hours she spent on treadmills and StairMasters, much to her dismay and his delight. God, but he mustn't think of her body now that she so obviously wasn't going to turn up. That would be a torment too far.

Where was she? Perhaps he should try to find her now and come clean. Tell her that he'd been in love with her from the moment he saw her. But then that wasn't strictly true, but then that had been because he hadn't known about love in the slightest. Maybe she was with that Charlie character. Jesus, have flash car, will shag birds. But surely not in her case . . .

Alice's fingers were shredded with papercuts and the once-white trouser suit was now dotted with puddles of blue ink and streaks of black print. All the desks sat empty and the phones had stopped ringing hours ago. The lamp on her desk was the only sign of life apart from the odd footsteps of the security guard pacing the floor. She slumped over her desk. Her clock told her that she was three and a half hours late for her date and even if she did turn up now she wouldn't be recognized. Apart from the suit she also had deep bags of tiredness circling her eyes like the rings of Saturn and, inexplicably, the paper disks from the bowels of the hole punch littered her scalp. She pulled out the note again and read it carefully. It was the closest she was likely to get to him tonight, if not ever.

Alice made her taxi driver swing by the Rose Garden when she left the office at midnight. But it was all shut up, the orange plastic chairs stacked up on the tables and black bagfuls of rubbish piled up in the street outside. She sank back into the seat and almost cried with tiredness and frustration. Life was indeed a bitch, as was her boss.

Tash hadn't put in an appearance since her disappearing act this morning and the room was still heavy with the smell of Alice's promised evening, perfume and hairspray. The answerphone light flashed away revealing one message. Alice held her breath, knowing that while there wasn't a hope in hell of it being him, as he probably didn't even have her phone number, this was the last hope of the day and if this came crashing down she might as well just go and slit her wrists now.

"Alice, it's Charlie here. I hope you're better after the other night. I feel so bad that you didn't get to go to L'Orangerie with me. So I've booked it again for next week. Thursday, eight o'clock. I'll pick you up." Oh Lord, pass me the razor blades, she thought.

"Presumptuous prick." Alice threw her shoe at the machine and burst into tears.

A car pulled up in the drive and moments later the front door opened. Tash looked almost as crumpled and careworn as Alice. Without a word she thudded down on the sofa next to Alice.

"A vino and chocolate moment?" she said, conjuring a bottle of red wine from her tiny handbag.

Please don't mention chocolates, Alice thought miserably; if only she hadn't trodden in them, then she'd have a gastronomic reminder of *him* that could sit at the bottom of her underwear drawer for all eternity to torment her with what could have been. She could pop the sweet reminders into her mouth one by one, savoring his affection for her. It would all seem more tangible than a broken date and a crumpled note. Tash was foraging for a corkscrew in the kitchen and came back with two glasses and a Toblerone the size of ancient Egypt.

"I think we probably deserve this." She handed Alice a

glass of sinfully expensive red wine and half of the Toblerone. "Is that my Versace suit by the way?" Alice nodded,
too exhausted to make promises of dry cleaning and good
as new. "I always hated it. It made my ass look huge."

"Is this to forget DP?" Alice asked, raising her wineglass.

"More of a substitute. He's taking his wife to dinner
tonight. God, I really think I can't give him up, Ally." Tash
was rarely vulnerable, but she was pretty close right now.

"Do you want him to leave his wife?" Alice asked the obvious question.

"No. I mean, well, he says he will. I've told him I
won't see him any more if he doesn't. I mean, Jesus, what
would that make me if I knowingly slept with a married
man?"

"Human," Alice said, wondering if perhaps her mystery
admirer might be married, hence the discretion.

"Anyhow, that's not my decision. But, Jesus, his arms,
Alice, did you see his arms? Anyway, enough of DP. How
are you and Charlie getting along?" Tash asked.

Alice wanted to come clean, "He's kind of clingy actually. Not really my cup of tea." Clingy. Now there was a eu-
phemism for a man who attaches you to his chair. Alice
slugged back a mouthful of wine and put in two triangles
of chocolate.

"I wish Alan had been clingy with me."

"Actually, Tash, I think I'm going to break up with him."
Alice came clean.

"Well, that's fine, I suppose, but he really is a great catch,
Alice. You know one of his clients is Mel Gibson?" Tash
patted her knee, and the girls just dwelled on their private
miseries and demolished the Toblerone.

"I don't think we should get up tomorrow. We should

just pull on the curtains and paint our toenails. The world can go screw."

"Deal." Alice shook hands with Tash. And since they weren't going to work they might as well stay up. Tash put the video of *Reservoir Dogs* on and they rocked with laughter, the psychopaths in their souls having being stirred up by evil males.

CHAPTER 22

Alice's date with Charlie loomed large again and there was nothing that anybody but herself could do to get her out of it. It was obvious that no amount of chucking up on his expensive suits was going to prove a deterrent. She hadn't realized that he was so keen. But as usual with problems she just buried her head as far down in the sand as she could and assumed the ostrich position. Her mind as usual was divided into males she couldn't bear to think about for fear of nausea, Tommy and Charlie, and those she thought about all the time, Paddy and her secret admirer. She'd been so close to kissing Paddy that night. Thank the Lord she didn't. It would have ended in certain humiliation. How did he end up with someone as malevolent as Izzy anyway? He's beautiful and clever and kind, and Izzy's beautiful, and Alice is clever and kind. Not hard to see what the most powerful asset to wield was then, thought Alice, looking at herself more closely in the mirror. She was sure that her nose was growing. Or had she just become accustomed to seeing all those retroussé Californian specimens? Maybe she should get one done herself, she wondered, pinching the end to see what it would look like with a few millimeters razed from the tip.

"I think we should have a party, just to prove to ourselves that we're still young and vital." Tash came in and sat on the corner of the bath as Alice experimented with various bits of plastic surgery. "It's about time I found myself a real man who doesn't have to send an absence note to his wife every time he takes me to dinner."

Alice wondered how long Tash could go without seeing DP. Even in the heady days of sixth form she'd never known her to be as absorbed by a man as she was by DP. And as for proving how young and vital they were: Tash's desire to talk about throwing parties was significantly greater than her desire to have people stubbing cigarettes out in her potted plants and spilling red wine down the walls; she was too much of a control freak.

"Sounds like a good idea to me," said Alice, giving herself a face lift with a very tight, high ponytail, secure in the knowledge that it would never come to aught.

"I thought that a sort of seventies-in-the-city theme would go down well."

"Sure," Alice said absently, "lots of flares and stuff." But she knew only too well the sheer horror of the fancy dress party, especially the seventies ones, where Abba is played to death and your thighs are squashed into the trousers your mother wore, which in photos make her look like a Charlie's Angel and make you look like a Hell's Angel who's ridden pillion too long and has the saggy bum to prove it. Never again. It'd be caftans or not at all for Alice.

But when Alice came home the next day she found a hundred gold-embossed invitations weighing down the telephone table and the kitchen cupboards stuffed with cocktail shakers and swizzle sticks. Strangely this party seemed to be making its way beyond the stage of abandoned guest lists on the back of Post-it notes. But Alice had bigger and badder things to worry about. Just a week until her date with Charlie and she still hadn't thought of a way to chuck him.

She'd listened to the song "Fifty Ways to Leave Your Lover" over and over again. "Get on the bus, Gus." Yeah, right. She wondered what rhymed with Alice but couldn't come up with anything—maybe that's why she couldn't leave her lover. Had she been called Sam all would have been well, she could have just made a new plan, Sam. She'd put her problem to Lysette that morning.

"Just tell him straight this time," Lysette said.

"But I can't. Tash thinks she's doing me a favor by setting us up. And she thinks it's all going really well."

"Which just shows how much Tash cares."

"Okay, I'll do it on Monday, but first . . ." Alice tugged at her earrings. "Tash seems to be having a party on Saturday night. Will you come and protect me from the hooded claw?"

"Pervy Charlie?"

"Who else?" Alice planned to wear the largest afro wig that Melrose Avenue had to offer and some white trousers with VPL in the hope that she'd be rendered an untouchable by Charlie. Having Lysette by her side wielding a very sharp cocktail stick would just be an extra precaution.

Saturday arrived and Alice and Tash set about re-creating Studio 54 in their living room. They borrowed from a friend in props at Paramount a disco globe that had last seen the light of day in John Travolta's bedroom in *Saturday Night Fever*, and Alice painstakingly skewered cocktail sticks through pieces of cheese and pineapple until her hand looked like a colander, she'd stabbed it so many times.

"I'm counting on other people to bring all the drugs they need," Tash said, snaking in wearing an off-one-shoulder sheeny top that made one wonder whether that seventies archhero Bryan Ferry was lurking in the bathroom. "What do you think?"

Alice sucked the blood from her palm and nodded. "Lovely. Can I borrow your white trousers?"

A look of undisguised horror flashed across Tash's face. "I have these very flattering black hot pants if you'd prefer." Subtlety was not Tash's strong point, but Alice took the news that she obviously looked ghastly in the trousers as a good sign. She wanted the sartorial equivalent of "Don't touch me with a bargepole" to be her message of the evening.

"So run through who's coming again?" Alice asked Tash, just to make sure there weren't any more nasty surprises lurking unprepared for on the guest list.

"Mimi, Fifi, Izzy, Tommy . . ."

It seemed to Alice that to be de rigueur at this party you had to have a name that ended in *eeee*. After the first fifty names had been read off the guest list, she switched off.

"Jordi, Suzy, and that's it." Tash put down her list and began to apply herself to the task of filling her plastic pineapple with ice. Alice wandered off to make sure that the cat hadn't made off with her wig.

By ten o'clock the house was throbbing to the beat of *Disco Daze* and *Disco Nites* and the party looked like a fashion shoot for retro chic. Not for the Angelinos the music of the Wombles and Brotherhood of Man to capture the era, and not for them the crocheted jackets and loon pants that graced any London seventies night. Oh no, this was just slick all the way. Boys kissed girls and girls kissed girls

and lines of cocaine seemed to evaporate into the haze
of fun. Satin trousers gleamed under the lights and a girl
was singing "Halston, Gucci, Fiorucci" to the palm tree
in the back garden. Cocktails were spilled down shimmering frocks and the queue for sex in the bathroom stretched
all the way along the corridor to Alice's bedroom, where
Tommy, enjoying his celebrity privilege and newfound
atheism, had refused to wait and was exciting moans of
delight from a Jerry Hall look-alike against Alice's door.
Pouring herself another ladle of punch, Alice made a mental note not to use her door handle till she'd been at it with
jiffy cleaner.

Most of the people in her house looked slightly too intimidating to talk to, so she sought out some of Tash's actor friends from the film set, who all seemed very nice but
hadn't really come out of character.

"I did enjoy being head of MI5," one chortled in a cut-
glass British accent.

"My God, that must have been thrilling," said Alice, surprised that he was so open about his profession. Things
had obviously changed since Bond's day.

"Yes, I usually play the baddies so it's rather a change,"
he said, and with a camp flourish wandered off and began
to nibble the earlobe of a man young enough to be his
grandson. Alice was tucking in happily to the Cinzano and
watching everyone from an inflatable-lips sofa when the
inevitable first drama of the evening began to unfold out
on the porch.

"I've left her, honey, I thought you'd be pleased," a man's
voice as thick and rich as molasses soothed. The woman
was obviously not on speaking terms with him anymore.

"C'mon, darling. I love you, that's why I did it. We can be

together now." Still no reply from the woman. At least Alice presumed that it was a woman, not a sound had been uttered yet. Then there was the resounding sting of flesh slapping flesh. A dramatic how-dare-you gesture on the woman's part, Alice presumed. God, darling, I love you. Alice would have been thrilled to have been on the receiving end of this romantic moment. Who was this ungrateful temptress who could lure a man on the one hand and slap him across the face with the other?

"Tash, I love you." Ah. So DP had finally left his wife for Tash. Why on earth wasn't she happy? Alice sank back into the cupid's bow and wished somebody would pursue her like that. Even Jamie, the alleged love of her life, had just gotten a friend to ask her along to the pub one night and then groped her while she was waiting for her white wine at the bar. So much for auspicious beginnings. She should have known it was a bad omen.

Alice was just nodding off on the sofa when Lady Marmalade began to play, *"Voulez-vous couchez avec moi ce soir?"* Forty girls who'd get a very loud yes any time they uttered that phrase were slinking around, all hips and hair, when Charlie lurched out from behind the minibar.

"Alice, wanna dance or, erm, would you prefer to *couchez avec moi*?" He laughed. At least somebody thought he was funny.

Alice slid along the sofa and teased up her afro wig into a clinically insane look. She also pressed her thighs together so that her cellulite was almost visible through the thin white cotton of her trousers. And a pickled onion. She quickly snatched one from the coffee table beside her and began to chew noisily on it. "Charlie, sorry about the other night. I'm forever chucking up on men." She'd hoped this would act as a deterrent, but it seemed to have the opposite effect.

"Good, then I won't take it personally. Hey, we should get some practice in before Wednesday or what? Wanna show me this famous bed of yours again?" Charlie sat down next to her and hurled an arm around her shoulders.

Alice was scouring the room for Lysette. Where in hell's name was she? Surely they hadn't invited some bit-part Merchant-Ivory actor who'd flop his floppy hair in her direction and elope with her? She looked beyond the swaying hips and saw the world's smallest bottom squeezed into a pair of the world's smallest hot pants. Izzy. As if on cue Izzy turned around to reveal just a fraction of a bikini top barely concealing the ubiquitous Californian stand-up-for-themselves bosoms. And, sod's law, Izzy spotted Alice. She strolled up to the sofa on teetering heels and hovered above Alice and Charlie.

"Tommy here?" She'd obviously abandoned all pretext of civility.

"Fucking some girl outside my room last time I saw." Alice couldn't be bothered with this.

"So he doesn't know that I'm here then?" It was rhetorical. Alice did her best Mona Lisa impression.

"Alice and I were just on our way there if you wanna come, too?" Charlie's double entendre was both predictable and repellent. Surely two of the state's largest egos wouldn't fit in one double bed. Alice munched in a bored way on another pickled onion as Charlie took in Izzy's legs. She couldn't help scouring the room for Paddy. Even if he was here with her, what was the harm? She'd still get to stare longingly at him from afar. Look longingly at his green eyes and imagine them lovingly taking in every detail of her. Just a fantasy like that was better than being up close and personal with Charlie.

"I wax them." Izzy was regaling a dazzled Charlie with the details of her hair-free legs. "And sometimes I get my lovers to do them for me."

"Painful?" Charlie asked, the flame of his desire flickering to life.

"Only if I'm lucky." Izzy's flesh goose-bumped with delight. Charlie's wick was lit.

Oh God, moaned Alice inwardly. Because if Izzy is into all that handcuff-and-mask business, surely Paddy is bound to have his finger in that particular pie, too, and I couldn't bear that, she thought, one sado-masochistic experience is quite enough for my lifetime. She eased herself from the sofa and left Izzy and Charlie to discuss the finer, thrilling nuances of pain thresholds.

"And when you take a Band-Aid off, do you do it quickly or sloowwlly?" Charlie's eyes were half closed with anticipation; Izzy was slumped on the sofa next to him in a swoon of ecstasy.

Alice wandered out and sat on a bench at the bottom of the garden. She couldn't hear the sea over the swell of music and laughter drifting through the open windows into the night, but she could smell seaweed and sand. She could also smell the onions on her breath. Just as well she hadn't seen Paddy in the heaving throngs beneath the glitter ball. Well, at least that got Charlie off my back, she thought, slightly cross to realize that she now looked like Vera Duckworth on an away day to Blackpool Tower Ballroom for no reason at all.

"I've been looking for you." A man's voice drifted up the garden. She didn't dare move in case she had inadvertently plonked herself in the middle of a tryst. She waited for the inevitable woman's voice: "Over here, darling, help me off with this bra." But it never came. Instead she heard the man again. "Away with the fairies, aren't you?" The voice laughed.

She knew that voice from somewhere. Hang on, she knew that voice from the other night. Another garden, another moon. Paddy.

"Izzy was on the inflatable sofa last I saw her," Alice said without turning around.

"Are we going to make a habit of meeting like this?" The voice was drawing closer. The footsteps had stopped behind her now. Alice didn't dare turn around. "Have I done something wrong?" His voice was slightly wounded. He swung his leg over the seat and sat down next to her, looking straight ahead.

She could tell because for about three seconds she was able to move her eyes far enough around in her head to see him. But after that she began to go dizzy, so it was three seconds maximum unfortunately, not long enough to discern significant things like a smile playing about the corners of his mouth or dangerously flashing eyes. And thank God he wasn't looking at her. She moved her legs onto tiptoes under the bench so that her thighs would look thinner, then she pulled her wig down on one side of her face to trap the lethal onion fumes that she was polluting the planet with. Then she spoke.

"Hello." Always a good start.

"Aha, so you are with us. I was beginning to think you were just a very pretty hallucination down here among the roses." I thought you were a mutant clown escaped from Jerry Cottle's touring circus would be one thing and certainly truthful; pretty with the roses was quite another and very blatant bollocks, frankly.

"So Izzy's got you playing that game again, has she? Well, if that's the way you get your kicks, then fine. But could you just leave me out of it?" Alice choked back a sharp tear and tried to tip her head back slightly so that her eyeliner didn't form rivulets of Harem Nights down her cheeks. And he laughed. Yes, the heartless bastard laughed.

"And why is it that every time I want to kiss you we end up talking about her?" Paddy asked, the romantic wind taken out of his sails.

"Possibly because the reason you say you want to kiss me is that she's making you. Kiss Alice thingy and then we can all have a hoot at her expense."

He laughed even louder. QED.

"Darling."

Oh God, he was turning around. Oh God, he had her chin in his hands. Her wig was slipping between them now, sliding millimeter by millimeter down her forehead, over her eyebrows, there, it was gone. It lay on the bench between them like a sad tribute to Coco the bloody clown. Alice bit back the tears and Paddy exploded into a raucous, bench-quaking laugh. Her hair was flat to her head and the onions were beginning to haunt her.

He saw her tears and fell silent for a moment. "Darling, the reason I was going to kiss you was because I thought you were beautiful. I have done since I first saw you."

Alice hiccuped back a sob now. This was all far too much for her. "But Izzy," she said, gulping.

"Izzy's a distraction." He longed to tell her the truth, how Izzy was merely a way to pass his days as he waited to win Alice around, but her emotional state was probably a bit unbalanced right now. He'd probably save it till later, at least until he'd had time to ease her mind about this stalker business.

"Oh, I'm sure she is. Come-to-bed-and-distract-me-forever kind of distraction." Alice was mortified now, there wasn't a hope in hell that Paddy could prefer her to Izzy, and in this state she resorted to the vocabulary of an over-tired parent whose seven-year-old has just claimed that the goldfish broke the Ming vase.

"I may be cabbage-looking but I'm certainly not green." Oh God. Alice wished that the wig was still on her head and she could hide behind its forgiving looks. Where did that come from? *At the moment of seduction take the opportunity to liken oneself to a green vegetable, this will undoubtedly send your paramour into paroxysms of longing.* Hardly.

"Mmmhhmmm." Paddy stared at her; she had those green eyes all to herself, what on earth was he thinking? They both lunged for the wrong side of the nose, but somehow they managed, somehow they kissed. And Alice could hear the strains of the party and taste warm martini on his lips and the faint remains of his last cigarette; she ran her tongue over his china-smooth teeth—God, she'd forgotten how wonderful a kiss could be. And she'd almost forgotten that she tasted of onion. They eventually pulled apart and looked at each other and laughed, through sheer joy.

"So we made it to the rose garden," said Paddy, plucking down one of Tash's precious blooms and tucking it behind Alice's ear.

It pricked, but she bit back her ouch with a "Thank you. It's lovely." Then he put his hand on the back of her neck and kissed her again. A petal fell from the rose onto her hand as it lay on Paddy's knee.

"This time I'm not going to let you just slip away," he

said, still holding the back of her neck for all he was worth, his lips only inches from hers. "But I have to go now," he said. Alice was too delirious to notice. She nodded her assent as he brushed his lips on her cheek and left. It must have been at least half an hour before she realized that he wasn't coming back.

"Well, where did you think he'd gone?" Lysette asked as she drained her third cup of black coffee. It was four in the morning and most of the partyers had moved on to other venues and other beds. Alice and Lysette were sobering up in the kitchen amid the empty beer cans and the odd piece of clothing.

"To the loo, I suppose. I don't know." Alice put a piece of dried-up cheddar into her mouth and promptly took it out again. "Men always vanish in the throes of passion. I've never been sure where they were going and it's always seemed presumptuous to ask. Anyway, it's usually just to get a condom or something, isn't it?" Alice asked.

Lysette, who had obviously never had a man vanish on her in the throes of passion save to delve under the bedclothes in order to provide a better service, looked at Alice as though she'd found the Holy Grail and then given it to a passing marathon runner to sip water from and toss away another mile down the course.

"Do you think maybe we should call the police?" Lysette was dissolving an aspirin on her tongue and trying to watch it at the same time.

"No, I think that maybe I should give up on men altogether. Even Charlie ran out on me tonight and he's supposed to enjoy pain. And let's face it, I must be the most painful girlfriend in the world, otherwise these ordinary, mild-mannered men wouldn't feel the need to cruelly dump me. Would they?"

"Don't say we haven't all warned you about the men out here. If you had any sense you'd go back home and find yourself a husband from those charmed shores of yours."

"Paddy's from Ireland. That counts." Alice almost screamed in frustration.

"Yeah, but it's not exactly England, is it? I mean he might as well be from New Jersey." Lysette obviously couldn't believe that anyone could be so unfortunate on the romantic front. "Oh, but don't forget your stalker, I bet he turns out to be the man of your dreams." Lysette sat in silence as Alice scrutinized a black lacy bra that some lucky lass had left behind.

"Maybe I'm just wearing the wrong underwear," Alice said, and suddenly remembered a similarly sexy garment she'd found on the television aerial at Bywater Street. "You haven't told me about Gareth yet," Alice said, longing to change the subject.

"I don't really want to talk about it, Alice," Lysette said, chomping another aspirin.

Alice raised her eyebrows. "Why?"

"I won't be seeing him again. His mother. She wasn't really from Wales at all. He just said it to impress me." She took a swig of water and Alice tried not to dwell on the complexities of Lysette's mind.

When Alice finally unstuck herself from the dried pools of Babycham on the kitchen table, it was just beginning to get light. She made her way to her bedroom, colliding with the minimum number of walls possible, given her extraordinary tiredness and quite ordinary inebriation. She opened the door with her hand tucked in her shirtsleeve, cleverly remembering the Tommy-against-the-door incident earlier. As she pulled off her shoes in anticipation of flopping onto the bed and only waking up when a handsome prince who'd promise to stay with her for more than five minutes was leaning over her, she saw the outline of a three-headed monster swirling on her bed. She screamed and froze as the monster disentangled itself to reveal not a monster at all—well, not one but three monsters actually. Charlie, Izzy, and Saffron the personal trainer were all glaring at her, their naked bodies covered, judging by the jar on her bedside table, in Nutella.

CHAPTER 23

Paddy hadn't seen Izzy since the night of Alice's party when he'd suddenly panicked and had to run away in case Alice's evil flatmate discovered him on the premises, and he wasn't about to break his silence now.

"Tell her my grandmother's died and I've gone back to London," he told Jack, who was holding one hand over the phone.

"You said that last week."

Paddy shrugged; he didn't care.

"He's gone back to England actually, Izzy . . . Did I see his passport? Well, no, but . . . Does it say Patrick Kennedy? I should imagine it says Patrick Wilde, that's his name after all . . ." A shrill burst escaped from the receiver and Jack had to hold it away from his head. "Off her rocker." He grinned, putting down the phone and finishing his beer.

"So you're taking her to L'Orangerie?"

"Who?" Paddy was miles away, trying to decide whether he should tell Alice to meet him there or to risk it and turn up in Jack's Volvo, which he'd been borrowing since Jack was now ferried from gym to café in Beatrice's Porsche. He opted for collecting her in a taxi; that way he could break it to her gently that it was he who'd sent her the notes and the chocolates. He was sure she wouldn't mind, it was just that banshee of a flatmate of hers he was a bit worried about.

A woman seen in rollers and face cream is the female equivalent of gloves off in battle. You've seen her at her worst and she'd not be beneath using the filthiest tricks to eradicate you from her life, or in this case the life of her best friend, who's probably too nice to protest. He'd have to be careful there. A woman's vanity is a dangerous thing. But first he had to ask Alice out. Yes, that would definitely be a step in the right direction.

Alice had lived in phone hell since the party. Now she knew that Paddy knew where she lived, there was an out-side chance that if he was determined enough he could ring her. It wouldn't be easy, but if he cared enough he'd find a way. All he had to do was find out Tash's surname, not hard since everyone in Southern California knew who she was, and then . . . tap tap tap . . . call her. Except of course that he hadn't. Maybe he wasn't even in the slightest bit keen on her.

As the week went by, phone hell reached insane proportions. She left the house having Sellotaped the answerphone plug into the wall just in case the cat pulled it out midmorning while she and Tash were at work. She would then reenter the house approximately three times before she drove away just in case the phone had rung just as she walked out of the door. When she got home she'd walk surreptitiously over to the machine so that Tash didn't suspect that she was waiting for a call and she'd casually look at the number of messages. She'd then listen as one by one they weren't Paddy. It was even worse when she was in the house because not only would she fly six feet in the air every time the phone rang, she'd also have to have her "hello" delivery just right, and then of course it would be somebody for Tash, and then the line would be engaged for a precious two hours. By Wednesday her nerves were shredded and she had no fingernails left and by Thursday morning she'd taken to biting off her split ends with frenzied twitchiness.

"Coffee or tea, sir?" The stewardess spat it crossly. She was in a filthy mood because she'd been put in economy, catering to the herd. Guido had told her that there was a rock star in business class but still wouldn't swap with her even though the rock star was straight and Guido obviously wasn't going to pull him.

"Got any lager?" Gibbo asked, grinning through his dreadlocks.

"No." She tossed her ponytail over her shoulder and moved on to the seats behind. "Coffee or tea?"

"We shouldn't be drinking, Gibbo, we need to be in full control when we arrive," Simon said, swirling his cocktail stick between his fingers.

"Mate, if you'd told me the name on your passport was Icarus I'd of thought twice about asking you to do this. I mean they're gonna be all over you like a bloody rash at customs."

"Gibbo, get off my case. I've got a bloody parcel in my underpants that's scratching like hell and I don't need you being a pain in the arse. We'll be fine—I know what I'm doing."

"And did you call that cousin of yours yet?" Gibbo asked, hoping that Alice might be a gorgeous L.A. babe that he could take back to Melbourne as a souvenir of his reckless youth.

"Nah, but she'd be cool. Anyway we don't make it to L.A. until we've got these guys out of our hair, right?" Simon pulled his eyemask down and tried to sleep, which was difficult with a plastic bag Sellotaped to his bum.

"Alice, it's for you," Tash yelled from the kitchen. Alice hadn't even heard the phone ring. Seven-thirty on a Wednesday morning—surely it had to be her mother. She didn't have time to spit out, so she ran to the phone with her toothbrush frisking away at her molars.

"Chullloooo," she gargled.

"Alice? It's Patrick here. Listen, I know it's really short notice, but would you like to come to supper with me tonight? About eight?" And it really was Patrick.

Alice spat out her Colgatey froth into a nearby plant. "Sounds great. Ermm . . ." She hadn't quite got the hang of conversation with him.

"I'll pick you up then, angel. See you later." He rang off. Alice looked mesmerized at the phone and chewed on her toothbrush until the bristles came out in her mouth. So much to think about, so little time. Tonight. That meant tonight. Which meant today, which meant in a few hour's time. Maybe she should have said no.

"But it's only about ten hours away. I don't have time to have braces put on my teeth, I don't have time to lose a stone, my hair's the color of dog . . . Oh my God, and what am I going to do about Charlie?" Alice was doing situps on the office floor. She'd forfeited lunch in a bid to have a sleeker torso by eight o'clock.

"I thought that Charlie was bopping Izzy and the personal

trainer," Lysette said, holding Alice's ankles down on the floor.

"He is, but he still wants me to go out to dinner with him tonight. I couldn't say no."

"Relax, I'll phone Charlie and tell him you've become Catholic. That bit's easy. And the reason Paddy's asked you out is because he likes you as you are." Lysette was the voice of reason, which however reasonable always seems to go unheard in such cases.

"Nooo. But I'm not ready to fall in love. Maybe in three months' time when I'm the person I should be, when I've learned French and brushed up on current affairs and my nails have grown back . . . Have you seen my nails, Lysette?" Alice managed between ferocious head-banging situps.

"Sit up a minute," Lysette instructed.

Alice shut up and did as she was told. She looked her in the eye, waiting for the inevitable words of wisdom, and Lysette whacked her across the face with the palm of her hand. Alice was totally silent.

"Why?" she finally asked, flabbergasted.

"Because," Lysette replied, and went back to her desk.

Alice wasn't sure if that was reason enough to physically assault your friends, but she was concussed for the afternoon and felt a whole lot better by five o'clock.

Seven o'clock found Alice covertly putting on her makeup in the wardrobe. She'd broken the news to Tash that she wasn't going out with Charlie anymore but still couldn't quite muster up the courage to tell her that she was seeing somebody else so soon. So now she had to pretend that a girlfriend from work was taking her out to dinner to cheer her up so she couldn't possibly be seen tarting herself up

too much for someone she'd described as plain Patricia
who was taking her to Koo-Koo-Roo. She'd assumed that
Tash would be working in the editing room until at least
midnight, but she'd dashed into the house delighted because DP's wife was seeing her shrink and they were going
to the theater.

"So it's all on again?" Alice asked, warily creeping out
from her wardrobe.

"I've told him no sex until his divorce is finalized, but we
can still enjoy intellectual pursuits together. Do you think
that's okay?" Tash asked.

"I expect so. So has he told her then?"

"He said so, but she's in denial. Refuses to believe him.
That's why she's got this emergency appointment with her
shrink. He's picking me up at seven-thirty." Then Tash vanished into the bathroom to floss her teeth for her intellectual pursuit.

While Tash was in a weak moral position at the moment
Alice almost told her about the date with Paddy but just
couldn't. It would be too like biting the hand that feeds,
she thought as she applied a free sample coral-colored lipstick by mistake.

"Do you think I should go for the mistress or the marry-
me look?" Tash appeared in the doorway of Alice's room
holding up two remarkably similar outfits as Alice crawled
out, revealing her coral lips in all their fluorescent glory.

"Oh, definitely the marry-me one," said Alice, hoping
that if DP proposed to Tash tonight she'd stay out longer
and not notice the alien Irishman cleaning his teeth in the
bathroom the next morning.

"Alice, what are you doing in the wardrobe in your underwear?" asked Tash sympathetically. The breakup with

Charlie had obviously hit her hard and she suddenly felt guilty. "If you want you can come out with us tonight . . ." Tash volunteered.

And Alice felt even guiltier. Here was noble Tash, prepared to allow pathetic Alice to come to her illicit dinner when all the time pathetic Alice was pulling the wool over noble Tash's eyes. She could have cried, had she not been so panic-stricken that she might actually have to go and watch Tash and DP spooning prawn cocktails furtively into each other's mouths instead of having the night of her life with Paddy. Paddy, whose kisses tasted of martini and who had practically melted the phone line when he'd just called to ask her to dinner. God, imagine how good it could get.

"That's so sweet of you, Tash, but Patricia'll be here at eight and it's a bit too late to cancel." Then the Judas line: "Besides, I'd hate to spoil your evening." Oh Alice, you're shameless, she thought, now Tash'll feel bad. Oh mean, ungrateful cow. She vowed not to use so much of Tash's expensive shower gel in the future, by way of atonement.

"Well, if you're sure. And, sweetie, that lipstick will look really unflattering in those lights at Koo-Koo-Roo."

Alice retreated to the wardrobe as she applied the regulation two coats of mascara and a third for luck. She then had to open the door slightly so that she could get enough light to see that her blusher was being applied only to the apples of her cheeks and not the whole leaves, branches, and tree, too. She had her back to the door so that Tash couldn't burst in as she struggled with the fastener around the waist of her suspender belt. Then she carefully arranged a cleavage in the cups of the bra she'd found on the kitchen table the night of the party. Well, she reasoned,

she'd washed it and it was no different from buying something from Oxfam really; besides, she could never have
afforded even the little lace rosebud that nestled between
the cups, let alone the whole thing. And the finishing touch,
a dusting of bronzing powder between her boobs—she'd
read that it did wonders for the décolletage and gave the il-
lusion of a formidable bosom. Good.

Five to eight and Alice was all but ready to go. But she
was sure she could hear Tash still padding around the
house. Maybe she'd left the radio on. Alice opened the door
just enough to poke half her nose and an eye out. Tash
was humming along to the radio and was very definitely
still in residence. She had gotten to the perfume stage,
which was a good sign. But God, supposing that DP was
coming to pick her up and had gotten caught in some traffic jam on the freeway, supposing he'd had a flat tire and
was going to be late? Shit. Supposing that his wife had
canceled her appointment with the shrink and decided instead that to stay at home and cook her husband's dinner
was much more effective therapy for a crumbling marriage? Alice wanted to yell out to Tash and ask her if she
wasn't worried that her date was twenty-five—Alice looked
at her watch, no, twenty-seven—minutes late.

Three minutes. Paddy would be arriving in three minutes
and would park his car and stroll up the drive, ring the
doorbell, and the full magnitude of Alice's treachery toward
her benefactor would be revealed. There was nothing for
it, Alice would have to wait by the front window and inter-
cept Paddy along the drive and steer him back toward the
car. No matter that she looked too keen or, even worse,
that he would imagine that she was harboring some murky
secret in the house. A jealous lover or, worse, a deranged

parent who might reveal to Paddy Alice's shameful genetic makeup, the shape of Alice to come, all wild hair and flashing eyes. Alice hoped that his imagination wasn't quite as potent as hers.

Tash hummed her way into the room in full battle regalia. She'd opted for the mistress look par excellence. Dagger heels, no underwear, and hair that would withstand any number of boudoir antics and a Force 9 gale to boot.

"Alice, you look lovely," said Tash as she took in Alice's almost human attire—a dress without holes in it, shoes from a shop and not ones spied at Portobello, which belonged to a 1940s war widow, and she'd made that extra-special effort to comb her hair. In short, Alice looked like any other girl being taken to dinner at L'Orangerie on that summer evening. "I think it's great that you're making an effort to look your best even though you're just off to Koo-Koo-Roo, it's really important not to take it too hard when a man dumps you. After all, just because you're not his type doesn't mean you're not somebody else's. Anyway, I'll have a word with Charlie tomorrow. I'm sure he'll see the error of his ways," said Tash sympathetically as she squirted Passion on her inner thighs.

"Thanks. You know, Tash, Charlie didn't exactly dump me, it was more . . ." Alice was stammering. She had to come at least halfway clean or Charlie would run into Tash and all would be revealed: how Alice had said she'd found God, how she had claimed to want to concentrate more on her studies of the saints' lives and be free to attend mass most evenings and that she might even change her name to Bernadette. It would be much simpler if she could tell the truth about finding him in a threesome in her bed covered in something that is far nicer on toast, but she couldn't, it was all too heinous.

"Alice, you just don't need to make excuses to me, I'm your friend. Charlie'll be putty in my hands—" Tash was interrupted by the honking of a horn in the drive. Both girls crashed heads in a bid to see who it was. Alice held her breath and squinted.

"It's a taxi, it must be Patricia," said Tash, going to open the door. Alice rammed in between Tash and the door and sprinted to the car as fast as her new shoes, which were rubbing already, could carry her. Just as she reached the car she saw the back door opening and two very male shoes emerging—shit, she jumped over the flower bed with the grace of a Thelwell pony over Beaches Brook and landed thud onto Paddy's toes.

"Oh my God, I'm so sorry," she said, but she didn't have time to stop her crusade, he must not get out, so she shoved him with both hands to the far side of the taxi seat and slammed the door behind her. After which spectacular display she turned to him, in a voice as smooth and cool as an afterdinner mint, and said, "Patrick, so sweet of you to come." Oh my God, now not only did he suspect her of harboring lunatic parents he could plainly see that she had inherited all their maniacal and schizophrenic ways.

"Alice, you look . . . different," he said, secretly rather disappointed that she hadn't thrilled him with some wild and wonderful outfit. "I suppose you've come straight from work."

Alice smiled sweetly and, regaining the breathing pattern of a human rather than a salivating dog, crushed her face against the window to make sure that Tash hadn't cottoned on to Paddy. Well, she wasn't tearing down the drive with a rolling pin, which was a start.

"My flatmate's got this protective thing about me, you see," she said as he looked quizzically at her. "We've had a few problems with some stalker and she likes to keep an eye on me."

Paddy blanched slightly and wondered how he was going to get out of this one. In his incarnation as a Don Juan, he'd hidden under a few beds as boyfriends tore through wardrobes looking for "that smarmy Irish bastard," but this one might prove to be a little more difficult.

CHAPTER 24

Alice could see instantly why L'Orangerie was such a big deal. The host showed them to a walled terrace that led out to an airy glasshouse. Orange trees blossomed and the air was steeped in their scent. This mingled with a hundred notes of Ombre Rose, Patou's Joy, and fragrances too rare and expensive to recognize. The tables were laced with the remains of lobster claws, dewy green salads, and near-empty bottles of Clos du Mesnil and Chardonnay. Even the piano player in the corner seemed to add to the romantic ambience and not make Alice feel that she'd just stepped into the Harrods food hall, as she usually did when she heard the soft strains of ivory keys. She and Patrick drifted into the room on a wave of lighthearted conversation. In fact, it was all quite perfunctory. That's the hellish thing about first dates: you've spent so many hours in your head lying under his duvet discussing how unimportant all his ex-lovers are now that he's met you and deciding whether your firstborn will have your nose or his eyes, that it's always quite peculiar when you have to start from scratch and relate your parents' occupations and where you went to school instead.

"So how long are you planning to stay in L.A. for?" asked Alice, ducking under his arm as he held the door to the main atrium for her.

"I really don't know. I just came out here for a week and I'm still here, so who knows." He approached the maître d'. "Table for two, Wilde."

Alice shivered. She was on a date with a man whose surname was Wilde. How great could life get? She followed him as he weaved through the tables to the most intimate and romantic corner of the restaurant. "Probably thought you were a film star or something with a name like that, that's why we got the best table." Alice laughed.

"Probably did." Paddy smiled. He'd pulled a few strings with one of the producers who was trying to lure him to Hollywood. In fact, he'd practically had to sign an eight-page document promising to work with this guy if ever he directed a Hollywood movie, but it seemed worth it. Worth it for Alice with her scruffy hair and beautiful, crumpled bedroom face, poetic dark circles under her eyes that made her look as though she'd had a permanently fabulous night before, and lips like slumber-down pillows. But for once he wasn't even sure what would happen next. Would she even want to kiss him at the end of the evening? My God but love was like the mumps, you became all swollen and uncomfortable.

Alice sipped her crystal-cool Chardonnay and took another forkful of her sweet potato mash, not even noticing the king prawns lurking beneath, every mouthful easing her closer to blissful intoxication. Paddy was telling her about Ireland and in her mind she was sitting beside a peat fire with his arm around her.

"And I think Bernard Shaw was absolutely right, Dublin is just an open-air madhouse. But we like it that way. And oh, but you have to see Trinity College, it's splendid, and there's this pub around the corner where . . ." He suddenly looked up at Alice and stopped. "God, I'm going on, aren't I? Am I boring you?" He smiled and his fatal green eyes creased up.

"Not at all. It sounds great . . ." she said, coming around, almost surprised to find herself in the light walls of the restaurant and not in some desolate farmhouse with a moss roof. And the voice—it was like having honey poured all over her naked body. She wasn't sure if it was the wine or some curious Celtic spell that had been woven over her. She smiled deliriously.

"And there's this great thing called—"

"The Blarney Stone?" asked Alice before she had time to think. But he did know how to talk.

"There, I told you I was boring you. I do talk a lot, you know, especially when I'm nervous. It doesn't happen often, but . . ." Then he stopped himself and laughed so loudly that Alice thought that wineglasses would start shattering. She looked around at her fellow diners to see if they'd noticed what she thought was his life-affirming guffaw but what they might think was a decibel-crunching racket. Nobody even blinked; in fact, they all seemed to be quite stuffed. Her taxidermist neighbor from Bywater Street must have filled them to the gills with horsehair or something: older couples who barely had a word to say to each other and looked as though they'd rather be at home with a good book; fashionable beauties in head-to-toe Armani; and then of course the rich men with the young women, these by far outnumbered the others. Alice just couldn't imagine herself ever being so desperate to eat in a good restaurant that she'd be willing to fumble with a man older than her father at the end of the evening. She'd take Koo-Koo-Roo with somebody she actually fancied any day. But today, today was the perfect exception.

"And how long will Alice stick it out in this Hammer Town of Horrors?" Paddy was asking her.

"Oh, who knows. I only came here to escape other horrors, but I'm not really sure if I fit in that well." Then she added, laughing, "Nobody understands me."

"Don't I know just what you mean," he said, dropping a lump of sugar into his cappuccino. "People keep asking me if I know how to Riverdance." He looked up at her and grinned, skyscraper cheekbones grazing the stratosphere.

Alice ran her finger across the dusty white top of her meringue and licked the sugar. "I just kind of miss things. Pubs for one—don't you just long to go and have a pint in a hovel with a swirly carpet and green velour cushions and then have a curry afterward?" Alice smiled, her head was spinning at the contrast between this fantasy and the one she was living. "Not that I'd swap this for anything right now." She gestured around the lavishly stylish room, taking in a horribly familiar figure at the far corner of the room. And as she did so the figure picked her up on his vanity antennae, which made him aware whenever a woman was looking at him, homed in on her and glared.

"What's up?" Paddy turned around to see what she was looking so wan-faced about.

"No, don't turn around—" But it was too late. Charlie had seen them and was making his way over.

"Is he your boyfriend or something?" Paddy asked, recognizing Charlie as the smooth bloke with the BMW that Alice had come home with one morning, and if he remembered rightly the one who'd taken Izzy off his hands at Tash's party. Maybe he had something to be grateful to him for after all.

"No, and neither are you, leave this to me," Alice blurted

out, breaking into a smile as Charlie's even-darker-than-usual face bore down on their table.

"Alice." It was not a greeting. "What are you doing here?" And in the tradition of many a novel his eyes flashed.

"Charlie." Alice gave him the benefit of her most beatific look. "How lovely to see you. This is my religious counselor, Father Patrick Wilde." She gestured toward Patrick, who didn't have a history of insanity in his family and the theater in his blood for nothing.

"To be sure we were just discussing the finer points of the catechism." He held out his hand to Charlie, who was obviously not going to take this well.

How could Alice have known that ever since childhood, rejection had been his issue? Christ, Charlie'd spent thousands of dollars talking to his shrink about it, but, unfortunately for Alice, to no avail. He wouldn't have tolerated being stood up even by the pope himself, let alone some halfwitted English girl. "And I do suppose you know, Father, that you are dining with a fallen woman," he snarled.

"There is more repenting in heaven over one sinner who is sorry," Paddy said plausibly, and Charlie just grunted and backed away to his table, where another fallen woman, obviously his date, was tucking into a slice of rock melon.

"Wow, you were great. Did you learn that stuff at school?" Alice asked, enchanted by Paddy's performance.

"I think I should be the one asking the questions, Sister Alice, don't you?" He grinned wickedly. "And we'll start with finding out what a sweet girl like you was doing with a treacherous bastard like him."

"The same as you and Izzy, I expect." Alice couldn't help it. She couldn't quite grapple with the specter of Izzy, and too much wine and pavlova had loosened her tongue. "I mean you're so lovely and she's such a cow." Oh hell, now she'd said it. Date over, she thought, as she closed her eyes and fainted.

The first thing she saw when she opened her eyes was a whiteness so bright that she thought she'd woken up too close to Charlie's bleached and capped teeth. But then a blurry shadow loomed over her and something was brushing against her face. A fly perhaps? She wafted her hand about. God, it must be a huge fly, maybe this was the lower region of hell.

"Steady on there, Doctor. I think she's coming round."

Alice woke to find herself watching an episode of *ER* from a prostrated position. George Clooney circled her head and green coats fuzzed around against the glaring-white walls.

"How are you feeling now?" asked an Irish voice. Oh God, it wasn't *ER*, it was Paddy. His hair flopped in her face as he leaned over and peered into what must undoubtedly be her face at its most hideous. The first sane thought that occurred to her was that nobody got away with wearing such an obscene amount of mascara only to find it still in situ after a bizarre fainting fit in a public place. Her second thought was for her life.

"What's wrong with me?" she asked the omnipresent Paddy, who was still inches away from her wayward eye makeup and was probably getting an eyeful of her less-than-flawless foundation, too, under these lights.

"The doctor reckons that you were allergic to something you ate." It was all coming back to Alice now. And it was quite obvious what had happened to her. She'd lied to Charlie about taking orders and she'd slandered Izzy.

"I was struck by a thunderbolt from the Almighty," she said.

Paddy laughed. "You're such a bloody nut. When was the last time you ate prawns?" he asked.

Alice furrowed her brow. "Never, I hate them. They bring me out in a rash."

"Fine. Then we can take you home, nothing more sinister than a bit of food poisoning. Bit bloody melodramatic though. At least we got to leave without paying the bill."

The wind blew cold and hard on her face as she rested her head on Paddy's chest. "Where are you taking me?" she asked. The color was returning to her cheeks and most of her faculties seemed intact, but she could swear that they were heading for the Hills and not Santa Monica.

"I've got some melatonin at home and thought that we should pick some up for you, give you a good night's sleep."

Alice wasn't sure she wanted a good night's sleep. If having fainting fits got you a broad chest to rest on and unquestioned access into a man's apartment, then she'd have to try it more often. The taxi driver pulled up outside an apartment block.

"Do you want me to wait?" he asked. Paddy looked at Alice.

She shook her head, "I don't think that I could withstand the journey all the way back to Santa Monica," she said, smiling, and he paid the driver. She also made the most of his supporting arm up the stairs; it wasn't a particularly brawny arm and most of the time it was guiding his cigarette to his lips, but still, it's the thought that counts.

"Here we are." He opened the door on to what Alice presumed must be a workshop.

"You mean it's meant to look like this?" she asked incredulously as she ran her hand along the workbench.

"Designed by California's finest, apparently. No expense spared." Paddy laughed as Alice picked up a rubber inner tube that adorned a bare concrete wall. "But the pièce de résistance"—he led her through the doorless rooms into the inner sanctum—"the bedroom, except for the fact that there's no bloody bed."

Alice gaped in horror. A Draconian mattress and not a curtain or frill in sight. She quivered in horror as she imagined the glare of unfiltered light on her cellulite tomorrow morning. She walked toward the only shelf in the room and scrutinized his books: *The Architect Within, American Architecture Today*. "Not yours, are they?" she asked nervously. There was something slightly intimidating about men who preferred light and space to curtains and rugs.

"Nah, those are." He pointed to a small pile on a particularly sugical-looking steel trolley: Brendan Behan's *Borstal Boy* and *Studies in Renaissance Fiction Making*.

Hmmm. Maybe she preferred the architect within. She was feeling slightly awkward; perhaps she shouldn't have been so eager for the taxi driver to leave. Her stomach was churning with Paddy's inevitable closeness. They'd kissed once, but he'd left her behind in the rose garden afterward. Everything else may just have been another dose of expatriate kindness. She blushed at the thought, and now she'd wangled her way into his room and he was nowhere to be seen.

"Found them." He walked toward her tossing a bottle of melatonin capsules in the air.

Alice turned around. Take the tablets and run was her first instinct. But she was totally welded to the spot. He'd taken off his shirt and his slightly too baggy trousers hung just below his navel. He just stood there watching her, throwing and catching the bottle as though he was about to play a Wimbledon warmup match. Alice wanted to run to the bathroom. Since when had physical attraction been this stomach turning? Certainly not with Jamie; with Charlie it had been but for entirely different reasons. This was grown-up, undiluted lust. And she wanted to be somewhere else.

"So do you think I should drug you before or after?" he asked, not taking his gaze off her. It wandered from her eyes to her mouth and, heaven help her, over her body. She wanted to laugh, but every sinew was paralyzed.

"Do they work?" Oh Alice, oh Alice. Just keep your mouth shut. She folded her arms in front of her and pinched herself on the back of her arm as a punishment for her idiocy.

"Are you trying to tell me something?" He laughed out loud at her outrageously hands-off pose. She'd broken the spell; he was no longer a wolfish lover waiting to pounce but just quite nice Paddy. She knew which one she felt comfortable with, but when he'd looked at her like that her body was mercurial, darting and dancing inside. He threw himself on the bed and lay back with his hands behind his head, staring at the ceiling. Alice could have screamed. Now he thought she didn't want him, now she'd have to take her tablets, get a taxi all the way back to Santa Monica, and never see him again. She'd rejected his one advance.

Alice stood by the shelf and buried her head in a copy of *Wallpaper* magazine, taking in the clean floor coverings and lean furniture on its pages as though it were Tolstoy. If she hadn't been in such a terrible state she'd have noticed that as he stared at the ceiling he smiled. He smiled because most women he knew would have been waiting in their bra and suspenders on the bed by the time he came back in, and Alice, even though she'd gone to the trouble to put on a suspender belt (he'd noticed with a faint groin-straining pleasure as she lay in the ambulance), wouldn't even have contemplated displaying it voluntarily. He wanted to marry this girl.

"Why don't you come and sit down?" he said, patting the white sheet beside him.

Alice put down the style bible. Game on again. She was determined to speak only when she had something interesting to say but instead found herself saying, "No more prawns for me then." She grimaced at herself as she wended her way to the bed via every piece of furniture on the way; there weren't many, so she took to stroking her hand along the very interestingly textured walls. "It's a kind of Polyfilla effect, isn't it?" She was almost there.

Paddy was looking at her with such amusement that he could easily have laughed for a week, but he didn't want to terrify her anymore. Was he really so intimidating? If truth be known he wasn't exactly straight-from-a-yoga-class calm himself. He'd imagined this moment for so long— hell, this was the reason he was here, if he was being honest with himself. He couldn't believe he'd never thought her beautiful when he'd first seen her, disturbing, yes, beautiful, no. But now she was the loveliest thing since . . . Helen of Troy? Juliet? Audrey Hepburn? Perhaps lovelier than all of them. How would it feel when he finally made it? Mission accomplished. Back to work, back to life, and the next unsure thing? Perhaps. That was the usual pattern, but he couldn't imagine having enough of Alice. She was sitting beside him now, perched on the edge of the bed as though it were burning coals. A condemned woman.

"Alice, you don't have to do this, you know." He smiled kindly at her.

She couldn't turn around and look at him; she'd probably faint again. Why of all days had her body chosen today to make her regress to adolescence? Grown women who'd had tons of sex in their time didn't behave like this.

"I mean, we could always get ourselves a glass of whiskey and just hang out for a bit." He pulled himself off the bed and kissed her on the cheek as he left the room.

Alice sunk back onto the bed and cursed the day she'd ever been given hormones. So much better just to lie back and think of Queen and Country than to endure all these weird bodily impulses. She pulled petals from an imaginary flower. He fancies me. He fancies me not. Where on earth would all this end up? Quite weak with all the effort, she lay back on his pillow and kicked off her shoes. Paddy came back into the room with two tumblers of whiskey. He deposited one in her hands and clambered over her to the other pillow.

As his body skimmed hers and the sip of whiskey caught in her throat she groaned.

"I'm so sorry, I don't know why I'm being like this, maybe it's because of Jamie, maybe I feel that if I like another man he'll betray me, too, or something," she spluttered, knowing that this had nothing at all to do with Jamie but feeling that Paddy deserved an explanation.

"Sweetheart, stop fretting. It's just a drink, it's just me. There's absolutely nothing to worry about."

Alice took another sip of whiskey and relaxed.

"It's weird, isn't it, the way your body revolts at times like this. Just won't do a bloody thing you want it to do." Alice giggled. You had to laugh or you'd cry.

"But it does want to, doesn't it?" He was looking at her again, this time just at her eyes. She nodded silently. He put his glass down on the floor beside the mattress and turned back around. Without another word he kissed her. And that was that.

Alice struggled with her whiskey glass and suspender belt at the same time, unhooking the fiddly catch that had been digging into her back all night with one hand and trying to put her glass on the floor without spilling it with the other, and all the while being locked face-to-face with Paddy. Paddy, who was thankfully no longer New Age man but total straight-down-the-line, knows-what-he-wants, age-old man. Alice ran her hands over the chest he'd so cleverly prepared earlier by removing his shirt. She didn't have the manual dexterity to deal with shirt buttons after such a harrowing half-hour of nonforeplay. Instead she went straight for the one button she cared about right now and eased his trousers off. Phew, back on form, she thought as her bra sailed across the room. A familiar-looking bra, thought Paddy briefly, as he collapsed on top of her.

CHAPTER 25

"**H**ello, Alice's phone." Lysette was keeping a lookout for Jennifer; if Alice didn't show up soon she was dead meat. "She's not here, I'm afraid. Can I help?"

"I really need to speak to her, does she have a mobile?" The voice was unmistakably English.

"No, she doesn't, but I can take a message." Lysette was dying to know who this was.

"My name's Simon Benedictus. I'm meant to be staying with her, only I'm at LAX and I'm a bit stuck. You don't have her address, do you?" Simon fed another fifty cents into the call box and looked around him nervously. He was in the luggage hall and they were still waiting for their bags to come through.

"Listen . . ." Lysette scoured the office, Jennifer was nowhere to be seen and there was still no sign of Alice. "Cabs are hopeless in this town, why don't I come and pick you up? It's really not far and would be no trouble."

"Well, that'd be really kind, thanks," said Simon, not in the slightest bit surprised that a total stranger would leave the office to give him a lift from the airport. Besides, he was far too busy looking at the man on the other side of the carousel, with his glossy black hair and Gucci loafers, chatting easily into his mobile but absolutely not taking his eyes off Simon and Gibbo.

.   .

Alice had already decided that she would take a sick day. Hadn't she had food poisoning last night? If pushed she'd just call the doctor at the hospital and get him to write her a note. She lay awake pondering the usual morning-after-the-night-before routine that she and her friends had endured since they were seventeen. It was designed by the man to make the woman feel better after committing an act of indecency only hours before. It's true, even in a day and age where what women get is what they bargained for and what they bargained for is what they wanted all along, men still feel that they're inevitably going to switch into regret mode upon waking up—which is terribly sweet on the man's part but also very wearing for the poor woman.

"Morning, how are you," says man, sidling up to woman.

"Fine, thanks," replies woman, wondering whether he's just after another round of indecent acts or whether he's inquiring about her mortal soul.

"Good," he says, nodding sensitively.

"Got any aspirin?" she asks, just in case it was sex he was after and not the latter.

"That was really nice last night, thanks," he says, ignoring the aspirin request.

"I thought so, too," she says, wishing he'd shaved beforehand and spared her the stubble burn.

"It meant a lot to me," he utters, looking into her eyes and wondering why her face is all red and lumpy.

"Arrrgghhh," she wants to yell, "leave me alone, stop treating me like a girl. I had sex because I wanted to, not for the greater good of mankind. Let's just leave it at that. Stop patronizing me." Except she doesn't say it because she's too polite, so he never learns and the next girl in his bed has to endure the same nonsense.

Alice lay in the sun-soaked folds of the white sheets thinking about this. Paddy lay asleep beside her and while she was indeed suffering from fairly hefty stubble burn not only on her face but her chest and pretty much every-where else, too, mysteriously including her right foot, she wasn't going to be demanding aspirin. Nor, she hoped, was Paddy going to be remotely considerate. She pulled her watch from the floor beside her and was knocked side-ways by the vapors from the remains of her whiskey. She'd already been lying there for about an hour, but it was only seven-thirty. They hadn't gotten to sleep until four offi-cially. Alice had spent another hour pretending to sleep decorously, which wasn't easy with a strange man behind you. If only the prawns would stop swimming around and gurgling inside her, she might feel a bit more elegant. But that was another new man problem: all sounds, be they slurping, burping, or churning, were amplified tenfold in his presence. And now she was dying for the loo. Her clothes were nestled beside a chest of drawers on the other side of the room, but it might as well have been Alaska, so far did it seem. She plotted her route again:

1. Move without disturbing Paddy.

2. Stand up and try to prevent half of Los Angeles from seeing me through the curtainless window.

3. More important, try to stop Paddy waking and scream-ing as my glaringly white body crosses the room.

4. Retrieve clothes without bending over, this is too hideous a prospect to contemplate.

5. Make it to the bathroom (which terrifyingly seems not to have a door) and have a silent pee before retracing steps and shedding clothes as though all of above had never happened.

.   .

She was filled with horror. Every time Paddy looked as though he was out for the count and a safe getaway could be made, he made some adorable but mission-preventing gurgling noise. Finally she did it. She took a slug of whiskey for courage and made it safely to the bathroom under cover of the jacket she'd worn last night. Then to flush or not to flush? She took a deep breath as she pushed the handle and flushed. The sound of rushing water obliterated every other noise in the world and Alice held her breath until peace returned to the bathroom. She tiptoed over to the very scratchy mirror and examined her face. All makeup was now safely deposited on Paddy's pillow except for the obligatory circles of mascara nestling comfortably in the bags under her eyes. She dabbed a blob of toothpaste in her mouth, swilled furiously, and headed back for the bedroom. She vowed to plant a flagpole with her knickers on the top at the end of her expedition if she made it back. But chance would have been a fine thing.

Paddy had his head propped up on a pillow and he eyed her with amusement as she came back into the bedroom with just her jacket on.

"Been somewhere nice?" he asked. A blush rose through Alice's body, but she bravely discarded the jacket and walked the full seven paces from the doorway back to the bed naked. He whistled appreciatively and she dove under the duvet as casually as she could.

"So, Miss Lewis, prawn cocktail for breakfast?" Oh praise the Lord, he wasn't going to talk "About last night . . ."

"Oh God, did the whole restaurant see me fall over?" She cringed.

He nodded cheerfully. " 'Fraid so, sweetheart. But you did it elegantly. I made notes for the next time I have to instruct some fey heroine to swoon in one of my plays." He planted a kiss on her shoulder. "Just gotta take a slash." He hopped out of bed and sauntered toward the bathroom.

Alice put her head under the duvet and let out a silent scream. He was gorgeous, irresistible. And he hadn't tried to talk about where their relationship was going or have sex with her yet. Something landed on top of the covers. She pulled out her head and Paddy was standing there with a glass of water in one hand. He'd tossed a little packet of Pain Aid at her and was busy tearing the wrapper off his own. Oh, I love you, she thought as she swilled hers down with water.

"I take it you're not going to work today?" said Paddy.

"I might try to make it in after lunch if I can get it together," she said feebly. Paddy looked at her with a that'll never happen look.

"There's this beach party at Malibu today, fancy it?" he asked as he sat down on the bed and clicked on his watch. Alice froze; she thought of Izzy.

"Izzy's not going to be there," he said, and lay back down beside her. "Or if you prefer we could just do recovery." He tucked a strand of hair behind her ear and waited for a response.

"Recovery?" she asked, not really sure what it entailed but hoping that it would mean she didn't have to put on a bikini or expose her pallid body to the sun.

"More Pain Aid, Bloody Marys, and sheer indulgence."

"Okay, then, recovery it is," she decided.

Paddy pulled the covers back over his head, slung his arm around Alice, and within five minutes was fast asleep.

Lysette wound down the window of her car as she pulled into the arrivals area of LAX. All she knew was that Simon was probably in his late twenties and might look a bit like

Alice would if she were a boy. Then again, she supposed, she didn't look a bit like her redneck cousins in Atlanta, thank God. Hmm, maybe she should have asked him to wear a carnation or something. She turned off her radio so she could concentrate better, and when she looked up she realized that she was getting the tingles in her fingers. She had always felt this when a psychic prediction was coming through. The last time she'd had those pins and needles had been when the chiromancer in Vegas had told her that she'd have a change of fortune and she went out onto the tables and lost four hundred dollars. And sure enough, standing by the trolley bay, his hands in his pockets, rucksack at his feet, stood a man who could only be Simon Benedictus. His navy-blue sweater and sunburned ears made her catch her breath.

"Simon?" she called out of the open window. Simon and Gibbo looked at her as though she was a mirage in the rippling heat of the Los Angeles morning.

"Hi, Simon Benedictus. This is really kind of you," said Simon, walking around the car and shaking hands with Lysette, who had jumped out of the car in a heartbeat. She was at least two inches taller than Simon and more Amazonian than anything he'd encountered in the rain forest.

"I'm Lysette and I guess Alice has vanished, so you can come back and stay with me." Gibbo, who just wanted to be somewhere cool with a tall beer as soon as possible, began to load the luggage into the trunk of Lysette's car as she and Simon just gazed at each other. The planes swooped low in and out of their eyeline, but they continued to gaze. Fate had thrown Simon Benedictus into Lysette's path and now she absolutely had to run with the baton.

"And you know what? We can go to this great little tea

shop I know in Beverly Hills. I guess after being away from home for so long you'd want to, like, reacquaint yourself with old customs," Lysette said, her hair flying in the breeze from a landing Boeing.

"Spot on, Lizzy. I'd love to reacquaint myself with a few old customs." Simon winked at Lysette and she smiled broadly.

"Okay, fellas, are we gonna just hang around here until we get beheaded or shall we get the hell off the flight path?" said Gibbo, slamming the trunk of the car. "So have you got any sisters, Lizzy?"

When Patrick and Alice eventually woke up at midday, he tossed Alice a pair of old jogging pants and a sweatshirt and vanished into the shower. He emerged soaking wet and twice as sexy and proceeded to remove Alice's jogging pants and sweatshirt. Oh well, if he hadn't been predictable in some way then she might have begun to suspect him of being a fraud, maybe married or gay. Besides, she was quite in the mood now that she'd had a few hours more sleep and knew that he wasn't going to be throwing her out onto the street. A whole day with him, nobody else, just Paddy, sofa, Pain Aid, and sex. What more could a girl ask for?

At four o'clock, as the afternoon movie came to an end, Alice suddenly remembered that she hadn't called Tash, who'd still think she was with Patricia in Koo-Koo-Roo.

"Can I use your phone?" she yelled to Paddy, who was getting a beer from the fridge.

"Sure. Want one?" He held a beer through the kitchen door.

"No thanks." Alice got Tash's voice mail at the studio,

thank God. "Tash, it's Alice. I'm, erm . . . out. With a friend, so I'll probably see you later. 'Bye," she said hastily in case Tash was about to pick up the phone to grill her.

"Are you afraid of her?" Paddy flopped down on the sofa next to Alice and fiddled with the cord of her jogging pants absentmindedly.

"No. It's just that it's easier not to tell her the truth. I will. When the time's right. But she really had hopes for me and Charlie and I don't want to disappoint her. Maybe when she meets you she'll feel happier," Alice said.

Paddy let go of the cord and turned to look at the television. Alice felt sick to her stomach. Oh God, she'd done that fatal thing of mentioning the fact that they might be together beyond tomorrow morning. It was all right for men to talk about beach parties in Malibu, but if a woman did she was sinking her claws in. Alice closed her eyes and contemplated putting her stuff together and just leaving now. It was Jamie all over again, that ancient incessant whinge, "I'm just not ready for commitment."

But Paddy was harking more upon the coming-clean debate. Should he tell her now that he was the stalker who'd sent her the flowers and chocolates, or should he wait until they knew each other better and all fears that there may be a psychopath lurking beneath his mild exterior were dispelled? If he didn't tell her, then Tash certainly would. He hadn't seen what was wrong with his pursuit of Alice; it had all been totally innocent and seemed like the most surefire way of wooing a stranger. It was the minds that turned what he did into something warped, which struck him as perverse not vice versa. Never mind. He'd wait a while longer. He snapped away from the cartoon on the telly just as Alice was coming back from the bedroom with her bag and dress under her arm.

"I'm off now, Paddy. Thanks for dinner." She stood in the doorway hoping he'd stop her.

He did.

"Where on earth are you going? We haven't even recovered yet." He attempted to laugh.

Alice was steely. She'd read all about behavioral cycles and repeating the mistakes of relationships over and over, and she wasn't going to fall victim to that, no matter how good the sex had been and how merry his laugh.

"I've got to go." She took a deep breath. "I've been in dysfunctional relationships before and I know how the trouble starts. I'm sorry." But instead of the look of horrified misery that she'd hoped for, Alice was greeted with a guffawing outburst of mirth.

"You've been in California too long!" She was floored. How dare he laugh at her when she was questioning the essential foundations of their relationship? "What did I do wrong?" His laughter had given way to a worried look.

"When I mentioned the future you went all silent and huffy."

"The future?"

"Yes. Dinner with Tash. I don't expect you to be leading me down the aisle or anything, but I would like to be able to mention tomorrow without you getting all fretful." Alice was quite pleased with her eloquent testimony. If only she'd been able to verbalize her feelings to Jamie with such honesty. So America had taught her something other than to steer clear of wheatgrass juice and men with fur-lined accessories.

"Come and sit here," Paddy said, patting the sofa next to him. Alice dithered in the door for a few moments before dragging her feet and plopping down at the opposite end of the sofa from where he was. "If I gave that impression, then

I'm sorry. If you want the truth, then you're the loveliest—
and I know you'll roll your eyes when I say this—most beautiful girl—" Alice rolled her eyes but was secretly thrilled at
the compliment.

"There you go—" He waited for her fit of obligatory modesty to pass. "Anyway, I have, I have to admit, had rather a
lot of experience with women, but you, Alice Lewis, take
the proverbial biscuit. You are quite the most brilliant and
lovely woman I've ever met. There, I've said it. I might
even mention the love word, but you'd just snarl across the
room at me and probably throw something." Then that
heartbreaking smile.

Alice bit her lip and thought she might cry. "So should I
stay then?" she asked quietly, wishing she was positioned
on the other side of the sofa now.

Paddy laughed and leaned over and kissed her. "Oh, and
here I was hoping that you'd leave and never come back."
he said.

Alice hit him spastically with her trapped arm. "Oh, very
funny."

Paddy pulled up the car at the bottom of the road and cast
a nervous glance at the front window of the house.

"Want to come in for a cup of tea?" asked Alice, hoping
that Tash would still be out.

Paddy leaned over and kissed her. He hadn't made it to
his razor today and his five o'clock shadow was rapidly approaching the early hours of the morning.

"No thanks, I'd better get going." He hadn't even put on
the handbrake and if Alice hadn't known better, she would
have sworn that he was dying to ditch her and run.

"Okay, well, then, maybe we'll speak soon."

"Most definitely, darling," but his foot was still hovering over the accelerator.

"Bye then." She picked her bag up from the floor by her feet and skipped out of the car. Stop being so paranoid, Alice, she told herself as she slammed the door behind her. Then he was gone. The most wonderful dinner date, man, sex all rolled into one green-eyed package had sped down the street in his dusty car leaving nothing but the smell of smoldering rubber.

"Oh well." She shrugged and sauntered down the road to her house, which was a good two minutes away. "I have his jogging pants. I snagged his best cashmere jumper, I'm bound to see him again."

CHAPTER 26

"**W**ell, nobody's forcing you to go!" Tash was yelling at the top of her voice.

"You don't understand. This is California. If I don't go, then it looks as though I don't want to save our marriage and she'd get even more in the divorce settlement. California law is that the woman gets half. I'd definitely lose the house in Martha's Vineyard." DP was whining now. Alice couldn't imagine why anybody would want to be married to him in the first place.

"And you're mistaking me for somebody who gives a shit." Wow, Tash could be ferocious when she wanted, too. Alice hadn't a clue as to what they were arguing about but was so happy that she'd willingly have gotten out her pom-poms and, yes, even a miniskirt, and played cheerleader to Tash.

"Listen, my going to the shrink with Marion won't make a goddamn bit of difference to our relationship, Tash honey."

"Oh, yuck," Alice said. He'd gone all conciliatory.

"Oh, but there you are wrong. You are totally dickless and now we don't have a relationship anymore—"

Alice stood frozen, waiting for the next installment, when out of the bedroom door hurtled DP, stark naked, and followed by a videotape. Alice watched as DP floundered, hobbling about with one trouser leg on and the other trailing him. He looked at her as though she were from Mars.

"Don't mind me," she muttered, and took another spoonful of Cheerios as she stood and watched from the doorway of her bedroom. A ribbed condom package sailed past and landed at her feet.

"Tash honey, just listen to me, please." DP now had his trousers up to his knees and was waddling back toward the bedroom door, which chose that second to slam resoundingly in his face. Excitement all the way on Fourth Street, Alice thought cheerfully.

"This is fantastic tea. Just like my nanny used to make." Simon smiled at Lysette, who was beaming back proudly at him. It was only eight o'clock, but she'd been up since six baking spotted dick.

"Is that a good thing?"

"Yeah, my nanny's fab. My mother, on the other hand, can't boil an egg. Is this Fortnum and Mason's?" He polished off the cup.

Lysette looked at him, his hair curling around his sticking-out ears and his aquiline nose. She looked at the holey gray sweater tied around his waist and knew that this was probably going to be the man she would marry. She couldn't remember what Alice's objection had been but presumed it was all very incidental.

"You got a gun, Lizzy?" Gibbo stumbled into the room rubbing sleep from his eyes.

"Shut up, Gibbo, we don't need a gun," Simon said, moving over to the window where Gibbo was peering from behind the curtain out into the street. "Well, we wouldn't bloody well need one if you hadn't got greedy. Christ, you're a moron." Simon walked off to the bathroom.

"Golly. Temper. I like that." Lysette noted the vibrating walls of her house with admiration.

"Oh, he's not usually like that, he's usually a real pussycat," said Gibbo quickly. He was quite keen on Lysette and didn't want Simon swiping her from under his nose. If she liked them tough, then he'd show her. "Actually, it's all my fault. Persuaded Simon to do it. We were carrying some stuff through from Venezuela for these completely psychopathic gangster guys, anyway, I thought, no bloody way am I risking me arse for nothing. So we sneaks through a bit more, y'know, smuggles it through. Anyhow, we didn't give it to them, but now they know, so they're after us. See that bloke in the Lamborghini outside . . ." But when Gibbo turned around Lysette had vanished. She was rattling the bathroom door,

"Simon, I think you're great and stuff, but y'know this is like a really big deal thing going down here and while a puff of grass with friends is one thing, smuggling narcotics is quite another—"

The bathroom door opened and Simon stood there stark naked smiling at her. "Come in a minute, darling," he said, locking the door behind them and then sitting on the side of the tub. "Now this may seem like a really forward thing to say and I accept your point about the smuggling, but it's not what you think. . . . Anyway, what I'm trying to say is that since I met you twenty-four hours ago—"

"Twenty-two if we're being precise," Lysette said, not thinking it at all strange that she was locked in her own bathroom with a naked, drug-smuggling member of the English aristocracy but thinking instead that this was perhaps the moment she'd dreamed of all her life.

"Okay, then, twenty-two. Anyway, the tea you made me this morning. The steak and kidney pie last night . . . the fact that you use Yardley's English Lavender." He picked up a bottle that he'd been studying from the side of the bath. "The thing is that I've been out with so many women, some beautiful, others not really. They were mostly bright or had great taste in shoes and stuff. We ate in great restaurants, had fantastic holidays in Mustique. The whole shooting match." Lysette was rarely jealous, but right now she would have traded all her years of orthodontia just to be one of those Englishwomen with their strange dress sense and Simon Benedictus on their arm. "But the thing is that none of them ever had that certain something. You see, my nanny . . . she was probably the first woman I ever loved, and she wore Yardley's English Lavender and made spotted dick like you couldn't dream of . . . and I suppose in the way that most men end up marrying their mothers I've always wanted to marry my nanny. In fact, possibly the only thing I did learn from my mother was to follow my instincts and live as large a life as possible, or you'll come back as an ant or something . . ." Lysette looked at him curiously as he bit his lip, he really did have terribly sexy crooked teeth.

"Go on . . ." she said.

"I think what I'm trying to say, Lizzy, is, will you marry me?" He looked almost sheepish now and wondered if perhaps he should be clothed for this rather pivotal moment in his life. But until a few minutes ago he'd not really known that he was going to do it. Now he couldn't wait to get her to the church on time. But before he had time to consider slipping on a bathrobe, Lysette was on top of him and the two of them tumbled backward into the empty bathtub, laughing and kissing.

"Hold on just one sec." Simon leaned over the side of the bath and picked his jeans up off the floor, reached into the back pocket, and pulled something out. "I thought maybe this would be a kind of engagement thingy," he said, handing her the biggest fuck-off diamond she had ever, ever seen.

"Simon, oh my God, a diamond as big as the Ritz . . . I love it." She kissed it and then kissed him. "How come it was in your pocket?"

"Well, like I said, there was a bit of a misunderstanding on the old narcotics front, not saying that my parents aren't actually users and that I haven't been known to in- dulge once in a blue moon, but the thing is, I'm not such a seedy character. . . . We were smuggling diamonds, me and Gibbo. But as I was the one saving Gibbo's neck, he won't mind me having it. So this, my darling, is all yours. With this rock I thee wed."

Alice was, to put it mildly, a new woman. She parked her car and tossed her car keys in the air like a cheap cinema commercial for a hatchback. She swaggered through the reception area of her office without so much as a cursory glance at Kelly, who blew an incredulous hubba-bubba bubble and vowed to listen in on all of Alice's personal phone calls that day and blackmail her with the evidence. When she got to her desk, Alice sat down and swiveled on her chair in a way that it had never been swiveled before. Sexy, swivelly, Paddy, she thought as her computer screen flashed to life.

"It would be useful if you and Lysette could manage to be in the office at the same time." Jennifer passed by Alice's desk and dropped a pile of papers. "I've taken you off

Tommy's publicity for a while and you're looking after Robertson O'Rourke. There's a press junket in New York; you'll be expected to attend," Jennifer said before dumping a manila folder spewing yellowing press clippings on Alice's desk. God, at least Tommy's folder was a more inspiring pink color. Robertson O'Rourke. Alice knew absolutely nothing about him save that he definitely fell into the has-been category, but she was, she suspected, about to learn absolutely everything about him in the next couple of hours. Still, though, nothing could break her spirit. She set about the folder with the enthusiasm most people would set about rereading *Pride and Prejudice* if they were lying in long grass nibbling a box of Dairy Milk.

"Alice, you've got to come down to reception now. I've got a surprise for you," Lysette called up from reception.

"I can't," Alice whispered. "Jennifer's shackled me to the desk."

"Fuck Jennifer, darling, this is bigger than her ass." Lysette had obviously spent the weekend downing dangerous cocktails of drugs.

"Okay, I'll be there in a second." Alice picked up the manila folder and took a pencil for good measure. If she was going to be caught fleeing her desk by Jennifer, she should at least look as though it was a purposeful flee. She strode toward the lift, pretending to examine a cutting from 1967 about Robertson's divorce and wondered what on earth Lysette was being so weird about.

"Surprise!" As she stepped out of the lift, Lysette and Simon, their arms around each other, stood there grinning inanely at her.

"Simon . . ." Alice stuttered for a few minutes, then frowned in puzzlement, but still they didn't really manage to fill her in on the salient details, such as why Simon was there with Lysette, why Lysette appeared to have lost her mind, and why they were both being pursued by South American gangsters. Eventually she gave up and merely kissed Simon on both cheeks and led a very reluctant Lysette to her desk. "Don't mean to be a killjoy, guys, but one of us has to keep our job. I'll have her in reception at one for lunch, Si. We'll catch up later. Great suntan, by the way."

Lysette put her coat on the back of her chair and managed to sit still at her desk and at least give the impression of a working woman to Jennifer, who was circling like a shark in the background.

"You're not just smiling because of me and Simon, are you," Lysette whispered. "I know a pathological love grin when I see it."

"I had a weekend to die for." Alice nodded matter-of-factly.

"Last I heard you were going out with Patricia from accounts." Lysette kicked off her shoes and typed her password on her keyboard.

"Oh, come on, we don't even have an accounts department," Alice said. "I only said that to Tash on the phone. It was Patrick."

"Who's Patrick?" Lysette was now completely confused.

"Paddy, Patrick, Paddy."

"What, Izzy's boyfriend? The sexy Irishman Paddy?"

"The very same. Except he's not Izzy's boyfriend." Then she added coyly, "But he might well be my boyfriend." Alice was suddenly every character in Wonderland rolled into one; certainly the Cheshire Cat was playing its part in her repertoire.

Lysette leaned over and hugged her. "Oh, darling, I'm so happy. For you and for me."

"So am I. For you and me, too." Alice almost cried. To an outsider it would have looked like an AA meeting at which Alice announced that she'd just completed her twelfth step.

Jennifer walked by and eyed them suspiciously. "Alice, Kelly tells me that you've been taking an unnecessary number of personal phone calls. Can we keep the office as a place of work and not . . ." She tried to work out what all the hugging and tears might be about, ruling out pregnancy because Alice just didn't look capable of attracting a man, let alone knowing what to do with him when she got him, honestly, these English girls ". . . enjoyment."

Alice and Lysette returned to their seats and Alice got on with typing out a press release for Robertson O'Rourke whom she now knew to be a crooner of seventy-nine who'd just married his niece.

Alice had just run off three hundred copies of "Robertson O'Rourke Keeps It in the Family" when an irate Jennifer put her head around her office door. "Alice, it's a call for you. A Patrick Wilde." She slammed the door and seconds later Alice's phone was ringing. She nearly hid under her desk in fear. On the one hand she had just received a warning glare from her boss, which wasn't exactly suggestive of a juicy pay raise and a Christmas bonus, and on the other hand the man of her dreams with bells on was on the other end of the phone—it was just too much to bear.

"Alice, answer that now." Lysette was glaring at Alice as she performed a sort of Scottish reel devoid of tartan between the phone and the underside of her desk.

"I don't know what to say to him."

"How about hello?" Lysette, patience at an end, picked

up the phone. "Hello. Sure, I'll just get her." Then sweet as pie, "Alice, it's Patrick Wilde." Alice shook her head furiously and mimed bloodcurdling screams, but her voice, like something from the *Exorcist*, belonged to somebody else.

"Just coming." Sweetness and light. She grimaced at Lysette and took the receiver from her.

"Patrick, hi, it's Alice."

Lysette rolled her eyes in despair. Were all English girls like this? She must ask Simon. Simon. At the very thought she pinched herself and then took the rock out of her pocket. Simon had a friend in Goa who would set it for them. She pictured herself in *The Tatler* on the steps of her ancestral home with Simon beside her and a Labrador or two for good measure. As long as he wasn't killed before teatime by the gangsters, she thought anxiously, and tried to remember whether you added your milk first or last when you were making a cup of upper-class tea.

Alice put the phone down and picked up her pathological grin again. "He's taking me to lunch. He's taking me to lunch." The girls smiled at each other like love-struck twins in a Doris Day movie.

Alice spent the rest of the morning in the loo trying to wash her fringe and blow-dry it under the hand dryer, which involved a frantic amount of ski-style exercises, propping herself up against the wall on an imaginary chair and leaning backward into those backbreaking crab things they'd done in gym at school. But after her fifth trip to the loo, when she'd accidentally soaked the back of her shirt through to transparent, Alice was collared by Jennifer.

"If you have cystitis, I suggest you take some medication," she had snapped as the sexy-at-a-pinch postboy deposited some internal mail on Alice's desk.

Alice blushed furiously and had to make do with a

beauty routine that consisted of giving herself a manicure with a pair of pinking shears she'd found in her middle drawer. She set about scraping off all of the purple polish she'd applied last night in a fit of wanton passion. In daylight it looked as though she'd trapped her fingers in a door. Finally her clock clicked to one o'clock. The office emptied as everyone set off with clients for expensive restaurants and friends called up from reception to announce their arrival. Alice was usually long gone by this stage, sneaking out at ten to with Lysette under the guise of visiting the mailroom to FedEx some packages. Lysette and Simon hung around to calm her nerves a bit but at ten past, with no Paddy in sight, they decided they really had to be heading off to Taco Bell to get to know each other a bit.

"If we don't go now, Ally, there'll be no chicken fajitas left," Simon said apologetically.

"Bye, darling, and good luck." Lysette pecked Alice on the cheek and thrust a halfpence into her fist. "It's a really old British coin. It'll bring you luck," she said as she ran toward the lift. "It brought me loads." She took Simon's hand and winked behind her.

Alice looked at the coin and thought fondly back to the days when everything had been ninety-nine and a halfpence and wished she were still eleven years old. He's just not going to turn up, she thought, he probably spotted Izzy at some traffic light with her roof down and her hair blowing tantalizingly in the breeze and thought better of spending lunch with Alice and her seafood intolerance. And by twenty-three minutes past Alice had rubbed off her lipstick and was contemplating getting some sandwiches from the shop downstairs.

Suddenly her phone shrilled around the silent office. She snatched it up. "Hello!"

"Alice, it's Robertson O'Rourke. How ya doing, baby?" Alice's eyes widened with horror. Please God, no. Robertson had been known to talk the hind legs off farmyards full of four-legged animals. "I was just going to have my siesta with Mimi, my wife"—he broke off into a machine-gun rattle of guffaws—"when I thought, hey, it's not fair just to limit my affections to my beautiful new wife, no matter how large her breasts. So I thought to myself, who can I share my happiness with this hot Vegas afternoon other than . . ." Alice struggled for an excuse but couldn't even find the space in the rapid fire to insert it. The clock now said twenty-eight minutes past. ". . . that's the great thing about sex with a younger woman, don't you agree?" he chirped on and on until Alice put the phone down. She just took the receiver and placed it down in its cradle. If anyone asked her later, she would just pretend that they'd been cut off.

Then it began to ring again. It was bound to be Robertson again, wasn't it? She let it ring. It rang and rang and began to mock her; it knew that she was there and wouldn't stop until she succumbed. Finally she just picked up her purse and ran for the lift. She'd get some sandwiches, force them down, and forget that Paddy had ever existed. He was undoubtedly now lying in Izzy's hammock with the warm glow of a satisfied man.

Alice dragged her heels across the lobby and contemplated a visit to a witch doctor she'd seen advertised in the *L.A. Times*. She had to get one of those things that warded off Kelly's evil eye; it was beginning to give her the creeps. And while she was there maybe she could pick up some powdered locust or something to slip into men's drinks to aid in successful seduction. It was obvious her technique fell short somewhere along the line.

But maybe it wasn't the seduction. She dragged her feet slowly and hitched up her tights. Maybe it was her ability, you know, in bed. She'd heard about performance anxiety on some television advert; maybe she had performance ineptitude. Maybe—why had it never occurred to her before—maybe she was doing something wrong. When she was younger she'd always wondered if perhaps her family had taught her something in a totally different way from everybody else. For many a month she had been plagued by the thought that every person in the world apart from her family sat on the toilet the other way around, kind of looking at the cistern and not the room. And what's more she'd never know any different. She was doomed to spend her life going to the loo the wrong way around. Was the same thing happening in her sex life, was she perpetrating some terrible mistake? How would she ever find out?

She tugged herself across the floor like a sack of old green potatoes.

"Alice, where have you been?" Alice spun around at the sound of the familiar voice. In the corner of the foyer, folding up his newspaper and standing up, was Paddy. Alice became the *Exorcist* woman again, her head spun around on her shoulders from Kelly, whose face was almost obliterated by a lime-green bubble, to Paddy, who looked slightly hurt.

"But how long have you been here?" she asked, wishing she hadn't chosen the moment before to hitch her tights up like an unhygienic school-dinner lady. "Did you call up to say you were here?" She turned to Kelly, who was still a resolute bubble.

"Your line was engaged," lied Kelly, displaying her embryonic Meryl Streep acting qualities again.

"What time did you get here?" Alice was determined to find out. Robertson hadn't phoned until well after Patrick was due and Alice had deliberately stayed off the phone since twelve-thirty for good measure.

"Listen, we don't need a postmortem, let's just go and have lunch. I'm starving." Paddy kissed her on the lips and she ducked under his arm as he held open the door.

Paddy had stopped at the deli on the way and filled a paper bag to bursting with amazing salads and cheeses and a bottle of white wine—warm, but who cared? They drove heartstoppingly quickly to a tiny bay near the beach and laid the food out on a rather spartan gray blanket that Paddy had snatched from his flat.

"I can't believe I have to be back in an hour. How much do you think we can fit in?" Alice asked.

"Not nearly enough." Paddy leaned over and grazed her lips with a kiss. Thank heavens there was no time for shyness. For not being sure if it was okay to refer to certain things. They just had to pack it all in. Food, kissing, talking. All before two-thirty.

The sun was beginning to catch Alice's cheeks and she laid down her fork and reached for a napkin. Her goat cheese and baby spinach salad was without doubt the most filling thing she'd ever eaten. After just one green leaf she was unable to eat a morsel more. And Paddy wasn't doing so well with his Roquefort and prosciutto focaccia either. They were mostly just looking at each other in a dazed and adoring way. Alice would stare blatantly when she thought he wasn't looking, if he was cutting a wedge of Brie or watching a glider high above the glittering ocean. And when he walked off to pee in the bushes, she committed every detail, from untied fraying shoelace to his lopsided lope, to memory. She'd play it back later as she sat at her desk daydreaming.

Paddy wasn't quite so carefree. He'd really wanted to take her to dinner tonight but knew that if he did he'd have to risk revealing himself to Tash and he still hadn't concocted a good-enough excuse for his previous loitering. He was just hoping that maybe she'd have to go away on a shoot to Mexico for six months or something, and by the time she came back Alice would be emotionally wedded to him and refuse to leave his side even for her best friend. And bloody Izzy wouldn't leave him alone. She'd invited him to go to her salsa class with her tonight, which from what he could gather was the equivalent of a full-blown serious relationship in this town. But Alice looked lovely as she surreptitiously tried to pluck a spinach stem from her front teeth with her fork, and although he was still in a state of shock that he hadn't even the slightest desire to bed a few of the golden beauties who paraded around Santa Monica beach, he wasn't in the least bit sorry that he was here. Although he should probably think about what he was going to do about *A Chaste Maid in Cheapside*, which he was due to start rehearsing in the West End in a few weeks.

They delved into their melting chocolate-fudge sundaes with flourishes of pleasure. Alice dipped her finger into the cream on top and sucked it clean; Paddy plucked the cocktail cherry and popped it into her mouth, gently tugging the stem out as the fruit fell away. Their spoons collided as they eased the ice cream from the tub and hot fudge dribbled down their throats. Finally they collapsed with satiety.

"Is this horsehair?" Alice winced as she rested her bare arm on the rug.

"I reckon it must be a prison blanket or something escaped from Alcatraz. It hurts like hell, doesn't it?"

"Kills." Alice pulled up her skirt and attempted the impossible. To turn her legs a darker shade of pale. "That was fantastic, so chocolatly." She closed her eyes and lay back.

Paddy looked longingly at the blond flecks of hair on her thighs and wondered when had been the last time he'd enjoyed a dessert so much. And how long it would be before they could stop substituting ice cream for sex and enjoy the real thing.

"So I guess I'd better get back to work." Alice held up her arm and squinted at her watch.

Paddy, who was still sitting beside her, nodded in a glazed way and rubbed his foot lightly up and down her ankle.

"You don't have to give me a lift back. I can get a cab if you want to stay and have a swim or something," said Alice, suddenly aware that it was fast approaching three o'clock and that wine and an afternoon in the office invariably spelled disaster. But Paddy seemed not to have noticed that her mind had reluctantly shifted back into work mode. He lay down beside her, propped himself on one elbow, cupped her chin in his hand, and just looked at her. Alice was shocked—it was all a bit too filmic for her to take—but he looked so beautiful and sincere that she eventually relaxed. He let his hand drop and picked up her hand instead; he laced his fingers through hers.

"Alice, I know you'll think that this is too soon to tell and that I'm just saying this, for whatever reason men usually say these things, but I'm not, I've thought about it a lot."

Alice was ready for almost anything. He wanted to put

her on his car insurance. He wanted her to help him choose some new shoes. Would she mind ironing a few shirts.

"Alice, I love you."

In which case she absolutely wasn't ready for anything. Her knees began to knock together and despite the blazing afternoon sun her teeth chattered. She looked around for the game-show host and waited for the screen to be drawn back to reveal the host of ex-girlfriends chortling merrily at this ridiculous girl who thought that Paddy Wilde could be in love with her. But none. Nothing. Just the long grass, the sea and a distant yacht, and Paddy still looking intently at her, his hand gripping hers tightly. She felt like one of his actresses. This was definitely her cue to say something that would stop the world in its tracks.

"Thank you," she managed. Not *Doctor Zhivago*, but then she wasn't Julie Christie. Paddy leaned forward and kissed her.

"Just thought you should know." He smiled and the intense specter of Laurence Olivier was gone from the table. In its place was charming Paddy. "And I've never said that to anybody before."

Naturally Alice didn't sleep for the next three days. They would speak at midnight, Paddy lounging in the moonlight on his white sheets, floundering in the midsummer heat with nothing on, Alice with the candles lit around her bed and the waterfall trickling behind her. They would laugh quietly at jokes exclusive to them. Alice would become so deliciously suggestive in her remarks that she could feel herself blush and they both longed to be together.

"You really should come over sometime. I have this amazing bed that I'm just dying to use," she would say.

"I can't wait," Paddy would reply, before telling her some little-known fact about the moon that would leave her staggered by the transitoriness of her own existence. And it was just as well that they hadn't seen each other this week because frankly work was hellish.

Alice had had to work until ten every night on the Robertson O'Rourke campaign because he'd phoned Jennifer later and told her, "You know, maybe I'm older than I realize. That there young woman, Alice, doesn't seem to find me in the least attractive, or else why would she be goin' an' puttin' the phone down on me? Well, least I got my Mimi, and that's a blessin' and you still wish I'd take you in hand, don't ya, Jenny?" Well, at least that's what Alice presumed he would have said, he wouldn't have been malicious, but Jennifer had been appalled at the incident and ordered Alice to make this publicity run as smooth as honey or else. Alice had duly been phoning journalists in at least ten different time zones in a bid to persuade them not to opt for the "dirty old man in incest scandal" line.

In fact, the only spare second that Alice had all week was devoted to celebrating with Simon and Lysette at L.A. Farm. Alice contemplated inviting Paddy but thought that maybe all the talk of marriage and babies-to-be might just be a little too full-on for the first week of their relationship. Hell, even the word *relationship* was a bit full-on for the first week. Instead Alice joined the blissful couple in the bar.

"Sorry we had to meet here, but it's kinda out of the way and it's unlikely that the guy who wants his diamond back will find us here," Lysette said, fearing more for her diamond than her life.

"Why don't you tell the police about him?" Alice asked.

"Christ, Ally, no wonder I always beat you at cops-and-robbers when we were little: that's called turning yourself in," Simon said, one hand on Lysette's knee, the other on his beer.

"Well, you haven't done anything wrong, have you?"

"He's smuggled diamonds, Alice," Lysette said proudly, as if it required the brains of a rocket scientist and the courage of a war correspondent.

"Okay, but just be careful, you two. These guys could be dangerous," Alice warned, but neither of them looked particularly worried. "So the million-dollar question: Will it be Saint Paul's or Westminster Abbey?" Alice asked, wondering whether she'd make it to a *Hello!* spread at least once in her life as "Alice Lewis, cousin of the groom and close friend of the bride." Or maybe she'd be overlooked by the picture editor in preference of Fifi or some other actress. She also wondered if she would dare to invite Paddy.

"Actually, we've kind of reached a life decision," Lysette said carefully, holding Simon's hand for reassurance. "We're getting married on a white-water raft in Nepal."

"You're what?" Alice tried to picture the ever-graceful Lysette in a crash helmet and a life jacket on her wedding day.

"It's kind of been a dream of mine," Simon said. "Then we're going to have the honeymoon at the Ritz. Don't worry, Ally bongo, I'm sure we can find a boat big enough for you." Simon hooted with laughter and prodded Alice in the now positively washboard stomach. He obviously hadn't noticed the change in Alice since she was eleven.

"Well, I think that sounds great. It's a fantastic compromise, isn't it? Shows that you really care about each other," said Alice.

"Exactly." Simon said, beaming, "And then we'll go and live in the ancestral home."

"Great. My God, Lysette, you'll just love it. Acres of garden, even has its own chapel, and there's this sweet little
wing where the servants used to live . . ."

"No, the houseboat, Ally. I was born there, it was the
happiest time of my life. I just really want to share it with
Lizzy." Alice looked at Lysette for a hint of disappointment.
What was the point of marrying a lord with crooked teeth
and Dumbo ears if you were going to have to live on a rot-
ting bamboo raft in Kashmir? But Lysette was all love and
ecstasy. Perhaps she hadn't really noticed what Simon had
said. Or even more surprising—perhaps she was really in
love with him.

Alice made her excuses and left L.A. Farm just before
midnight so that she could catch Paddy before he went to
bed. It was hard enough having to spend the evening with
love's young dream. To then have been deprived of speaking to her own only hope for such a thing would have been
unthinkable. Her cab pulled out onto the freeway with Burt
Bacharach on the radio and a man in a black Lamborghini
on its tail.

At eleven o'clock on Thursday night Alice flopped, exhausted, onto her desk. She buried her head in her hands
and closed her eyes for a few blissful seconds. Only a press
junket left to arrange now and she'd be done for the night.
She flipped through her directory of hotels and thought
that Trump Tower might be fun; she'd heard that they had
gold makeup bags in the hotel bedrooms and she was desperate for somewhere to put her lip liner. She drew a ring
around the number with a red pen and flicked off her computer screen. It could wait until tomorrow. Besides, she
needed her beauty sleep. Tash and DP were going away for

a dirty weekend in Palm Springs to celebrate his wife's admission to the Betty Ford clinic, so Alice and Patrick were going to have a love-in at Fourth Street. Alice bought strawberries and croissants at the 7-Eleven on the way home along with some Pop-Tarts for her dinner.

"Don't those things really gross you out, Alice? I swear you'll rot inside." Tash was sitting on the kitchen counter removing the nail polish from her toes and strewing the floor with manky pieces of cotton.

"Why don't you just get a pedicure in Palm Springs?" Alice winced as she burned her tongue on the Pop-Tart. Now she'd have a horrible blister and wouldn't be able to appreciate kissing Patrick quite so well.

"Palm Springs is off. His wife's managed to persuade her shrink that it's not Pain Aid dependency, just unhappiness, so they both have to go to some seminar on rediscovering joy in your life in Vegas."

"Oh, Tash, I'm sorry," Alice said honestly. She was sorry. Should she tell Patrick that they might have to put up with confining themselves to the bedroom rather than have access to every tabletop and stick of furniture in the house for their revels, or should she just omit to mention it? The thought of waking up in the stark, staring brightness of his workshop was enough to make up her mind. A diet of Pop-Tarts and no sleep had taken its toll on her under-eye circles and *peau d'orange* thighs and she didn't want to risk making Paddy head for a cellulite-free zone like Izzy. So it was decided then. She would just forget to tell him that Tash would be home all weekend. She put the croissant dough in the freezer and was throwing the strawberries in the bin when she saw a cockroach blinking in the daylight as it emerged from the bottom of the carton.

"Tash, I've kind of got a friend coming over this weekend, is that okay?" Alice asked as she pulped the cockroach under the bottom of her shoe. Working in PR had obviously hardened her heart and toughened her stomach more than she'd realized.

Tash looked up from her middle toe. "Are we talking the male of the species?" she asked. Alice nodded. "That male wouldn't be Charlie, would it?"

"He's called Paddy." Alice held her breath. She knew that honesty was supposed to be the best policy, but she just couldn't bring herself to confront these situations. But this one had to be dealt with owing to the fact that she was planning to spend most of the next two days confining herself to her room with this man. She had a Charlie Brown calendar on her desk at work that declared, "There is no problem too big or too complicated that you can't run away from it." This was the premise with which she'd conducted most of her life. This was one problem that unfortunately didn't comply with the rule.

"So is he, like, a friend over from London or something?" Tash asked, splodging nail polish on the tip of her big toe. "I don't know why I don't just get a pedicure. He can have the sofabed for as long as he likes."

"He won't be needing the sofabed," Alice uttered with the courage of an extra in *Braveheart*.

"Really?" Tash's eyes shot up, and Alice nearly evaporated on the spot.

Do or die, Ally. "I've been seeing him for a few weeks. I think he may have a girlfriend, but I like him and so far he hasn't tried to tie me up, which is more than can be said for Charlie." There. She'd said it.

"Charlie tried to tie you up?" Tash yelped, choking back the giggles.

"It's not funny, Tash, it was really embarrassing." But now Alice was laughing; the idea of Charlie's fur-lined handcuffs seemed preposterous.

"And he growled!" she squealed.

"Growled?" Tash had knocked over the bottle of polish, which was dribbling down the countertop. "Like how?"

"Like . . . gggggrrrrr . . . like a bear." Alice bit back tears of mirth and the girls spent the next ten minutes growling like bears to each other, then every growl from grizzly to pussycat.

"But I think I was meant to think it was sexy," Alice hooted.

"Oh God, sweetheart, I'm so sorry. Why didn't you tell me earlier?" Tash asked, mopping up the spilled varnish. "I'm so glad you've met somebody else. Charlie's such an ass-hole, all talent agents are. I should have known better." So Alice happily took this as carte blanche to welcome Paddy to the bosoms of her household, the fake and the humble alike. Maybe she'd have to start telling the truth more often.

"You know, there are such freaks in the world. I didn't really want to tell you this, but this morning I found a box on the doorstep. Really pretty with this pink bow," said Tash. Alice wondered if maybe her mystery admirer had returned. Typical, just when you've met the man of your dreams along comes a second one. Talk about number II buses. "Anyway, inside the box was"—Tash looked nervously at Alice—"was a toy gun. The note just said: 'Or else.' It's such a cheap thing to do and if it weren't for your stalker, I'd guess it was just a prank. I've called the police and they're putting us on the patrol route, but we have to be real careful, Alice. Okay?"

Alice sat back and breathed in sharply in shock. God, could that be the same man she'd had daydreams about running away with, the one she'd contemplated meeting at the Rose Garden that evening? She really had had a narrow escape. She vowed to learn her alarm code by heart this weekend and to start going to kickboxing classes again. Thank heavens Paddy was coming for the weekend, he wasn't exactly a mountain man but he could probably throw a good stage punch if called upon.

Alice lay in bed, peppermint tea in one hand, the phone in the other. "I have to go to New York on Monday," she told Paddy during their late-night call.

"How long for?" He sounded pleasingly devastated.

"I have to do a press junket with Robertson. I'll bring you back a shower cap from my hotel though. I'll be back on Wednesday. Will you miss me?" It was extraordinary how much more one could say on the phone that one couldn't have brought oneself to utter in the flesh.

"Goes without saying. I'll be desolate. So are we still on for tomorrow night?"

"Tonight," Alice reminded him. Her alarm clock shone out one-thirty in the darkness. "Yes, we're still on. Come around at about six." If Alice had been a Hardy heroine, she would have felt the puppet strings bobbing away, the gods having their sport with her. For little did she know then that six o'clock that evening was to prove the most fateful moment of her trip so far.

Alice was just putting the finishing touches on her room. She turned on the waterfall and plumped up the duvet to look as though a sleeping Venus had just woken up, stretched, and wandered off to the bathroom. The white linen lay in delicate folds and she had a taper ready to light the candles when night fell. She was chilling the green olives for the martinis she would serve, and a sprig of jasmine she'd collected from the garden filled the room with scent every time a breeze wafted in through the window.

There were reports of a possible earthquake tonight, which filled her with tremors of excitement. She couldn't wait to feel the bed shake and the candles blur into one flame and to wake in the morning and joke, "Did the earth move for you?" She slipped on her dress and padded barefoot down the hall. Tash was lounging in her room listening to the Go-Gos and applying lime-green polish to her fingernails.

"Is he here yet?" Tash asked as Alice passed by the door.

"Any minute." Alice plumped up the cushions and casually tossed herself on the sofa like a nymph at rest. "You might remember him from the party except that you were too busy with DP. We were in the rose garden."

A shriek escaped from Tash. "You fucked him in my rose garden?" She pretended to be outraged but was secretly pleased for Alice. After all, she was the one who'd pushed her into the arms of Pervy Charlie.

"I did no such thing. We kissed," Alice replied. "You'll really like him, Tash." And with that Alice fled to her room to begin lighting the candles, which would take at least half an hour and couldn't be done in the throes of passion later. She contemplated the bed. The holy grail of every male in Southern California, even if Alice wasn't exactly the preferred vintage to be supped from it as far as most of them were concerned. And tonight was indeed the night. She struck the first match and lit the taper. She could hardly wait.

Paddy sped along the freeway as fast as his ancient car would take him. He picked a dusty polo mint out of the cassette holder and sucked happily on it. So this was

the weekend. He knew now that when he told Alice about
the stalker misunderstanding she'd just laugh and ask him
why he'd sent her chocolates and not Cartier diamonds,
even though she'd secretly loved the notes he'd sent her.
Then she'd rebuke herself for not having turned up at the
Rose Garden that night and the whole thing would be forgotten. Just part of the misunderstanding of early love. Like
Alice not realizing what he thought of Izzy and the pair of
them being chain-smoking alcoholics at that dinner party.
God, he really did like her a lot. Which was more than
could be said for the others whom he'd only fallen in love
with. Maybe now they could go back to London and become the most dynamic theatrical duo in town. She wasn't
happy publicizing incestuous geriatrics and he had to get
on with sorting out *A Chaste Maid in Cheapside*. They could
live in a garret in Bloomsbury and fall in love slowly in the
backs of black cabs or over long chats and pints of Guinness in The Nelly Dean.

Paddy pulled up outside the house on Fourth Street and
felt strange that for once he didn't have to be furtive. And
never would he again after tonight, he could be a full-
fledged boyfriend who didn't have to park his car a mile
away and hide behind cheeseplants at parties.

Alice had lit all the candles when she suddenly noticed
that she'd left a pair of graying knickers hanging on the
washing line in full view of her bedroom window. She
wanted the perfect rose-garden vista to be on view from
the bed so she darted out of the back door and down to the
washing line to extract them.

The front doorbell rang and Paddy stood hopping from foot
to foot. Should he have brought something other than tor-

tilla chips and his toothbrush? he wondered. This all felt very formal.

"I don't fucking believe it. What do you mean this is closure? One minute you're leaving your wife, the next you're calling me on the speakerphone from your seminar in Vegas to tell me it's over!" Tash paced across the kitchen with the portable phone.

"Natasha, I'm sorry. I've been hurting real bad since my children were born but hadn't the insight to realize why. Now I have. I need to be with my family." There was a faint round of applause in the background as the rest of the seminar group who had gathered in the Elvis Presley Memorial Hall offered their support to DP. His wife smiled and wiped away a grateful tear.

"And have you told everyone in your class just how much you like to be hurt? Have you told them that not only do you like to be hurt but that I can send them the video, too? Recreational Caning for Beginners. Wouldn't that be fun at your next meeting! They could all see just what you, Mr. Masochist, like to do with his *very* little prick. 'Cause I'm telling you, it's the tiniest one I've ever seen!" Tash spat, and put the phone down.

In the dusty hall twelve overweight couples looked thoroughly relieved that it wasn't them who had to share tonight. The men made mental notes to conveniently misdial their mistresses' telephone numbers when it was their turn. DP turned purple and contemplated enlargement surgery.

Patrick buzzed the door again. He began to walk around into the back garden to see if Alice was there when the door flew open and Tash stood deathly white and livid before him. It was hard to tell who was the more shocked.

Alice began to deadhead a few roses. They looked quite sorry for themselves close up. She clamped the knickers under her chin and held the stem with one hand and plucked with the other. It would only take a second and there was no way Paddy would be on time, she thought, as she tossed the deadheads over into the next-door neighbor's garden. Maybe she'd pick one of the livelier blooms off and pop it on Paddy's pillow. No, on second thoughts maybe that was just too Jane Seymour. But she could put one in a vase.

"You must be Patrick . . ." Tash put out her hand perfunctorily to shake Patrick's. Patrick took a step backward in shock. Then they both froze in full comprehension. Tash was looking straight at Alice's stalker. Another bastard male.

"You!" Tash blasted. Patrick contemplated bolting but hoped that any second Alice would appear in the hallway and save him.

"You!" This time she screamed and lunged for Patrick, who carefully stepped aside. "You're the pervert who came around here that day!"

"I can explain." Patrick smiled in a bid to charm her— bad move under the circumstances.

"So you think it's funny, do you? You think that scaring women is an amusing pastime? You think sending grubby notes and death threats will make you more of a man? You're a loser. Now get the hell out of here before I call the police. And if you ever call Alice again I will personally wield the knife that castrates you!" She glared at Patrick, who began backing away toward the drive.

"I'm not a stalker, I'm perfectly normal. Where I come from it's called wooing a woman. In fact, most women seem to enjoy it!" How on earth had Alice managed to hook up with this paranoid crazy anyway? He contemplated making a dash inside and rescuing Alice and eloping with her, but there was a garden fork dangerously close to Tash's elbow. Was it worth dying for love? Possibly, but there was no room for mistakes in this game. He wouldn't be much good to anybody in a perforated state. He decided to make a run for it and call Alice later when Tash had gone to Palm Springs as planned. Jesus, that woman was scary.

"Just get off my property or I'll have armed-response security guards on your case in fifteen seconds." She almost seemed to relish the idea of tearing Paddy limb from limb. In truth it was DP she was seeing in the middle of her lawn, DP in his jeans and cowboy boots with his camera slumped sexily over his shoulder. I'll show you, you smug bastard, she was thinking as Paddy leaped into his Volvo and fled.

Alice threw the knickers into the laundry room as she passed. The front door was wide open.

"Tash, we have to get some manure for the roses, they're at death's door." Alice wandered through into the hallway, where Tash was standing, staring out onto the street. "What are you doing?"

"Alice, we have to talk." Tash turned around and closed the door behind her. "Let's sit down."

"What are you talking about?" Alice laughed nervously,

wondering why Tash was being so weird. Tash sat on the
sofa with one leg tucked underneath her, making a space
for Alice, who reluctantly perched on the edge of the cushion with one eye on the door. She really hoped that Tash
wasn't going to go all psychoanalytical on her when Paddy
was here just because she didn't have anything else to do
with her Friday night.

"Is it about DP?" Alice asked calmly.

"It's about that Irishman." Tash couldn't bring herself to
say his name.

"Paddy?" Alice was beginning to get butterflies in her
stomach. What on earth was going on?

"Whatever. He was just here," Tash said calmly. Alice
tried to stand up to see if his car was outside. She was
feeling increasingly panic-stricken. Tash put her hand
on Alice's knee. "No. He's just left. Alice, this is really
serious."

Then Alice got the picture, phew, she'd been thinking
that something serious had happened. "Oh God, you think
that he's still going out with Izzy, don't you? I should have
said something, Tash. He's not. It's over. We're officially together." Alice smiled triumphantly, glad they'd gotten to
the bottom of that one.

"I haven't a clue about Izzy and I'm afraid it's more serious than that, sweetie. That man is the stalker. He's the
psychopath who's been following you and watching the
house, sending death threats and heaven knows what
other horrific things. I guess if we sent the police around
to his apartment they might find walls full of photographs
of you or something." Tash was genuinely shocked and
worried for Alice.

"He's my what? Tash, what on earth are you talking

about? I've been to his apartment. There's only Polyfilla on the walls. Where has he gone?" Alice got up and walked over to the window. This had to be some sick joke. Was Paddy hiding behind the tree in the front garden? She pressed her face against the glass and tried to see if he was there.

"You mean you've been to this guy's apartment? Oh my God, thank the Lord you're safe! Shit, imagine if I'd gone away this weekend, he could have done something really fucked up." Tash contemplated the narrow escape that Alice had just had.

"Tash, how do you know he's the stalker?"

"Because I saw him that day. He drove away in a Volvo and I'm positive it was him. I'll identify him to the police. They can arrest him when he arrives home. What's his address?"

"Are you sure?" Alice dropped heavily onto the sofa. "Did he admit it?"

"He said he thought that there was nothing wrong with terrifying a woman. Said they enjoyed it!"

Alice lay on the bench in the rose garden. Tash had been in bed for the last two hours and she could feel the darkness lift into tomorrow. They'd spent the evening vacillating between arguments about Paddy not being that type of person and then comforting each other with the all-men-are-the-same adage. Neither way of coping made Alice feel any better. She willed Paddy to suddenly turn up beside her in the garden and tell her that it had all been a huge mistake and kiss her. She also longed to scream at him and kick in the hubcaps of his wretched Volvo. She had no idea if he was really her stalker. And was it such a bad thing? She had after all quite liked her stalker for a while, longed for him to be somebody as handsome and bright as Paddy. And the flowers had been beautiful and now she understood the significance of the Rose Garden. Not just a dodgy place on Venice Beach. But just as she ran with the gorgeous notion of a man who cared about her so much that he'd do those things, the bile rose in her stomach again and Tash's words came back to her.

"So if he really loves you and he's not just messing with your mind on this power trip of his, then how come he didn't tell you? He is dangerous, Alice. And he lied to you." Then Alice remembered the toy gun in the box. Surely that couldn't be Paddy. Not in a million years. But then who was it? Alice's shoulders hunched into another stifled sob and she buried her head in her arms and cried.

Why did the first man she'd fallen in love with—because that was exactly what had happened—since the treacherous Jamie have to be a psychopathic weirdo who preyed on pitiful women? She should have kept up the kickboxing classes after all. And she should have known that any normal man wouldn't have fallen in love with somebody as gauche and odd as her when every other woman in town looked like an advert for exotic beachwear.

Santa Monica Boulevard was deserted apart from an eco warrior who was holding a vigil outside the Lobster Pot for the souls of departed crustacea. Paddy dialed Alice's number for the hundredth time. The answerphone clicked on again. He hung up. If he left a message, that would be tantamount to abusive phone calls in Tash's book, and he wasn't going to risk that just yet. He still had other avenues to explore, though what they were he wasn't quite sure yet. He opened the package of tortilla chips he was still clutching and got back into his car to ponder his next move. Though even Patrick Wilde wasn't feeling wildly optimistic tonight. It was half past four in the morning and if Tash had decided to stay in town for the weekend, then he was basically stuck. He had to go back to London on Monday. No two ways about it. The play began in a matter of weeks and every theater critic in the West End would be watching.

"Bugger. Bugger." He banged the steering wheel and tugged at his hair. Bugger.

CHAPTER 27

"**C**hicken or beef?" the air hostess asked Alice.

"Not for me, thanks." Alice refastened her earplugs and tried to ignore the very loud lip smacking of the man next to her as he attacked his beef. The man on her other side had some kind of nervous twitch in his leg that had been making the whole row of seats tremble since they'd left LAX three hours earlier. Alice had heard such bad things about the red-eye, but it had seemed like the best way to have a bit of peace.

"Don't even think about phoning him!" Tash had barked every time Alice had gone within a seven-meter radius of the telephone. And Alice realized that this was for the best. Tash knew more about men than Alice. And she'd worked in the movie industry for the past six years; she recognized a warped mind when she came across one.

"And you don't really love him. Listen, when you get back from this business trip to New York, we'll book you an appointment with my shrink and get you on the straight and narrow again. There is a reason why you're attracted to abusive men, Alice, we just have to work out what it is," Tash reassured her. "And we can do it together, honey. I've learned a lot from DP, and the most important thing is that girls should stick together. My next film starts shooting in

Europe in three weeks and I intend to have a full-blown lesbian affair."

Alice nodded and slid off to her bedroom again. She put another seven drops of Bach Rescue Remedy under her tongue and wondered if she could somehow mainline it. Lovely though it was, it wasn't quite potent enough to deaden her aching heart and body. Her bed remained un-slept in and her face was equally unslept in. She looked closely at herself in the mirror.

"I love you, Paddy. I really do," she uttered, hoping that she could somehow conjure him up. "No I don't. No I don't. You lied to me, you Izzy-worshiping weirdo. I hate you." If only she could make up her mind, then she could make a decision as to whether she'd phone him or send his per-verted gifts and notes back by FedEx.

The beef slurper in the next seat sent a yellow foam earplug flying into her lap. She tossed it back in his general direction and pulled down her Lone Ranger eye-mask and tried to sleep. But Paddy just churned through her mind and stomach. How on earth would she be able to organize the press junket in this state? It was probably just as well that she was going a day early so that she'd be able to get her head together before she faced the world again. Hiding out with Tash in L.A. was not conducive to clear thinking.

Had she felt this bad when she'd broken up with Jamie? It was hard to remember. How clever and cunning our Cre-ator was when He made pain something that is quickly for-gotten. If we didn't, nobody would fall in love again or have babies or undertake any of those things that cause you immeasurable pain. But this time Alice was sure it was the worst she'd ever felt. Ever.

·   ·

The Volvo's exhaust pipe was trailing dangerously close to the ground as Paddy pulled up in Izzy's gravel driveway. If he was going to make it home, he'd have to borrow some string to tie it together. Leaving the key in the ignition, he walked around to the back of the house.

"Izzy, you have to let me in. Please," Paddy hollered through the half-open window in the dead of night. "Izzy sweetheart, don't do this to me."

"Patrick, what are you doing here?" Izzy appeared naked at the window, her face bathed in pale moonlight, her tousled hair falling about her shoulders. She looked like an imprisoned princess in a fairy tale. A relieved smile flickered across Paddy's face as she opened the window and leaned out to find him standing on the lawn beneath her window. "This is just like *Romeo and Juliet*!" Her confident laugh echoed in the garden.

"Izzy. Can I come in?" Paddy pleaded.

"And what makes you so sure I don't have company already?" She winked. Gone was the virgin damsel and in her place the wily temptress.

"I'll completely understand." Paddy moved closer to the window and caught her hand. "Please, Izzy."

He looked so very like JFK Jr. in this light, she thought, almost his spitting image, in fact. Would he mind if she called him John-John? she wondered. A picture of them together on the cover of *People* magazine flashed into her head. "Well, okay, honey. But this better be worth it." She winked and made her way to the French windows to let him in.

Alice unpacked her plastic bag of underwear and a crumpled business suit and lay back on her bed and cried.

Trump Tower with its luxuriant suites and she was here alone without even the joy of being able to lie in bed and burn up the phone lines with dirty nothings to Paddy. She looked out and saw the yellow cabs blur past in the afternoon rain. What was he doing now? Was he thinking about her? Missing her? She could pick up the phone and call him. Just to tell him that she never wanted to see him again after he'd lied to her. She wouldn't listen to any excuses, but at least he'd know that it would be a waste of time if he were to try to get in touch with her ever again. And as for trying to win her around by sending her poems and flowers and chocolates . . . well, he could forget about that. Yes, maybe she should call him so that he'd know.

She held the receiver in her hand, took a deep breath, and dialed the first digit of his mobile number. She'd been chanting it like a precious mantra for the past thirty-nine hours: 1-310-555 . . . She stopped. Her heart couldn't take it. She walked over to the minibar and extracted a miniature Jack Daniel's.

The phone rang. She dropped the bottle on the carpet and froze. "Please God let it be him . . . please please please . . ." She lived in bliss for approximately three seconds: It was Paddy, he was sorry, it was all a fantastic mixup and he'd take her to the bar at Chateau Marmont tomorrow night to celebrate their getting back together.

"Hello?" But it was a woman's voice. Alice's heart plummeted all five floors to the lobby. And beyond.

"So you have to be on the ball at this press junket or you're fired. I've taken over the supervisional role on this project and we'll reassess your contract when you return to Los Angeles. The word in the office is that you couldn't organize a tab of ecstasy in the Viper Room." Kelly polished off her hatchet job with a flourish. "I'll be in town in the morning. Just vacate your suite and I'll take over. Jennifer will fax you with an official disciplinary warning."

Alice swigged back the Jack Daniel's and then set to work on the mini Coke and Diet Sprite. Was there caffeine in Sprite? How could she have done this? How could she have mailed Tommy's signed Sex Addicts Anonymous testimony out to seven thousand journalists without even noticing? She buried her head in her hands. She must have done it last week when she was in blissful intoxicating love. When she was being inane. Poor Tommy. That'd teach her. She could probably have mailed herself to the *Herald Tribune* without noticing last week, she was so tired. She must have had the seven-page document attached to the back of Robertson's press release. No wonder the photocopying had taken so long.

Well, that was it, wasn't it? No job. No man. Nowhere to stay in the city with the highest crime rate in the world. Wasn't life just a bowl of cherries? Alice picked up the phone to call Tash but couldn't face the tirade. She wanted to talk to Paddy, she wanted to tell him that she'd as good as been fired for spoon-feeding the piranhas of the press the salacious and unimaginably lurid details of Tommy's multiple-hooker-famous-actress-naming-kinky-enough-to-put-you-off-your-breakfast sexploits. And that the man she had fallen in love with was actually a card-carrying pervert. And Paddy would have laughed until tears rolled down his cheeks. But she couldn't. Instead she called Lysette. Lysette who believed in love and who would tell her what to do.

"Lysette. It's me, Alice."

"Honey, how's your dirty weekend? Did you feed each

other strawberries by candlelight in a bubble bath yet?" Lysette laughed.

"I'm in New York. Paddy's my stalker. Can you believe it? He's been the one sending me notes and flowers and—"

"God, that is so romantic I could die," Lysette said, taking another three minutes to relay this romanticism to Simon, who was scouring the For Sale columns for an authentic Silver Cross pram for their firstborn.

"So why New York? Shouldn't you guys be celebrating this together? Wow, he must be really crazy about you."

"Yeah, but Tash thinks that it's really unhealthy," Alice said, wondering if maybe Lysette was right and that rather than being an evil act it was in fact merely gorgeous.

"Well, excuse me for speaking out of turn, but Tash is hardly Miss Wiseass when it comes to love, is she? I mean, she let Simon slip through her fingers, didn't she?" Lysette had managed to overlook Simon's adolescent penchant for kissing his classmates, quite rightly, as a side effect of the English public school system.

"The thing is, Lysette, he also sent a gun in a box. It was a death threat," Alice said, knowing that even Lysette's optimism wouldn't be able to see the bright side of this.

"Death threat, my ass. Did it have this kind of tacky note attached saying 'If you dare' or something?" asked Lysette as she straddled Simon's back and massaged his shoulders.

"It said 'Or else' I think."

"That's the one. Well, the thing is, that stupid Donatello got his victim confused and followed you home. He felt really bad about it. He's Catholic, you know. I should have called you only we've been so busy. . . ."

"Donatello?" Alice was now totally confused.

"Yeah, he's actually really sweet. He wanted the diamond back, but I told him that as that was out of the question he could come to the wedding instead. We'd even hire his white-water-rafting helmet for him. Anyway, he had some of my home-baked shortbread and said he'd think about it. He's still asleep downstairs."

"God. I do love you, Lysette. I really do. I'll see you Wednesday. Okay?" And Alice hung up. Now she could call Paddy and explain and tell him that the bed was too big without him and she missed him. Dialed 1-310-555-73 . . . 4 . . . huge breath and swig of mini-vodka . . . 6. There.

"Hello." Female. Not Paddy.

"Hi . . . erm . . . is Paddy there?" Alice gulped back the vodka in surprise.

It was late morning in Malibu and it had been a veeerrryyy long night for Izzy, but she knew an English accent when she heard one. And she guessed instantly who this accent belonged to.

"Is that Alex? You don't want to talk to Patrick, do you?" Her voice was patronizing and cloying.

"It's Alice. Is he there?"

"Let's just see. Paddy? No, I think he's in the shower. Can I get him to call you back?" She smiled broadly as she saw Paddy cross the corridor from the bathroom to the spare room, where he'd determinedly spent the night, whistling Van Morrison.

"No. Don't bother." Alice hung up the phone.

"Ciao." Izzy pushed in the aerial on Paddy's mobile phone and put it back on the coffee table next to his car keys. She looked around for some clothes to wear. Where on earth had she left that great bra?

·   ·

Alice packed up her carrier bag and put it by the door ready for a speedy getaway when Kelly arrived tomorrow morning. It was worse than she had ever imagined. If she stayed in this hotel room one more minute, she'd hang herself from the light fixtures. She'd never been to New York before, she really should see something of the city. How could he have gone straight back to Izzy without more than a backward glance at Alice? Maybe he'd never left Izzy in the first place. Tash's words reverberated through her head as she wandered along West 44th Street. Was she really a victim? Perhaps she should see a shrink. The behavioral patterns weren't looking so good, really, were they?

"Well, Doctor . . ." She imagined herself hesitating. "Do I call you doctor?" The generic shrink would nod his head in a generic shrink fashion. His balding pate reflected the light, which shone into Alice's eyes as she lay on his chaise longue. "The problem here is that the last three men in my life treated me badly and I'm starting to worry. Is this pattern going to repeat itself throughout my life?"

The generic shrink muttered something incomprehensible about moths to flames and potty training, but Alice didn't really take it in.

"You see, I have to know if there's some kind of inherent flaw in my attitude toward men because they just keep on being shit. The first one dumped me only moments after sexual intercourse had taken place and said he had found more excitement with a lawyer with a bob."

The shrink was puzzled by the bob. Was this perhaps some unusual form of foreplay?

"No." Alice enlightened him. "It's just a particularly pedestrian hairstyle. That was the sad twist of irony. How boring must I have been if my boyfriend left me for somebody with a bob?" The shrink didn't respond. "Anyway.

Eventually we split up. I'd like to be able to say that I left him, but in fact I didn't, so I can't. Anyway. I lived without him. I wasn't always the cheeriest of souls, but I survived. Then I met Charlie, who wanted my bed more than my body, I suspect, but that was short-lived. Then there was Paddy. I love him."

"Ah, good. Yes. This is healthy." The shrink nodded.

"But even if he weren't a pervert he'd still prefer Izzy to me, so that's out of the question. Do you think I'm incurable, Doctor?" Alice asked.

But the generic shrink had gone. Only to be replaced by a fat NYPD cop muttering into his walkie-talkie. Alice actually felt much better. Maybe therapy would work for her after all. If she embarked upon a course of self self-help, then she could be happy in no time. She made a point of scheduling an appointment with herself again tomorrow. Then she rounded a corner into what was obviously a less salubrious part of town and felt as though she'd arrived in Gotham. The drains in the road sent smoke snaking out into the rainy air and men loaded boxes onto the backs of lorries and wolf-whistled her. If only she could lose herself in New York for a while, she might never have to face work or men again.

CHAPTER **28**

Robertson put his arm around his niece and posed ecstatically for the cameras. Mimi grinned for all she was worth. She was thinking that she and Robertson could swing by Tiffany's later and pick up some of those adorable baubles she'd seen in *Seventeen* magazine.

"So is this your fountain of youth?" asked one journalist, pointing at Mimi.

"Sure is." Robertson lit his cigar and puffed away proudly. His hand was firmly welded to Mimi's bottom.

"And Mimi. Are they real?" the journalist continued. Alice was about to throw this woman out. She'd already got far too close to the bone with her question about the mysterious disappearance of Robertson's seventh wife off a brothel ship in Cannes thirty years ago.

But Mimi smiled sweetly. "Robertson gave them to me," she said, proudly heaving up her bosom. "Aren't they great?"

Alice sat back down in her chair. Thank God that this wasn't too taxing. She didn't feel up to wrestling with journalists today. Perhaps their being so well behaved now was a mark of their gratitude that Alice had handed them the scoop of the century like John the Baptist's head on a plate. Here you go, guys. All yours.

"How do I please him?" The hint of a blush rose from Mimi's cleavage at this point and crept up to the roots of her peroxided locks. "Well . . ." She wound a tendril around her finger and pondered.

"Alice. I need to see you outside. Now." Kelly appeared in the doorway in full Demi Moore scary-executive-boss-woman mode. The assembled journalists turned to look at her for a second and then resumed interviewing. Alice clambered over the notepads and cameras and heads of people strewn across the floor and made her way over to Kelly.

"Outside!" Kelly barked. Alice complied. She was not obeying, she told herself. Merely complying. "What in hell's name do you think you're doing in there? You're not the star attraction. You should be sitting on the floor. And you're letting way too many dubious questions go un-checked. Robertson is senile and the girl is a dunce. You're meant to do the thinking for them. Not let the fucking mob attack them at will." The hotel corridor was dark, but Alice noticed that Kelly had wasted no time in making herself a name badge with Alice's job title on it.

"I happen to think that Robertson and Mimi are doing fine on their own. This is a PR agency, not a kindergarten."

"You obviously can't cut it in this town. You're some pa-thetic excuse for a woman from Bumblefuck, England, and you're trying to compete with the big boys. Give it up." Kelly popped a blueberry bubble in Alice's face.

"You know what?" Alice asked.

Kelly rolled her eyes. Did she even need to listen to this brain-dead moron?

"Sod this for a game of cards. You can look after Robert-son yourself. In fact, you can have my job. I'm leaving."

And with that Alice stormed away, not realizing that she still had her microphone pinned to her chest and switched on. She walked back into the room to collect her carrier bag. The posse of journalists stood up and clapped as she walked in.

Robertson prized himself from his wheelchair. "You did great, kid. Don't you let them get you down." He clasped her hand warmly. "And if you ever need another job, call me."

"Thanks, Alice, you've been sweet." Mimi stood up and hugged Alice to her chest. Alice wiped away an emotional tear from her eye and ducked from the room.

Kelly was waiting in the corridor. "Hotel room keys please," she demanded, her hand open before her.

Alice ruffled through her bag and found the breezeblock with its attendant key.

"Catch." In no mood to behave herself now, Alice tossed the key to Kelly.

But Kelly wasn't quick enough off the mark. The key and concrete fell bang onto Kelly's perfectly pedicured big toe. *Crunch.* "Ouch. I'll sue you for this, you irresponsible bitch!" Kelly threw at her as Alice sauntered down the hotel corridor with nonchalant bravado. She kept on walking until she reached the lift. Then she burst into tears the second the door closed behind her. What on earth was she meant to do now?

Alice didn't even have a map of the subway. She had no phone card so couldn't ring Tash. She just had her carrier bag with her jeans in it. Where did people like her go to? In London she'd probably have been a case for the Salvation Army. Or at least she could have stowed away on the train to Norfolk and been in her mum's kitchen in no time. But this was the Big Bad Apple. Alice walked for at least half an hour before the idea struck her. Central Park. That was where all the people like her went. People who kept their cigarettes and gin bottles in plastic bags.

"Excuse me, can you tell me the way to Central Park, please?" she asked a man who automatically confirmed her suspicions that she was now living outside the law.

"You don't know where the park is? What are you, some kind of freak?" He laughed and pointed over her right shoulder. She'd been right next to it all along. She turned and made her way to the nearest entrance. Apparently there was a whole life beneath the streets of New York. Alice wasn't sure if you exactly got your own unit, but she'd heard that some famous dress designer who'd fallen on hard times had been living under the city for five years now. She might have to explore that as an option. Then she changed her mind as the man who was walking three paces behind her began to bark like a dog.

Then suddenly she was there. At a gateway to Central Park. The Diana Ross playground. Alice looked up and saw the blossom trees swaying. She saw the nannies sitting on the benches as their charges hurtled up and down the climbing frames. A dog walker untangled his leashes as two puppies yapped deafeningly at each other. Talk about an oasis of calm in a chaotic world. Perhaps not exactly calm but certainly refreshing. She wandered on and crossed the road.

"Get outta the way!" At least sixty Rollerbladers nearly lost their limbs as Alice ignored the Don't Walk sign and stepped off the sidewalk into their paths.

"Sorry." She stumbled back again and smiled. This was lovely. She felt almost sane. No job, etc., etc. Yeah, Alice, change the record. She was even beginning to bore herself with her incessantly miserable life. She was back in the psychiatrist's chair.

"You see, I've got to stop running away from things. I should confront my problems. I've spent years trying to worm out of things. Worming out of going to parties. Worming out of dates with disastrous men. A better woman would have made something of living in L.A. with its cheap manicures and organic supermarkets. But not Alice Lewis. Oh no, Alice Lewis makes a royal cockup of it. So, Doctor, I think that what I have to do is to go back to California. I think I still have my ticket in here . . . Hold on a sec." Alice sat down on a nearby bench and fumbled in her bag. She shook her tights and bra to make sure that it wasn't tucked away inside them. "Ah yes, Doctor, here it is." She kissed the ticket briefly.

"So now I shall go back, get another job, and tell Paddy that if he still wants to stalk me after I've been such a wet blanket, then he's very welcome to. Oh, you don't agree, Doctor? Why not?" Alice furrowed her brow. "You think that I'm not in my right mind? Well, you're probably right there, but this is just something that I absolutely have to do."

"Too bloody right you're not in your right mind." A voice in Alice's right ear. Oh no. A fellow wino? Had she invaded somebody else's turf?

"I'm sorry, but you see I won't be . . ." Alice turned around to face her accuser. There, large as life and at least seven times as handsome, was Paddy.

"Mind if I join you?"

Alice was much too shocked and embarrassed to jump up and hurl her arms around him as though he were a long-lost love on a wartime railway platform. But she did shift her underwear off the bench so that he could sit next to her. "Help yourself," she mumbled. What was she meant to say? He'd just caught her talking to herself like ten kinds of lunatic on a bench next to the Diana Ross playground. It was difficult to find the right words to express how she felt.

"How did you find me?" Seemed like a good, logical

start. And she had a lot of ground to make up for on the common sense front.

"It was like the twelve labors of Hercules, I have to confess, but I made it." Not much common sense going on there either.

Alice decided on a more specific approach. "You're back with Izzy then?" she asked, her eyes glued to a dog that was peeing against a woman's Bloomingdale's shopping bag. She waited for the thud of pain to wallop her in the stomach.

"How did you know?" Paddy frowned. There. Boom. It got her just below the rib cage. She reeled backward. "I mean, of course I'm not back with Izzy. But I went there last night . . ." he began to explain.

Alice let out a wildwoman of Borneo in distress chortle. "Ha heee haw!" She snorted on the *haw* part. "You expect me to believe that you're not back with her? Well, I may have been the most gullible fool you ever had the misfortune to go out with, Paddy, but I've changed. You see, I've realized . . ."

"You're forgetting that I just sat in on your session with the shrink." He smiled. She could have hit him, had she not wound her bra around her hand so tightly that she couldn't move her fist. The woman opposite had just discovered the dog pee on her new Ferragamo jacket. The dog sailed through the air with the imprint of a Timberland boot on its bottom.

"Alice." He took her bra-bound hand and made her look at him. "I went to Izzy's to get Lysette's sister to help me find Lysette to help me find you. She said you were definitely in New York, so we went to your office and found Trump Tower circled in the phone book on your desk and I have just signed a check for five hundred dollars to a

woman claiming to be your boss, as an out-of-court settlement for damage that you just inflicted upon her, and then
I was pointed in your general direction by a man in a wheelchair who told me that if he didn't have Mimi he'd snap
you up. I've been tailing and losing you for the past hour.
So I suppose in a way I am your stalker, however . . ." Alice
stared at Paddy, who was obviously more than a bit bewildered by what had happened. ". . . this of course is not
even to begin to address the accusations of gross indecency leveled at me by your demonic flatmate or the fact
that when I realized I might never see you again I considered becoming a monk."

"Really?" Alice bit her lip to stop herself from breaking
into a smile.

"Well, not really. Not really a monk, but I still love you,
Alice. And I like you. And I think that this will probably last
longer than five nights and a lunch date." Paddy kissed her
gently on the cheek.

"So what do we do now?" she asked. She felt that she'd
made as many life-altering decisions as she could for one
day and couldn't quite face another.

"Well, I vote that we go back to London, since we're just
as far from there as we are from L.A. right now, and between us we have enough Wanted posters scattered around
that town to make a cowboy movie. Izzy, Tash, and probably half of the LAPD are out for my blood after I sent you
death threats."

"Speak for yourself." Alice laughed. "I don't have any
enemies."

"Your boss, Izzy, Charlie . . . to name but a few." Paddy
had started to kiss her hand. "If we go back and hide out
for a while, then we can come back here when we're no
longer pariahs."

"And what will I do in London?"

"Well, there's this theater company that I've been meaning to tell you about. They're in need of a great publicist. Then there's this guy who has this great big flat in Soho and really wants somebody to share it with him, except he's very particular, not any old person will do." Paddy smiled expectantly at her.

"If you think that I'm about to leave my life behind to follow you halfway across the world just because it happens to suit you and the production schedule of *A Chaste Maid in Cheapside*, then you're sadly mistaken." She smiled. "You see, I want more from a relationship. I want a man who'll prove he loves me, who'll pursue me to the ends of the earth, woo me—maybe even send me flowers or a poem or two."

"In which case you'll have to forget it, I'm afraid," said Patrick, shaking his head. "You see, I've given up on being romantic. It's too dangerous."

"Oh, all right then," Alice conceded as he began to kiss her hand softly. "I suppose I can be persuaded to live without all of that romantic bit. . . ."

About the Author

CLARE NAYLOR worked as an editorial assistant at a major British publishing house. When her first novel, *Love: A User's Guide*, was bought for the movies, she left her job to write full time. Her novels include *Love: A User's Guide*, *Catching Alice*, and *Dog Handling*. Clare lives in England and is currently working on a new novel.